# CINNAMON ROLL MURDER

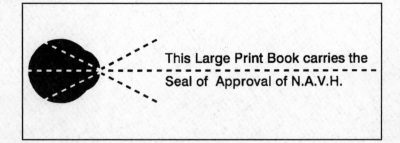

This Large Print Book carries the
Seal of Approval of N.A.V.H.

# CINNAMON ROLL MURDER

## JOANNE FLUKE

**THORNDIKE PRESS**
*A part of Gale, Cengage Learning*

GALE
CENGAGE Learning·

Detroit • New York • San Francisco • New Haven, Conn • Waterville, Maine • London

## GALE
### CENGAGE Learning®

**LIBRARY OF CONGRESS CATALOGING-IN-PUBLICATION DATA**

Fluke, Joanne, 1943-
    Cinnamon roll murder / by Joanne Fluke. — Large print ed.
      p. cm. — (Thorndike Press large print mystery)
    "A Hannah Swensen Mystery with Recipes."
    ISBN 13: 978-1-4104-4619-0
    ISBN 10: 1-4104-4619-0
    1. Swensen, Hannah (Fictitious character)—Fiction. 2. Women private
investigators—Minnesota—Fiction. 3. Cooking—Fiction. 4. Large type
books. I. Title.
PS3556.L685C56 2012
813'.54—dc23                                       2011047456

Published in 2012 by arrangement with Kensington Books, an imprint
of Kensington Publishing Corp.

This book is for my favorite composer,
Billy Barnes,
my favorite musician,
Bob Menadier,
and my favorite jazz singer,
Laurie Gral.

# ACKNOWLEDGMENTS

Big hugs for Ruel, my in-house story editor and chief taste tester.
And hugs for the kids who don't seem to mind helping with the taste testing.
Hugs and kisses for the grandkids who don't suffer from butter, sugar, or chocolate deprivation thanks to Hannah Swensen's recipes.

Thanks to my friends and neighbors:
Mel & Kurt, Lyn & Bill, Lu, Gina, Adrienne, Jay, Bob, Laura Levine (Jaine Austen mysteries) & Mark, Danny, Judy Q., Dr. Bob & Sue, Richard & Krista, Mark B., Angelique, Daryl and her staff at Groves Accountancy, and everyone at Boston Private Bank.

Thank you to my Minnesota friends:
Lois & Neal, Bev & Jim, Lois & Jack, Val, Ruthann, Lowell, Lila & Curt, Dorothy &

sister Sue, Mary & Jim, Tim Hedges,
and that great guy from KARE-TV
whose name I never can remember.

Special thanks to my wonderful
Editor-in-Chief and good friend,
John Scognamiglio.

Hugs all around to Steve, Laurie, Doug,
David, Adam, Peter, Robin, Karen, Vida,
Lesleigh, Adeola, Darla, Rosanna, Mickie,
Alex, and all the other folks at Kensington
Publishing who keep Hannah sleuthing
and baking up a storm.

Thanks to Hiro Kimura, my superb cover
artist, who's drawn scrumptious desserts
for the covers of every Hannah Swensen
mystery. This one is the best ever! I just
hope no one eats the cover before they
read the book!

Thank you to Lou Malcangi at
Kensington for designing all of Hannah's
incredibly gorgeous dust jackets and
paperback covers.

Thanks to John at Placed4Success.com for
Hannah's movie and TV spots, and for
handling my social media.

Thanks to Kathy Allen for the final
testing of Hannah's recipes.

Thank you to Sally Hayes (and Gary, too)
for sharing wonderful recipes.
And a big hug to my friend Trudi Nash for
helping me on book tours.

Thanks also to all the wonderful media
guides in the cities I've visited. Without
all of you I'd be totally lost, both
figuratively and literally.

Hugs to superb food stylist Lois Brown, for
making my recipes look scrumptious in
Phoenix. And thanks to my Chicago food
stylist, Judy Krug, for keeping that frozen
yogurt frozen.

Thank you to Dr. Rahhal,
Dr. and Kathy Line, and Dr. Wallen.

Thanks to Jamie Wallace for keeping my
Web site, MurderSheBaked.com up to date
and looking great.

And many thanks to all the readers who
love Hannah almost as much as I do. I just
wish that I had the time to test every single
one of the great family recipes you send.

# CHAPTER ONE

"The only problem with leaving four car lengths in front of you is that four cars come in to fill up the space!" Hannah Swensen complained to her sister Michelle, who was riding in the passenger seat of her cookie truck. "I'm going forty. Do you think that's too slow?"

"Absolutely not. It's nasty out there, and anybody who drives faster than forty on a night like this is crazy."

"Or they come from other states and they don't know anything about winter driving in Minnesota. I think I'll pull over as far as I can and let that whole herd of cars behind me pass."

"Good idea."

Hannah signaled and moved over as far as she could to encourage the other drivers to pass her. They probably thought she was being too cautious, but a thin film of water glistened on the asphalt surface of the highway, and the temperature was dropping fast. The water would turn into slick ice in a matter of minutes and there was no way Hannah wanted to sail off into the ditch and land in the mud that was just beginning to refreeze from the afternoon thaw.

Some people said that Minnesota had two seasons; Shovel and Swat. Hannah knew that wasn't the case. The land of the frozen north had four seasons — Fishing Season, Duck Season, Deer Season, and Mud Season. This was the first Thursday in April and Lake Eden was having the worst Mud Season on record. In the past three days, Earl Flensburg had used his Winnetka County tow truck to pull eighteen vehicles out of the muddy ditches. This number included Hannah's cookie truck. Twice.

The current road conditions had been brought about by an extremely snowy winter that had yielded a record number of inches. Then, just last week, the days had turned warm with temperatures approaching a positively balmy fifty degrees. This unseasonably warm snap had melted the banks of hard-packed snow that lined the sides of the roads and had turned the shoulders into mud pits. To compound the problem the nights, like tonight, were cold enough to refreeze the water from the afternoon runoff, but the mud in the ditches took much longer to refreeze. Hapless motorists on the highways skidded on the icy film. If they were lucky, they simply ended up in the ditch in need of a tow truck. If they were unlucky, they sideswiped several other cars, resulting in multiple injuries. Warnings about the hazardous road conditions filled the KCOW-TV evening news, but some drivers seemed perfectly oblivious. Until the weather evened out, one way or the other, accidents on the highway would continue to be more common than lost mittens.

Hannah gripped the wheel tightly. Road conditions would improve once they turned onto the gravel road that led to the Lake Eden Inn, but they still had over five miles to go on asphalt that resembled nothing so much as an improperly frozen hockey rink.

The two sisters rode in silence for several minutes and then Hannah glanced over at her sister. There was a smile on Michelle's face and Hannah assumed that she was thinking about Lonnie Murphy, the youngest member of the Winnetka County Sheriff's Department detective squad. They were on their way to meet Lonnie and his cousin, Devin, at the Lake Eden Inn. There they'd enjoy a preview of Sally and Dick Laughlin's first-ever weekend jazz festival by listening to the headliner band, the Cinnamon Roll Six, rehearse for their performance the following night. When the rehearsal was over, the Swensen sisters would help Sally serve Hannah's Special Cinnamon Rolls to the small crowd that had been invited to the musical sneak-peek.

The cinnamon rolls smelled wonderful and Hannah's stomach growled. She hadn't taken time for lunch, and she did her best to resist an almost overwhelming urge to reach in the back and snag one for herself. Only the fact that she had to keep both hands on the wheel kept her from indulging that urge. They'd taken the sweet treats out of the oven at The Cookie Jar less than thirty minutes ago, frosted them, and covered the pans with foil. Then they'd secured them in the back of the cookie truck and headed for the highway. Now the interior was filled with the mouthwatering scents of warm bread, cinnamon, and chocolate, and Hannah was getting more ravenous by the minute.

Michelle gave a wistful sigh. "I don't know how much longer I can hold out. Those rolls smell scrumptious."

"I was thinking the same thing myself. Maybe we should . . . uh-oh!" Hannah stopped speaking abruptly as brake lights began to flash on the roadway ahead. "Holy . . . !"

"Cow!" Michelle supplied, finishing the phrase with a much more socially acceptable word than the one that Hannah had been about to utter. "What's going on up there?"

"I don't know, but it looks like trouble. And we're not sticking around to find out!" That said, Hannah reacted almost instantaneously as she wrenched the wheel, pumped the brakes, steered out of a skid, and managed to fishtail onto the curvy access road that led to the Winnetka County rest stop.

Hannah barreled past a speed limit sign that warned motorists to slow to fifteen miles an hour. She knew she was going much faster than that, but she didn't take her eyes off the road to check as she muscled her truck around the icy curves. When she reached the straightaway that ran past the rest stop, she skidded on a patch of ice and came very close to crashing into the faded Minnesota state map with the red YOU ARE HERE arrow pointing to Lake Eden. Still going well over the posted speed limit, her truck whizzed past the metal picnic table and barely missed wiping out on the corner of the concrete block restrooms.

They were deep in the pine forest now and the ice and snow lay in patches on the road. Hannah, the taller of the two sisters, felt her hair graze the top of the truck. For the first time in her life, she was grateful for the masses of curly red hair that cushioned her head. She was seriously wondering how much more swerving and skidding her truck could take before it shook apart, when they hit a pile of snow that slowed them, and the cookie truck came to rest scant inches from the massive trunk of a magnificent Norway pine.

"We made it," Hannah said in a shaky voice, stating the obvious.

"We did. I really don't know how you managed to get us here in one piece."

"Neither do I." Hannah realized that she'd been holding her breath and she took a deep gulp of air. And then, because she felt decidedly lightheaded, she lowered the window for a breath of fresh cold air.

Michelle did the same and then she turned to give her sister an unsteady smile. "That could have been bad, but you turned off just in time, and we . . ." Michelle stopped short and leaned closer to the open window. She listened for a moment, and then she frowned. "What's *that?*"

"More trouble," Hannah answered, listen-

16

ing to sounds of metal striking metal with considerable force. "It's a good thing we got off the highway when we did. It sounds like a really bad accident."

"More than one accident. It's a chain reaction. They're still crashing over there and it must be a massive pileup. Do you think we should go back and try to help?"

"Yes, but first we need to call the sheriff's station. Do you have your cell phone?"

"Right here." Michelle pulled it out of her pocket. "What do you want me to say?"

"Tell them it's a multi-vehicle accident and to come out here right away. There are bound to be injuries, so they should put in a call for ambulances. Tell the dispatcher to alert Doc Knight at the hospital so he can set up to receive the accident victims."

"Got it," Michelle said, pressing numbers on her phone.

"I'm going to try to get turned around and drive up there."

"Okay. It's ringing now. I'll tell the dispatcher what's happening."

As Michelle began to relay the information to the sheriff's station, Hannah turned the truck around. This took several minutes as the road was narrow, and they couldn't be of much help if they wound up stuck in the ditch. Her window was still down and

17

she realized that the squeal of brakes and loud crashes had stopped. With the exception of a car horn that had stuck, the night was eerily silent. And then, just as she was about to pull out onto the access road that paralleled the highway, sirens wailed in the distance. Help was coming, and from the sounds of the breaking glass and impacts they'd heard only seconds before, it wasn't a moment too soon.

Hannah and Michelle traveled forward on the access road, grateful that they weren't in the path of the approaching emergency vehicles. They spotted three squad cars, two ambulances, and the Lake Eden fire truck. All had sirens wailing and lights flashing as they approached the accident scene.

"It's bad," Michelle said, as they got close enough to see the twisted wreckage.

"I know. Look up there on the left about fifty feet ahead. There's a bus upside down in the ditch. And there's so much wreckage spread out on the road, I don't think the emergency vehicles can get to it."

"You're right. They'll have to hike in and it's a ways. Let's get as close as we can on the access road and walk in through the ditch. I took a class in first aid and maybe I can do something to help. At least we can try to get the bus doors open so the passengers can get out."

Hannah drove forward until she was adjacent to the overturned bus. Then both sisters got out of Hannah's cookie truck and hurried down the steep, tree-lined bank.

"Careful," Hannah warned. "It could be muddy at the bottom of the ditch."

Michelle reached the bottom first and turned back. "It's still frozen. It must be because it doesn't get any sun with all these trees."

The snow was deep at the bottom of the ditch and the two sisters waded through it with some difficulty. Then they started up the steep bank on the other side and made their way toward the overturned bus.

"I don't hear anything," Michelle said as they got closer to the bus. "Maybe everyone inside is okay and they're just waiting for someone to come and help them get out."

*Or maybe everyone inside is unconscious or dead,* Hannah thought, but she didn't say it. That was speculation on her part, and there was no sense in upsetting Michelle until they were able to get inside the bus and assess the situation for themselves.

"It looks like a charter bus," Michelle commented as they got closer. "There aren't any regular busses painted gold. I wish I could read what it says on the side, but the letters are upside down and backwards."

"It's the band bus."

"What band?"

"The Cinnamon Roll Six."

"How do you know that?"

"It says Cinnamon Roll Six on the side."

Michelle was silent for a moment, trying to make out the letters. "You could be right. Can you actually read it, or are you just guessing?"

"I can read it. I taught myself to read backwards and upside down when you and Andrea were kids and I was helping you with your homework."

"But why did you have to learn to read upside down and backwards?"

"It was easier than getting up and walking around to read over your shoulders." Hannah reached out to grab Michelle's arm. "Careful of that pine branch. The bus snapped it off and it's sticking up like a spear."

Another twenty feet and they had arrived at the back of the bus. It was wedged between two trees and it had obviously rammed into a third, even larger tree. From the wide swath the bus had cut through the spirea and gooseberry bushes, it had obviously rolled over and slid on its top to the place where it was now lodged.

"We can't get in the passenger door," Michelle said, walking around the bus. "It's blocked by those tree branches. Don't most charter busses have an escape hatch cut into the top?"

"Yes, but the top of the bus is now the bottom, and it's buried in several feet of snow. We'll have to get in through the back door. Come on, Michelle. Let's go."

Both sisters headed around the bus, lifting pine branches as they went. When they arrived at the rear, Hannah attempted to open the door. "I can't get it open," she reported, stepping back with a disappointed sigh. "The handle won't budge."

"It must be locked from the inside."

"You're right. Let's see if anybody inside can hear us."

"Hello?" Michelle called out. "Are you okay in there?"

They waited a moment or two, but there was no answer. Hannah stepped closer and yelled as loudly as she could. "We need someone to open the back door. Can anyone get there to unlock it?"

The only sounds they heard were the distant sirens of emergency vehicles speeding to the accident site, and the wind whistling through the pines. Inside the locked bus, all was ominously silent.

# CHAPTER TWO

The two sisters waited breathlessly. Hannah was almost positive that they were thinking the same dire thought. *Was everyone dead inside the bus? Or were they so badly injured they couldn't even call out?*

"I can do it," a faint voice came from the interior of the bus. "I was riding in the back. Give me a minute and I'll get there."

Several moments later there was the sound of a lock clicking, and the back door swung open to reveal a handsome but haggard-looking man with strips of cloth wrapped around his wrist. The cloth strips were holding a screwdriver in place as a makeshift brace. "Are you doctors?"

"No," Michelle answered. "I've had first aid training, but that's about it."

"Who *are* you then?"

"Two passing motorists who came to help," Hannah explained as quickly as she could. "It may take the paramedics some time to get to you. The road's blocked by the wreckage and they'll have to hike in over half a mile. Is anyone inside badly injured?"

"No. We've all got bruises, but I'm the worst . . . unless you count the bus driver. Lynnette made this splint for me. She used to work in a doctor's office."

"Lynnette's a nurse?" Hannah asked.

He shook his head. "She was in charge of the appointment desk, but she used to help the nurses when they got really busy. You know, hand them things and stuff like that."

"Do you think your wrist is broken?" Michelle asked.

"I don't think so, but I'm no doctor. I guess I can find out for sure from the paramedics, or the doctors . . . if they ever get here."

*You're pretty impatient considering the accident happened less than five minutes ago,* Hannah thought, but she didn't say it. He'd been injured and she should make allowances for that. "I'm sure they'll come just as soon as they can," she said, giving him a comforting smile. "Two ambulances and a fire truck passed us on the way here."

Michelle stepped closer and examined his splint. "Your splint looks just fine. It's holding your wrist immobile and that's exactly what it's supposed to do. You'll probably need X-rays when you get to the hospital, but you're fine for now. Just be careful not to bang it against anything or try to use your right arm. You don't want to risk injuring it further, especially since you play keyboards."

"You know me?" he asked, looking pleased.

"Not personally, but I know your music. You're Buddy Neiman, the keyboard player with Cinnamon Roll Six."

"That's right." Buddy gave her a long, assessing look. "So you're a fan?"

"I certainly am. Your music is great."

"Thanks. Hey . . . maybe you want to get together for a drink or something after we play tomorrow night."

Hannah held her breath. She hoped Michelle realized that Buddy was trying to pick her up.

"That would be nice. I'll be there with my boyfriend and his cousin, Devin. Devin's your biggest fan, and he's the one who introduced me to your music. He's got everything the Cinnamon Roll Six ever recorded, and he plays keyboards with the Jordan High jazz band. He told me he can hardly wait to meet you and tell you how great he thinks you are."

Hannah watched the play of expressions

cross Buddy's face. There was disappointment in the fact that Michelle had a boyfriend, regret that he'd asked her to have a drink since she'd assumed he was open to including her boyfriend and Devin, and pleased at the compliment to his musical talent. Flattery must have won out in the end, because he smiled.

"I'd like to meet your boyfriend and his cousin," he said, going into fan mode. "Devin sounds like a nice kid."

"Oh, he is. He's pretty talented, too. He's got a job playing the piano at the Lake Eden Inn during the dinner hour on weekends."

*Enough chit-chat,* Hannah's mind prodded. *Get to what's important.*

"You said there weren't any other serious injuries unless you counted the driver," Michelle said, almost as if she'd read Hannah's mind. "What did you mean by that?"

"He's dead."

"The driver is *dead?*" Hannah repeated, just to make sure she'd understood his response.

"That's what Lynnette said. She went up there to see if he was okay, and when she came back, she told us he was dead. It's probably why he went off the road in the first place. I'm thinking it must have been a heart attack or something sudden like that.

One minute we were traveling along as smooth as silk, and the next minute we were fishtailing across three lanes of traffic and crashing sideways into the ditch."

"We'd better take a look at the driver to make sure there's nothing we can do for him," Michelle said.

"Sounds good. Come on in."

Buddy held out his uninjured arm, and Michelle hopped nimbly into the bus. It took Hannah a bit longer to get inside, but soon the two sisters were standing at the very back of the bus in the space where the band stored their instruments. The locked cabinets, which had been bolted to the floor, were now hanging upside down over their heads, and they were standing on what looked like a shallow trough, but was really the slightly arched ceiling of the bus.

It was a bit disorienting. The shadows were deep, the interior illuminated only by two strips of emergency LED lights that had been installed on the floor. Those lights were now above their heads, and Hannah could see that close to a dozen people were huddled against the windows on either side.

"The back door's unlocked if anybody wants to get out," Buddy announced, "but it's warmer in here."

"I think we should all stay here," an older

man spoke up. There were several nods from the group huddled around him, and Hannah could see that he was the leader, unofficially or not. "Better hold onto the pup. He's so little, we could lose him in the snow."

Buddy shrugged. "We're going to have to lose him anyway now that Clay's dead. He's the one who stopped to rescue him. And he's the one who said he'd find him a home."

"Maybe we can take him," a girl with long black hair spoke up. "He's so cute."

Hannah moved a step closer and saw a tiny puppy face with impossibly big ears peeking out from a blanket on the girl's lap.

"You know we can't take him," the brown-haired guy sitting next to her said. "We're on the road all the time."

"We can just turn him loose once we get to town," Buddy suggested. "Maybe somebody will feel sorry for him and take him in."

"You can't do that! It's cold out there, and you know he was almost frozen to death when Clay rescued him. He's got to have a warm place to sleep and food to eat. He's so thin I can feel his little ribs right through the blanket. We've just got to find somebody to take him in."

"I'll take him," Hannah said, surprising everyone including herself.

"Who are you?" the older man asked her.

"Hannah Swensen. And this is my sister, Michelle. We spotted the bus in the ditch and we came to see if we could help."

"Nice of you," the man said. "I'm Lee Campbell, the band manager."

"Karl Reese. Drums." A tall gangly redhead with hair almost as curly as Hannah's spoke up. "And this is my girlfriend, Penny."

"Glad to meet you," Penny said. "Thanks for coming to help us out."

The girl holding the puppy gave Hannah a shy smile. "I'm so glad you're taking this little guy. He's been through a lot, and he's really a good puppy."

"My wife, the patron saint of anything with fur," the brown-haired man sitting next to her said. "She's Annie and I'm Tommy Asch. I play sax and clarinet."

"Conrad Bergen. Bass," the guy who looked like the boy next door in so many old movies introduced himself.

"I'm Eric Campbell," the guy with long, dark hair pulled back into a ponytail gave them a smile. "And he's Drake Mason," he introduced the bald, slightly heavyset guy sitting next to him. "We're brass."

"I'm Cammy." The girl with an extremely

28

low-cut sweater told them. "I travel with the band."

The bleached blonde sitting next to her gave both of them an assessing look to see if they might be competition. "And I'm Lynnette. We help the boys set up and . . . uh . . . things like that."

Hannah was not about to ask what *things like that* meant. Instead she said, "I understand the driver is dead?"

"Yeah. I went up there to check on him. He was dead."

"Did you try to find a pulse?" Michelle asked her.

"Do I look like an idiot? Sure I tried to find a pulse. There wasn't any, and he wasn't breathing either. I've got some medical training, you know."

*Of course you do,* Hannah's mind replied. *You know how to say "Doctor will see you at ten on Thursday, Mrs. Smith. Please let us know twenty-four hours in advance if you can't keep your appointment."* But instead of voicing her thoughts, she asked, "Do you mind if I take a look, Lynnette? Sometimes those pulse points can be very difficult to find, especially if the patient is comatose. It's not that I don't trust you. I'm sure you know what you're doing. It's just that if I don't check to make certain, I could lose my

29

license."

"Oh. Well . . . sure! *That's* different. Have at it." Lynnette dismissed her with a wave. "No way I'm going up there again. Clay looked really creepy."

*Wonderful!* Hannah's mind replied. *I can hardly wait to see what you think is creepy.* But of course she didn't say a word. She certainly wasn't looking forward to a trip to the front of the bus. It would be a test of agility because she'd have to walk in the metal trough that formed the high part of the upside down ceiling, but she wanted to spare her sister the sight of the dead driver. She turned to Michelle and chose her words carefully. If Michelle thought she was needed, she'd come along even if the prospect was daunting. "I'll go check on the driver. You stay here and see if you can help anyone else."

"No way. I'm going with you."

"But you don't have to . . ."

"Yes, I do." Michelle insisted. "I don't want to lose my license either."

The trip up the nonexistent aisle wasn't easy. The way Hannah assessed it, they had two choices. They could walk upright, putting one foot directly ahead of the other and risk losing their balance, or they could straddle the very center of the ceiling and walk with their feet spread out several feet apart. Hannah opted to straddle the steepest part of the ceiling and they preceded forward, small step by small step, with their arms extended out from their sides for balance.

Michelle waited until they were out of earshot and then she tapped Hannah on the arm. "What license are we in danger of losing if we don't do this?"

"Uh . . ." Hannah thought fast. "I think that would be our Good Sense license. I'm willing to bet that Lynnette didn't even know *how* to check for a pulse."

"I'll buy that."

The two sisters made their way toward the front of the bus. The dim glow from the strips of LED lights was cold and blue, and everything, even ordinary things like bus windows and shades, seemed eerie and unreal. Most of the bus seats had fallen open into a reclining position, and hung above their heads flapped out like giant prehistoric bats.

When they reached the front, Michelle glanced around. There was no one slumped by the walls or spread out on the ceiling that was now the floor. "I don't see the bus driver. Where is he?"

"There," Hannah answered, pointing

31

upward at the driver still strapped in his seat above them.

For a moment neither sister said a word. They just stared at the driver, suspended by his seat belt, with one arm dangling down so far the fingers almost touched their heads. His mouth was open as if in surprise, and he appeared to be regarding them fixedly with his sightless eyes.

Michelle shivered, and then she turned to Hannah. "Lynnette's right. He's creepy," she whispered.

"No argument here," Hannah replied, taking Michelle's arm and turning her around. "Let's go."

"But . . . shouldn't we check for a pulse?"

Hannah was about to point out that the driver's neck was twisted at an impossible angle and no one could live with his neck turned halfway around like that, but Michelle looked shaken enough as it was. If Michelle wanted her to feel the dead driver's wrist for a pulse, she'd do it.

She was about to reach up for the driver's wrist to search for signs of life she knew weren't there when Buddy hailed them from the back of the bus.

"Come on back! The paramedics just arrived!"

# CHAPTER THREE

"Is everybody okay back there?" Hannah asked as she turned onto the highway.

"We're fine," one of the wives responded. Hannah wasn't sure which wife it was since there were two married couples riding in the back of her cookie truck. They were part of the group that Doc Knight's interns had asked her to take to the hospital, since there were only a few vehicles available and the ambulances were transporting the more seriously injured.

Luckily, the two couples had escaped with minor scrapes and bruises. One of the husbands had a cut on his leg that might require a couple of stitches, and the other husband had suffered a blow to his head and would be watched for several hours for signs of a concussion. The wives had scrapes and bruises, but their injuries were minor. They had been on their way to the Tri-County Mall to see a movie when they'd come upon the accident and been unable to avoid becoming part of the massive pileup.

"How about you, Buddy?" Hannah asked. The keyboard player had the most serious injury in her little group of what Ben Matson, one of Doc's interns, had called the "walking wounded".

"I'm okay, except those cinnamon rolls are driving me crazy. Usually we stop somewhere on the road, but we were supposed to have dinner out at the Lake Eden Inn before our practice."

"All he had was some of my vegetable chips," Lynnette, the final member of Hannah's group reported. She was completely uninjured, but she was riding along so that she could rejoin the rest of the band at the hospital.

"We were going to have dinner at the food court out at the mall," one of the husbands told Hannah, "so we're pretty hungry, too. How long until we get there?"

"No more than fifteen minutes. I have to make a quick stop to drop off the puppy, and then we'll go straight to the hospital. We'll get you all something to eat from the vending machines just as soon as we get there."

"Forget the dog, just get us some food," Buddy said, sounding more than a little petulant. "I want one of those cinnamon rolls right now."

Hannah shook her head. "I'm sorry, but I can't do that. The cinnamon rolls are part of an order that's been bought and paid for. But I do have some cookies in the back. How about a couple of Triplet Chiplets?"

"What are those?" one of the wives asked.

"Cookies with three kinds of chips. These have white chocolate, semi-sweet chocolate, and milk chocolate chips."

"Too bad that white chocolate's not peanut butter chips," Buddy complained.

*Well it's not, and there's not a lot I can do about it at this late date,* Hannah thought, but she snapped her mouth tightly shut and reminded herself that Buddy had been in a traumatic accident. It was true that his injury wasn't life threatening, but he was probably afraid that his wrist was broken, and that might end his musical career.

"Try one. You'll like them," Michelle said, just as Hannah pulled into Lisa and Herb's driveway. "Hannah's going in with the puppy, but I'll stay here and find all the extra cookies she has in the back. Then you can choose the ones you want to try."

"Hannah! What are you doing . . . oh! How precious!" Lisa held out her arms to take the puppy.

It was precisely the reaction Hannah had been hoping for. She stepped into her business partner's warm kitchen and put the puppy into Lisa's waiting arms. "This poor little guy was on the band bus when it went into the ditch. He was part of that accident on the highway. Someone was holding him and he's not hurt."

"Thank goodness for that! I know all about the accident. Herb got a call about twenty minutes ago, and he left to go out there to help transport people to the hospital." She looked down at the puppy with a concerned expression. "Are you *sure* he's not hurt?"

"I'm sure. One of the paramedics checked him out. I think he's really hungry though. The driver of the band bus found him shivering in the cold and stopped to pick him up. The wife of the bass player wrapped him in a blanket and held him. They were going to take him to a shelter."

*"Were?"* Lisa asked, carrying the puppy to Dillon's dog bed, tucking the blanket more securely around him. She opened a can of dog food, put some into a bowl, stirred in some chicken broth to thin it, and heated it in the microwave. "So does he belong to anybody?"

"No. That's why they were going to take him to the shelter. And when they told me that, I said *I'd* take him. I don't know why I did that. I have no idea if he'll get along with Moishe. And even if he does, he'll be alone all day in the condo while I'm at work. And since I'm on the second floor, I can't even have a doggy door."

"I have a doggy door," Lisa said, stirring the bowl of warm food and picking up the puppy again. She nestled the little guy in her lap, dipped her finger in the bowl of food, and let him lick it.

"I know you have a doggy door, but I didn't come here to ask you to take me off the hook. I can try it and see how it goes. I just need you to babysit while I take some of the accident victims to the hospital to get checked out."

"Okay, I can do that. But I'm serious, Hannah. I can take him. We only have one dog and we've been talking about getting another one. When you have two, they're company for each other."

"But will a dog this little get along with Dillon?"

"Of course he will. Dillon loves other dogs and he's crazy about puppies. He'll adopt this little one in no time flat."

"Well . . . I don't want you to feel you

*have* to take him."

"I don't feel I have to. I *want* to take him. Dillon's always with Herb. He rides in the squad car with him and he goes on rounds. They're practically inseparable. Dillon loves me. I know he does. But Herb trained him and spent more time with him than I did. Dillon's really Herb's dog, and I'd like a dog of my own. This little guy could be *my* dog."

"Well . . ."

"Come on, Hannah. The only reason you said you'd take him is you felt sorry for him. And now you're having second thoughts and . . ." Lisa stopped talking and narrowed her eyes. "You figured I'd take him right from the start, didn't you!"

"Who, me?" Hannah put on her most innocent expression.

"Yes, you. You knew I'd take him, and that's why you said that *you* would. And you brought him over here so I'd fall in love with him and keep him. Don't deny it, Hannah. We've been partners for almost three years and I know you."

"Okay. Maybe I had you in mind. You *did* say you wanted a dog that was all your own. And this little guy is so small, we could keep him down at The Cookie Jar during the daytime."

"How about the health regulations?"

"Your husband is in law enforcement. Police dogs are in the same category as service dogs. You know the rules. Service dogs can go into places that normally don't allow dogs."

"But Sammy isn't a police dog or a service dog."

She'd named him already! Hannah felt almost giddy with success. "Sammy could be a service dog in training. Why did you name him Sammy anyway?"

"It's his markings. He looks like he's wearing a little Sam Browne belt. Are you sure I can bring him to work?"

"I'm sure. All we need is a crate for when we're super busy, a bed and some toys, and a leash and harness for when he wants to visit in the coffee shop."

"You had this all planned out, didn't you?"

"No, at least not everything. I was just hoping, that's all. So do you think it'll work?"

Lisa glanced down at little Sammy. He'd finished most of the food and fallen asleep snuggled in her arms. "Oh, yes," she said, giving a happy smile. "It'll work just fine."

When Hannah pulled up by the emergency entrance to Lake Eden Memorial Hospital, she was met by Freddy Sawyer, who had been pressed into service as an orderly, and Marlene Aldrich, one of Doc Knight's interns.

"Ben's inside running triage," Marlene said, motioning for Freddy to help the two couples out of the back of Hannah's cookie truck. "Any serious injuries, Hannah?"

"A possible concussion, a cut that may need stitches, and bumps, scrapes, and bruises. Nothing life threatening. The most serious is Buddy Neiman." Hannah watched as Freddy carefully helped Buddy down from the cookie truck. "He plays keyboards with the Cinnamon Roll Six, the jazz band. Their band bus went into the ditch. Buddy hurt his wrist and we're hoping it's not broken."

Marlene inspected Buddy's splint and gave a quick nod. "It's fine for now. Get your whole group settled in the waiting room, and I'll come to take Buddy to X-ray myself."

"I'll get everyone settled," Michelle said, and led the little group away. As soon as they were out of earshot, Marlene turned to Hannah. "I heard them play at Club Nineteen in the Cities, and Buddy was terrific. The whole band was terrific. Are any of the rest of them injured?"

"Just Buddy. Someone else is bringing the rest of them in. Is there anything I can do to help out, Marlene?"

"Just get your group coffee, or something to eat if they're hungry. The kitchen's closed, but the vending machines in the lobby have sandwiches and fruit, and things like that. We'll be by to check out your people just as soon as we can."

"How's Freddy doing?" Hannah asked as they entered the emergency room doors. Ever since the mildly retarded young man had started to work for Doc Knight and his staff at the hospital, he'd seemed more relaxed and cheerful.

"Freddy's great. He really loves to work, and once he learns how to do something, he never forgets. This place couldn't run without him. I tell him that every day, and he always gives me that big smile of his and says his mother used to tell him that." Marlene stopped and gave a little sigh. "And speaking of mothers, I almost forgot to tell you. Yours is here, and she said she wanted to see you right away if you came in. I think she's in Doc Knight's office making phone calls to bring in the Rainbow Ladies."

"Okay. I'll find her."

Hannah helped Michelle get beverages and snacks from the vending machines for

41

the two couples, Lynnette, and Buddy. Once she'd made sure they were comfortably settled, she went off in search of her mother.

Delores Swensen had taken over as leader of the group of women now called the Rainbow Ladies, a hospital auxiliary that helped patients fill out paperwork, acted as companions to those who didn't have family present for their treatments and procedures, visited anyone who didn't have visitors, read books to patients who were bored with watching television, and generally served as a liaison between patients, family members, and the hospital staff.

The new responsibility their mother had taken on had come as a surprise to all three of her daughters. Hannah, Michelle, and Andrea all knew that their mother was not known for her charity work. Andrea thought that their mother might have become more sympathetic to those less fortunate now that she was older, but Hannah and Michelle still thought there must be another motive. Delores wasn't a joiner and she certainly wasn't a do-gooder. There had to be a reason for this sudden change, and they had yet to discover what it was.

Before Delores had taken over this charitable group, it had been known as the Gray Ladies. The gray smocks the women wore were definitely not to their mother's liking. Delores preferred bright colors, and she immediately indulged her preference. The Gray Ladies, now known as the Rainbow Ladies, wore blazers in their favorite bright color. As the leader of the group, Delores had her choice of colors, and she'd ordered three blazers for herself. Tonight she was wearing one in a bright cherry color, and Hannah spotted her coming out of Doc Knight's office.

"Hannah!" Delores exclaimed, giving a relieved sigh. "I knew you were driving out to Sally's tonight and I hoped you and Michelle weren't involved in that big accident."

"We weren't. I managed to turn off at the rest stop just in time."

"Well! That's the last time I complain about that rest stop and all the money the state wasted." Delores gave her eldest daughter a sharp look. "You should have called me immediately. I was worried about you and Michelle."

"Sorry, Mother. We were busy trying to get to a bus that was overturned in a ditch, and we didn't even think of it. We didn't mean to make you worry and we apologize."

"All right then. I'm just glad you two girls are all right. Tell me about the bus."

"It was the band bus carrying the Cinnamon Roll Six. The rest of the cars in the accident were blocking the road, and it took the paramedics a while to get to the bus. Michelle and I took the access road and walked across through the ditch. We were the first ones there."

"Oh, my!"

"The driver's dead, but everyone else seems to be okay except the keyboard player. He may have a broken wrist, but they won't know for sure until he has X-rays."

"Oh, dear! Have you called Sally?"

"No, Mother. Why would I call Sally?"

"To tell her the band bus was in an accident. She's probably worried because they haven't shown up."

Hannah reached for her cell phone, hoping she'd remembered to charge it. "I can call her right now."

"I'll do it. You can call her the minute you find out if that keyboard player's wrist is all right. If the Cinnamon Roll Six can't play, she'll have to hire another jazz band."

"All right, Mother. I'll do that."

"Is the rest of the band here at the hospital?"

"I think so."

"Good. Where are those cinnamon rolls Sally ordered?"

"They're in my truck."

"How many do you have?"

"Ten dozen. That's what she ordered."

"Come with me," Delores said and headed back into Doc Knight's office. She sat down behind his desk, picked up the phone, and punched in a number. "Sally?" she asked when her call was answered. "This is Delores Swensen from the hospital. Your jazz band has been in an accident, a big pileup out on the highway, and they're here at the hospital. The bus is overturned in a ditch and the driver is dead, but the only other serious injury is that the keyboard player may have a broken wrist. We'll find out when he has X-rays and Hannah will call to tell you. In the meantime, she has your cinnamon rolls here. Do you want her to pass them out to the band and the other people who were in the accident?"

Delores listened for a moment, and then she gave a little nod. "Of course we'll heat them, Sally. And I'll have Hannah tell the rest of the band members that Dick is coming right out to pick them up and bring them to the Inn."

Hannah listened as Delores ended the conversation and said goodbye. It was the shortest and most succinct phone call she'd ever heard her mother make. Perhaps acting as the head of the Rainbow Ladies was very

45

good for Delores. It appeared that the extra responsibility had taught her to be less conversational and more efficient. If this call was any indication, it had reduced her tendency to gossip.

"All right, dear," Delores said when she'd hung up the phone. "Sit down and spill it."

"What?"

"Sit down and spill it. If you and Michelle were the first ones at the scene, you're bound to have some inside information and juicy details about the Cinnamon Roll Six."

"But I really don't know that much . . ."

"You probably know more than you think you do. Carrie got a call from a friend in Uppsala this afternoon. This lady said that the bus driver, Roger somebody-or-other, had a girl traveling with him, and she was a twelve-year-old-runaway!"

"That's not true, Mother. There were girls on the bus, but none of them were *that* young. Besides, the driver's name was Clayton, not Roger."

Delores gave an exasperated sigh. "See? That's how gossip gets started! The wrong information gets spread around by people who don't really know anything."

"You're right."

"I know I'm right. And the worst of it is . . ." Delores stopped speaking and stared hard at Hannah. "You said *was.* You said the driver's name *was* Clayton."

It was Hannah's turn to sigh. She'd spoken without thinking, and now she was stuck. There was nothing for it but to tell Delores what she already suspected. "The driver's dead, Mother."

Delores gave a sigh so deep, it seemed to come up from her toes. "You found another body!"

"Not exactly. Someone else found him first."

"But you *saw* him?"

"Yes, I saw him." Hannah knew what was coming next. It always did.

"Then tell me all about it. I want to know all the details so I can pass them on to the other Rainbow Ladies. I want you to meet me in the kitchen in fifteen minutes. And do hurry, dear. We have to get started passing out those cinnamon rolls."

## SPECIAL CINNAMON ROLLS

DO NOT preheat oven. This dough needs to rise before baking.

**Hannah's 1st Note: From start to finish, these cinnamon rolls will take about 3 and 1/2 to 4 hours before they're ready to eat. Your work time is only about 30 minutes, but there's a lot of down time while you wait for the dough to rise and to bake.**

**Ingredients for the Dough:**

1/2 cup hot coffee

1/2 cup whole milk

1 Tablespoon white *(granulated)* sugar

1 packet *(1/4 ounce)* dry active yeast *(I used Fleischmann's Active Dry yeast)*

1/4 cup salted butter *(1/2 stick, 2 ounces)*

1 Tablespoon vegetable oil

1 large egg

1 teaspoon salt

1/4 cup white *(granulated)* sugar *(yes, that's in addition to the sugar above)*

3 to 3 and 1/2 cups all-purpose flour *(pack it down in the cup when you measure it)*

## Ingredients for the Filling:
1/2 cup **(1 stick, 4 ounces, 1/4 pound)** salted butter, softened to room temperature

1 Tablespoon ground cinnamon

3/4 cup white **(granulated)** sugar

1 cup semisweet **(regular)** chocolate chips

## Ingredients for the Pan:
2 Tablespoons softened butter

2 Tablespoons white **(granulated)** sugar

1 teaspoon ground cinnamon

## Ingredients for the Icing:
1 cup powdered **(confectioner's)** sugar

1 Tablespoon salted butter, melted

1 Tablespoon milk

1/2 teaspoon vanilla

In a small microwave-safe container, combine the hot coffee with the half-cup milk. Microwave it on HIGH for 30 seconds.

Stir in the Tablespoon of white sugar. Then pour a half-cup of the mixture into another container.

Add the packet of yeast to the microwave-safe container and gently stir it in. Let it sit on the counter to proof **(that's what they call it when yeast starts working and** *bubbling)* while you . . .

Melt the butter in another small microwave container. It should only take about 30 seconds on HIGH. Add the Tablespoon of vegetable oil and let it sit on the counter to cool.

In a medium-size bowl, use a wooden spoon or a fork to beat the egg with the salt, the white sugar, and the coffee and milk mixture that does NOT contain the yeast.

Feel the small bowl with the butter and oil mixture. If it's not so hot it could cook the egg, stir it into your work bowl.

Add 1 and 1/2 cups of the flour. Stir it in and continue to stir until the mixture is smooth.

Now add the yeast mixture. *(See how puffy it is? Your yeast is working.)* Stir it in gently.

Add 1 and 1/2 more cups of flour in half-cup increments, stirring after each addition. *(Remember to pack it down in the cup!)* If the dough seems sticky, add that last half-cup of flour and stir that in.

Now comes the fun. Clear a space on your counter for the bread board. If you don't have a bread board, just clear a nice clean space on your counter.

Dust your work space with flour, spreading it out in a circle with your impeccably clean palms. Then upend your work bowl and plop the dough down on your floured circle. Sprinkle more flour over the top of your dough. Then grab it and flip it over so the bottom is now the top.

Think about that old boyfriend who broke up with you in high school, or anyone else in your past you'd really like to slap or punch. Visualize that person's face in the center of your mound of dough, pick up one edge and punch it down hard in the center of the dough. Fun, wasn't it?

Turn your dough clockwise and do it all over again. Keep turning and punching and pummeling that dough for the whole 5 minutes, flipping it over every minute or so to make sure you're also kneading the bottom.

When 5 minutes are up, gather the dough into a ball on the board or counter.

Wash and dry your hands.

If you haven't already done so, take 1/2 cup of salted butter out of the refrigerator so that it will be softened by the time you need to make the filling for your rolls.

Spray the inside of a much larger bowl with Pam or another nonstick cooking spray. Pick up the dough and nestle it right down in the bowl you prepared.

Wash and dry your bread board *(or your*

**counter if you didn't use a bread board).**
Tear off a sheet of plastic wrap that's larger than the surface of your dough, and stretch it out on the space you washed. Spray it with nonstick cooking spray, lift it up, and cover the dough in your bowl, sprayed side down, so it's touching the surface of the dough. Tuck it in around the dough so that the dough will stay nice and warm.

Set the bowl in a warm, draft-free place and let it rise for 1 to 1 and 1/2 hours or until it's doubled in size.

Sprinkle your bread board or counter again with a light coating of flour.

Turn the work bowl upside down on the floured board so that the dough will come out. *(If it sticks, just scoop it out with your hands.)*

Sprinkle the mound of dough lightly with flour, punch it down with your palms, and roll it out with a rolling pin into a 9-inch by 13-inch rectangle. *(That's the size of the cake pan you'll be using to bake your Special Cinnamon Rolls.)*

Spread the surface of the rectangle with the softened butter. *(If you forgot to soften it, give it 30 seconds in the microwave on HIGH to half-melt it and then spread it out on your dough.)* Let your dough sit there in all its buttery goodness while you make the rest of the topping.

Mix 3/4 cup white *(granulated)* sugar with the Tablespoon of cinnamon. *(I do this with a fork.)* Sprinkle this sugar and cinnamon mixture over the top of the rectangle of dough.

Sprinkle the cup of chocolate chips on top of the sugar and cinnamon mixture as evenly as you can.

Starting from one of the long sides of the rectangle, roll it up tightly like a jelly roll. Since you don't have 8 hands, you'll have to work from side to side, rolling a little bit up at a time in order to get it nice and even. Pinch the edge to the surface of the roll so that it will stay closed.

Spread the bottom of a 9-inch by 13-inch rectangular cake pan with the 2 Tablespoons of softened butter. Sprinkle in the 2 Tablespoons of sugar and tip the pan so it's evenly distributed. Sprinkle in the teaspoon of cinnamon as evenly as possible.

Use your sharpest knife to cut the roll of dough into 12 slices. Arrange the slices in the cake pan 3 rows across and 4 rows down.

Spray another sheet of plastic wrap with nonstick cooking spray and use that, sprayed side down, touching the surface of the rolls. Tuck it in and set your Special Cinnamon

Rolls in a warm, draft-free place for 45 minutes or until they're doubled in bulk.

When your rolls are ready to bake, preheat the oven to 350 degrees F., rack in the middle position. Leave the plastic wrap on your rolls until your oven comes up to temperature.

Remove the plastic wrap and bake your rolls at 350 degrees F., for 30 minutes or until nicely browned. Then take them out of the oven and place them on a cold stove burner or a wire rack to cool while you make the icing. You'll want to frost your rolls while they're still warm so that the icing can run down into the crevices.

Put the cup of powdered sugar into a small mixing bowl. Using a fork, mix in the melted butter, milk, and vanilla. Whisk it with your fork until it's smooth and creamy, and has the consistency of icing.

If the resulting mixture is too thick, whisk in a little more milk. If the resulting mixture is too thin, whisk in a bit more powdered sugar.

**Hannah's 2nd Note: Mother thinks I should frost these with Neverfail Fudge Frosting. I'm convinced that Mother would eat a dill pickle and insist that it was delicious if I frosted it with fudge frosting.**

# CHAPTER FOUR

When Hannah got back to the waiting room, she found Michelle sitting between Lonnie Murphy and his cousin Devin. Devin was a tall, lanky young man with an endearing grin, the bluest eyes Hannah had ever seen, and a shock of black hair that that fell in waves over his forehead. Devin had the chair next to Buddy Neiman, and there was a big smile on Buddy's face. Hannah figured that Devin must be regaling the Cinnamon Roll Six's keyboard player with compliments. Perhaps it would sweeten him up a bit.

"Hi Devin," Hannah greeted him, and then she turned to Lonnie. "Did they call you in to help?"

"Yup. We were only a mile from here when I got the call. The dispatcher told me to go straight to the hospital, and I was turning in the driveway before she even finished telling me about the accident."

Marlene came in just then and walked quickly to Buddy's side. "You can come with me," she said. "The other intern, Doctor Matson, wants to have a look at your wrist, and then someone will take you down to X-ray. There's a little wait, but it's not that long."

"I'll come with you," Lynnette offered, but Buddy shook his head.

"Stay here and wait for the rest of the band," he said. "You need to meet up with them when they come in. Devin here can come with me to X-ray . . . right, kid?"

"Sure!" Devin jumped up immediately. Then his delighted expression faded somewhat as he turned back to Lonnie. "Is it okay? I mean, do you need me to help you with anything?"

Lonnie shook his head. "Not a thing. We're here to help the patients. Buddy's a patient, at least for right now, and you're helping by keeping him company."

"Bring the rest of your group and follow me," Marlene instructed Hannah and Michelle. "We'll take them all into emergency together. Once they're cleared, the Rainbow Ladies can arrange for transportation."

It was only a short walk to the emergency room. Everyone handed over the paperwork they'd completed, and they all took seats in the uncomfortable green plastic chairs that were set aside for patients. Hannah wasn't sure if the chairs were an attempt to keep people from coming to the emergency room with non-emergency ailments, or an attempt to generate business by causing more complaints like backache, stiffness in the neck and shoulders, and loss of mobility from sitting on such a hard, unyielding surface.

The interior of the emergency room looked different tonight. Two sets of ugly tan curtains that could be drawn to cordon off a cubicle, had been tied back, out of the way. The resulting space was filled with medical personnel who were lined up against the back wall. She recognized three of the nurses, but the rest were strangers to her. They must be the extra nurses from nearby communities that had been called in to augment Doc Knight's small staff.

Vonnie Blair, Doc's secretary, was sitting at a desk in the far corner of the room. A copy machine sat next to her desk and once she made copies of a patient's paperwork, she stapled it to a folder. The doctor in the front of the line came forward to take the folder and call a patient to be seen.

Lonnie watched for a moment or two, and then he turned to Michelle and Devin. "I'm going to make the copies for Vonnie. It'll go quicker that way."

When Lonnie had left their little group, Michelle turned to Hannah. "Isn't that Norman near the back of the line?"

"I don't see . . . oh, yes. It's Norman. They must have called him in for any dental emergencies. I think I'll go over and . . ." Hannah stopped speaking and gave a little sigh. "No, I won't. *She's* with him."

"I wasn't going to mention that. I know how you feel about her. But you probably should do it anyway. Lake Eden's not that big, and you have to get along with her if you want to stay friends with Norman." Michelle stopped and frowned. "Unless you *don't* want to stay friendly with Norman."

"Of course I want Norman to be my friend. He's going to need to come over and see Cuddles."

"How's that going anyway?"

Hannah gave a little smile. She'd agreed to take Norman's cat, Cuddles, when he'd said that he had to find a new home for her, that his fiancée, Doctor Bev, was allergic to cats and she was going to move in with him. Hannah's cat, Moishe, and Cuddles were best friends so it wasn't an imposition at all. "Moishe's happy to have Cuddles with him. He really likes her you know. And Cuddles is crazy about Moishe."

"Does Cuddles miss Norman?"

"I think so. I know my place is the second-best home for Cuddles, but Norman's house, with Norman, is the best home for her. It's just a pity that . . ." Hannah stopped speaking as tears came to her eyes. She blinked several times and managed to keep them at bay. "Never mind. We can talk about that later tonight. You're staying with me, aren't you?"

"Of course. I know I could stay at Mother's, but she's never home. She's either at the hospital with the Rainbow Ladies, or over at Doc's house. It wouldn't be as much fun to stay there by myself."

Hannah blinked, and this time it wasn't to blink away tears. "Mother stays over at Doc's house?!"

"Oh, no. I didn't mean *that*. I just meant that Mother spends a lot of time with him at his place, at her place, at the hospital, or out doing something. That's all."

Hannah gave a relieved sigh. It wasn't that she was concerned about her mother's behavior. It was just that she didn't want the other members of the phone tree they'd unofficially dubbed The Lake Eden Gossip Hotline to gossip about their founding member, Delores herself!

"Buddy Neiman?" a voice broke into Hannah's thoughts. "The doctor will see you now."

"Come on, kid." Buddy got up from his plastic chair with an agility Hannah wished she could emulate, and motioned to Devin. "He's probably going to send me to X-ray. Let's go."

Hannah got to her feet. "I'll go with you. I want to make sure your wrist is okay."

They walked in pairs, Buddy and the nurse in the lead, and Hannah and Devin following behind them. As they passed by Norman and Doctor Bev, Norman's fiancée stepped behind him quickly, almost as if she didn't want Hannah to see her.

Bev's maneuver couldn't have suited Hannah better. She gave a little wave as she passed them, said a quick "Hi, Norman." And then they were on their way to see Doctor Ben Matson.

"Hello, Hannah." Ben greeted her. "You weren't injured, were you?"

"Not me. Your patient is Buddy Neiman. He's with Cinnamon Roll Six."

Ben glanced down at the chart. He took the time to read it through, and then he turned to Buddy. "So you're the keyboard player. Let's see what's going on with that wrist of yours."

As Ben began to examine Buddy's wrist,

Hannah glanced at her watch. Almost fifteen minutes had passed since she'd left her mother, and it was time to get the cinnamon rolls, meet Delores, warm the rolls, and then pass them out. "Is it okay if I leave you here, Buddy?" she asked him. "The lady who ordered the cinnamon rolls said to bring them inside and pass them out."

"Sure, if you bring me one. No problem."

"I'll catch up with you," Hannah promised, and with that said, she was off, hurrying across the floor to Michelle and the rest of their group of patients. When she got there, she saw that Bertie Straub, one of the Rainbow Ladies, was sitting in the chair that she had vacated.

"Your mother sent me to take over your group," Bertie told her. "She wants all three of you to help her pass out the cinnamon rolls."

"All *three?*" Michelle asked.

"Andrea must be here," Hannah said, drawing the obvious conclusion.

"That's right. She's in the kitchen with your mother and they're making the coffee."

Hannah drew a sigh of relief. At least they weren't trying to cook anything! Both Delores and Andrea were culinarily challenged in the kitchen.

"She said to tell you to drop everything else and bring her the cinnamon rolls," Bertie added. "And she said to do it right away."

"Right," Hannah said, exchanging glances with Michelle. That was a command, and commands from Delores were not to be ignored. They thanked Bertie for taking over their duties, said goodbye to their charges, grabbed an unused hospital cart, and rushed outside to retrieve the pans of rolls.

Less than five minutes later, they were pushing the cart down the hospital corridor with ten dozen Special Cinnamon Rolls on the top shelf, and every bag of leftover cookies that Hannah had loaded into her truck on the bottom shelf.

"What's in the box?" Michelle asked, eyeing the distinctive bakery box that Hannah had set on top of a pan of rolls.

"Sinco de Cocoa Cookies. They're chocolate and avocado drop cookies."

"Chocolate and avocado? That's a strange combination." Michelle opened the box and peered inside. "They smell really great. Are they good?"

"Would you like to taste one?"

Michelle gave a little laugh. "I thought you'd never ask! Do you want me to get one out for you?"

"Absolutely. We're running late, and Mother's probably beside herself. It'll be easier to deal with her if we have a little chocolate. You taste first and I'll push the cart. And then you push the cart and I'll taste."

"Sounds like a plan to me." Michelle took a big bite of her cookie and an expression of total bliss crossed her face.

"Good?" Hannah asked.

"So good I could live on these for the rest of my life. Now I'll push and you taste." Michelle popped the rest of the cookie into her mouth, handed the second cookie to Hannah, and grabbed the cart.

Hannah took a bite and savored it for a moment. Then she chewed, swallowed, and smiled, accomplishing all three almost simultaneously.

"You like it as much as I do?"

"You bet I do! This is a great combination! I don't know why, but the avocado seems to makes the chocolate taste more intense."

"I think it does something to the texture, too."

"You're right. The texture is smooth and almost creamy."

Michelle looked a bit puzzled. "I didn't

actually taste the avocado the same way I would in guacamole."

"I didn't taste it either, but it's clear it's influencing the other ingredients. I'm not really sure why it works that way, but it does."

"And how!" Michelle agreed as they turned the corner and arrived at the double-wide kitchen doors. "Do you think we should give Mother one to sweeten her up?"

"Not yet. Just move the box to the bottom shelf. If she asks what it is, we'll tell her it's a special order."

"But it's not a special order . . . is it?"

"Yes, it is. It's a special order for the whole Swensen family."

"I get it." Michelle looked pleased. "It's for later, when we're through with the patients, and everything's nice and calm, and we can relax with a cup of coffee and something yummy."

"You got it," Hannah said, pushing in the swinging style kitchen doors and holding them open so that Michelle could wheel in the cart.

"About time!" Delores greeted them.

"Hi, Mother. Hi Andrea." Hannah gave them a big smile. "We're here, and we're all ready to cheer up some hungry patients."

# SINCO DE COCOA COOKIES
## (CHOCOLATE AVOCADO COOKIES)
Preheat oven to 350 degrees F.,
rack in the middle position.

**Jo Fluke's Note: Davene Mainwaring came up with the name for these delicious cookies. The "Sinco" refers to the five main ingredients: avocado, butter, flour, eggs, and sugar(s). The "Cocoa" refers to the other main ingredient, chocolate. I know that "Sinco" is really spelled "Cinco," but I couldn't resist a little pun since these cookies are so "Sin" fully delicious.**

1/2 cup salted butter *(1 stick, 4 ounces, 1/4 pound)*

3 one-ounce squares unsweetened chocolate *(I used Baker's)*

3/4 cup white *(granulated)* sugar

1 cup brown sugar, firmly packed

2 large eggs

1 teaspoon vanilla extract

1/2 teaspoon salt

1 teaspoon baking powder

1/2 cup mashed avocado *(that's 2 medium or 1 very large avocado)*

3 cups all-purpose flour *(pack it down in*

*the cup when you measure it)*
1 cup semi-sweet or 60% cocoa chocolate chips *(that's a 6-ounce bag)*

Melt the butter with the squares of chocolate in a microwave-safe bowl on HIGH for 2 minutes. Stir to see if the chocolate has melted. If it hasn't, microwave it again in 30-second increments until you can stir it smooth. You can also melt the butter and chocolate in a saucepan on the stovetop at MEDIUM heat, stirring frequently. *(I did this and it made my kitchen smell SO good!)*

**Hannah's 1st Note: If you cut the one-ounce squares of chocolate in half, they'll melt faster.**

When everything is melted, take the mixture off the heat *(or out of the microwave)* and let it cool on a cold burner.

Combine the white sugar and the brown sugar in a mixing bowl. Stir, or mix with an electric mixer until they're a uniform light brown color.

Add the eggs, one by one, mixing them in after each addition.

Mix in the vanilla extract, and beat the mixture until it's light and fluffy.

Mix in the salt and the baking powder, and beat until they're thoroughly combined.

Mash the avocado until it's a smooth puree. Measure out a half cup. Add it to your work bowl and mix until it's well blended.

Feel the outside of the bowl containing the butter and the chocolate mixture. If it's not so hot that it might cook the eggs, add it to your mixing bowl. *(If it is, have a cup of coffee and wait until it cools some more.)* Beat until everything is thoroughly incorporated.

Add the flour, 1/2 cup at a time, mixing after each addition. Continue to mix until the dough is smooth and well-blended.

Remove the bowl from the mixer and stir in the chocolate chips by hand. Stir until they're evenly distributed throughout the cookie dough.

Drop the dough by rounded teaspoons onto greased cookie sheets, cookie sheets sprayed with Pam or another nonstick cooking spray, or cookie sheets covered with parchment paper.

**Hannah's 2rd Note: I covered my cookie sheets with parchment paper — it was a lot easier!**

Bake at 350 degrees F. for 13 to 15 minutes, or until the cookies feel dry when LIGHTLY TOUCHED on the top. Be careful doing this. They will be very hot. If the very top of the cookie feels dry, take them out of the oven immediately. Like brownies, you don't want to overbake them. (Mine took exactly 14 minutes.)

Cool the Sinco de Cocoa cookies on the cookie sheet for 5 minutes. This will firm up the bottom. Then remove the cookies to a wire rack to cool completely. *(If you use parchment paper, you can just pull it off the cookie sheet and onto a wire rack.)*

Yield: 4 to 5 dozen delectable, chocolaty cookies that taste silky smooth and rich.

**Hannah's 3rd Note: I'd say that Sinco de Cocoa Cookies are so rich that nobody can eat more than one or two, but the last time I took a baker's dozen (that's 13 cookies) to Granny's Attic as a special treat for Mother and Carrie, they finished them all at lunchtime and called to ask me for more!**

# CHAPTER FIVE

"These are really good, Hannah." Lynnette popped the last bite of cinnamon roll into her mouth and gave a sigh of satisfaction. "I don't even feel guilty for breaking my diet."

"Uh-oh." Hannah went on red alert. She'd dieted before, more times than she wanted to count, and she certainly didn't want to tempt anyone to stray from their weight-loss plan. "I'm sorry, Lynnette. I should have asked if you could have a cinnamon roll. I just assumed that everyone wanted one, and . . ."

"And I *did* want one," Lynnette interrupted her. "It was delicious. If I had one of these every morning, I'd probably ditch my diet for good."

"Is it a weight-loss diet?" Michelle asked.

"Not really, but how much tofu can you eat? It's just something my friend Cammy talked me into trying when we started traveling with the band. Maybe it's time for

69

a change, anyway. I'm sick of eating nothing but tofu and vegetables. You don't happen to have an extra one of those cinnamon rolls, do you?"

After leaving another roll with Lynnette, Hannah and Michelle went up the corridor, dispensing their delectable wares. When they came to the end, they still had one pan of cinnamon rolls left, and Hannah turned to Michelle. "Why don't you find the nurses and give them some? A lot of them came in early, and they probably didn't have time to eat."

"Good idea." Michelle looked down at the cart and assessed the contents. "I think I've got enough," she said.

"If you don't, go back to the kitchen and get the cookie bags. That's why we brought them in. There should be enough to give cookies to everyone in the waiting room." Michelle turned to go, but Hannah called after her. "Just don't bring the box with the Sinco de Cocoa Cookies. They're for later."

Hannah watched as Michelle pushed the cart down the hall. After her sister had disappeared around the corner, Hannah stood there in the middle of the corridor, unsure of exactly what to do next. She supposed she could check on Buddy to see if he'd enjoyed his cinnamon roll, or perhaps she could go back to the emergency room to ask Bertie if she needed any help with the patients. She was just considering her options when the decision was made for her.

"Hannah?" One of the nurses came bustling up. "Your mother wants you. She's in treatment room seven. By the way, those were great cinnamon rolls."

"Thanks," Hannah said, walking down the hall toward the adjoining corridor. She had no idea what her mother wanted, but it was bound to involve something that would keep her from her condo and her bed when that was the only place she really wanted to be. She turned the corner at the end of the corridor, started down a second corridor that veered off at a ninety degree angle, and spotted Delores about twenty feet ahead, just emerging from one of the treatment rooms.

"Mother?" Hannah rushed forward to put her arm around her mother as Delores slumped heavily against the wall. Her mother's complexion was the same color as the all purpose flour that Hannah used at The Cookie Jar, and the makeup on her face stood out in sharp relief.

"Hannah," Delores said in a trembling voice. She shook her head as if to clear it and took a deep breath. "I need you, Hannah."

Alarm bells went off in Hannah head. Something was drastically wrong. "What is it, Mother? Are you ill?"

"No."

"Then what is it? You're shaking."

"He's dead," Delores said, giving a sigh that seemed to go on forever. "I just looked in at him to see if I could bring him anything. And he's dead!"

"Are you sure?" Hannah asked, preparing to go in and substantiate her mother's words.

"I'm very sure."

Hannah gave her mother a little hug. Delores was still shaking, and she looked as if she were about to pass out. "I'm sorry, Mother," she said in a comforting voice. "I know how hard this must be for you, but people don't come to the hospital unless there's something really wrong with them. Some patients are critically ill, and the doctors can't save them."

"I know that. You don't understand!" Delores stared at her eldest daughter for a moment, and then she shook her head. It appeared to be a massive effort and she took several deep breaths. "You don't understand!" she repeated.

Hannah held her mother tighter, afraid that she might faint. This was obviously the first time since Delores had started to do volunteer work at the hospital, that she'd come face-to-face with death. "I think I *do* understand," she said. "And I know it's a shock when a patient dies. It's terribly sad, but it happens, especially when you work at a hospital. Do you want me to call a nurse?"

"No."

"All right, but you need some help. You're still shaking and you're as pale as a ghost. I'd better call Doc Knight."

"No, call Mike," Delores insisted. And then she began to slide downward on the wall, as if her legs were no longer capable of supporting her.

Hannah couldn't hold her up, even though she tried. Delores was close to fainting and she was slumping like a rag doll. All Hannah could do was help her sit down on the linoleum floor with her back against the wall. Hannah crouched next to her and patted her mother's shoulder. "It's okay, Mother. You've going to be okay. I'm going to call Doc Knight to take a look at you."

"No! Call Mike!"

"But . . . why should I call Mike?"

Delores took a deep breath and visibly struggled to compose herself. A little color

73

came back to her complexion, and she turned to give Hannah a glare. "I told you why. He's dead!"

Hannah was thoroughly mystified by her mother's words. Mike was a detective with the sheriff's department. She didn't think it was standard hospital procedure to call the sheriff's department every time one of the patients died.

"Do it! Call Mike!" Delores insisted again.

It was fairly clear that her mother's mind had slipped a cog or two from the shock of discovering the dead patient. Perhaps, if Hannah could encourage Delores to talk about her traumatic experience, the shock would fade and her mother would calm down and think clearly again.

"All right, Mother," Hannah said in her most reassuring tone. "I'll call Mike, but first I need some information from you. Do you know the patient's name?"

"Of course I do. I looked at his chart the moment I came in. We're supposed to do that. It's more personal if we call the patients by name. And then I looked at *him,* and . . ." Delores stopped speaking and shuddered. "His name was Buddy Neiman."

"Buddy Neiman?! Are you sure?" Hannah was so shocked, it took a moment for it to sink.

"That's what it said on his chart."

"But I brought Buddy a cinnamon roll just a couple of minutes ago! The technician was wheeling him out of X-ray, and he said it was just a bad sprain. He was going to take Buddy to a treatment room to wait for someone to put a splint on his wrist. They wanted him to keep it immobile for a day or two. Once the splint was on, he could leave the hospital." Hannah began to frown. "Are you absolutely sure the patient was Buddy Neiman?"

"I'm sure. I remember thinking it was strange that he didn't use his full name. Usually Buddy is a nickname. He's dead, Hannah. I told you that."

"But the only thing wrong with him was a sprained wrist. Nobody dies from a sprained wrist!"

"That's true," Delores said, "but he didn't die from a sprained wrist. He died from the pair of surgical scissiors somebody buried in his chest. Call Mike!"

# CHAPTER SIX

Hannah sat at the round table in the hospital kitchen, the one the cooks used for their coffee breaks, waiting for her mother and sisters to join her. It was almost ten at night, and everyone who'd been admitted to the hospital was resting comfortably. Those who'd been treated and discharged were on their way home. Dick Laughlin had driven in with the Lake Eden Inn van to pick up the surviving members of the Cinnamon Roll Six and their entourage and Hannah had no doubt that Sally had given them a hot meal and shown them to their rooms.

It was snowing again, and Hannah stared out at the scene outside the kitchen window. Doc Knight had built his hospital in a lovely wooded area of Eden Lake's shore. Every one of the rooms for patients had a view of the pines and the lake because Doc believed that hospitals should be designed to make the patients comfortable and relaxed.

The outside of the hospital was illuminated by what the farmers in the area called yard lights. They were bright lights on tall poles that lit up the surrounding countryside. Doc's lights didn't seem to bother the wildlife around the lake. Patients who didn't draw their drapes could catch glimpses of deer browsing in the woods, raccoons scurrying across the snow, and an occasional porcupine waddling between the trees. Birds of every color and size flitted here and there, and others perched on the tree branches. If you had to be in the hospital, this was the nicest one Hannah had ever seen. It was no wonder that Freddy Sawyer was so happy living and working here.

Hannah caught sight of her reflection and frowned. She really ought to get her hair trimmed. It was a mass of unruly red curls that could not be tamed, and usually sent hairdressers running for the hills. Her face looked fuller and she knew that wasn't due to an imperfection in the glass windowpane. She'd gained a little weight after losing so much last year when she'd gone undercover at the spa in the mall to investigate a murder case. She was five feet eight inches tall, and that meant she could carry more weight than her shorter sisters. But her jeans were starting to feel tight around the waist and she knew she was doing what Delores lived in fear of doing. She was letting herself go.

She really should pay more attention to her personal appearance. It would help to wear clothes that were slimming, rather than shapeless and comfortable. She could get a new, flattering hairstyle, and while she was there at the beauty salon, she could learn the basics of makeup. But when could she find time do all this? She rarely got more than five or six hours sleep, and she didn't want to give up an hour of sleep time just to look more attractive. Her customers in her coffee shop and bakery were used to her just the way she was.

The wind whipped up loose snow and pelted it against the windowpane. Hannah jumped and immediately felt a little foolish, but it was an eerie sound made even more chilling by coming at the heels of murder right here in the hospital.

It was a big relief when the kitchen doors opened to admit Delores, Michelle, and Andrea. Hannah got them settled with cups of fresh coffee and motioned for Michelle to get the box of special cookies they'd stashed in a cupboard.

"Here, Mother. Have one of these," Michelle said, opening the box of Sinco de Cocoa Cookies.

"Thank you, but no. I'm not hungry."

"Come on, Mother," Hannah urged, pushing the cookie box closer so that her mother could catch a whiff of the tantalizing scent. "It'll help, I promise. Just try one, okay?"

"Chocolate?" Delores asked. And when Hannah nodded, she reached for a cookie.

"They're double chocolate," Hannah told her. "These cookies have chocolate chips and more chocolate in the dough. Down the hatch, Mother. I have three dozen in the box and they're going to go fast."

"You're right," Andrea said, reaching for a cookie. As usual, the third Swensen sister was dressed fashionably and oh-so-appropriately for a night helping her siblings at the hospital. Her light blond hair was fashioned in an intricate braid that was formed into a circle very like a chignon, and her makeup was flawless. She wore a soft pink sweater, grey tailored slacks, gray leather shoes that matched them perfectly, and the string of pearls her husband Bill had given her for Christmas two years ago.

"What do you think, Mother?" Michelle asked, noticing that Delores had finished her cookie.

"I think they're just what I need. And I

think I'll have another. Please hand me one, will you, dear?"

"Ready?" Michelle asked, inserting the key in the lock on Hannah's condo door, but not opening it.

"I'm ready." Hannah stood several feet in front of the door, her legs spread out a bit for balance.

"How about Cuddles? Does she do it, too?"

"Not yet. I'm hoping she doesn't learn it from Moishe. I don't know if I can handle two cats at once."

"Here goes." Michelle opened the door and stood to the side to make room for the orange and white blur that leaped out and hurtled into Hannah's waiting arms.

"Oof!" Hannah said quite involuntarily. "I think he's gotten heavier."

"You could weigh him to see. Just stand on the scale with him in your arms. And then put him down and weigh yourself."

"Not a good idea." Hannah walked into her living room and set her cat down in one of his favorite places. Moishe loved to sit on the back of the couch and peer through the living room window.

"Why isn't it a good idea?"

"Because I don't want to weigh myself.

And if I want to find out how much Moishe weighs, I'll have to do it."

"Oh." Michelle walked over to the arm of the couch where Cuddles, a much smaller grey tabby, was sitting. "Hi, Cuddles," she said, giving her a scratch under the chin. "When's Mike coming over? And shall we feed him?"

"I think we'd better. He made a point of telling me he didn't have time to eat dinner."

"Good. I'm hungry, too."

"But you had a cinnamon roll and four cookies," Hannah reminded her.

"I know, but now I need something substantial, something with meat, something really good. What shall we make?" Michelle hung her coat in the closet, rubbed Moishe's ears as she walked by, and headed to the kitchen.

"I don't know." Hannah followed her.

"Then let's see what you've got, and maybe it'll give us some ideas."

"I doubt it. I've been so busy, I haven't been to the Red Owl for at least a week."

"I can see that," Michelle said, surveying the nearly empty refrigerator shelves. "Do you have any hamburger?"

"I think there's some in the freezer." Hannah opened the door to look. "Here's a one-pound package of lean ground beef. Will that do?"

"It's perfect. Let's thaw it right in the frying pan."

"Okay. I'll put it on." Hannah got out a frying pan, unwrapped the frozen hamburger and plunked it in, covered the pan and turned the burner on medium heat. "What are we making?"

"I don't have a name for it yet. Do you have any frozen veggies?"

Hannah went back to the freezer and looked. "Broccoli, cauliflower, frozen chopped onions, and a bag of peas and carrots."

"Is that last one a mix?"

"Yes. It's the kind with green peas and carrots cut in little cubes."

"Great! I need a cup."

Hannah carried the bags to the counter. She opened the peas and carrots, poured out a cup for Michelle, and put a twist tie on the bag. "How many chopped onions do you need?"

"Forty-seven."

"What?" Hannah paused, the open bag of onions in her hand.

"Just kidding. Take out a quarter cup or so. I don't think that proportions will be that critical."

Hannah measured the onions, twist tied the bag closed, and put the bags back into the freezer. "You have a recipe for whatever you're making, don't you?"

Michelle laughed. "Not really. I'm winging it."

"What kind of meal do you think it'll be?"

"A hamburger bake. I do bakes every week or so at college. Most of the time they turn out to be good. If they're not, we just smother them in ketchup and eat them anyway."

Hannah began to smile. Michelle was turning out to be a real Minnesota cook, using whatever was in the refrigerator, freezer, or pantry and coming up with her own dish. "Do you want the onions in the frying pan with the hamburger?" she asked.

"Yes. Do you have any canned soup?"

Hannah added the frozen onions to her frying pan. "I'm pretty low on canned soup. I was going to pick some up last week, but I forgot." She opened the cupboard door and surveyed her canned goods. "I've got split pea, cream of asparagus, and cheddar cheese. Will any of those work for you?"

"Sure. I'll take the cheddar cheese. It's condensed, right?"

"That's right. You have to add milk."

"We will, but not as much as it calls for.

Do you have a quarter cup of milk?"

"I'm sure I do. And if it's too old to use, I've got a can of evaporated milk."

"That'll do. I think I saw half a package of shredded cheese in the meat drawer. Will you check to see what kind it is?"

Hannah went to the refrigerator while Michelle flipped the hamburger and onions. "It's cheddar," she reported.

"Great. Do you know how to make a biscuit crust from scratch?"

"I think I can handle that. Do you want it now?"

"Start it now, and I'll watch the hamburger. We need to use the biscuit dough as a bottom crust in the cake pan."

"I like that. And then the hamburger, onions, veggies, and cheddar cheese soup go on top of it?"

"Right. It's all mixed up together and then the shredded cheese goes on top of that. It should look nice, and I bet it'll taste good too."

The two sisters worked in companionable silence for several minutes. Then Michelle gave a long, drawn-out sigh.

"What is it?" Hannah asked her.

"I was thinking about Norman. You two made such a nice couple. I know you like Mike. I like him, too. But I always kind of hoped that you and Norman would get married. And now it won't ever happen. Because of *her!* She's going to make sure he never sees you again. She's holding that daughter of hers over his head like a carrot!"

*Or like an albatross,* Hannah thought, swallowing past the lump in her throat. The last time she'd been alone with Norman, the day he told her about the daughter he had, he'd looked so miserable it had almost broken her heart. "It's a very sad situation," she said, trying to be charitable. "I'm sure she has her daughter's best interests at heart. And I *know* Norman wants to do the right thing by Diana."

"*Is* it the right thing? But maybe Diana's not Norman's daughter. Maybe she just said that so she could latch on to a nice successful guy who wouldn't even question it."

These same thoughts had been running through Hannah's mind lately, but she didn't want to talk about it now. It was too late. The die was cast. Norman was going to marry Doctor Bev, and that was that.

The phone rang to disrupt Hannah's unhappy thoughts, and she hurried to answer it. It didn't really matter who was on the other end of the line. She was grateful for the interruption. "Hello?"

"It's me, Hannah," Andrea said in a voice

85

that was little more than a whisper.

"Andrea? What's wrong with your voice?"

"I don't want Bill to hear me. He's upstairs changing his clothes to go back to the sheriff's station."

"He's going back tonight?" Hannah glanced at the clock. It was already eleven-thirty.

"You know how it is. If something big happens, the sheriff has to be there. And this is big!"

"*What's* big?"

"It's that bus driver, the one who went off the road with the band and got killed."

"Clayton Wallace?"

"Yes, that's his name. Doc Knight just called. He finished the autopsy, and he said that the accident didn't kill Clayton Wallace, that he was already dead when the bus went off the road."

Hannah remembered what Buddy had told her, that he thought the driver had suffered some kind of sudden attack and that's why the bus went off the road. "Was it his heart?" she asked.

"Yes. How did you know?"

"When Michelle and I got to the bus, Buddy Neiman told us that they were traveling along just fine. And then all of a sudden, they were barreling into the ditch. He thought the driver must have had a heart attack or a stroke."

"Well, he was right. Doc's running some tests again to make sure, but he told Bill the results of the first blood test."

"What was it?" Hannah did her best not to sound impatient. Andrea would tell the story in her own way, and she knew from past experience that trying to speed up the process was useless.

"If the first test was accurate, Mr. Wallace overdosed on his heart medicine."

"Was it an accidental overdose?" Hannah asked, hoping that it had been a simple mistake, but not at all convinced it was, especially after Buddy's murder. Two people on the same bus were dead and it wasn't due to the traffic accident.

"There's no way for Doc to tell whether it was accidental or deliberate. And you know the rules. If there's the possibility that it could be a homicide, the department has to investigate."

"So now they have two homicide investigations."

"That's right. I know Bill . . ." Andrea stopped talking and gave a little gulp. "I have to go. He's coming down the stairs."

"What is it?" Michelle asked, when Hannah got off the phone.

"There's the possibility of another murder."

"Who?"

"Clayton Wallace, the band bus driver. Doc Knight thinks he was dead before the bus crashed into the ditch."

"You mean . . . somebody on the bus killed him?"

"Maybe. And maybe not. All Doc Knight knows at this point is that Clayton took an overdose of his heart medication."

"You mean he could have taken extra pills by mistake?"

"It's possible. Sometimes pills look alike. But it's also possible that someone could have tampered with his medicine."

"I wonder what he did when he traveled with the band?" Michelle looked thoughtful. "Did he take his pill bottles with him? Or did he have one of those matrix things marked with the days of the week, and . . ."

"Uh-oh!" Hannah gasped as an image of the dead bus driver, still strapped in his seat, flashed across the screen of Hannah's mind. There was something directly below him on the floor, and she'd reached down to pick it up. Even though the light was dim, she'd noticed that it was square and had little compartments. It sounded a lot like the pill matrix that Michelle had just described.

"What's the matter?" Michelle asked when Hannah didn't explain further.

"I think I saw that pill matrix."

"Where?"

"On the bus, right below the driver. If he had it on his lap, it could have fallen down when the bus overturned."

"That's right. You'd better call Mike and tell him to go out to the accident scene. It could be important evidence."

"I know, especially if the pills have been moved around."

Michelle waited a moment and then she frowned. "Well? Aren't you going to call him? He has to get out there right away before they haul the bus away."

"There's no reason to call him," Hannah said with a heavy sigh.

"Why not?"

"Because it's not there anymore. It's right here. I picked it up without thinking, and I zipped it into my parka pocket."

# HAMBURGER BAKE

Preheat oven to 400 degrees F.,
rack in the middle position.

## The Filling:

1 pound lean ground beef

3/4 cup chopped onion *(you can also use frozen chopped onions)*

1 can (10 and 3/4 ounces) condensed Cheddar cheese soup *(I used Campbell's)*

1 cup frozen vegetables *(I used peas and carrot mix — I've also used a corn and chopped bell pepper mix)*

1/4 cup whole milk

## The Crust:

1/2 cup butter *(1 stick, 4 ounces, 1/4 pound)*

3/4 cup whole milk *(in addition to the 1/4 cup used in the filling)*

1 and 3/4 cups all-purpose flour *(don't pack it down — just scoop it up in a measuring cup and level off the top)*

2 and 1/2 teaspoons baking powder

1/4 teaspoon salt

## The Topping:

1 cup shredded cheddar cheese

Spray a 9-inch by 13-inch cake pan with

Pam or another nonstick cooking spray. *(You can also grease it generously if you'd rather not use the spray.)*

The filling takes the most time, so you'll start that first by crumbling the raw hamburger into a 10-inch or larger frying pan.

Add the chopped onion to the hamburger in the pan.

Fry the meat and onions over MEDIUM heat on the stovetop until the hamburger is nicely browned.

Drain the hamburger and onions. *(You don't want a lot of hamburger fat in this dish.)*

Add the condensed soup, frozen vegetables and the 1/4 cup milk to the hamburger and onions. Stir well. *(You can do this right in the frying pan.)* Cover the frying pan and set the mixture aside.

Put the 1/2 cup of butter in a microwave-safe bowl. Add the 3/4 cup whole milk and heat it on HIGH for 1 minute. Stir. If the butter isn't melted, heat it for another 30 seconds and stir. Continue to heat in 30-second increments until the butter has melted. Then take the bowl out of the microwave and set it on the counter to cool slightly.

**Hannah's 1st Note: Michelle and I used a 4-cup Pyrex measuring cup to**

melt the butter with the milk. You could also do this in a saucepan on the stovetop, if you wish.

Measure out the flour and put approximately half of it in a mixing bowl. *(You don't have to be exact — nobody's going to complain if it's less or more than half.)*

Sprinkle the baking powder and salt over the top of the flour in the bowl. Add the remainder of the flour and stir the bowl with a fork until all of the dry ingredients are thoroughly combined.

Add the butter and milk mixture to the mixing bowl, and mix until the resulting dough is well moistened.

**Hannah's 2nd Note: In case you haven't guessed it, you're making baking powder biscuit dough.**

Spoon the dough into the bottom of the cake pan you prepared earlier. Spread it out so that the dough forms an even layer in the pan. This will be the bottom layer of your Hamburger Bake.

Spread the hamburger mixture on top of the biscuit dough. Do this as evenly as possible.

Sprinkle the shredded cheddar cheese over the top of the hamburger layer.

Bake the Hamburger Bake at 400 degrees F. for 30 minutes. Then take it out of the oven and let it cool on a cold burner on the stovetop or on a wire rack for at least 10 minutes before serving. *(It's just too hot to serve straight out of the oven — eager eaters could burn their mouths.)*

**Hannah's 3rd Note: This dish is perfect to take to a potluck dinner. All you have to do is prepare a cardboard box big enough to hold your baking dish and line it with a bath towel. When you take the Hamburger Bake out of the oven, place it in the box, and cover it with the towel. It should stay warm for at least 30 minutes.**

Yield: This delicious, quick, and easy main dish makes 10 servings if you pair it with a green salad.

**Hannah's 4th Note: If there's any Hamburger Bake left after dinner, cover the pan with plastic wrap and refrigerator it right in the pan. You can simply reheat it in the microwave the next day for lunch.**

**Hannah's 5th Note: If you invite Mike to dinner and serve Hamburger Bake, don't plan on having any leftovers. When Michelle and I made it for him, he ate half a pan all by himself!**

# CHAPTER SEVEN

"That was good," Mike said, putting down his fork. He took a sip of his coffee and a wistful expression crossed his face. "I don't suppose you have any cookies left. I saw you passing out rolls and cookies to the accident victims."

Hannah shook her head. "No cookies, but I *do* have some Kentucky butter cake."

"Great! I'll take a piece of that. What's Kentucky butter cake?"

"You want it without even knowing what it is?" Michelle sounded surprised.

"Sure. Hannah's never made anything I didn't like." Mike turned to Hannah. "What is it?"

"It's a white cake with loads of butter. Mother's friend, Cassandra, sent her the recipe. I made it in two pans, gave one to Mother, and put the other in the freezer for emergencies."

"So I'm an emergency?" Mike asked with

a devilish grin.

Hannah was lost for an answer. Mike's grin always made her heart beat faster. He was indisputably the most handsome man in Lake Eden. The only problem was, he knew it!

"Am I an emergency?" Mike asked again.

*You're an emergency, all right! I can't decide what to do with you. Sometimes I love you, sometimes you exasperate me, and when I'm not stuck trying to decide how I feel about you, I just want to throw my arms around you, and . . .* but she wouldn't think about that. At least not now.

"Well?" Mike's grin was devilish. He knew he'd thrown her completely off balance.

Hannah's mind jumped into overdrive, and she settled for the safest course. "I'd say the whole *night* was an emergency. Michelle and I almost got killed in a car crash, we were a hospital corridor away when Buddy got murdered, and then we found out that the dead bus driver could be a another murder victim. If that's not a night of emergencies, I don't know what is!"

*Uh-oh!* Hannah's mind sounded a warning, and she clamped her mouth shut. She didn't want Mike to know that Andrea had eavesdropped on Bill's conversation with

Doc Knight and called to tell them about it. She shot Michelle a glance, silently urging her to change the subject and hoping that sibling nonverbal messaging was working.

"Hannah didn't tell you, but there's a little problem with the cake," Michelle said, causing Mike to turn and focus on her.

"What's the problem? Isn't it any good?"

"It's wonderful, but the name is wrong. You know how patriotic some of the people in Lake Eden are. If Hannah wants to serve it at The Cookie Jar, we can't call it by another state name."

"Well . . . what does it taste like?"

"Butter. And butter's really good. Mother's friend in Kentucky says she bakes it, glazes it with melted butter and sugar, and sprinkles it with powdered sugar."

"But you don't do it that way?" Mike asked Hannah.

"No. I decided to frost it with our Great-Grandma Elsa's Brown Butter Icing." Hannah turned to Michelle. "Mike's dying to taste it. I can tell. Why don't you go to the kitchen and get him a piece?"

"So what was all *that* about?" Mike asked, the moment that Michelle had disappeared into the kitchen.

"All what?"

"All that about the bus driver and how it could be murder? Who told you that?"

Hannah thought fast. There was no way she was going to finger Andrea. She relied on her sister to give her the scoop when Bill had information about an investigation.

"Hannah? Who told you?"

The man had a lot in common with an elephant. He'd noticed her slip and he hadn't forgotten it.

"Everybody knows. It's already on the Lake Eden Gossip Hotline."

"No!"

"Yes," Hannah said, stretching the truth a bit. After all, Delores was the founding member. And Andrea *was* their mother's daughter.

"But Doc told Bill, and Bill didn't tell anybody but me. When I called Lonnie in, I didn't tell him why. I just said to meet me here. That means Doc, Bill, and I are the only ones who knew."

Hannah thought fast. "Not necessarily. One of the interns could have been there when Doc did the autopsy. Or a nurse could have helped him. I know he records his findings on tape so that Vonnie can type them up, so Vonnie must have known, too. There could be several people at the hospital who knew."

"Hmm. I didn't think of that. I guess it doesn't really matter, not in the long run. The news always gets out one way or the other."

"Here you go!" Michelle came back with a large piece of cake on a plate and handed it to Mike. She refilled his coffee cup, took a seat, and waited for him to taste it.

"Wow!" Mike said, after his first bite. "This is a really good cake, and I love the frosting."

"We like it, too," Michelle said. "Do you have any idea what Hannah should call it?"

Mike took another bite and chewed thoughtfully. "I'm thinking. What's in this frosting?"

"Browned butter, sugar, vanilla extract, and cream," Hannah answered him.

"Butter in the cake, and butter in the frosting?"

"And a butter sauce poured on top before you frost it," Hannah added. That's what gives it that little crunch on top."

"There sure is a lot of butter in here," Mike commented as he took another bite. "Whoa! I got it!" He took a swallow of coffee, and grinned at them. "Butterama Cake," he said.

"Butterama Cake?" Hannah repeated, and then she began to smile. "I like it. From now on I'm calling this cake Butterama Cake."

"Okay, Hannah," Mike said, pulling out his notebook. "Tell me everything you saw and heard from the moment you entered the bus until the moment you left the scene."

Hannah knew Michelle was answering a similar question for Lonnie. They'd separated into couples so that Mike could take Hannah's statement in the living room. Michelle had taken Lonnie in the kitchen to feed him some of the Hamburger Bake. She'd heard Michelle put Lonnie's dishes in the sink and start another pot of coffee. Undoubtedly Lonnie had also begun to take Michelle's statement.

Mike was looking at her expectantly, and Hannah thought back several hours, replaying the scene in her mind. "The bus was upside down. You probably already know that." She waited until Mike nodded and then she went on. "Buddy Neiman unlocked the back door from inside and that's how Michelle and I got in. We asked if anyone was injured and he said that he had the most serious injury. He showed us the splint Lynnette made for him."

"Lynnette?"

"She's one of the . . ." Hannah stopped

and frowned slightly. "I guess you call them groupies. Lynnette and another girl named Cammy travel with the band. She told us they help the band set up, and . . . I don't know what else."

"I'll bet I do," Mike said under his breath, and Hannah pretended not to hear him. "You said Lynnette put a splint on Mr. Neiman's wrist. Is she a nurse?"

"No, but she used to work in a doctor's office. Anyway, Michelle asked Buddy if there were any other injuries, and that was when he told us that the driver was dead. We asked how he knew that and he said that Lynnette had gone up to the front of the bus to check on the driver, and when she came back, she said he was dead."

"Okay. I'll have to get her prints in case she touched anything on or around Mr. Wallace. Do you know if she felt for a pulse?"

Hannah shook her head. "I don't know for sure. We talked to her about that. She said she did, but I don't think so."

"Why not?"

"Because she said it was creepy and she didn't want to see him again. I don't think she would have had the nerve to touch him."

"All right. Describe the scene for me."

Hannah took a deep breath. "The only

light was an LED strip on the ceiling. Of course the ceiling was upside down, and we walked on it like a floor. There were things all over that had fallen from the seats. The bus had a vaulted ceiling, so we were walking in the trough. It was hard to keep our balance, and we took small steps, one foot in front of the other, the way you'd walk on a tightrope. Since there was so much debris that had scattered all over when the bus tipped upside down, we had to be careful not to trip over anything."

"Okay. I understand. Go on."

"I didn't want Michelle to come with me, but she insisted. If I'd known how creepy it was going to be, I would have ordered her to stay put. When we got to the front of the bus, I spotted the driver." Hannah took another deep breath. "It was a horrible sight."

Mike reached out for her hand and squeezed it. "I know. We cut him down. I'm sorry you had to see that, Hannah."

"So am I, but I'm even sorrier that Michelle saw it."

"Me, too." Mike put his arm around her and leaned back on the couch. He shut his eyes and gave a big sigh of contentment. "I knew once I got out here, I could relax for a couple of minutes."

Hannah noticed that there were dark circles under his eyes. For a reason she didn't fully understand, they made him look even more handsome. Maybe it was the nurturer in her coming out, or at least that was what her former psychology professor would have said. Whatever the reason, she felt a new tenderness toward him. Mike was usually so strong and self-confident that it was difficult to imagine that he could ever really need comfort and tenderness from anyone. Before she quite realized that she was going to do it, she reached out and gently stroked his forehead. "Stay as long as you like," she said in a soft voice. "I know you're really tired."

Mike opened his eyes and smiled at her. "Careful what you offer, Hannah. All I need right now is a twelve-pack and the remote, and I'll never leave."

Hannah laughed, and her tender mood disappeared. Mike was okay if he could crack a joke. "Are we through with my statement?" she asked.

"Almost." Mike flipped to a fresh page in his notebook. "Do you remember seeing anything at the scene that was curious, or suspicious?"

"Yes, but I didn't realize it until I heard that the driver had overdosed on his heart medication. There was a pillbox on the floor, one of those plastic ones with little compartments for the days of the week."

Mike reached for his cell phone. "The crime scene techs are out there now. I'll call and tell them not to miss it."

"Don't bother. I have it."

"What?"

"I almost tripped over it, so I picked it up and zipped it in my parka pocket. I didn't know it was important then, but I thought someone might need the pills and I'd better take them with me. And then, with all the confusion at the hospital, I forgot I even had them."

"Did you touch them?"

"Only to pick them up. And I was wearing gloves because Michelle and I had just waded through the ditch and it was cold."

"Did you take off your gloves when you stuck the pillbox in your pocket and zipped it up?"

Hannah did her best to remember, but that part was a blank. "I don't know. Buddy was calling us, and we were in a hurry to meet the paramedics, and . . . I just don't remember."

"That's okay. Don't worry about it. If you did, we can eliminate your fingerprints."

Hannah heard a familiar scratching noise

in the hallway, and she knew she had to warn Mike. "Put your feet up. Quick!"

"What?"

"Just do it. Prop them on the coffee table and tuck in your arms. And hurry!"

"Okay," Mike agreed, sounding amused. "What's going on?"

"You'll see. It's the midnight cat crazies."

"What are cat craz . . . oof!" Mike let out a gasp as Cuddles landed on his chest. He watched in obvious amazement as the two cats raced in circles across the living room rug, Cuddles in the lead and Moishe chasing her. "Hey guys," he said. "What are you do . . . oof!"

Hannah laughed. She couldn't help it. This time Moishe had landed on Mike's chest. "You're a launch pad," she said. "Usually they stick to the floor. That's why I told you to put your feet up. But I guess this time they're performing for you, and they're trying something new."

There was a loud scratching noise as the two cats barreled into the laundry room, and a thump followed by a louder thump as they jumped up on Hannah's washer and dryer, and then down again.

"I don't remember the Big Guy doing that before," Mike said, putting his feet back down on the floor.

"He never has. It's Cuddles. She goads him into it. They love their game of chase and they haven't broken anything . . . yet. But I don't really care because they're having so much fun."

There was a bang from the kitchen, and they heard Michelle gasp.

"What the . . ." Lonnie exclaimed, stopping short. "Cuddles just jumped up on the refrigerator and Moishe skidded straight into the door! He seems to be okay, though. He just shook his head a couple of times, and then he leaped up on the counter."

Hannah laughed. "It's kitty crazy time. Don't worry. It'll be over soon. They'll tire themselves out in a couple of minutes, and then they'll sleep all night."

"Cuddles seems to be having a great time here," Mike said, snapping his notebook shut.

"She's fine." Hannah knew the interview was over and she was relieved. Recalling the sight of the bus driver dangling above her had not been pleasant.

"Do you think she misses Norman?" Mike asked the same question that Michelle had earlier.

"Yes. I've seen her go to the window by the stairs and look out, as if she's waiting for him to come and pick her up. She looks sad. And before you say anything, I don't think I'm imagining things."

"I believe you, and I think you're right. Cuddles just adores Norman. Every time I went out there to see him, she was right there. If we went into the kitchen, she followed us. And if we went into the den, she tagged along. My sister has a cat and he doesn't do that. How about Moishe? Does he follow you around?"

"Not unless it's breakfast and he wants his food. Or dinnertime and he's hungry. Moishe's more independent. He's not waiting for anybody to come and get him. He knows he's home."

Mike looked away for a minute. When he turned back, there was a sheen of moisture in his eyes. "It's sad," he said. "Cuddles really loves Norman, and Norman loves Cuddles. I've been out there a couple of times for dinner since Bev and Norman got engaged."

Hannah was perfectly silent. She didn't know if she wanted to hear what was coming next.

"Norman's not happy. I think he's making a big mistake by marrying her."

Again, Hannah was silent. She agreed completely and there was nothing for her to say.

"They're not good together. As much as Norman tries, his heart's not in it. And she's . . . clingy. I don't know what she's doing, what she's up to. But I do know she's not right for Norman."

"Sour grapes?" Hannah asked, and then she regretted it. Mike had dated Doctor Bev, and she was prying.

"Not sour grapes. I wouldn't go out with her again on a bet. There's something wrong there, something that gets the cop in me anxious."

"You think she's a criminal?"

"No, nothing like that. It's just she's not . . . real."

"What do you mean?"

"My instincts tell me she's playing a part. I thought I knew her. I really did. But she's different with Norman than she was with me." Mike's eyebrows furrowed in a frown. "The way things are now, I wouldn't trust her as far as I could throw her."

Hannah wasn't about to touch that one with a telephone pole. She just sat and waited for Mike to say more.

"I know why they're getting married. Norman told me. We're friends, good friends, and we talk. I'm all he's got now. He needs someone to talk to, and Bev won't let him see you anymore. Norman told me that every time he says he wants to see Cuddles, she begs him not to. She told him that the cat dander gets into his clothes and gives her a terrible allergic reaction."

*Oh sure!* Hannah thought sarcastically. *If she's that allergic to cats, she couldn't treat any of her patients who have cats. And she certainly couldn't visit Norman at his place, because Cuddles once lived there.*

"You don't believe that?" Mike asked, noticing Hannah's suspicious expression.

"Not really."

"Well, neither do I. I think it's just an excuse to keep him from coming out here and seeing you."

Hannah thought back. Norman had come to see Cuddles a total of twice since he'd gotten engaged to Doctor Bev. On both of those occasions, he'd acted terribly guilty, and Hannah was convinced that Bev hadn't known where he'd gone. "You could be right," she said.

"Norman told me about Diana and how, after they broke up, Bev didn't tell him she was pregnant. My question is . . . why didn't she? Why didn't she tell him? He would have married her back then. What was she waiting for? And why did she wait this long to find him and tell him? It just doesn't make sense, Hannah. There's something wrong

108

there. And I don't want to see my best friend hurt."

# BUTTERAMA CAKE

Preheat oven to 325 degrees F.,
rack in the middle position.

**Hannah's 1st Note: Cassandra told Mother she got this cake recipe from her aunt. They made it in a Bundt pan and called it Kentucky Butter Cake.**

**The Cake Batter:**

1 cup softened butter *(2 sticks, 8 ounces, 1/2 pound)*

2 cups white *(granulated)* sugar

4 whole eggs★★★

1 teaspoon salt

1 teaspoon baking powder

1/2 teaspoon baking soda

2 teaspoons vanilla extract

3 cups all-purpose flour *(pack it down in the cup when you measure it)*

1 cup buttermilk *(If you don't have buttermilk on hand, you can use cream. The cake will taste a bit different, but it'll still be wonderful.)*

*★★★ If Andrea were making this cake, I'd have to tell her to crack the eggs and take them out of the shell before adding them to her mixing bowl.*

Get out a 9-inch by 13-inch cake pan

*(metal or glass, either will do)* and either spray it with Pam or another nonstick baking spray or butter it generously on the inside. *(If you use butter, this could bring the total butter count up to a pound!)*

To make the cake batter:

By hand in a large bowl or with an electric mixer *(it's easier with a mixer, of course)* beat the butter for a minute or two.

Sprinkle in the white sugar, beating as you sprinkle. Mix the butter and the sugar together until they turn into a light, fluffy mixture.

Add the eggs, one at a time, beating after each addition.

Add the salt, baking powder, baking soda, and vanilla extract. Mix them in thoroughly.

Add 1 cup of the flour and beat it in.

Mix in half (1/2 cup) of the buttermilk. Mix it in thoroughly.

Add the second cup of flour and mix well.

Mix in the rest of the buttermilk (1/2 cup).

Add the remaining cup of flour and beat until the batter is smooth and without lumps.

Pour the cake batter into the 9-inch by 13-inch cake pan you prepared. Smooth out the top with a rubber spatula so that it's evenly distributed in the pan.

Bake the cake in a preheated 325 degree

F. oven for 50 minutes. Then take it out of the oven and set it on a cold burner on the stovetop or a wire rack to wait for its Butter Sauce.

## The Butter Sauce:
1 cup white *(granulated)* sugar

1/4 cup water *(I'll just bet you could use Kentucky Bourbon instead of the water here, but I haven't tried it yet.)*

1/2 cup butter *(1 stick, 4 ounces, 1/4 pound)*

1 Tablespoon vanilla

## To make the Butter Sauce:
Put the cup of sugar, the 1/4 cup of water, and the 1/2 cup of butter in a medium-size saucepan.

**Hannah's 2nd Note: Don't use a saucepan that's black or brown on the inside. You'll be using it again later when you make the frosting and you need to be able to see when the butter you'll heat in it turns brown.**

Heat the three ingredients on MEDIUM heat until the butter is melted, but DO NOT let the mixture come to a boil.

**Hannah's 3rd Note: You can also do this in a microwave-safe bowl on HIGH for 90 seconds. (I used a 4-cup Pyrex**

measuring cup.) **If the butter is not melted at the end of that time, microwave it on HIGH in 20-second increments until it is.**

Pull the saucepan over to a cold burner, shut off the hot one, and add the Tablespoon of vanilla extract. *(Be careful — it could sputter a bit)*

Use a fork, food pick, or a thin wooden skewer to poke holes all over the top of your cake. Don't be too gentle. You want the holes to go all the way down to the bottom of the cake pan. *(I used a thin wooden skewer and poked about 45 holes in mine.)*

Pour the warm butter sauce over the top of the cake as evenly as you can. If you used a saucepan, don't bother to wash it. You'll be using it again when you make the frosting.

**Hannah's 4th Note: So far there's 3/4 of a pound of butter in this cake. Add it up if you don't believe me. If you frost it with Great-Grandma Elsa's Brown Butter Icing, it'll be only a quarter cup shy of a whole pound!**

Let the cake sit out on the wire rack or cold burner for at least 10 minutes so that the Butter Sauce has time to soak into the holes you poked.

Refrigerate your Butterama Cake for at

least 2 hours. At the end of that time, just leave the cake in the refrigerator and start the Brown Butter Icing.

## Brown Butter Icing:

1/4 cup butter *(1/2 stick, 2 ounces, 1/8 pound)*

2 cups powdered sugar *(confectioner's sugar — pack it down in the cup when you measure it)*

1 teaspoon vanilla extract *(you could also use Kentucky Bourbon)*

2 Tablespoons heavy cream *(that's whipping cream, but you could also use half and half which is light cream)*

1/2 cup chopped pecans or walnuts *(optional — to sprinkle over the top of the cake after you frost it.)*

## To make the frosting:

Put the 1/4 cup butter into a medium-size saucepan. *(You already have one sitting on a cold burner if you made the Butter Sauce on the stovetop.)* If you used the microwave instead, make sure that the saucepan you choose is not colored black or brown inside. *(I made that mistake and I couldn't see when the butter had browned.)*

Place the saucepan on the stovetop and heat it at MEDIUM-HIGH heat. The butter will melt and then it will brown. Continue to heat it until it has browned.

When the butter is a nice caramel color, **(this took about 5 minutes for me),** remove it from the heat and shut off the burner.

Stir in the 2 cups of powdered sugar.

Stir in the vanilla extract.

Put the 2 Tablespoons of heavy cream in a small cup and drizzle them in, stirring as you go until the frosting is smooth and spreadable.

This is another one of those wonderful no-fail frostings. If it turns out to be too runny, add a bit more powdered sugar. If it turns out to be too thick and stiff, add a bit more cream. Continue to adjust these two ingredients until the frosting is the right consistency.

Take the Butterama Cake out of the refrigerator and frost it with Brown Butter Icing. If you like, you can sprinkle some chopped pecans or walnuts over the top to decorate your cake.

Return the cake to the refrigerator until you're ready to serve it. Like revenge, this dish is best served cold.

# Chapter Eight

When the alarm went off the next morning, Hannah woke up to discover that she ached all over. In other circumstances she might have thought that this had something to do with the fact that two pillow-hogging cats, who seemed to morph into much bigger creatures in the dark of night, had shared her bed. But in this case, she was almost certain her soreness and stiffness was caused by last night's trek through the ditch with Michelle, when they'd waded through the deep snow to get to the band bus.

"Come on, you lazybones. It's time to get up," Hannah said to the two cats who were stretched out sideways on her mattress, taking up much more than half the bed. They didn't move. They didn't even flicker a whisker in her direction, so Hannah tried again. "Daylight in the swamp. Time to get up and chase all the mice that came in during the night."

Moishe opened one yellow eye and looked at her. His mouth remained closed, but Hannah could have sworn she heard him say, *Good try Hannah, but there's no mice in here. All I smell is the leftovers from the Hamburger Bake you made for Mike. Let us sleep for gosh sakes! Just because you have to get up before the crack of dawn doesn't mean that Cuddles and I have to lose sleep.*

"All right. You can sleep," Hannah said, bowing to that penetrating one-eyed stare. "I'll fill your automatic feeder before I go."

She needed coffee. She'd probably die without it. Hannah thrust her feet into her moccasin slippers, thrust her arms into the faded chenille robe she'd purchased at Lake Eden's only thrift store, Helping Hands, and shuffled down the hall.

The door to the guest room was closed. Michelle must still be sleeping. She certainly couldn't blame her! Lonnie and Mike hadn't left until almost two in the morning.

As she entered the living room, she saw that the light was on in the kitchen. She must have been so tired that she'd forgotten to turn it off before she'd gone to bed. It was a good thing that her mother didn't know, or Delores would tell her best friend, Carrie. Norman's mother was "green" through and through, and she would be terribly worried about the number of kilowatts that Hannah had wasted. Carrie was concerned about pollution, global warming, the state of the economy, and the size of the global footprint that everyone but her was leaving. Delores had called Hannah on Christmas morning to tell her that Carrie had given her a goat. This wasn't a real goat, Delores had rushed to explain. It was a goat that an international organization shipped to an impoverished family in a country neither Hannah nor her mother had ever heard of, so that they could have milk for their children to drink.

Carrie was a nice woman. Hannah liked her a lot. She had an abundance of good qualities, but she was a little crazy. It was wonderful that her new husband, Earl Flensburg, thought her eccentricities were charming.

Coffee. She needed it so much she could almost smell it. Hannah padded across the living room carpet and stepped into her white-walled kitchen. She put her hands over her eyes for a moment. The banks of florescent lights overhead seemed as bright as the sun in a cloudless sky.

"Good morning," an angel said to her. "Would you like some coffee?"

"Yes," Hannah answered in a weak voice,

squinting as she made her way to the Formica table that would be an antique in about fifteen years. Of course it wasn't really an angel. It was her youngest sister Michelle. But Hannah thought Michelle was *acting* exactly like an angel should act as she set a mug of lifesaving brew directly in front of her.

One sip and Hannah felt almost human. Two sips and she remembered her name. Three sips and she was capable of doing simple sums in her head. Five sips and she could *not* do quadratic equations. Of course she'd never been able to do quadratic equations, but she did remember the failing grade she'd gotten in algebra.

"More?" Michelle asked, wisely speaking in one-word sentences. She'd stayed at her older sister's condo many times before, and she knew Hannah's routine in the morning.

"Yes, thanks," Hannah said. And then she waited, her head resting on her folded arms, until Michelle had brought the second mug of coffee. She took another sip, and a smile spread over her face. Perhaps this day wouldn't be such a horrible day after all!

Michelle had insisted on coming to The Cookie Jar with Hannah to help, and by the time they arrived, it was six in the morning.

Hannah pulled up, into her spot, plugged in the heater that kept her oil and transmission fluids at a workable temperature, and waited for Michelle to join her before she inserted her key in the lock.

Hannah turned the key, but there was no familiar click. The door was already unlocked. "Behind me, Michelle," she warned. "Somebody opened this door."

"What are you going to do?"

"I'm going in, but you're not. Stay out here. Here's my key ring." Hannah handed it to Michelle. "If you hear anything that doesn't sound right, head for the van and get out of here as fast as you can."

"No!" Michelle grabbed Hannah's hand as she reached for the doorknob. "You're not going in there alone. It could be a robbery in progress. Or who knows what else. You should call Mike and have him check it out first."

Hannah shook her head. "I'm probably being overcautious and there's nothing to worry about. Maybe Lisa came in really early."

"Her car's not in her parking spot."

"I know. But there aren't any other cars either. And there weren't any tire tracks in the snow when we drove in."

"But I *still* don't think you should go in

alone. Let's call Lonnie if you don't want to bother Mike. He'll come right out here and . . ."

Michelle stopped speaking as they heard the sound of a car engine.

"There's a car coming down the alley," Hannah pointed out quite unnecessarily.

"I hear it. Maybe it's a volunteer coming to open Helping Hands early."

"That's possible. Or maybe it's . . . Andrea?" Hannah caught sight of her sister's Volvo and simply stared. Andrea *never* got up this early. Ever since Andrea and Bill had hired Grandma McCann to live in to take care of Tracey and Bethie, Andrea had been sleeping late.

Andrea wheeled her Volvo into the space next to Hannah's cookie truck, and got out of her car. "Hi Hannah. Hi Michelle."

"What are *you* doing here at this time of the morning?" Hannah asked before Michelle could voice the question.

"Mother called me and told me to meet her here. They even unlocked the back door for me."

"Who unlocked it?" Hannah asked her.

"Lisa. Mother's having an early morning meeting with Lisa to tell her everything about finding the body. She wants Lisa to tell the story because she knows it brings in lots of business for you."

Just then the back door opened and Delores poked her head out. "What are you doing out here? It's really cold this morning, and you're going to freeze to death. Come on in. Lisa and I have fresh coffee and cookies for you."

Hannah had expected Delores to visibly show the signs of the traumatic experience she'd suffered the previous evening. But her mother was smiling. Her hair and her makeup were perfect, and she was wearing another of her designer suits.

Andrea took off her coat and hung it on a hook next to the back door. She was also dressed to perfection in a lovely dark green pantsuit that set off her light blond hair.

Hannah glanced down at her jeans and rather heavy lavender sweater. Then she turned to look at Michelle, who was wearing corduroy slacks and a dark heavy brown sweater, and she thought she understood why she loved her youngest sister so much.

"Sit down. Both of you," Delores ordered.

Hannah and Michelle took seats at the stainless steel work island in the center of the kitchen. It was obvious that Delores was in charge, even though it was Hannah's domain.

"Why are you here so early?" Hannah asked Lisa.

"Your mother called me last night and asked me to meet her here. I had Dad drop me off, and I came early to start the baking. I've got a batch of Short Stack Cookies coming out in a minute or two if you want a fresh cookie."

"I do," Michelle said immediately.

"I'd like one, too," Hannah echoed the sentiment.

"So would I," Delores said, smiling at Lisa. "I've been up for hours and I'm ready for breakfast."

There was a moment of silence. Then all three sisters turned to stare at their mother in shock.

"Cookies for breakfast?!" Michelle was the first to recover enough to ask.

"You never let us have cookies for breakfast when we were kids," Andrea complained.

Hannah gave her mother a searching look. "Don't tell me we finally managed to convince you that cookies are breakfast food!"

"Of course not. But some cookies are more acceptable than others. Delores gave all three of them a smug smile. "Lisa told me that Short Stack Cookies taste just like pancakes. And pancakes are perfect for breakfast."

# CHAPTER NINE

After Lisa's Short Stack cookies were eaten and everyone had declared them delicious, Delores cleared her throat.

"I have something to discuss with you girls," she said, looking very serious.

"I'll just go out in the coffee shop," Lisa said, getting to her feet. "It's almost time to set up the tables."

Delores held up her hand. "Don't leave. This concerns you, too. I just want to make sure that you're all going to help investigate Buddy Neiman's murder. I need to know who did it as soon as possible."

Hannah was puzzled. "Why is that, Mother? You told me last night that you never met him. Until you found him dead, that is."

"And that's true. But I spoke to Doc at the hospital this morning, and he said they're all at *sixes and sevens*."

Hannah knew what that phrase meant.

She'd read it in one of her mother's Kathryn Kirkwood Regency romances.

"Doc actually put it that way?" It was obvious that Andrea had read the books too, or she wouldn't have asked the question.

"Yes, he said that. He loves to read my romances. As a matter of fact, he's going to help me with my next book."

"Doc's going to help you write your Regencies?" Michelle's eyebrows shot up in surprise.

"No, but he's going to do some research on the healing arts in Regency England for me. He wants me to be accurate when it comes to medical things."

"Why is the whole hospital at sixes and sevens?" Hannah asked, pulling them back to business.

"Because it's a murder scene. Doc says that's not very good for business."

The four women just stared at Delores. None of them knew how to respond.

"Doc was *joking*. Hospitals don't solicit business. They provide a community service. But then he got serious and he said he wished that whoever stabbed Buddy Neiman had used a different murder weapon."

"Why?" Andrea asked.

"The sheriff's department detectives are still out there interviewing anyone who had access to those scissors. And unfortunately, that includes everyone who was at the hospital last night."

"But how could just anyone have access?" Andrea asked her. "Aren't surgical scissors just used in the operating room?"

"Not necessarily," Delores explained. "There's a pair of sterile surgical scissors in every treatment room. And the treatment rooms aren't locked."

Hannah went to the drawer, took out a new stenographer's notebook, and grabbed a pen. Delores was giving her new information and that meant it was time to write it down in the notebook she called her *murder book*. She flipped to the first page and turned to her mother. "So it could have been someone on the staff who took them, or even someone who was walking down the hall and saw the opportunity."

"Exactly."

"Or another patient could have taken them," Lisa suggested.

"You're right, Lisa. Or it could have been someone from a patient's family. Or . . ." Michelle paused, looking worried. "Or anyone who came out to the hospital last night and volunteered to help . . . like the Rainbow Ladies, or like us."

Hannah turned to her mother. "Do you

know if they're keeping everyone in the hospital until they can question them?"

"Not everyone, but they took names and addresses. And I heard Mike tell Dick Laughlin that everyone on the band bus had to stay put at the Lake Eden Inn until he said they could leave."

"This is probably inappropriate under the circumstances, but do you know if the band is going to play tonight?" Lisa asked. "Dad and Marge planned to drive out there to have dinner and hear them."

"How could they play?" Andrea answered her. "Unless they can find a substitute, they won't have anyone on keyboards."

Michelle looked thoughtful. "You're right. I wonder if . . ."

Hannah turned to her sister when she stopped speaking. "You wonder what?"

Michelle gave a little shrug. "I just had an idea, that's all. It's nothing. Really."

Hannah stared hard at her youngest sister. She was sure that the idea wasn't *nothing*. There was definitely something on Michelle's mind. Hannah was just getting ready to ask her about it again when Delores stood up.

"I'd better go. I want to run out to the hospital and tell Doc that you're already working on the murder case. You are, aren't you?"

"We are," Andrea replied, patting her briefcase-sized purse. "I've got the crime scene photos right here."

"How did you get them so soon?" Delores asked her.

"Everything's digital now. They sent them to Bill over the Internet, and he downloaded them to a disk before he came home last night."

"And he gave them to you?" Delores was clearly shocked.

"Not exactly. Let's just say that I managed to copy the disk and print them out while he was sleeping."

"Andrea!"

Andrea just shrugged as Delores gave her a stern look. "Come on, Mother. It was the only way I could think of to get them. And you *do* want us to work on the murder case, don't you?"

"Of course I do. I told you that."

"Well, having the crime scene photos is bound to help. Would you like to see them?" Andrea offered, pulling a manila envelope out of her purse.

"No!" Delores said definitively, and then she gave a little shudder. "I was there. That's quite enough for me! Just let me know if I can do anything to help your investigation. I'm good at undercover work, you know. And I'm at the hospital almost every day." She turned to Lisa. "I'll be back here around one to see your new puppy. Little Sammy sounds just darling."

"He's a love." Lisa smiled a proud smile, almost as if her new puppy was a newborn baby she'd just brought home from the maternity ward.

"When I come, I'll bring a copy of the autopsy report," Delores promised. "I've got a key to Doc's cabinet. I can copy it right at the hospital."

"Mother!" Andrea treated her to the same stern look that Delores had given her earlier. "You thought I was wrong for copying Bill's disk of the crime scene photos without his permission. Now you're going to do the almost same thing to Doc Knight."

"Doc's not my husband," Delores pointed out. "That's different."

Hannah exchanged glances with her sisters, and they all began to smile. Since they'd been little, they'd known that what their mother thought was bad behavior for them wasn't necessarily bad behavior for her.

"Don't forget your cookies," Lisa reminded Delores.

"I won't." Delores hurried to the counter and picked up one of Hannah's bakery boxes. "Doc and the nurses are going to love these. Thanks so much, Lisa."

Hannah waited until Delores left, and then she turned to Lisa. "What kind of cookies did you give her?"

"Chocolate Chip Crunch. I figured the chocolate would do them some good. It's got to be a madhouse out there."

"Right. Mother said she'd come back at one to see Sammy. Where is he?"

"Herb's got the morning off, so he's taking Sammy to Doctor Bob's for a complete checkup with blood work and everything. I told him that the paramedics said that Sammy was fine, but he insisted. He said you can't be too careful with a little guy like Sammy."

"Very true," Hannah said, smiling at her partner. It sounded as if Herb had fallen in love with Sammy, too.

"Let's get started," Lisa said. "We've got a lot of work to do."

Hannah glanced over at the bakers' racks. They were filled almost to overflowing with freshly baked cookies. "But the racks are full. Didn't you already do all the baking?"

"I did. Sammy was snuggled up in bed

with Herb and Dillon, so I came in to work early. And I baked extra cookies because I knew we'd be jam-packed with customers today."

"Because you're going to tell the story of how Mother found the body?" Andrea asked.

"I'm definitely going to do that. Your mother told me to make it just as theatrical as I wanted, and she's going to come in and listen." Lisa turned to Hannah. "We always get tons of customers when I tell murder stories."

"I know," Hannah said. "But we don't open the coffee shop until nine, and it's only seven. What else is there to do before we open?"

"We have to start working on this murder investigation right away. And after we get everything organized, I want you and Michelle to tell me exactly what it was like when you went up to the front of the bus to see the dead bus driver's body. Our customers are going to want to hear about that, too."

"You're doing a double feature?" Michelle asked her.

"You betcha. Now let's get back to business. You met Buddy last night and so did Michelle. Andrea and I need to know your impressions of him. And then we need to figure out a reason why somebody wanted to kill him."

Hannah was greatly relieved when Andrea slipped the crime scene photos back into the envelope. This was definitely a crime of passion. Buddy had been stabbed multiple times with the scissors, and some of the wounds hadn't bled. This led her to believe that the killer had kept stabbing him even *after* he was dead. Of course she wasn't a doctor or a forensic specialist. She'd have to wait for Delores to bring in the autopsy report to make certain she was right. Lisa and Michelle had gone into the coffee shop to open it for business, but not until they'd talked about the direction their investigation would take, and Hannah and Michelle had told Lisa about entering the overturned band bus and seeing the dead driver.

"I'm going to mix up more cookie dough," Hannah said, rising from her stool at the stainless steel work island.

"But don't you have enough?" Andrea asked her.

"Maybe for Lisa's rendition of *Delores Finds the Body,* but not for *Michelle and Hannah Discover the Dead Bus Driver.* Two stories will take a while, especially if Lisa embellishes."

"And she will."

"Naturally. She'll probably take a break between the two, and customers will order more coffee and cookies."

"What kind of cookie are you going to make?"

"I thought I'd try a new recipe I thought of when I made JoAnn Hecht's recipe for Nutmeg Snaps. They were so popular, I decided to make more cookies with spices. I'm going to call these Cardamom Cuties."

"That's a nice name for a cookie. I don't think I've ever had cardamom. What does it taste like?"

"It's a little like cinnamon but it's deeper and more intense. And it's used more widely in European countries than it is here. Do you remember Great Grandma Elsa's sticky buns?"

"Maybe. I was pretty little when she was alive. I remember that I liked going out to the farm because she always had cookies and things for us."

"That's a good place to start. Think about her kitchen table with the red and white tablecloth on top."

"I remember that. It had little red flowers."

"You got it. Now try to remember the

afternoon that she gave us warm rolls and fresh-churned butter. Those were her sticky buns. They stuck to our fingers, and you dropped yours on the floor."

"I remember! I cried."

"And she told you not to cry because she'd just washed the kitchen floor. She picked up your roll, put it back on the plate, and you finished eating it."

"I remember that whole thing."

"Okay. See if you can remember the taste of that roll. It had caramel and pecans on top, and the inside was filled with cardamom and sugar."

Andrea shut her eyes. When she opened them, she was smiling. "I remember. Those rolls were delicious. Are the cardamom cookies going to taste like that?"

"We'll find out. They'll be ready to eat around noon."

Andrea glanced at the clock. "It's going to take you over three hours to make the dough?"

"No, that'll go fast. But it has to chill for two hours or more in the refrigerator."

"Can I help you make it?"

"Sure, as long as you crack the eggs and take them out of the shell before you add them to the bowl."

Andrea sighed loudly. "You're never going

to let me forget that lemon pie, are you?"

"Probably not," Hannah said, heading for the pantry to gather the ingredients.

## CARDAMOM CUTIES

DO NOT preheat the oven yet — this cookie dough must chill before baking.

1 cup salted butter, softened *(2 sticks, 8 ounces, 1/2 pound)*

2 and 1/2 cups brown sugar *(pack it down in the cup when you measure it)*

2 large eggs

1 and 1/2 teaspoons baking soda

1/2 teaspoon salt

2 teaspoons ground cardamom

3 and 1/2 cups all-purpose flour *(pack it down in the cup when you measure it)*

1/2 cup shredded coconut

1/2 cup white chocolate chips

extra brown sugar *(about 1/2 cup)* for rolling dough balls before baking

**Hannah's 1st Note: Although you can certainly make this recipe by hand, it's a lot easier with an electric mixer.**

Place the softened *(room temperature)* butter in a mixer bowl and beat it until it's smooth.

Add the dark brown sugar and beat it until it's nice and fluffy.

Mix in the eggs. Make sure they're thoroughly incorporated.

With the mixer running on LOW speed, add the baking soda, salt, and cardamom. Keep beating until you're sure they're evenly distributed.

Add the flour in half-cup increments, beating after each addition.

If you have a food processor, put the shredded coconut and white chocolate chips in the bowl. Process with the steel blade in an on and off motion until the coconut and white chocolate are cut into smaller pieces.

If you don't have a food processer, lay the coconut and white chocolate on a cutting board and chop them into small pieces with a sharp knife.

Take the cookie dough out of the mixer and stir the small pieces of coconut and white chocolate chips into the dough by hand.

Cover your mixing bowl with a sheet of plastic wrap and press it down over the top of your dough, tucking it in on the sides so that no air gets in.

Refrigerate the Cardamom Cuties cookie dough for two hours *(overnight is fine, too)* so that it is thoroughly chilled. Chilling the dough makes it much easier to work with.

When you're ready to bake, preheat the oven to 350 degrees F., rack in the middle position.

Take your cookie dough out of the refrigerator and set it on the counter.

Line your cookie sheets with parchment paper, or spray them with Pam or another nonstick baking spray.

Put some brown sugar, a half-cup should do, into a small bowl. You'll be rolling dough balls in the sugar before baking.

Roll the dough into 1-inch balls.

Roll each dough ball in the brown sugar, covering it completely.

Arrange the dough balls on your cookie sheets 2 inches apart. You should be able to get 12 dough balls on each cookie sheet.

Flatten each ball with the bottom of a glass, or the flat blade of a metal spatula.

Bake at 350 degrees F. for 8 to 12 minutes or until the cookies are golden brown. *(Mine took 11 minutes.)*

Remove the cookies from the oven and let them cool on the baking sheets for a minute or two to firm up. Then remove them to a wire rack to cool completely. *(This is very easy to do if you've used parchment paper — all you have to do is slide them off the cookie sheet onto the wire rack by pulling on the edge of the paper.)*

Store the Cardamom Cuties in an airtight container or in a covered cookie jar. They should last for at least a week. *(But of course they won't last for a whole week because everyone in your family will love them!)*

These cookies freeze beautifully if you stack them like coins in a wrapper, roll them in foil, and place the rolls in freezer bags.

Yield: Approximately 6 dozen cookies, depending on cookie size.

# CHAPTER TEN

The Cardamom Cuties had just come out of the oven and Hannah was indulging herself with a cookie and a cup of coffee when Michelle came through the swinging door that separated the kitchen from the coffee shop. "Norman's here," she announced.

Hannah drew a deep breath. She wasn't exactly sure how to react to Norman now that he was engaged to Doctor Bev. The easy caring relationship they'd shared in the past suffered an abrupt reversal, and she felt as if she were walking on eggshells. Now, instead of saying exactly what was on her mind, she was forced to think before she spoke, and she'd never felt the need to do that with Norman before.

"He wants to see you," Michelle continued, shrugging slightly. "I said I'd check to see if you were still here."

Michelle was giving her an out, and Hannah was grateful. But just as her youngest sister had pointed out the previous night, Lake Eden was small and they were bound to run into each other. She closed her eyes for a moment, took another deep breath to try to calm her pounding heart and said, "Send him back."

"Are you sure? You don't look as if you really want to see him."

"I do, and I don't," Hannah admitted. "But I don't want to shut any doors between Norman and me right now. Go ahead and send him back here, Michelle. I'll handle it."

Michelle looked a little worried. "Okay if that's what you want me to do. I'll go tell him right now."

When Michelle had gone back into the coffee shop, Hannah poured a cup of coffee for Norman. Her hands were shaking slightly and she spilled a few drops on the counter, but that was no surprise. She was nervous about seeing him. What did he want with her? Was he going to be perfectly friendly and simply ask her about Cuddles and how the cat he loved so much was doing? Or was he going to tell her that he couldn't endure being ostracized from her, and despite the fact that he had a child with Doctor Bev, he was going to break off their engagement for the second time and banish his ex-ex-fiancée to the Hull Rust Mahoning mine, the only open pit iron ore mine still operating in Minnesota?

Hannah gave a little laugh as she carried Norman's coffee to the stainless steel work island. She was letting her imagination run away with her. She fetched two Cardamom Cuties for Norman to try and set them on a napkin next to the coffee. Then she sat down on the stool across from his and took a deep breath. She was nervous. There was no denying that. But she had to force herself to calm down, and maintain her composure for whatever came next.

The door between the coffee shop and the kitchen opened, and Norman came in with a grim expression on his face. "Hi, Hannah," he said, sounding every bit as serious as he had on the day he'd told her he had a daughter with Doctor Bev. "It's good to see you. How's Cuddles?"

"She's just fine," Hannah reassured him. "She's playing, she's eating, and she's adapting very well. Mike saw her last night and she was playing chase with Moishe. If you ask him, I'm sure he'll tell you all about it."

"Good. That's good."

Hannah stopped and debated what to say

next. Should she tell Norman that Cuddles missed him? Or would mentioning that just upset and depress him?

It only took a moment for Hannah to decide. Norman needed to know. "Cuddles still looks out the living room window as if she expects you to come and pick her up."

Norman blinked several times. "You're probably right," he said. "It's what I used to do."

"Maybe, if you came out to see her on a regular basis, she'd know what to expect, she'd adjust to the new schedule, and she'd be more content."

"I can't do that, Hannah. I was afraid that Cuddles would miss being at home, but . . . well . . . she can't be at home any longer. Bev's allergic. The last time I saw her after seeing Cuddles, she had a full-blown allergy attack. She said it was from the cat dander on my clothes. And now she gets upset when I even mention visiting Cuddles."

*Then maybe you shouldn't mention it to her,* Hannah thought, but she didn't say it. Perhaps Bev really was allergic to cats. "Can't her doctor prescribe some kind of medication? They have a lot of new allergy drugs on the market."

"I know, but nothing seems to work for Bev. Every allergy drug she's tried makes

144

her so groggy and dizzy, she can barely walk across the room. It's not that she doesn't *want* me to see Cuddles. She knows how much I miss her, and she feels really terrible about all this."

Hannah didn't believe that for a second. Hannah knew she had cat dander all over her clothes, especially since shedding season for Moishe seemed to be at least eleven and a half months long. Yet the last time Hannah had talked to Doctor Bev at her birthday party in February, Norman's fiancée hadn't even sniffled. Perhaps Hannah didn't have the right to pass judgment when she wasn't an expert on allergies, but she was almost positive that Doctor Bev's allergies were fake. She was also almost positive that Doctor Bev had Norman buffaloed into thinking they were real.

"Well," Hannah said, determined to be cheerful and upbeat. "You don't have to worry about Cuddles. She's having a good time with Moishe and you know how well they get along."

"Oh, I know. They're best friends. You know . . . I miss Moishe, too. I used to love it when you brought him to my place. Remember how they used to sit on the kitty staircase I built, and stare out at the birds in the trees?"

"I remember."

The only sound in the kitchen was the hum of the motor in the walk-in cooler. Hannah could tell that Norman was lost in his thoughts, and she was lost in hers. She thought about the house they'd designed together. In a way, she regretted even hearing about the Minneapolis paper's Dream House contest. The idea that Norman would actually build it hadn't crossed her mind. The house had turned out to be perfect. She'd loved taking Moishe out there and spending time with Norman in the house they'd designed for the contest. But now that Norman was re-engaged to Doctor Bev, everything was different. If she'd been able to see into the future, she might never have agreed to enter the Dream House contest with him in the first place. She'd put countless hours and a lot of hard work into collaborating on the blueprints. It just wasn't fair that Doctor Bev would be marrying Norman and living in Hannah's dream house with him.

There was a long silence, and finally Norman spoke. "Those were really good days, weren't they, Hannah."

Hannah nodded. She could tell that Norman was depressed, and she decided to change the subject. "So why are you here,

Norman?" she asked him.

"I just came to tell you that Bev put the wedding invitations in the mail yesterday. You should get yours today. I know it's awkward, but I hope you'll come. Bev doesn't want a church wedding, so we're holding the ceremony upstairs in the community center. The reception's downstairs in the banquet room."

Hannah tried not to look too dismayed. She'd been hoping that something, anything really, would happen to break up Norman and Doctor Bev, but the chance of that happening was growing slimmer by the day. "When's the wedding?" she managed to ask, forcing the words past the lump in her throat.

"Two weeks from now, on Saturday. Anyway, I just want to say that I'm still here for you, Hannah. I always will be. And if there's anything I can do to help you investigate Buddy Neiman's death, just let me know."

"Thanks, I'll do that," Hannah said, even though she knew she wouldn't call on Norman unless she absolutely had to. There was no point. And even if she had to call on him, there was the distinct possibility that Doctor Bev wouldn't let him help her anyway.

■ ■ ■ ■

"Here's the autopsy report." Delores plunked an envelope down on the kitchen counter. "Now where's Lisa's new puppy?"

"Sammy should be here any minute. Herb called Lisa to say he was leaving Doctor Bob's office, and Sammy got a clean bill of health. They won't have the results of the blood work until tomorrow, but Doctor Bob says there are no signs that there's anything seriously wrong."

"That's good. I picked up a few things for him at the mall."

"That was nice of you," Hannah said. And then she turned to look at her mother. Delores was carrying an enormous bag from the pet store. "That looks like more than a few things. What do you have?"

Delores opened the bag and pulled out a fire-engine red quilted dog bed with a detachable pillow. "There are zippers," she said, pointing them out. All you have to do is pull the foam out, it's all in one piece, and put the quilted part in the washing machine."

"That's a very nice present, Mother."

"I thought so. I chose red because I know it's your favorite color."

Hannah was confused. "But Mother . . . Sammy is Lisa's dog, not mine."

"I know that. Bu Lisa told me that little Sammy is going to be spending a lot of time here at The Cookie Jar. And he might as well have a bed that's your favorite color, don't you think?"

"I think . . . why not?" Hannah gave a little laugh. "Thank you from Sammy, Lisa, *and* me."

"Oh, that's not all. I bought some toys, too." Delores reached into the bag and pulled out a plush duck. "If Sammy bites down on its stomach, it quacks."

"That's cute," Hannah said, taking the duck and squeezing it around the middle. It made a series of quacking noises that sounded so realistic that Lisa came rushing into the kitchen. "What's . . . oh. It's a toy! Let me see it."

Hannah tossed her the duck, which quacked several times on the way. Lisa caught it around the middle and it issued another volley of quacks.

"Look at this one," Delores said, pulling toys from her bag. "Here's a stuffed rooster. And this one's a horse that whinnies. And I've got a pig that oinks, a cow that moos, and a sheep that does . . . whatever it is that sheep do." Delores turned to her eldest daughter. "What is it called, Hannah?"

"It's called a bleat, Mother."

"Really? I don't think I ever knew the name for the sounds sheep make."

"They're not the only animals that bleat. It's also the word for the wavering sound made by a goat or calf."

Lisa reached out and squeezed the sheep and it started to bleat. Not to be outdone, Hannah grabbed the duck and the pig, and activated them. Then Delores entered into the fun with the rooster and the horse. Michelle, who was still in the coffee shop, heard the racket in the kitchen and came in to check. When she saw what they were doing she hurried in to activate the plush cat and plush dog. The four women were having so much fun, squeezing the stuffed animals and laughing, that they didn't hear the back door open. They were perfectly unaware that Herb was standing there watching them until he said, "And what do we have here? Wannabe farmers?"

Lisa giggled, Hannah winced, Michelle blushed, and Delores tried to look as if she were merely an observer of three other women making fools of themselves.

"They were trying out the toys I bought for Sammy," Delores explained.

"Right." Herb glanced at the toy rooster

and the toy horse in Delores's hands and grinned. It was clear that he wasn't fooled by her uninvolved observer act.

And then she quickly changed the subject. "Where's your new little guy?" Delores asked, changing the subject before he could comment.

Herb smiled. "Right here," he said, flipping his coat back to show Sammy snuggled in a baby carrier, his ears sticking up in two sharp points and his black eyes moving from face to face.

"Adorable," Delores pronounced, stepping forward to stroke Sammy's head. "He's just darling."

"Yes, he is." Lisa beamed like a mother accepting compliments on her newborn.

"I can hold him while you go out to my car," Delores said, sitting down at the workstation and holding out her arms. "The keys are over there on the counter and the crate's in the backseat."

"Crate?" Lisa asked, looking surprised.

"Two boys from the pet sore loaded it for me, but it's too heavy for me to carry in. It should go perfectly in that corner," she pointed to the corner closest to her, "and it's made out of wood so that it can double as a table."

"That's clever," Hannah said.

Lisa smiled. "Yes, it is. We can always use another flat surface for stacking cookie boxes."

The swinging door opened and Mike stepped into the kitchen. "What's everyone doing back here? The coffee shop's packed with customers. Marge and Jack can't handle everything alone."

"My fault," Michelle said. "I was only going to be gone a minute, but we were having so much fun, I lost track of time."

"Me, too," Lisa admitted. She hurried over to give Sammy a little kiss on his head, and then she turned to Herb. "Do you think you can bring in that crate by yourself? I really should be up front. It's time for another performance."

"I can probably do it. And if it's too big for me to handle alone, I'll snag Mike to lend a hand."

"Sure. I'll help," Mike agreed. "Where's the crate?"

"In Mother's car," Hannah answered him.

"My keys are on the counter," Delores added. "It was too big for the trunk so they put it in the back seat."

"What's in the crate?" Mike asked.

"It's empty," Delores told him. "I bought it for Sammy."

"Sammy?"

"This Sammy." Delores lifted a corner on the blanket so that he could see the puppy in her arms. "Sammy is Lisa's new puppy, and he's going to be staying here during the day."

"I take it Sammy's another police dog in training?" Mike asked, winking at Hannah. He was the one who'd told her that it was okay to bring Dillon into the kitchen as long as he was a police dog in training.

"That's exactly what he is," Hannah said. "Either that, or he's a service dog in training. We'll just have to wait for him to grow up a little before we decide."

"Fox terrier?" Mike asked.

"That's what Doctor Bob thought," Herb said. "Grab the car keys, will you Mike? Once we get that crate in and set it up, Delores won't have to hold Sammy any longer."

"Oh, I don't mind," Delores said. "He's a little angel. He just licked my hand."

Hannah stared at her mother in surprise. Delores seemed to be developing a soft spot in her heart for animals. Come to think of it, she was also getting much more compassionate about other people's problems, and more generous with her friends. Something was changing her mother's outlook on life, and Hannah liked the change.

Mike turned around to grab the keys. "What's this?" he asked, noticing the envelope with the autopsy report. "It's from Lake Eden Memorial Hospital."

"Oh, it's just something Doc Knight wrote," Delores told him. "I didn't have time to read it when I was out there this morning, so I brought it with me to read later."

*Smooth,* Hannah thought. *And everything you said was perfectly true and terribly misleading. That's a real art form and I wish I could do it.*

It didn't take long for the men to bring in the crate. It took even less time for Hannah to grab the envelope with the autopsy report and slip it into a drawer.

When the men came in with the crate, Hannah had them put it in the corner and slip Sammy's new dog bed inside. Then Herb settled the little dog inside.

"You can leave the crate door open," Hannah told Herb. "I'm through baking for now, and I can keep an eye on him."

"I don't think he's going anywhere right now," Delores reported. "The minute he got settled in that bed, he closed his eyes, gave a big sigh, and went straight to sleep."

Hannah glanced at the puppy in the crate. Her mother was right. Sammy was fast asleep. He looked warm and comfortable cuddled up in his new soft dog bed, and she found herself wishing that she were small enough to crawl into the crate and snuggle up next to him.

"Where's your parka?" Delores asked, jogging Hannah out of her fantasy.

"It's on the hook by the back door."

"No, it's not. And I don't see it anywhere in the kitchen."

Hannah glanced at the hooks by the back door. Delores was right. Lisa's quilted coat and Michelle's heavy wool jacket were the only things hanging there. "Don't worry, Mother. It's got to be around here somewhere."

"I've heard *that* before," Delores said, and then she laughed. "When you were a child, you lost at least one thing a week in the winter. You took off your parka, or your scarf, or your mittens and then you promptly forgot where you put them."

"But they always turned up," Hannah defended herself even though Delores seemed amused by the memory. "Don't worry, Mother. I didn't lose my parka. The only thing I've lost lately is sleep!"

# CHAPTER ELEVEN

"What did Mike say when he saw Mother's envelope from the hospital?" Andrea asked, turning on the access road that led to the Lake Eden Inn.

"What's this?"

"It's the access road for the Inn. Weren't you paying attention?"

"I was, and I wasn't asking you what this road was. I was repeating what Mike said. He saw the envelope with the autopsy report and he asked *What's this?*"

"Did you have to lie to him?"

"Not me. Mother answered Mike's question, and she managed not to lie either. She said it was something Doc wrote, and she brought it with her to read later."

"Smart."

"It certainly was. Mother's a master at skirting the truth."

"That's true, but Mike's a detective. He was trained to be suspicious."

"I know. I think he probably guessed what it was."

"But then why didn't he follow up?"

"Because he didn't want to know for sure. If he'd known for sure, he would have had to take it. He told me a long time ago that only authorized people are allowed to have access to autopsy reports."

Andrea gave a loud sigh. "That means Mike knows we're investigating. And he's going to read you the riot act about it."

"No, he won't. I think he knows it won't do any good."

Andrea chuckled. "Well, he's right. Telling you not to investigate is like telling the wind not to blow."

They were very close to the Inn now. Hannah could see it through the trees. She expected Andrea to drive past the front and turn down the road that led to the parking lot, but she drove behind the building and parked her Volvo in a spot clearly marked for deliveries.

"You can't park here," Hannah said. "It's just for deliveries."

"I'm delivering you. You don't want to walk all the way from the parking lot in those ratty blankets, do you?"

"No. They're not very warm. Are you going to drop me off and drive down to the parking lot by yourself?"

Andrea didn't say a word. All she did was shut off the motor and reach for the handle to open the driver's door.

"Sally's going to be mad if she gets a delivery and this spot isn't clear."

"No, she's not. While you were looking for your parka, I called Sally on my cell phone and asked her if I could park here. Now hurry and shrug off those awful blankets. There's no way I'm walking into the Inn with someone who looks like a street person!"

Hannah sighed heavily and shrugged off the blankets she'd taken from the back of her cookie truck. "I just don't understand what happened to my parka," she said as Andrea opened the back door and they stepped inside, into the warmth. "I looked all over and it's just not there."

"Are you sure you wore it?"

"Of course I wore it. It was cold this morning."

"Then maybe somebody took it?"

"Who?"

Andrea shrugged. "A thief opened the back door when you were using the mixer? When he saw that your back was turned, he grabbed it and ran off with it?"

"Why mine, when there were better jackets

hanging there? Mine was really old. And that tear in the sleeve was already there when I got it from the thrift store. I still say it's there somewhere. It just has to be."

"We'll look again later," Andrea promised, leading the way to the lobby and crossing it to the cloakroom so that she could hang up her coat.

"Nice outfit," Hannah said once Andrea's coat was off and hanging on the rack. "It's a good color on you."

"Thanks." Andrea turned around in a circle so that Hannah could see that the embroidered border of pink roses on the jacket of her wine-colored pantsuit went all the way around the bottom. "Who did you want to talk to first?"

"I'll talk to Sally first to get her impression of the band."

"That's a good idea. Let's see if she's in her office."

When they got to Sally's office just off the kitchen, she was on the phone. Hannah and Andrea sat down in the chairs facing her desk and waited for her to end her conversation.

"They just walked in. Hold on a second and I'll ask her." Sally turned to Hannah. "Did you find your parka yet?"

"No."

"No, she didn't," Sally said into the phone. She listened for a moment and then she smiled. "I'm sure she'd appreciate it. Come right out."

Hannah waited until Sally had hung up the phone before she spoke. "That was Lisa, she found my parka, and she's bringing it out to me?"

"No, no, and yes. It was your mother, she didn't find your parka, but she bought you a new one and she's bringing it out to you because she's afraid you'll catch a cold."

"You don't catch a cold from the cold," Andrea said. "I heard that on television last night. You have to be exposed to some kind of virus."

Sally nodded. "I heard that, too. It was on the medical segment of the KCOW Evening News." She turned to Hannah. "Andrea told me you girls were investing the hospital murder last night. I'm guessing you're here to talk to the band. Am I right?"

"You're right."

"Who do you want to talk to first?"

"You," Hannah said, pulling out her steno notebook and turning to a fresh page. "Tell me your impression of the band."

"Together as a group, or individually?"

"Individually."

"Shall I include the newest band member?"

"There's a new band member?"

"Yes. They held an audition, and they found a new keyboard player. He'll be playing with them at the show tonight. I saw Eric in the hall right after the audition and he said the new guy was even better than Buddy."

"Is it someone local?" Andrea asked.

"It certainly is!"

Sally gave a smile that reminded Hannah of one of the phrases Delores used in her Regency Romance books. She looked like *the cat that got into the cream pot.* "Who did they hire?" Hannah asked, unable to stand the suspense any longer.

"Devin Murphy. Bridget called me a little while ago and made a reservation for ten. The whole Murphy clan is coming out here tonight to hear him."

"That's just wonderful!" Hannah turned to Andrea. "You'd better call Michelle to let her know. She's going to be very excited. And will you ask her to call Lisa and tell her that the band is going to play tonight? Her dad and Marge want to come out here for dinner and stay to hear them."

"Sure." Andrea pulled out her cell phone and got up from her chair. "I'll call from the lobby. The reception's better out there."

"The band certainly moved fast," Hannah commented.

"I'll say! But that's not surprising. Lee told me they've been looking for a replacement keyboard player."

"Buddy Neiman was leaving the band?"

"That's right. He gave notice the day after Dick and I heard them in Minneapolis. They were so good, we booked them to headline our jazz festival."

"Did Buddy give any reason for leaving?"

"Not specifically. He told Lee he wanted to get out of the Minneapolis area for personal reasons, and he refused to discuss them. He wanted to leave right away, but Lee talked him into giving them two months to find another keyboard player."

"How long ago did you hear them play in Minneapolis?"

"Give me a minute and I can tell you exactly." Sally flipped pages on her date book and then she looked up. "Here it is. We went to Club Nineteen on the second Saturday in February."

Hannah calculated quickly. "So Buddy was leaving the band right after they played here?"

"That's when the notice Buddy gave Lee was up. So, yes. Unless Buddy reconsidered and he hadn't told Lee yet, he was leaving the band right after they finished our gig."

Hannah scribbled a few notes, and then she flipped to a fresh page in her notebook. It was time to move on to another subject. "I know they've been here for less than a day, but will you give me your impressions of the band members so far?"

"Of course," Sally agreed quickly. "For what it's worth, I like Tommy the best."

"Tommy Asch," Hannah said and waited until Sally nodded. "Why do you like him best?"

"He seems the most genuine, and he doesn't have an oversize ego like Karl does."

"Karl's too full of himself?" Hannah used an expression that was common in Lake Eden.

"I'll say! That young man thinks he's Art Blakey and Max Roach all rolled into one, and he doesn't have one tenth the talent they did."

Hannah understood. She knew a bit about the legendary jazz drummers. "What do you think of Tommy's wife?"

"Annie's as sweet as they come. She told me she helped the bus driver rescue the puppy." Sally stopped and looked slightly worried. "She also told me that you took him. How's that working out?"

"It couldn't be working better. Lisa adopted him."

"That's perfect! The last time she was out here with Herb, she told me that Dillon needed a companion dog."

Hannah glanced down at her sheet again. "How about Conrad Bergen?"

"Connie's okay, and he's going to be very popular out here. He's so handsome, he'll have plenty of the Lake Eden girls trying to pick him up. I know a couple of my younger waitresses tried last night, but that didn't work. Lynnette stuck out her claws and ran them off."

"Let's talk about Lynnette."

"That girl is big trouble. Last night she was hanging all over Connie, but this morning she switched her attention to Karl. I was there at rehearsal, and there was some heavy tension going on between Connie and Karl. Lynnette seemed to enjoy setting the two of them against each other. She's an instigator, pure and simple."

Sally stopped speaking, and her eyes seemed to focus at a point just above Hannah's head. She gave a little nod, and then she made a thumbs-up gesture.

Hannah stared at her, thoroughly mystified. "What does *that* mean?"

"It means I approve."

164

"You approve of the fact that Lynnette is an instigator?"

"No!" Sally gave a little laugh. "Did you forget that the window behind you looks out on the kitchen?"

"I forgot all about that window. Did someone show you something?"

"Yes. It was a Pucker Up Lemon Cake, and it looked just wonderful. They have to check with me before I'll let them put it on the dessert cart."

Hannah made a note to try the cake the next time she came out to the Inn for dinner. Then she got back to business. "Let's talk about Eric. What do you think of him?"

"I didn't really get any strong impression of him. He's not sinfully good looking like Connie, but he's not bad looking, and my waitresses seem to like him. A couple of them told me he was really funny. I know he cracks jokes during their performances, and I don't think they're rehearsed. He's just really quick on his feet."

"How about Drake?" Hannah asked, since Sally hadn't mentioned him.

"I'm not sure. Drake seems to be a nice boy, and I know he's the youngest member of the band. He's talented, and he seems very serious about his music. He'd be a handsome guy if he lost a little weight, but I

165

don't think he really cares that he doesn't get very much female attention. I don't know if that's because he discourages it, or because he's totally focused on the music."

"Lee's next. Tell me about him."

Sally's eyes narrowed, and she frowned slightly. "I don't like him," she said.

"That sounded pretty definite for a first impression."

"It wasn't a first impression. I dealt with him when Dick and I booked the band. He's very cold and businesslike, and I'm almost sure he's got money."

"From managing the band?"

"Maybe, but I don't think they've hit it big enough for that. My guess is that Lee has another source of income."

"An illegal source?"

"I wouldn't put it past him. I don't think Cammy would be that interested in waiting on him hand and foot, and doing the other things she does for him if money weren't involved. He's really not very nice to her, you know."

"I didn't know. Give me an example of what you mean."

"She said something last night about the bus driver and how awful she felt that he was dead, that he was almost like a father to her. I was bartending and I heard the whole thing. It was plain that she was grieving, but Lee just told her to shut up and stop bellyaching about it."

"That's cold."

"You bet. And the surprising thing is, she did exactly what he told her to do. She put on a smile and didn't mention the bus driver at all for the rest of the night. Lee's got some sort of control over her. I'm just not sure what it is."

Hannah jotted a few more notes, and then she stood up. "Thanks, Sally. You've been a big help. Can I get a list of the band's room numbers?"

"Of course. I'll call Ruth Ann at the desk and tell her to print out a list for you. Just don't leave without poking your noses in the kitchen. I've got something I want you to taste."

It was beginning to snow again by the time Hannah finished questioning Lynnette, Cammy, and the band members. She'd learned only one more thing of interest during these interviews, and it was that Buddy had told Lynnette that if she was very nice to him, he'd send for her when he got settled in a new place. Lynnette hadn't fallen for that old line. She'd told Hannah that she'd heard the same thing before from other guys, but the moment they'd left town, they'd forgotten all about her.

"We'll go talk to Lee now," Hannah said to Andrea as they walked down the hall toward Lee's room. "I need to find out more about the day that Buddy gave notice to Lee. Everybody in the band seemed to think he was happy playing with them. And they didn't understand why he wanted to leave."

"And we'll go home after we talk to Lee?"

"No, we'll go back and find Sally. She said she wanted us to taste something before we left."

"Oh, good! When Sally says that, it's always something wonderful."

The two sisters walked down the hall toward Lee's room. "What took you so long with that phone call to Lisa?" Hannah asked her.

"I called home and checked on the kids."

Hannah waited a moment, but Andrea didn't go on. "And?" she asked.

"The kids are fine. I told Grandma McCann I was with you out here, but she could reach me on my cell phone if she needed me. And after that, I called Bill to see if he was planning to be home for dinner. He's not. They're calling in pizza and having a strategy meeting about Clayton Wallace."

"The results of Doc Knight's second

blood test came back?" Hannah guessed.

"That's right. It was the same as the first one Doc ran. And he talked to Clayton's doctor to see what dosage he'd prescribed."

"Twice his normal dosage?"

"No. *Three* times his normal dosage. He was taking two other medications and the one pill for his heart. That's three pills every evening. Add two more heart pills to that total, and Clayton must have taken five pills. Think about it, Hannah. Wouldn't you realize that something was wrong if you shook your pills out into your hand and there were five instead of just three?"

"Normally . . . yes. I'd notice. But what if it was dark and you were driving a bus at the time? You might shake out your pills and just swallow them. If highway conditions were bad, you'd probably want to keep your eyes on the road."

"You're right. It could have happened that way. And if Clayton was the one who filled his own pill matrix and he put three heart pills in one of the little compartments by mistake, it's accidental death, not murder."

"That's true. But on the other hand, maybe somebody redistributed that heart medication in his pill matrix on purpose."

"I get it. The killer sets Clayton up with three times his normal dosage and hopes

Clayton will take it without noticing."

"Right. And that's murder."

"Okay. But what if . . ." Andrea stopped speaking and gave a frustrated sigh. "I'm getting confused."

"You're not alone. Quite frankly, I think we should leave the whole question of how Clayton died to the professionals."

"You mean you don't care?" Andrea sounded shocked.

"Not at all. I mean that we don't have all the resources the sheriff's department has, and we can only do so much. I really think we should concentrate on Buddy's murder."

"Because we *know* it's a murder?"

"That's part of it. I'd like to solve both cases. You know that. But Mother found Buddy's body. And Buddy was somebody Michelle and I both knew personally. Not only that, we were all right there at the hospital when it happened. That gives us more of a personal stake in finding his killer."

Andrea thought it over for a moment. "You're right. Let's solve Buddy's murder first. And then, if we have time and they haven't wrapped it up yet, we can work on figuring out what happened to Clayton."

# CHAPTER TWELVE

"I hope you don't have too many questions," Lee said as he answered Hannah's knock on the door. "I scheduled a rehearsal ten minutes from now."

"It won't take longer than that," Hannah promised, stepping into the room even though she hadn't been invited, and motioning for Andrea to follow her. While the other band members had been staying in rooms that were basically bedrooms with an attached bathroom, Lee had one of Sally's mini suites. There was a balcony and a view of Eden Lake. French doors separated the living room area from the bedroom, and, if Hannah remembered correctly, there was a bathtub and a walk-in shower.

The living room was large. There was a couch against one wall and a conversational grouping with a low table surrounded by four club chairs. A flat-screen television was positioned in front of the leather couch, and a desk sat on an inside wall.

"Let's get to it then," Lee said.

There was no invitation to sit down, but Hannah did so anyway. She knew how to deal with people like Lee. "Did Buddy give you any reason for wanting to move out of the Minneapolis area?" she asked him.

"No. He just said . . ." Lee stopped speaking abruptly as Cammy came out of the bedroom.

"Hi, Hannah." She gave them a smile.

"Hi, Cammy. This is my other sister, Andrea."

"Glad to meet you," Cammy said. "Did you come out to listen to the rehearsal?"

"Not exactly," Hannah told her, but before she could say any more, Lee held up his hand.

"Now that the introductions are over, get lost," he told her.

Cammy seemed to take that in stride because she nodded pleasantly. "Okay. I'll go down to rehearsal early."

Lee shook his head. "I don't want you there. And if you see Lynnette, tell her I don't want her there, either."

Hannah began to frown. Lee's tone was nasty. She turned her attention to Cammy and saw that her lower lip was trembling slightly. Her feelings had been hurt, and Lee could have told her to leave nicely.

"I'm going, but . . . why don't you want me at rehearsal?" Cammy asked him.

"That's *my* business. Now go."

*No way to treat a lady!* The thought popped into Hannah's mind. Perhaps it was because she'd recently watched the nineteen sixty-eight Paramount movie of the same name. Of course Lee might not be a serial killer, but this *was* a murder investigation. In any event, Lee's treatment of his girlfriend bordered on cruel, and Hannah decided that she was going to find Cammy just as soon as they finished interviewing Lee, and try to make her feel better.

The moment the door shut behind Cammy, Hannah turned to Lee. "I need to know exactly what Buddy told you when he said he was leaving the band."

"He said, *I gotta leave the band. I need to get out of the Cities.* I asked him why and he said, *It's personal. I don't want to talk about it.* I figured it was a woman."

"What makes you say that?" Andrea asked him.

"It's usually a woman when a guy pulls up stakes that fast. And Buddy had his share of groupies when we were on the road."

"Did he have a regular girlfriend?"

Lee shook his head. "Not as long as I've

173

known him. Buddy didn't want any commitments. He told me that once. And I never saw him with a woman more than once or twice."

"How long had you known him?" Hannah asked.

"Almost three years. I started putting the band together three years ago. I started with Eric. He's my little brother, and he's got real talent. All he needs is someone to channel it for him. We auditioned for a keyboard player first, and Buddy was my first choice."

"Were you happy with the way Buddy performed?" Hannah asked.

"Yeah . . . for the most part. He wasn't a genius like Brubeck or Garner, but he had good stage presence and the ladies loved him. The only thing that bothered me about Buddy was he had a temper when he drank. Since he didn't drink a lot and never on the nights we were playing, that was okay."

"Would you say you were good friends?" Andrea asked.

Lee gave a little shrug. "Sure, we were friends. I liked him and he liked me. That's not to say we never had disagreements."

"Disagreements over what?" Hannah followed up.

"Buddy wanted to hog the whole show. Then I'd have to remind him that we were a group and the *group* was the star, not just Buddy Neiman."

"Did Buddy's tendency to hog the show cause problems with the rest of the group?"

"Sure it did, but most of them have the same problem. From time to time, one or the other gets to thinking that he should have the spotlight. When that happens, I have to put the hammer down. That's what managing is all about. You have to know when to let it go, and you have to know when to kill it."

*You have to know when to kill it?!* Andrea looked horrified as the elevator doors shut behind them. "Do you think that was a Freudian slip?"

Hannah pulled out her notebook and pen. "Probably not, but I'll write it down anyway."

"Let's go find Cammy," Andrea suggested, as the elevator made its slow descent to the lobby. "She was really upset when she left Lee's suite, and she might be angry enough to give us some dirt about him."

"My feelings exactly, but I thought you were going to say that you wanted to find her to make her feel better."

"We can cheer her up, too. It's just that she's fragile right now and I think we can capitalize on that."

Hannah stared at her sister. She'd never seen Andrea in go-for-the-jugular mode before.

"Don't look at me like that. I'm just practicing something I read in one of Bill's detective magazines. Besides, I can't stand Lee. If he's the one who murdered Buddy, I want to get the goods on him and lock the cell door behind him myself!"

"I can understand why you didn't like Lee, but I've never seen you react to anyone that way before."

"I know. He just rubbed me the wrong way, that's all. Guys like Lee give me a royal pain. He treats Cammy like she's his servant, or even worse, like she's not a real person. Just think about what happened up there in his room. Lee never even considered what Cammy was feeling and what she might want from him. It's all Lee, Lee, Lee, and nobody else exists."

Hannah didn't say a word. Andrea was right.

"When we find Cammy, I'm going to ask her, but I'll bet anything that Lee's only nice to her when he wants something. And when he does, he's *really* nice until he gets it! He probably buys her a big bottle of expensive perfume every time he thinks she's fed up with him and about to leave him. He's just that spoiled, rotten type of guy who tries to bribe everyone around to his way of thinking."

*Buys her a big bottle of expensive perfume.* The phrase Andrea had uttered struck a bell. "Just like Benton Woodley?" Hannah asked, naming Andrea's first real boyfriend.

"Yes! *Exactly* like Benton! He even looks a little like . . ." Andrea stopped speaking, and Hannah watched as her face turned bright pink. "I really got hot under the collar about it, didn't I?"

"You did."

"It's just that I hate to see anyone get hurt And . . . I'm a little down on men in general right now."

"You had a fight with Bill?"

"No. Bill and I are fine. We never fight about the big things. It's always over something stupid and we laugh about it later. He's a good husband, Hannah. I'm happy I married him. It's just that I hate to see anybody taking unfair advantage of anybody else, and I can see that Lee is taking advantage of Cammy."

It was a reasonable explanation, but Hannah had the feeling there was something else wrong, something that Andrea wasn't telling her.

"I don't know about you," Andrea said, frowning slightly, "but I'd love to see Cammy refusing to take it and fighting back. Everybody should fight back when someone else hurts them, don't you think?"

Hannah thought about that for a moment. "I think you're right," she agreed. "At least I can't think of any exceptions."

"I'm glad you said that." They were about to pass the door to the coffee shop part of Sally's restaurant, and Andrea hesitated. "Let's go in and have a cup of coffee before we talk to Cammy."

"Okay," Hannah agreed quickly. If they sat down and had coffee, perhaps Andrea would spill whatever was on her mind.

But the sisterly confab was not to be. The moment they entered the coffee shop, Andrea grabbed Hannah's arm. "There she is, Hannah."

"She's with Lynnette," Hannah pointed out.

"That's okay, isn't it? You said they were friends and we probably need to talk to her, too. Let's go ask if we can join them."

A few moments later, Hannah and Andrea were seated at a four-person table with Cammy and Lynnette. Both young women looked dejected.

"How about some dessert to go with that

tea?" Hannah offered, noticing that both Lynnette and Cammy were drinking herbal tea. "I'm buying if there's anything on Sally's menu that's allowed on your diet."

Lynnette and Cammy exchanged a long look, and then Cammy spoke. "The diet's off, at least for today. Can we see a dessert menu? And can we have coffee instead of this awful tea?"

Hannah looked down at the contents of Cammy's cup. It was partially filled with a greenish liquid that reminded her of dog days at Eden Lake when the algae was in full bloom. "What kind of tea is it?" she asked.

"It's a mixture of herbs and spices that's supposed to calm us down when we're upset," Lynnette explained. "Cammy gets it from a special store in the Cities."

"Does it work?" Andrea asked.

"Not today," Cammy said with a frown. "Actually, I'm not sure it ever works."

Andrea gave her a commiserative smile. "What does it taste like?" she asked.

"Like somebody took lawn clippings, put them in an old sock in the dryer, and sold them as tea."

"She's right!" Cammy declared, and then she started to laugh. That was contagious, and all four of them laughed until they were gasping for breath.

When Hannah had regained some measure of control, she motioned for the waitress. But instead of coming over to their table, the waitress motioned to someone in the kitchen, and Sally came bustling out.

"No dessert menu for you," she said, smiling at them. I need all four of you to do a taste test for me. I tried a new dessert this morning, and I need to know if it's good enough to put on the dessert cart in the dining room."

"What is it?" Andrea asked her.

"Tapioca Pie with dark chocolate and white chocolate drizzled on the top."

"Oooh!" Lynnette's expression was almost beatific. "I just *love* tapioca!"

"Me, too," Cammy agreed. "My grandma used to make it all the time. She put chocolate chips on top."

"My grandma did the same thing, and it was a great combination. That's why I thought I'd dress up the pie with two kinds of chocolate." Sally turned to Hannah. "Do you girls want coffee?" When both Hannah and Andrea nodded, she turned to Lynnette and Cammy. "How about you? More hot water?"

"Not this time," Cammy told her. "This tea isn't good enough to be on the same table as your pie. Lynnette and I would like coffee, the stronger the better!"

# TAPIOCA PIE

You don't have to preheat your oven. This pie doesn't have to bake!

**For The Crust:**

2 cups vanilla wafer cookie crumbs *(measure AFTER crushing)*

3/4 stick melted butter *(6 Tablespoons, 3 ounces)*

1 teaspoon vanilla extract

**Hannah's 1st Note: If you want a change from vanilla wafers, you can make a shortbread crust using Lorna Doone shortbread cookies. You can also use chocolate wafer crumbs. They're both good. And if you don't feel like making a cookie crust yourself, or you simply don't have time, you can buy one ready-made at the grocery store in the baking section.**

To make the crust yourself, pour the melted butter and vanilla extract over the cookie crumbs. Mix them up with a fork until they're evenly moistened.

Spray a 9-inch pie pan with Pam or another nonstick cooking spray.

Place the moistened cookie crumbs in the bottom of the pie pan and press them down. Continue to press them until they reach up the sides of the pan. Place the pie pan in the freezer for 20 minutes while you prepare the rest of the pie.

**For The Tapioca:**

1 can *(13.5 ounces)* coconut milk *(I used Dole)*

2 large eggs

1/4 cup quick-cooking tapioca *(I used Kraft Minute Tapioca)*

1/2 cup white *(granulated)* sugar

1 teaspoon coconut extract *(If you don't have coconut extract, you don't have to rush out to buy it — just use vanilla extract instead. Or if you'd like to try a combination of both, use 1/2 teaspoon coconut extract and 1/2 teaspoon vanilla extract.)*

**Hannah's 2nd Note: You don't absolutely positively have to use coconut milk. You can substitute half and half or heavy cream if you can't find it in your store. And if you can't find the quick-cooking tapioca, you can still make this pie. Just use the amounts given in the recipe and follow the directions on the box of regular tapioca to cook it.**

In a medium-size saucepan, off the heat, whisk the coconut milk and eggs together until they're a uniform color.

Add the dry quick cooking tapioca and the sugar. Mix it all up and leave it on a cold burner for 5 minutes. *(Don't worry — I didn't forget the coconut extract. It won't be added until AFTER the tapioca is cooked.)*

Cook the tapioca mixture over MEDIUM-HIGH heat, stirring CONSTANTLY. *(Be careful — it's easy to burn.)* Bring it up to a boil and then pull it off the heat, give it a couple more stirs until it's no longer boiling, and add the coconut extract. Let it cool while you whip the cream.

**Hannah's 3rd Note: You can take another shortcut here if you want to. You can buy a container of frozen sweetened whipped cream and use 1 and 1/2 cups of that instead of whipping your own cream. If you decide to do it yourself, the instructions are below.**

**To Make Homemade Whipped Cream:**
3/4 cup whipping *(heavy)* cream
1/3 cup white *(granulated)* sugar

Whip the cream with an electric mixer until it holds soft peaks. *(When you shut off your mixer and you dip the blade of your rubber spatula in the bowl and pull it back up, soft peaks kind of slump over. They're there, but they nod their heads. Hard peaks stand straight up like little spears.)*

With the mixer running on HIGH speed, GRADUALLY add the sugar. When it's all mixed in, shut off the mixer and give the bowl a final stir with the rubber spatula.

**Hannah's 4th Note: Of course you can whip cream by hand with a copper bowl and a whisk, but it does take some time and muscle. Lisa and I wimp out and use an electric stand mixer.**

Take the bowl out of your mixer and set it on the counter. Feel the sides of the bowl with the tapioca and see if it's room temperature. If it's not, slip the bowl with the whipped cream into the refrigerator and let the tapioca mixture cool to room temperature.

When the tapioca mixture is cool enough, remove a bit of whipped cream *(about a quarter cup),* and add it to the bowl with the tapioca mixture. Stir it in gently. This is called "tempering." If you simply mix the whipped cream and the tapioca mixture together all at once, you'll flatten the whipped cream too much and it will lose its volume.

Now use your rubber spatula to scrape all the tapioca into your bowl with the whipped cream. "Fold" it in, keeping as much air in the mixture as you can. To "fold," dip your rubber spatula into the center of the bowl, and bring it along the bottom up to the side. Turn the bowl a bit to change the orientation, and do it all over again, "folding" the cream into the filling, so that you leave in as much air as possible.

Take the pie plate out of the freezer and scoop in the filling. Your Tapioca Pie, which has probably taken you a half hour or less if you used the shortcuts, is going to be a surefire hit.

Your pie probably looks a bit anemic. *(It tastes great, but it doesn't scream "I'm the Best!")* Decorate it a little. You can sprinkle it with toasted coconut, scatter the top with chocolate curls, do a little shave with white chocolate, or sprinkle the top with chocolate or shortbread crumbs. You can also decorate the top with seasonal fruit or candied fruit.

**Hannah's 5th Note: To toast coconut, preheat oven to 350 degrees F., spread 1/2 cup out on a foil-covered baking sheet, and bake it for 10 to 15 minutes, stirring occasionally, until it's golden brown.**

Refrigerate your pie until you're ready to serve. Tapioca Pie should be served chilled.

Yield: The pie can be cut into 6 to 8

pieces. *(If you're serving this pie after a big meal like Thanksgiving dinner, you should probably cut it into 8 pieces, especially if you're also serving another type of pie like pumpkin, or pecan, and your guests will want some of each).*

# CHAPTER THIRTEEN

Lynnette put down her fork and smiled from ear to ear. "That tapioca pie was the best. I vote we ditch the diet and start eating desserts again."

"I'm with you," Cammy said. "The only thing is, I have to be careful not to gain weight."

"Because Lee likes you thin?" Andrea asked.

"He *does* like me thin, but that's not why. At this point I'm not really caring a lot what Lee thinks."

"Why's that?" Andrea leaned forward, waiting for Cammy's answer.

"Because I'm tired of being treated like dirt, and the nice stuff he buys me isn't worth that. You were there for some of it today, and Lee toned it down a little for you. It gets a lot worse when we're alone."

Hannah reached out and patted her hand. "That's abuse, you know."

"But . . . all he did was insult me."

"It's still abuse," Andrea told her. "Hannah and I have a friend who was always getting injured. When she had a black eye, she said she'd run into a door. And when her arm was broken, she claimed she'd fallen down on the ice. She finally admitted to Hannah that her husband did all those things to her."

Hannah knew Andrea was talking about Danielle Watson, and she took up the story. "She told me it started out gradually. Her husband would get mad at her and insult her. He was always sorry later, and he'd apologize and be really sweet for a while. He'd even buy her gifts and flowers."

"That's what Lee does!" Cammy looked concerned. "Whenever he's really nasty to me, he'll tell me he's sorry and buy me a really nice present."

"Their marriage would go along just fine for a while, but then it would start again. He'd find fault with her for no reason and slap her around. When he calmed down, he'd apologize and surprise her with a new outfit or a piece of jewelry or something else he thought she'd like. She loved him so she forgave him. The big problem was that each time he lost his temper, the abuse would escalate."

"That's awful!" Cammy gave a little shiver. "Did your friend leave her husband?"

"She didn't leave, but he ended up dead."

Lynnette's eyes widened. "She killed him?!"

"No," Hannah answered. "Somebody else did, and for a completely different reason. But anybody who knew about the abuse *thought* she did it. She was the prime suspect in the murder investigation."

Cammy took another sip of her coffee. "Well, I don't think I'll stick around long enough to find out if Lee's going to start hitting me. I was thinking about leaving him anyway. I thought it would be so much fun traveling with the band, but it's not."

"That's exactly what I thought," Lynette said. "And then Buddy and I had that thing going for a little while. I was hoping that if I was around all the time, maybe we could get back together. But that didn't work."

"I told you it wouldn't. Buddy didn't want any attachments to anybody. I found that out early on."

"How early?" Hannah asked, jumping into the conversation. And then, when Cammy looked at her in consternation, she added, "I mean, when did you first meet Buddy?"

"I met him when he auditioned for the band."

"Both of us did," Lynnette added. "We were there because of Eric."

"We went to school with him," Cammy told them.

"Eric came into the doctor's office where I worked," Lynnette explained. "He recognized me right away and we started talking while he was waiting for the doctor to see him. That's when he mentioned that his parents had been killed and his brother was going to start a jazz band for him."

Cammy added, "Lynnette called me, all excited, and said that Eric had invited her to sit in on auditions for a keyboard player. And she told me that Eric said I could come along, too. So I did, and that's when we met Buddy."

"Was that when you dated him?" Andrea asked Lynnette.

"No, not then. He went out with Cammy first."

"That lasted a total of three nights," Cammy said with a laugh. "And then he moved on to Lynnette."

"And you moved on to Lee," Lynnette reminded her, and then she turned back to Hannah and Andrea. "Cammy's been with Lee for as long as Cinnamon Roll Six has been in existence."

Hannah watched Cammy closely as she

asked the next question. "You said Lee bought you presents. Do you know where he got his money?"

"Sure," Cammy said. "Their parents set up a trust. If they died, the kids inherited. But Eric was only twelve at the time and Lee was twenty-one, so they named Lee as executor until Eric reached legal age."

"So you think that Lee is using Eric's half of the inheritance to buy things for himself?"

"I don't know that for sure. Lee never said how much money there is. I think there's plenty. You ought to see the home theater setup Lee has at their condo. It's on Lake Harriet and it's a real showplace. Lee bought them a speedboat, a Harley, and a Jag. Eric doesn't spend much, but Lee's going through money so fast it'll make your eyes swim."

"Does Eric know that?"

"Yeah. Eric says it's okay with him as long as he can live with Lee at the condo. He's got that brother thing going with Lee. And . . . I don't know . . . maybe because Eric's always looked up to Lee, he thinks Lee loves him back."

"But you don't think Lee does?" Hannah got right to the important question.

"Maybe Lee does, and he thinks he's doing the right thing. And maybe he doesn't, and he's taking advantage of Eric because he has control of the money for another two years. Whatever."

"Can you think of any reason why Lee might have killed Buddy?"

"I really couldn't say for sure."

"But I can." Lynnette spoke up. "Cammy's too loyal to tell you this, but Lee was jealous of the fact she dated Buddy before she wound up with Lee. Every time Lee drinks a lot after a performance, he accuses her of flirting with Buddy."

"But I *didn't* flirt with Buddy!" Cammy insisted. "Buddy was just a friend . . . sort of. Lee's a late sleeper so Buddy and I used to meet for breakfast in the morning. He'd tell me all his problems, and I'd tell him mine. It was almost like a brother and sister thing. And before you ask, Lynnette," she turned to her friend, "we never talked about you. Buddy didn't bring it up, and neither did I."

"But you talked every morning over coffee?" Hannah asked.

"Over tea for me and coffee for Buddy, but yes, we talked every morning."

"Did Buddy ever tell you he was worried about anything?" Hannah held her breath, waiting for the answer.

Cammy thought for a moment. "Yeah.

Buddy told me he was worried about something that happened to him in Seattle. And he said that if anybody ever found out about it, he'd have to leave in a hurry."

"Did he tell you he was leaving the band?"

"Yes, he told me."

"Do you have any idea *why* he was leaving?"

"I have an idea, but I don't know if I'm right."

"Tell me," Hannah said, leaning closer.

"I think it had something to do with the woman who came to the show at Club Nineteen. I saw Buddy backstage with her after the performance, and he looked really upset. I just grabbed my purse, that's what I came backstage to get, and left before Buddy could see me. I didn't want him to think I was spying on them, you know? And then, the next morning, right before noon rehearsal, Buddy told Lee that he was leaving the band."

"Did you ask Lee why Buddy was leaving?"

"Yeah, but he said he didn't know, that Buddy wouldn't tell him."

"How about Buddy himself? Did you ask *him?*"

"Sure, I did. I figured that since we were such good friends, he might tell me. But all he'd say was that it was personal."

"Did you ask him if the woman had anything to do with it?"

"No. I figured I'd been nosy enough. I thought I'd wait a couple of days and then I'd mention it casually."

"Did you?" Andrea asked, leaning forward expectantly.

"I didn't have the chance. Buddy never met me for breakfast again. And he . . . well, there's no other way to say it . . . Buddy avoided me. It was like he didn't want to be alone with me anymore."

"Let's talk about the woman," Hannah told her. "Can you describe her for me?"

"I can try, but you've got to understand that the lighting's not very bright backstage. And they were standing a ways away."

"But you said you saw that Buddy was upset, so you must have seen his expression."

"Actually . . . no. His face was in the shadows. I saw his hands and he was clenching his fists. That's how I knew he was upset."

"How about her?"

Cammy shook her head. "She was standing with her back to me. All I can tell you about her is that she had dark hair, and she was shorter than Buddy. That's all, Hannah. I'd tell you if I could, but I don't know anything else."

Hannah bit into her herb-encrusted, center cut pork chop and gave a little sigh of pleasure. It was tender, succulent, and flawlessly seasoned, exactly what she'd grown to expect from any of Sally's entrees.

"How is it, dear?" Delores asked, forking some of her wild salmon.

"Incredible, exquisite, and totally delectable."

"I think you're describing my entree, not yours," Andrea said with a smile. She'd almost finished her slow-roasted chicken with sherry cream sauce, and now she was eating some of Sally's perfectly cooked vegetable medley. "Mine's the best."

"No, mine is," Michelle insisted. "I just love Sally's duck with crispy skin. And these Stuffin' Muffins she serves with it are incredible."

Delores flipped up the corner of the napkin covering Michelle's personal bread basket. "You didn't tell us that Sally gave you *four!*"

Michelle looked perfectly innocent. "Didn't I mention that? Goodness gracious! Let's pass them around."

All of them laughed, including Michelle.

"You're a piggy, Michelle," Delores accused her youngest daughter, as she took a muffin from the basket.

"I'll say she is!" Andrea commented, taking her muffin and passing the basket to Hannah.

*"Didn't I mention that?"* Hannah repeated, still smiling as she took the last muffin. "I don't know what they're teaching theatre majors now at Macalester, but you didn't fool us."

"Not even for a second," Andrea said, breaking open her muffin and buttering it. "That *Goodness gracious!* was really fake. I think you'd better take another acting class next semester."

For a few minutes everyone was silent, concentrating on their food. Andrea finished first, and put down her fork, then Hannah and Michelle did the same. They waited for their mother to finish.

At last Delores put down her silverware and smiled. "That was just excellent. It always is." She turned to Michelle. "That muffin was simply delicious."

"Yes, it was." Michelle agreed. "Why do you think I tried to keep them all for myself?"

Andrea turned to Hannah. "You need to get the recipe from Sally. These would be perfect at Thanksgiving. Maybe it's an easy recipe that even I could make."

"Maybe," Hannah said, doing her best not to sound doubtful.

"I know you don't think I can bake, but you liked those Double Puffs I made for Mother's cookie exchange, didn't you?"

"I liked them a lot. They were great cookies."

"I thought so, too," Michelle added quickly.

"Simply marvelous, dear." Delores reached out to pat her daughter's hand. "They were the hit of the afternoon. *Everyone* loved them. You know how we trade cookies afterwards, don't you?" She waited until her daughter had nodded, and then she continued. "Before we left the community center, five different ladies came up to me and offered to trade any other cookie they had if I'd give them your Double Fudge Drops in return."

"Really?" Andrea asked, looking very pleased.

"Really. And of course I turned all the offers down. And then I went home and I ate every one of them myself."

Hannah watched as Andrea flushed pink with pleasure. Her pleased smile was so luminous, it made Hannah smile, too.

Delores didn't compliment her daughters that often. When Hannah had called her on it once, she'd said that she expected her daughters to be competent young ladies who did everything well, and if she had no criticism, that was a compliment in itself. Now, suddenly, all that had changed. Hannah liked this new, softer side of her mother. She wasn't sure what had caused it, but she hoped it wouldn't change back.

"I'll ask Sally for the recipe," Hannah promised. "And if you think you can't do it alone, I'll be glad to help you make them."

"What recipe do you want, Hannah?" Sally asked, arriving with their coffee just in time to hear the comment.

"Stuffin' Muffins. Andrea wants to bake them for Thanksgiving."

"No problem. I'll run a copy and you can have it. It's so easy, even . . ." Sally stopped when Hannah gave her a warning glance. "I shouldn't say it. It's not that my sous chefs are dumb. It's just that only one of them knows how to bake."

Hannah smiled. She knew that what Sally had been about to say was, *It's so easy, even Andrea can do it.* Thanks to Sally's quick thinking, she'd stopped in midsentence and then implied that her sous chefs couldn't bake!

"Speaking of baking, my other chef tried a new cake this afternoon." She turned to Hannah. "You were there, as a matter of fact."

Hannah was puzzled for a moment, but then she remembered Sally's two thumbs up gesture. "Was that the Pucker Up Lemon Cake?"

"That's right. I tried a sliver a few minutes ago and I liked it a lot, but I'd like a Swensen family opinion."

"I'll order a piece for dessert," Delores offered. "Lemon's my second favorite flavor . . . after chocolate, of course."

"You don't have to order it. I'll send a sample piece to the table."

"And we'll all taste it," Hannah promised, not even bothering to check with her mother and sisters. She knew they were all in agreement that any sweet treat that came out of Sally's kitchen was bound to be wonderful.

# STUFFIN' MUFFINS
Preheat oven to 350 degrees F.,
rack in the middle position.

4 ounces salted butter *(1 stick, 8 Table-spoons, 1/4 pound)*

1/2 cup finely chopped onion *(you can buy this chopped or chop it yourself)*

1/2 cup finely chopped celery

1/2 cup chopped apple *(core, but do not peel before chopping)*

1 teaspoon powdered sage

1 teaspoon powdered thyme

1 teaspoon ground oregano

8 cups herb stuffing *(the kind in cubes that you buy in the grocery store — you can also use plain bread cubes and add a quarter-teaspoon more of ground sage, thyme, and oregano)*

3 eggs, beaten *(just whip them up in a glass with a fork)*

1 teaspoon salt

1/2 teaspoon black pepper *(freshly ground is best)*

2 ounces *(1/2 stick, 4 Tablespoons, 1/8 pound)* melted butter

1/4 to 1/2 cup chicken broth *(I used Swanson's)*

**Hannah's 1st Note: I used a Fuji apple this time. I've also used Granny Smith apples, or Gala apples.**

Before you start, find a 12-cup muffin pan. Spray the inside of the cups with Pam or another nonstick cooking spray OR line them with cupcake papers.

Get out a 10-inch or larger frying pan. Cut the stick of butter in 4 to 8 pieces and drop them inside. Put the pan over MEDIUM heat on the stovetop to melt the butter.

Once the butter has melted, add the chopped onions. Give them a stir.

Add the chopped celery. Stir it in.

Add the chopped apple and stir that in.

Sprinkle in the ground sage, thyme, and oregano.

Sauté this mixture for 5 minutes. Then pull the frying pan off the heat and onto a cold burner.

In a large mixing bowl, combine the 8 cups of herb stuffing. *(If the boxed stuffing you bought has a separate herb packet, just sprinkle it over the top of the mixture in your frying pan. That way you'll be sure to put it in!)*

Pour the beaten eggs over the top of the herb stuffing and mix them in.

Sprinkle on the salt and the pepper. Mix

them in.

Pour the melted butter over the top and mix it in.

Add the mixture from your frying pan on top of that. Stir it all up together.

Measure out 1/4 cup of chicken broth.

Wash your hands. *(**Mixing the stuffing is going to be a lot easier if you use your impeccably clean hands to mix it.**)*

Pour the 1/4 cup of chicken broth over the top of your bowl. Mix everything with your hands.

Feel the resulting mixture. It should be softened, but not wet. If you think it's so dry that your muffins might fall apart after you bake them, mix in another 1/4 cup of chicken broth.

Once your Stuffin' Muffin mixture is thoroughly combined, move the bowl close to the muffin pan you've prepared, and go wash your hands again.

Use an ice cream scoop to fill your muffin cups. If you don't have an ice cream scoop, use a large spoon. Mound the tops of the muffins by hand. *(**Your hands are still impeccably clean, aren't they?**)*

Bake the Stuffin' Muffins at 350 degrees F. for 25 minutes.

Yield: One dozen standard-sized muffins that can be served hot, warm, or at room temperature.

**Hannah's 2nd Note: These muffins are a great accompaniment to pork, ham, chicken, turkey, duck, beef, or . . . well . . . practically anything! If there are any left over, you can reheat them in the microwave to serve the next day.**

**Hannah's 3rd Note: I'm beginning to think that Andrea can actually make Stuffin' Muffins. It's only April now, so she's got seven months to practice. I'll let you know how she does right after Thanksgiving dinner.**

# CHAPTER FOURTEEN

"This is the lemoniest cake I've ever tasted!" Delores exclaimed, and Hannah could tell that her very proper mother was dangerously close to smacking her lips in appreciation.

"I agree. It's just great!" Michelle turned to Sally who was waiting for their opinions. "How does your chef get all that lemon flavor into one slice of cake?"

"He grinds up the whole lemon," Sally told them, "minus the seeds, of course. But everything else goes into the grinder. That's pectin, zest, everything."

Hannah tasted another bite. "You'd think it would be bitter, but it's not."

"He says that's offset by the sugar and raisins."

"Well, he's right," Michelle said, taking another bite. "It's wonderful!"

"I'll tell him you said that. And I'll definitely add it to the dessert menu."

When Sally left, Hannah saw her signal to their waitress. The girl was there almost immediately to take their dessert and coffee order.

"Have chocolate," Delores told Hannah.

"I was planning on it, but why do *you* want me to have chocolate?"

"Here's one reason." Delores pulled a large box out from its hiding place under the table. "I know how much you liked your old parka. I'm sorry it's gone for your sake, but not exactly for mine. It really was disreputable, Hannah. It certainly didn't reflect the fact that you're a smart, successful businesswoman."

*Mother took my old parka, so that she could buy me something that she liked better!* The thought flashed through Hannah's mind. *She probably threw it in the trash. Or maybe she took it back to Helping Hands.*

"What's the matter, dear? You're frowning."

"Was I?" Hannah responded with the first excuse that came to mind. "I was just trying to decide between Sally's flourless chocolate cake and her chocolate angel pie."

"Have both then. If you can't finish them, I'm sure one of your sisters will help you out." Delores gave a little laugh. "But first, open this." She thrust the box into Hannah's hands. "I do hope you like it."

*I don't care what kind of parka it is. What I'd really like is to have my old parka back!* but she didn't say that. Instead she forced a smile and said, "I'm sure it's lovely, Mother." And then she lifted the lid of the box.

Hannah blinked in surprise. It was her old parka reborn. It had come back to life as a smart, stylish quilted coat with exactly the same number of pockets her old parka had possessed. There were two large patch pockets with zippers, two side pockets sewn into the side seams, and even a small breast pocket for handy access to sunglasses or keys.

They were seated in one of Sally's private booths with curtains that could be drawn for privacy and a lovely chandeliertype light fixture directly overhead. As Hannah slipped her fingers into one of the side pockets to see how deep they were, the material of the parka glinted in the light. "Oh, wow!" she said, realizing that what she'd thought was simple olive drab, the same color as her old parka, was completely different. This olive drab wasn't drab at all! It had a design embossed on the material in gold.

"I was wondering if you'd notice," Delores said with a smile. "It's your favorite flower."

"Lilacs." Hannah tipped the box slightly so the light caught the design. "It's beautiful!"

There was a hood. Hannah felt like cheering. She loved parkas with hoods. That was probably because she often forgot to bring her hat, and winter mornings in Minnesota, an hour or so before the daybreak, were frequently the coldest part of the day.

"Fur?" Hannah's fingertips touched the trim around the ends of the sleeves and the collar.

"It's not real fur. I thought that might be a bad idea with Moishe."

"You thought right. He leaves fake fur alone, and so does Cuddles."

Hannah looked up just in time to see her mother and sisters exchange glances. "What?" she asked.

"Your sister has something to tell you, Hannah." Delores nodded toward Andrea.

The waitress chose that instant to arrive with the coffee pot. Once they'd given their dessert orders, everyone fell silent while she refilled their cups. Hannah was just as silent as her mother and sisters, but her mind was a claxon blaring out a warning. *They all know something that you don't know. And that can't be good!*

"Well?" Hannah said, the moment their

waitress had left them.

"Well . . ." Andrea faltered, and she turned to Delores. "Why do *I* have to do it? The last thing I want to do is hurt Hannah's feelings!"

"None of us want to hurt Hannah's feelings. We all love her."

"Yes, we do," Michelle said with a little sigh. "But I know exactly what you mean, Andrea, and I don't envy you a bit. I don't want to hurt Hannah's feelings, either."

This had gone on long enough. Hannah stood up to get their attention. "Hello? You're talking about me as if I'm not here. It's like a wake. And I'm not dead yet. Quit talking *about* me and talk *to* me!"

"You're right." Andrea turned to her. "Remember when I told you I called home and talked to Grandma McCann?"

"Sure. You said the kids were fine, Grandma McCann was fine, and Bill was fine."

"They are. What I didn't tell you was that the mail came. Grandma McCann said there was something that looked like an invitation, so I had her open it. It was an invitation to Doctor Bev and Norman's wedding and it's taking place next Saturday."

"I know."

"You *know?*"

"Yes. Norman came in at noon and told me that Bev had mailed them. Mine will probably be waiting for me when I get home tonight."

Michelle looked confused. "But . . . aren't you upset? They actually set a date. And it's only eight days away!"

"What are you going to do, dear?" Delores asked her.

Hannah gave a big sigh. "I'll have to go. I don't want to, but it wouldn't look right if I didn't. And that brings up an even bigger problem."

"What's that, dear?" Delores leaned forward in anticipation.

"I don't know what I should wear. I want to look good, but I don't want to be over-dressed."

"Wear white," Delores said, her eyes narrowing.

"But Mother! Isn't that a fashion boo-boo? I thought only the bride should wear white."

"That's right. And *you* should have been Norman's bride!"

"Please, Mother. Let's not get into that now. It just didn't work out that way."

"You should wear blue," Michelle offered, "because that's what you're going to be when Norman's new bride won't let you see him anymore."

Andrea shook her head. "I think Hannah should wear black. She might as well start mourning Norman now, because Doctor Bev is going to be the death of him!"

"So what are you going to *do* about it?" Delores asked, facing her eldest daughter squarely.

"I . . . don't know. Maybe I shouldn't go at all. Or maybe I should skip the ceremony and just go to the reception."

"I didn't mean *that*," Delores said. "I meant what are you going to do about Norman and Bev getting married?"

"What *can* I do? You know why he's getting married. Bev won't let him be a part of Diana's life unless he marries her. And since Norman's her father, he *wants* to be a part of her life."

"So you're just going to look the other way and do nothing." Delores summed it all up the way she saw it. "You're going to be polite, and nice, and take the crumbs Bev is willing to give to you. A little *hi* if he happens to see you on the street, a wave if he drives by, a Christmas card from the newlyweds."

Hannah shrugged. "I hope it's not that

bad, but if it is, I'll just have to cope with it."

"You even took his cat!" Andrea said accusingly.

"What *else* could I do? Norman loves Cuddles and so do I. I couldn't bear to see him agonize over finding her a new home. Norman and I are still friends. It's just that we won't see each other as often. He feels terrible about that, and so do I."

"We all talked about this," Michelle said. "All three of us think you're enabling Norman."

"Enabling?" Hannah snapped her mouth shut as their waitress arrived with their desserts. The flourless chocolate cake had lost its appeal, and so had the chocolate angel pie. She picked up her fork anyway, but put it back down on her plate when the waitress left them alone again. "How am I enabling him?" she asked.

"For one thing, you're making things easy for Norman," Andrea said, and Hannah noticed that she hadn't taken a bite of her own dessert either.

Michelle shoved her dessert to the side. "You let him take the easy way out with Cuddles. He never even had to *try* to find a new home for her. You said you'd take Cuddles right away."

"But . . ."

"Just listen to me," Michelle interrupted her. "Because of you, Norman never had to make a hard decision through this whole thing with Bev. If he'd been forced to make those hard choices, he might have decided that it wasn't worth it."

"Let me," Delores said, shushing Michelle. "Think about it, dear. Norman didn't have to give up Cuddles to a stranger because the minute he mentioned it, *you* took her. He might have had second thoughts if you hadn't volunteered so quickly."

"And how about the birthday party?" Andrea reminded her. "Norman didn't have to find somebody else to make a dessert for Bev's birthday party, because you told Mike *you* would. Norman might have realized exactly how upset you were if you'd refused to bake something for Bev."

"Your problem is you're just too understanding," Michelle accused her. "Last night you told me you thought Bev was just saying she was allergic to cats to keep Norman from seeing you. Isn't that right?"

"Well . . . yes. I *do* suspect that she isn't as allergic as she tells Norman she is."

"Then why didn't you act on that suspicion?" Delores asked. "You could have set some kind of trap for her and proved that she was faking it. You let her get away with it. Norman thinks she's allergic to cats. He might have thought twice about believing anything Bev told him if you'd set a trap to prove that her cat allergy was fake."

"I *thought* about doing that."

"But you didn't do it," Andrea pointed out. "Do you really think Norman's going to be happy with Bev?"

"Well . . . no. No, I don't. But he's doing the right thing."

"Is he?" Andrea asked.

"Yes. I told you all before. Norman wants to be a part of his daughter's life."

"How do you *know* she's his daughter?" Michelle spoke up again.

"Bev was pregnant when they split up in Seattle, but she didn't tell Norman about it."

"Let me get this straight." Delores took over again. "You *do* suspect that Bev is lying about her cat allergy to keep Norman from you. But you *don't* suspect that Bev is lying about her daughter's paternity to keep Norman from you."

"Well . . . when you put it like that . . ." Hannah's voice trailed off.

"You say you're going to miss Norman a lot if you don't get to see him very often,"

Andrea said.

"It's true. I *will* miss him." Hannah blinked away the tears that threatened to form in her eyes.

"But don't you see what you're doing?" Michelle asked. "You're making things easy for Bev by not confronting her. Because you're polite and you don't want to make waves, you're shoving Norman straight into her arms."

"If you really care for Norman as much as you say you do, you'll fight for him!" Andrea said.

"But . . . I don't know what I can do at this point."

"We do," Delores informed her. "The way we see it, you have two choices. You can either fight for Norman, or you can roll over and give up."

"But I wasn't trying to roll over and give up. I was just trying to be nice."

"There are times to be nice, and times to stand up for what you really want from life. Did I raise my daughter to be a spineless quitter?"

"You did not!" Hannah said. And as she said it, she felt a giant weight slide off her shoulders. "You *certainly* did not!"

"Atta girl!" Delores said, reaching out to touch Hannah's cheek. Then she picked up

Hannah's dessert fork, cut off a generous bite of flourless chocolate cake, and handed it to her. "Have some chocolate. And after we finish our desserts, we'll tell you all our ideas for giving Doctor Bev the boot."

## PUCKER UP LEMON CAKE

Preheat oven to 350 degrees F.,
rack in the middle position.

**Hannah's 1st Note: I think it's possible to make this cake by hand, but it will take a strong arm to do it. Lisa and I use an electric stand mixer. Some people may still have a food grinder in their kitchen cabinet. If you do, get it out and use it. If you don't, use a food processor and the steel blade.**

1 large lemon *(choose one with perfect skin — you'll be using that, too!)*

1 cup golden raisins *(Regular raisins will also work.)*

1/3 cup pecans

2 cups all-purpose flour *(Don't pack it down. Just scoop it out and level off the top of your measuring cup with a table knife.)*

1 teaspoon salt

1 teaspoon baking soda

1 and 1/2 cups white *(granulated)* sugar

1/2 cup *(1 stick, 4 ounces, 1/4 pound)* softened butter

1 teaspoon lemon extract *(Use vanilla if you don't have lemon.)*

3/4 cup whole milk

2 large eggs

1/4 cup whole milk *(This brings the milk total up to one cup.)*

Grease and lightly flour a 9-inch by 13-inch rectangular cake pan. *(Alternatively, you can spray it with baking spray, the kind with flour in it.)*
Wash the outside of your lemon. Then juice it and save the juice. *(You'll use it in the cake topping.)* Pick out the seeds and throw them away, then cut the pulp and rind into 8 pieces.

If you have a food grinder, grind the lemon pulp and rind with the raisins and the pecans. If you don't have a grinder, simply put the lemon pulp and rind into the bowl of your food processor, and add the raisins and the pecans. Process them with an on and off motion until they're chopped as finely as they'd be if you'd used a food grinder.

Set the ground lemon, raisin, and pecan mixture aside in a bowl on the counter.

Measure out one cup of flour and put it in the bowl of your electric mixer. Add the salt, baking soda, and white sugar. Mix them together at LOW speed.

Add the second cup of flour. Mix that in

at LOW speed.

Add the softened butter, the lemon extract, and the 3/4 cup of whole milk. Beat at LOW speed until the flour is well moistened. Then turn the mixer up to MEDIUM HIGH speed.

Beat for 2 minutes. Then shut off the mixer and scrape down the sides of the bowl.

Turn the mixer on LOW and add the eggs, one at a time, beating all the while. Then beat in the rest of the whole milk. Once the eggs and the milk are incorporated, turn the mixer up to MEDIUM HIGH.

Beat for 2 minutes. Then shut off the mixer, and scrape down the sides of the bowl.

Remove the bowl from the mixer. You're going to finish this cake by hand.

Gradually add the ground lemon, raisin, and pecan mixture to the mixing bowl, folding it in gently as you go. The object is to keep as much air in the cake batter as you can.

Pour the cake batter into the pan you prepared earlier, smoothing out the top with a rubber spatula.

Bake the Pucker Up Lemon Cake at 350 degrees F. for 40 to 50 minutes, or until a thin wooden skewer or a cake tester that's been poked into the center of the cake comes out clean. *(I started testing my cake at 40 minutes, but there was still sticky batter clinging to the tester. The last time I baked this cake, it took the full 50 minutes.)*

When your cake is done, take it out of the oven and place it on a wire rack or on a cold burner on the stovetop.

**Pucker Up Lemon Cake Topping:**

1/3 cup lemon juice *(from the lemon you juiced earlier)*
1/2 cup white sugar
1 teaspoon cinnamon
1/4 cup finely chopped pecans

**Hannah's 2nd Note: You must make the topping and put it on your cake while the cake is still piping hot from the oven.**

Drizzle the 1/3 cup of lemon juice over the top of your hot cake.

Mix the 1/2 cup of sugar with the 1 teaspoon of cinnamon. *(I usually mix them together with a fork.)*

Sprinkle the sugar and cinnamon mixture over the top of your cake.

Sprinkle the finely chopped pecans on top of the sugar and cinnamon.

Let your cake cool to room temperature. Cover it, and refrigerate it. You want to keep it nice and moist.

You can serve Pucker Up Lemon Cake at room temperature or chilled. It freezes well if you wrap it in foil and put it in a freezer bag.

# CHAPTER FIFTEEN

"Ready?"

"Ready." When Michelle opened the door, Hannah braced herself for the orange and white, fur-covered bundle that would arrive in her arms with the same impact as a bowling ball. But nothing, absolutely nothing, happened.

"Where is he?" Hannah asked, racing inside to see why Moishe hadn't greeted her in his usual way, and leaving Michelle to follow her.

"Moishe?" Hannah called out, but there was no answering meow. "Where are you?"

"Hiding," Michelle said, coming into the living room from the kitchen where she'd been looking for Moishe.

"Hiding? Why?"

"You may not want to know. Let's just say that you need a new flour canister and new flour to go in it."

Hannah turned, intending to go into the

kitchen to see for herself, but Michelle stopped her.

"Here," Michelle said, holding out her cell phone. "A picture is worth a thousand words. You've had a rough day already, and I thought I'd better prepare you before you saw the actual disaster."

Hannah stared at the small screen on Michelle's phone and groaned loudly. It *was* a disaster, even in miniature, and Hannah groaned again. It was clear that a game of chase had included the kitchen as a venue. Her plastic flour canister was on the floor on its side. The top had popped off and flour was spread all over the floor. To add to the mess, one of the cats had tipped over the water dish, and there was a puddle of flour mixed with water in front of the sink. Moishe's self-feeder was also on its side, and red and brown kitty crunchies had spilled out all over the mess on the floor.

"At least it's colorful," Michelle commented, taking her phone out of Hannah's hands and turning it off.

"That's true, but I really didn't need floor art. Let's go clean it up before it turns into a permanent sculpture."

Thirty minutes later, Hannah's kitchen floor was clean. With both of them working, it hadn't been the impossible task it had appeared to be at first glance. The cats had emerged from hiding and Hannah thought Moishe looked guilty. That made her feel bad. He'd only been playing, after all, and she'd cuddled him and told him that she wasn't *that* mad at him. She'd filled the self-feeder with fresh kitty crunchies and the water bowl with water. Everything was back to normal, except for the cracked canister and the lack of flour.

Hannah had picked up the pieces of the cracked flour canister and dumped them in the garbage. When she got a new one, it would be the unbreakable kind with a lid that screwed on tightly. She knew Moishe was having a good time with Cuddles here, but if they kept on going the way they were, the toll on her breakables could become simply astounding.

"Do you think Cuddles is a bad influence on Moishe?" Michelle asked, tying the top of the garbage bag closed.

"No. It's just that Norman's house is all set up for a young, active cat. It's big, there's thick carpeting, and not much furniture to get in the way when Cuddles is dashing around playing chase. Moishe and Cuddles never break anything in Norman's house, because they have enough room to run. My condo is a lot smaller, and it's packed with things."

"Well, it's really too bad that you lost all your flour. Do you have any more?"

"I don't think so, at least not here. The last time I ran out of flour, I just took the empty canister to work with me and filled it up at The Cookie Jar. It's silly to buy flour for home, when I've got fifty-pound sacks there."

"Too bad you don't have any here. I was going to bake cookies for Mike."

"For Mike? Why were you going to do that?"

"Because he should be knocking on your door in about an hour."

Hannah stared at her sister in surprise. "Why didn't you tell me Mike called?"

"Because he *didn't* call."

"Then why do you think he's coming over?"

"Because there's been a murder, and Mike always drops in at your place to see what we've found out."

Hannah thought about that for a moment. "You're right," she said. "Now I wish I hadn't thrown away that flour in the bottom of the cracked canister. We can't bake cookies without flour. And we don't have any flour, unless . . ."

Hannah stopped speaking, and Michelle waited for her to continue. "Unless what?" she finally prompted.

"Check my freezer. There may be some loose flour in a double freezer bag. I think I brought home too much when I was doing my Christmas baking. I seem to remember that rather than taking it back to The Cookie Jar, I froze the leftover flour."

"Makes sense," Michelle said, opening Hannah's freezer. "That's what I do at our house to keep the weevil eggs from hatching. It's really gross if you think about it."

"Not necessarily. You're getting extra protein."

"Eeuw!" Michelle made a face.

"If it really bothers you, sift your bag of flour into a bowl before you put it into your canister."

"And that'll get rid of the weevil eggs?"

"Some of them."

"Why would I go to all that trouble to get only *some* of the weevil eggs out?"

"Because you're compulsive and it might make you feel better."

"I'm not *that* compulsive!" Michelle declared, starting to look for the frozen flour, removing items from Hannah's freezer and then putting them back again. "Here it is," she said, holding the bag up triumphantly.

"It was in the last place I looked."

"It always is. That's an unwritten law. How much flour is there?"

Michelle held the bag aloft so that Hannah could see. "Four or five cups. Maybe a little more. It's hard to tell without measuring."

"If you think we've got one and a half cups, we'll make Eleanor Olson's Oatmeal Cookies. They're some of Mike's favorites, especially when I add raisins."

"I think there's that much. How about oatmeal? Do you have that?"

"I've got it. And I know I've got sugar and eggs. Let me get out the recipe and we'll start mixing up the dough."

Hannah took her three-ring binder from the spot next to the stand mixer and paged through it. "Here it is. I had one of these cookies almost every Thursday when Mrs. Olson was the head cook at Jordan High. The grade school got the cafeteria from eleven to twelve, and the high school came in from noon to one. I can't think of anybody who didn't like her oatmeal cookies."

"Mrs. Olson wasn't there when I started school," Michelle said with a frown. "Then the head cook was Edna Ferguson, and we never got cookies every Thursday like you did."

227

Michelle sounded a bit jealous and Hannah couldn't blame her. It was great to have a school cook who made special treats. "What I liked best about those cookies was that every once in awhile, Mrs. Olson put a surprise inside her cookies."

"Like what?"

"There would be small bites of sweet things like a square of Hershey's chocolate, or a little piece of pineapple or apple. One week it was even M&M's. We really liked those!"

Michelle didn't say a word. She just walked over to her purse and opened it. And then, as Hannah watched, she drew out several small packages of M&M's.

"Where did you get those?" Hannah asked.

"From the hospital vending machine last night. I brought back candy for everybody, and these were left over. Do you want to use them in the cookies?"

"Three guesses, and the first two don't count," Hannah said, grabbing the bags out of Michelle's hand.

# ELEANOR OLSON'S OATMEAL COOKIES
Preheat oven to 350 degrees F.,
rack in the middle position.

1 cup *(2 sticks, 8 ounces, 1/2 pound)* salted butter, softened

1 cup brown sugar *(pack it down in the cup when you measure it)*

1 cup white *(granulated)* sugar

2 eggs, beaten *(just whip them up in a glass with a fork)*

1 teaspoon vanilla extract

1 teaspoon salt

1 teaspoon baking soda

1 and 1/2 cups flour *(pack it down in the cup when you measure it)*

3 cups quick-cooking oatmeal *(I used Quaker Quick 1-Minute)*

1/2 cup chopped nuts *(optional) (Eleanor used walnuts)*

1/2 cup raisins or another small, fairly soft sweet treat *(optional)*

**Hannah's 1st Note: The optional fruit or sweet treats are raisins, any dried fruit chopped into pieces, small bites of fruit like pineapple or apple, or small soft candies like M&M's, Milk Duds, chocolate chips, butterscotch chips, or**

any other flavored chips. Lisa and I even used Sugar Babies once — they're chocolate-covered caramel nuggets — and everyone was crazy about them. You can also use larger candies if you push one in the center of each cookie. Here, as in so many recipes, you are only limited by the selection your store has to offer and your own imagination.

Hannah's 2nd Note: These cookies are very quick and easy to make with an electric mixer. Of course you can also mix them by hand.

Mix the softened butter, brown sugar, and white sugar in the bowl of an electric mixer. Beat on HIGH speed until they're light and fluffy.

Add the beaten eggs and mix them in on MEDIUM speed.

Turn the mixer down to LOW speed and add the vanilla extract, the salt, and the baking soda. Mix well.

Add the flour in half-cup increments, beating on MEDIUM speed after each addition.

With the mixer on LOW speed, add the oatmeal. Then add the optional nuts, and/or the optional fruit or sweet treat.

Scrape down the sides of the bowl, take the bowl out of the mixer, and give the cookie dough a final stir by hand. Let it sit, uncovered, on the counter while you prepare your cookie sheets.

Spray your cookie sheets with Pam or another nonstick cooking spray. Alternatively, you can line them with parchment paper and spray that lightly with cooking spray.

Get out a tablespoon from your silverware drawer. Wet it under the faucet so that the dough won't stick to it, and scoop up a rounded Tablespoon of dough. Drop it in mounds on the cookie sheet, 12 mounds to a standard-size sheet.

Bake Eleanor Olson's Oatmeal Cookies at 350 degrees F. for 9 to 11 minutes, or until they're nice and golden on top. *(Mine took 10 minutes.)*

Yield: Approximately 3 dozen chewy, satisfying oatmeal cookies.

# CHAPTER SIXTEEN

"These are really good cookies!" Michelle exclaimed, biting into a warm oatmeal cookie. "I'm glad you said that about the M&M's. Chocolate candy is perfect in oatmeal cookies. What else did Mrs. Olson use? Can you remember?"

"Once she put a slice of banana inside each cookie and sprinkled the top with cinnamon and sugar. Another time it was chopped dates. I think she did chopped dried apricots, too. That's the beauty of this cookie. It's one of those good, basic recipes that you can embellish almost any way you want."

"Well, this embellishment certainly worked!" Michelle finished her cookie and stood up. "I suppose we'd better pack up the dishwasher, and . . ." she stopped, as the phone rang. "Do you want me to get that?"

"Go ahead. I'll put on a fresh pot of coffee."

"Hannah's place. Michelle speaking." She listened for a minute and then she gasped loudly. "Are you *sure?*"

Hannah turned around to glance at Michelle. Her sister looked positively shocked. "What is it?" she asked.

"It's Mother. Pick up in the living room, Hannah. Mother's with Doc Knight and he says Buddy Neiman wasn't who he said he was!"

Hannah flicked the switch to turn on the coffee pot, and rushed to the living room to pick up the remote phone. "Hello, Mother. What's all this?"

"It's exactly as I told Michelle." Delores sounded a bit breathless. "I'm out here at the hospital doing some paperwork in Doc's office, and he just popped in to tell me that Buddy Neiman couldn't have been that keyboard player's real name."

"How does Doc know that?" Hannah asked.

"When Doc took a blood sample during the autopsy, it turned out to be B negative. And that didn't match the blood type on Buddy's hospital records. At first Doc thought Vonnie had made a mistake with the form, but he found a blood donor card in Buddy's wallet that said he had A positive blood."

"What was the name on the card?" Michelle asked.

"Bernard Alan Neiman. Everything in his wallet said Bernard Alan Neiman, including his Minnesota driver's license. And the blood type on his blood donor card was A positive."

"That's strange," Michelle said, clearly puzzled.

"Who tested the blood sample Doc took during the autopsy?" Hannah asked.

"Marlene. She carried it to the lab right after the autopsy. Doc did the second test himself. Both samples came up B negative."

"So Buddy was using fake identification," Hannah said, drawing the obvious conclusion. "Does Doc have any idea who Buddy really was?"

"Not yet. The only facts he has so far are medical. I wrote them down so I could tell you."

"Hold on while I get a pen." Hannah reached in her purse and pulled out her shorthand notebook. She grabbed a loose Rhodes Dental Clinic pen that was near the phone, and flipped to a fresh page. "I'm ready, Mother."

"Buddy's tonsils were removed, and he had an appendectomy scar. And he broke his left leg in three places when he was quite young. He had a birthmark on his left calf, and a mole on his neck. Norman noticed that Buddy still had all four of his wisdom teeth, which was unusual for his age, and he had a crown that was made of an experimental amalgamate that never made it to the commercial dentistry supply market."

"How would a dentist get it if it wasn't sold commercially?" Michelle asked.

"Norman told Doc that free dental clinics and dental schools sometimes hold clinical trials of experimental dental supplies. He's going to call around to see which company made it and which schools and clinics ran trials for them."

"Norman could tell all that by just looking?" Michelle asked, sounding impressed.

"Not exactly. He said he knew it was experimental because it had yellowed, and approved amalgamates don't change color. So Doc gave him permission to remove the crown and take it to a dental lab for analysis."

"Was Norman there when Doc did the autopsy?"

"No. Doc called Norman in later to see if he could spot anything distinctive about Buddy's teeth."

"Doctor Bev wasn't there?" Hannah asked, surprised that Norman's fiancée had let him out of her sight.

"Doc said he invited her to tag along, but she said she'd wait for Norman in the lobby."

*That must be because there's no real competition for her in a morgue,* Hannah thought. "Has Doc called Mike to tell him yet?"

"Not yet, dear. I'm passing it on to you first."

"Thanks, Mother. When is Doc calling Mike?"

"Right after I hang up, but he'll probably get Mike's voice mail. If you see Mike before he gets the message, will you tell him to call Doc at the hospital?"

"Sure, but what makes you think I might see Mike before he gets his messages?"

"Whenever Mike has a murder case, he always drops by your place to see what you've learned. Not only that, he's probably been working all day and he knows you'll feed him. He really shouldn't expect you to stay up and cook for him."

"That's no problem. Michelle always helps and she's great at thinking up quick meals. If I sound tired, it's probably because of all the cleaning we had to do when we got back here."

"What do you mean? Did the cats make a mess while you were gone?"

"And how!" Michelle said, laughing.

"What happened?"

"They were playing chase, and they knocked my flour canister on the floor," Hannah explained. "And then they knocked over their water dish, and we had kitty play dough to clean up."

"Oh, my! Well . . . that just goes to show we were right, dear. Cuddles needs to go home to Norman. She's got more room to run there. And the only way Cuddles can go home is for you to send Doctor Bev back where she belongs!"

"Food," Hannah said to Michelle after she'd hung up the phone and gone back to the kitchen.

"You're hungry?"

"Not me. Mike. We've got cookies, but what can we fix for a main course? Since we didn't stop at the Red Owl today, the food situation is the same as it was last night."

"Minus the hamburger," Michelle pointed out. "But I think you've got some elderly bacon in the refrigerator."

Hannah laughed. "Elderly bacon? I like that! How elderly is it?"

"I'll see." Michelle rummaged in the refrigerator for the package of bacon she'd spotted. "You're in luck. The sell-by date is today. But there's only half a package left. That's not going to be enough for Mike, is it?"

"Not *just* the bacon, no. But I've got something in mind that ought to work. How many eggs are left?"

Michelle opened the egg carton. "Four."

"That's perfect. And how much flour is left in the bag that was frozen?"

"A little more than a cup. I measured it before I dumped it back in."

"Do I have milk?"

Michelle shook her head. "All you have is whipping cream. Will that work?"

"I don't see why not." Hannah took out a frying pan and plunked it on the stovetop. "If you'll hand me that bacon, I'll start frying it."

"I can do that. What else do you need to make whatever you're making?"

"Salt and vanilla. That's it. Although . . ."

"What?"

"Was there any cheese left in that package of shredded cheese we used last night?"

"No. We used it up, but I saw a package of cream cheese in the back behind the whipping cream."

"That'll do. Mike likes cream cheese."

"Flour, whipping cream, eggs, bacon, salt, vanilla, and cream cheese . . ." Michelle stopped and shook her head. "What *are* you making?"

"What Grandma Elsa used to call German pancakes."

"But Grandma Elsa wasn't German."

"Neither were the pancakes. At least I don't *think* they're German. I just thought it would be easy to make them because they're baked in the oven. I can remember her beating them with an egg beater, but I'm going to use the mixer. It'll go a lot faster that way. Everything except the bacon and cream cheese goes into the mixer."

"What do you want me to do with the bacon."

"Fry it hard, and then cool it off and crumble it. It'll take me a while to beat the batter. I need a lot of air in it."

In a minute or two the kitchen was redolent with the smell of bacon frying. It smelled wonderful, and Hannah realized that the bacon was the new applewood smoked bacon that Florence at the Red Owl had begun to carry right after Christmas. Surprisingly, the sweet smokiness of the bacon and the scent of vanilla combined to create a breakfast perfume that made Hannah's mouth water even though she wasn't at all hungry.

"It sure smells good in here," Michelle

said, mirroring Hannah's thoughts exactly.

"I know. How's that bacon coming?"

"Almost done. I'm going to stick it in your freezer on a paper plate to cool it down fast. Do you want me to get out a pan?"

"Yes. I need an eight-inch square metal pan. I would have doubled the recipe and made it in a nine-inch by thirteen-inch if we'd had more ingredients, but we didn't."

"That's okay. I'm not hungry. It just smells good, that's all."

Ten minutes later, Mike's breakfast was assembled and Hannah slipped the pan in the oven. "Done," she said. "Now we can have a cup of . . ." She stopped and gave the phone an unhappy glance as it rang. "If that's Mike and he says he's not coming, we've just made something for nothing."

Michelle plucked the phone from its wall cradle and answered it. "Hannah's place. Michelle speaking." She listened for a minute and then she laughed. "I don't believe it! You never get up that early, especially two days in a row! Hold on for a second and I'll get her for you."

Michelle didn't have to tell Hannah who it was. Only one person they both knew deserved the comment Michelle had made about never getting up early two days in a row. She took the phone from Michelle and said, "Hi, Andrea. What's up?"

"Me, but I'm going to bed right after this phone call. I'm picking you up tomorrow morning at six. We're driving to the Cities."

"Why?"

"Because Bill says we're going to run into traffic from all the weekday commuters and we have to leave that early if we want to get there by nine."

"Okay. I'll buy that. Why do we have to get there by nine?"

"Because I have a meeting with Swartznagel Realty."

"Why?"

"Because I want to show my client a house they just listed in White Bear Lake."

"Why do I need to go with you?"

"Because you're the client, but don't tell Bill. He thinks you're just going with me to keep me company."

"Why *am* I going with you? And why am I pretending to be your client? I'm not in the market for a house."

"Because I can't tell Bill the *real* reason we're going to see the Swartznagel house."

"Cut to the chase, Andrea. We're going in circles. What's the real reason you're taking me to see this house?"

"Because it's right next door to Doctor Bev's mother's house, and we need to see

Diana. Then we'll go to breakfast, and then we'll drop in at Club Nineteen at noon."

"Are they open that early?"

"They are tomorrow. I just called and they're holding auditions for new jazz bands starting at noon. They do it one Saturday a month, and this is the Saturday for April. The waitress I talked to said everybody's welcome and the audience fills out comment cards on the band. I made a reservation for us. I'm pretty sure that between the sets, we can find a way to talk to the management and ask some questions."

"Okay. That's worth doing, but I have to be back right after that. Lisa's still telling her stories tomorrow, and the second day is just as popular as the first. She's going to need lots of cookies."

"That's not a problem. I called Lisa, and she said that Marge, Patsy, and Jack are coming down to help her. Pasty and Marge will take turns baking, and you know what great bakers they are. Michelle will be there, too, so Lisa says you don't have to come in at all tomorrow."

"That's fine, I guess, but I'm still a little confused about something. I can understand talking to the people at Club Nineteen. They might know more about the woman with the brown hair that Lynette saw with

Buddy backstage. We should ask them about Buddy's background, too. Maybe he mentioned where he came from, or anything that might help us find out . . ." Hannah stopped short. Perhaps Andrea wasn't up to speed yet. "You *do* know that Buddy wasn't Buddy, don't you?"

"Of course I do. Mother called me right after she called you."

"Good. What I don't understand is why we need to see Diana. I don't think it'll do us any good."

"It'll do a lot of good! We can't very well get a DNA sample if we don't see her . . . now can we?"

"But how are we going to get a DNA sample? I think her grandma might notice if we swabbed the inside of her cheek."

"We'll just. . . ." Andrea stopped and frowned slightly. "I'll think of something tomorrow, don't worry. I'm good at subterfuge. All you have to do is be convincing as my real estate client."

"How do I do that?"

"Look interested when I ask about the neighborhood. And be kid-friendly, especially if Diana's right there with her grandmother."

"Okay. Anything else?"

"Not really, unless . . . yes, a couple of

things. Don't wear jeans, whatever you do! Do you have any slacks?"

"One pair."

"Pull-ons?"

"Yes, with an elastic waist."

Andrea muttered something that sounded vaguely like, *Great! Just great!* to Hannah, and then she asked, "What color are they?"

"Dark grey. Claire picked them out for me."

"Okay, then they're fine. Wear them with a sweater under your parka. A *nice* sweater, not one that's all stretched out."

"I've got the sweater you gave me for Christmas last year. That's a *nice* sweater, isn't it?"

"Yes. That'll do just fine. Do you have any dress boots?"

In Hannah's mind the phrase *dress boots* translated into boots that wouldn't keep the snow off your feet. "No," she said.

Andrea sighed deeply. "All right, she said. "Wear those moose-hide boots of yours. If everything else is totally acceptable, you can have one fashion eccentricity."

"Thanks," Hannah said, chomping down on the inside of her cheek to keep from laughing.

"Be ready at six. I'll call you from my cell phone when I pull into the garage. And don't be late."

"Right," Hannah said, grinning as she hung up the phone.

"What's so funny?" Michelle asked.

"Andrea. She's planning out this undercover operation, and she even told me what to wear."

Michelle just shook her head. "That's our Andrea. We love her, but she can be a royal pain. But you got off light."

"What do you mean?"

"She could have told you to dye your hair!"

# GERMAN PANCAKES

Preheat oven to 375 degrees F.,
rack in the middle position.

Prepare an 8-inch square pan by spraying
it with Pam or another nonstick cooking
spray, or coating the inside with butter.

**Hannah's 1st Note: You can double
this recipe if you like, so that it will
serve 8 people. If you double this recipe,
it will take approximately 55 minutes to
bake.**

**Hannah's 2nd Note: This dish works
best if you use an electric mixer.**

6 strips bacon *(I used applewood smoked
    bacon)*
4 large eggs
1 cup whole milk *(I've used heavy cream
    and that works also)*
1 cup flour *(Just scoop it up and level it
    off with a table knife.)*
1 teaspoon vanilla extract
1 teaspoon salt
4 ounces cream cheese *(half of an 8-ounce
    package)* minced parsley to sprinkle on
    top *(optional)*

Fry the bacon in a frying pan on the
stovetop until it's crispy. Let it cool to room

temperature, and then crumble it into the bottom of your baking pan.

In an electric mixer, beat the eggs with half of the milk *(that's 1/2 cup).* Continue to beat until the mixture is light and fluffy.

Add vanilla extract and salt. Beat until they're well combined. Mix in the flour and beat for 40 seconds.

Add the second half of the milk *(another 1/2 cup)* and beat until everything is light and fluffy.

Pour half of the mixture over the bacon crumbles in the 8-inch square pan.

Cut the cream cheese into 1-inch-square cubes. Place them evenly over the egg mixture in the pan.

Pour the second half of the mixture over the cream cheese.

Bake at 375 degrees F. for 45 to 55 minutes, or until it's golden brown and puffy on top.

**Hannah's 3rd Note: This breakfast entree is excellent when served with biscuits or crispy buttered toast.**

# CHAPTER SEVENTEEN

It was eight-fifteen the next morning and the winter sun was already melting the snow at the sides of the exit ramp when Andrea turned off the highway.

"Why are we stopping here?" Hannah asked, as they pulled into a parking spot right next to the green and white striped awning over the front entrance of Perkins Family Restaurant.

"You need to get ready. My meeting with Swartznagel Realty is in forty-five minutes."

"But I *am* ready . . ." Hannah stopped and stared hard at her sister. "At least I thought I was ready. Tell me, Andrea. What is there about me that's *not* ready?"

"It's your hair. It just won't do, Hannah."

Hannah had a sinking feeling in the bottom of her stomach. Michelle had predicted this. "What's wrong with my hair?"

"It's too . . ." Andrea paused and Hannah could tell she was searching for a word. "It's just too memorable."

"What does *that* mean?"

"It's like when witnesses give descriptions of somebody they saw holding up a bank, or breaking into a house. They always notice a person's most memorable feature. Sometimes it's a tattoo, sometimes it's a birthmark, and sometimes it's the fact the perp had a scar. You know what I mean. In your case, it's your hair."

"My hair is a disfigurement?"

Andrea gulped. "No! Of course not! It's just that it's . . . distinctive. People notice it because it's so . . . unusual."

"By *distinctive* you mean bright red, kinky, and unruly?"

"Well . . . yes. And I want you to remember that you put it that way. I didn't. Don't get me wrong, Hannah. Your hair looks good on you. You wouldn't be our Hannah without it. But the thing is, I don't want Doctor Bev's mother to be able to describe you that accurately."

"So?" Hannah held her breath. If Andrea had brought a bottle of black hair dye, she was going to refuse to use it. There was no way she was going to color her hair.

"So Bertie Straub gave me a wig for you to use as a disguise."

Hannah couldn't help it. She laughed.

249

She'd never worn a wig in her life and all she could think of was the fake blond wig Delores had worn when she'd gone under-cover in her black leather biker chick outfit at the Eagle.

"What's so funny?" Andrea asked. "A lot of people wear wigs."

"I know. I was just thinking about the blond wig Mother wore out at the Eagle."

Andrea laughed. "I agree that was pretty awful, but she was *trying* to look cheap to fit in out there. This wig isn't like that one at all."

"I'm glad to hear that. Tell me what kind of wig you brought for me."

"It's a brown wig. I thought brown would be the best color because it's nondescript. This wig is streaked with blond because Bertie didn't have any plain brown ones, but a lot of people with nondescript brown hair streak it with another color."

"Don't let Michelle hear you say that! She has brown hair."

"I know, but her hair isn't nondescript. It's not really brown, either. It's more of a . . . a chestnut color. And it shines in the light like . . . like . . ." Andrea stopped, lost for a descriptive metaphor.

"Like liquid chocolate?" Hannah suggested.

"Exactly! And that's distinctive. I'm talking about plain brown here, the kind of brown paper bag brown."

"Okay, but I still wouldn't mention it to Michelle."

"I won't. Now let's go in and try on that wig. I can hardly wait to see what it looks like on you."

"Can't I just leave my hair as it is and have Doctor Bev's mother *think* I'm wearing a wig?"

"Hannah! You know that won't work!"

Andrea stared at her in such dismay that Hannah relented. "Okay. Fine. This is your show, and I'll wear the wig. You'll have to help me get it on, though."

"Oh, I will! That's no problem. Let's go in and have coffee. I could use another cup. And then we'll go to the ladies room and you can try on your wig. It's going to look great on you, Hannah. You'll see."

Less than a minute later, they were seated in a four-person booth. There weren't many people in the restaurant, and their waitress came up to them almost immediately.

"Good morning," she said, giving them both a big smile. "Would you like coffee to start?"

"Yes, please," Andrea replied. "And I think coffee is all we're going to have." She turned to Hannah. "Unless you want something."

"Just coffee for me, too. Black."

"Cream and sugar for you, Ma'am?" The waitress turned to Andrea.

"Cream, unless it's that coffee whitener."

"It's real cream and it comes in those little covered cups. Do you want one, or two?"

"Two please. Where's your ladies room?"

The waitress gestured toward the rear of the restaurant. "Back there. The ladies is the first door on your right."

"Let's go," Andrea said as soon as their waitress had left. "I want to see how that wig looks on you. Bertie gave me a sock for your hair."

Hannah was puzzled as she slid out of the booth and followed her sister. "A sock?"

"It's like a hairnet, but she called it a sock. It's made out of stretchy material, and you just gather up all your hair into a high ponytail on top of your head. Then you fasten the ponytail inside the sock. It's easier to put on the wig if your own hair doesn't get in the way."

"Makes sense," Hannah said gathering her hair into a high ponytail the way Andrea had instructed. She took the fastener Andrea gave her and secured the ponytail. "Can you put on the sock?" she asked. "I can't see to do it."

"No problem. Just crouch down a little, will you? You're a lot taller than I am."

*A lot taller, a lot heavier, and a lot less pretty,* Hannah thought to herself. Andrea and Michelle had inherited their mother's petite frame and classic good looks, while Hannah looked more like her tall, big, gangly, and unhandsome father. When they were children and Delores had taken her three daughters out to lunch, or for an afternoon outing, everyone commented on the family resemblance and how you could certainly tell that Andrea and Michelle were Delores's daughters. No one ever made that comment about Hannah. They probably assumed that she was a step-daughter, or perhaps a friend who'd been kindly included in the mother-daughter outing.

Hannah crouched, and Andrea slipped the elastic sock over her ponytail. She took the wig out of the wig box and settled it on Hannah's head. Then she did something with a comb, pulling down sections of hair to frame Hannah's face. At least Hannah thought that was what she was doing. Since her back was to the mirror, she had no way of actually knowing.

"All done," Andrea said. "You can stand up and turn around now. I want to know what you think of it."

Hannah stared at the stranger in the mirror. She blinked several times, and then she stared some more. It had to be her reflection. When she raised her arm, the stranger in the mirror raised her arm. And when she turned toward Andrea, the stranger mirrored her motion.

"Well?" Andrea prompted her. "What do you think?"

"I think I need a new name."

"What?"

"I said, I think I need a new name. And then I think I need to go down to CIA headquarters and fill out an application for deep undercover work. Nobody will ever recognize me in this wig."

"I knew it." Andrea looked proud. "But you didn't tell me. Do you *like* it?"

"I love it! The minute we get back to Lake Eden, I'm going to buy this wig from Bertie."

"Because you like your new look so much?"

"Not exactly. I'll buy it because it'll be so much fun to wear it to the next potluck dinner, and see if Mike tries to pick up the new gal in town."

"Here we are." Andrea pulled up in front of a house that was eerily similar to the one the Cleavers had owned on every *Leave it To Beaver* rerun that Hannah had watched.

"It's awfully big for just one person," Hannah commented.

"It's not just one person. You're moving your whole family here. I told you that you were married with children, didn't I?"

"Yes. My husband's name is Phillip and I have two kids. They're both in school so I'm concerned about the local elementary schools in the area."

"Good. And your name is?"

"Joyce Newhall."

"And you're from?"

"Royalton. I drove up here today to house hunt while my husband's at work and the kids are in school."

"That's just fine. You sound very convincing. Now why are you moving to Minneapolis, Hannah?"

"It's Joyce, and I'm moving to the Cities because my husband just accepted a job at Xcel Energy. It's a Fortune Five Hundred company, and Phillip is a tax attorney."

"Excellent. You're ready."

"I know, but are you?"

Andrea looked puzzled. "What do you mean?"

"Do you have a plan for getting the DNA sample?"

"Not yet, but don't worry. I'll think of something when we get there. Now let's hurry up and take a look at this house so that we can go next door."

After a quick glance in the mirror on the passenger side visor to make sure her wig was on straight, Hannah got out of Andrea's Volvo and followed her up the front walkway. Once her sister had retrieved the key from the lockbox and opened the front door, they stepped inside.

"Gorgeous!" Hannah said, catching sight of the massive curved staircase that led up to the second floor. Then she turned to shut the front door, and noticed the round, faceted window that was at least fifteen feet above the front door. "Look at that window, Andrea."

Andrea glanced up. "It's beautiful and it must have cost a bundle."

"Not that. I can tell it's expensive. But it's way up there. How do you clean it?"

"I should have known that would be the first question you'd ask." Andrea gave a little laugh. "The answer is, you don't clean that window. You hire someone to come in every month with a special ladder, and *they* clean that window."

"But . . . wouldn't that be expensive?"

"Of course it would be expensive. But you

don't care about that because Phillip makes huge pots of money, and he needs to impress everyone with his expensive home."

"Right." Hannah trotted obediently after her sister as Andrea led the way to a massive kitchen that would be almost impossible for one ordinary housewife to keep clean, several powder rooms on the main floor, and a small bedroom, living room, and bathroom that Andrea called the *maid's suite.*

The second floor was next, and Hannah counted six roomy bedrooms with walk-in closets and three full bathrooms. The master suite was behind doors and boasted a Jacuzzi in the massive bathroom, and a double fireplace that was built into the wall between the sitting room and the bedroom. There was even a refrigerator and a wine cooler in the sitting room, presumably there so that the master and mistress of the manor wouldn't have to trek all the way down the stairs to get their late-evening libations.

Hannah was glad when Andrea locked the door behind them. All this luxury coupled with the enormous asking price of the house they'd just seen was making her head spin. It was a relief to go next door to the modest two-story home that belonged to Doctor Bev's mother.

"If Diana's not home, I'll have to find something of hers to take with me," Andrea said as she prepared to ring the doorbell. "I hope she invites us in."

Hannah wasn't sure what she expected when Mrs. Thorndike answered their knock on the door, but it certainly wasn't the woman standing there. Bev's mother was the polar opposite of Delores although they were roughly the same age. Doctor Bev's mother was pleasantly plump, while Delores was sleek and svelte. And while Delores dressed in designer outfits, Doctor Bev's mother was wearing pull-on slacks and an old University of Minnesota sweatshirt that had seen better days. Doctor Bev's mother wore no makeup, and she'd had, in Hannah's opinion, a total of zero facelifts.

"Hello," she said cheerily. "I'm Judy Thorndike. I saw you looking at the house next door."

"Grace Benson from Up-Front Realty," Andrea introduced herself. "This is my client, Mrs. Newhall."

"Call me Joyce," Hannah held out her hand. "I'm glad to meet you, Mrs. Thorndike."

"Judy. So what did you think of the house?"

"It's just beautiful," Hannah said truth-

258

fully, "but I think it might be a little too large for us."

"How many children do you have?"

"Two," Hannah replied. But at almost the same time, Andrea said, "Three."

Hannah's mind went on red alert. Andrea had strayed from the script. She latched on to the first explanation that occurred to her, and gave a little laugh. "I'm afraid Grace is guilty of counting chickens before they're hatched. Or in this case, counting babies before they're born. Our third won't be making an appearance until right after Christmas."

"Joyce was wondering about the schools in this area," Andrea said, returning to the script.

"Oh, they're very good. There's a private elementary school, Scott Academy, only three blocks from here. It has an excellent reputation although it's not inexpensive, if you know what I mean. The public schools are also very good, but the nearest, Taft Elementary, is almost a mile away. There's an excellent preschool called Ready-Set-Learn that's only two blocks from here. My granddaughter, Diana, goes there and she absolutely loves it. I just know she's going to be terribly upset when we have to leave."

"You have to leave?" Hannah asked.

"Yes. My daughter's marrying a dentist, and his clinic is over forty miles from here. She's a dentist too, and she works there now. They're getting married next weekend, and she wants me to move into his house with her to take care of Diana while they work. But Diana and I have made such a nice life for ourselves here, that I just hate to give it all up and start over."

"Oh, dear." Hannah gave her a sympathetic glance. "Have you lived here long?"

"Over forty years. It's a wonderful neighborhood. I can tell you all the names of the neighbors and where the best grocery stores are, and . . . would you like to come in and have a cup of coffee with me? I just put on a second pot."

"We'd love to," Hannah accepted quickly. It was exactly as they'd hoped. Doctor Bev's mother was friendly, and she'd invited them inside the house where Diana lived.

# CHAPTER EIGHTEEN

The house they entered was neat and tidy, the sort of home that welcomed visitors in from the cold. The decor wasn't designer perfect, but it was comfortable and soothing. Judy led them to the kitchen, where a close relative to Hannah's Formica table and padded chrome chairs sat in a breakfast nook.

"I love this kitchen set," Hannah said as she pulled out a chair and sat down. "I have one almost like it at home. Mine's yellow, but I wish it was red, like yours."

"You should buy my house. I'll probably have to leave all my furniture." Judy turned to face her. "I'm going to put it up for sale, but not for couple of months. I want to wait to see if this works."

"You mean . . . the marriage?" Andrea asked, jumping to the obvious conclusion.

"Yes." Judy carried mugs of coffee to the table and went back for cream and sugar. "I have some Raspberry Drop Sandwich Cookies Diana and I baked last night. Would you like one?"

"I would," Hannah said. "I've never met a cookie I didn't like."

"This is a good recipe," Judy said, bringing a plate of cookies to the table. "Raspberry is one of Diana's favorite fruits."

Hannah bit into a cookie. It was fabulous. The raspberry taste was intense, and the cookie was soft and utterly delicious. There was a little frosting in the middle. It tasted like tart raspberry, and it went perfectly with the sweetness of the cookie. "They're wonderful cookies, Judy. Could I have a copy of the recipe?"

"Of course." Doctor Bev's mother opened a three-ring binder and took out a sheet of paper. "Here you are," she said, handing it to Hannah.

As Hannah accepted the printed recipe, she began to feel a bit guilty for deceiving Judy, but Norman's happiness was at stake. Anything they could learn about Doctor Bev and Diana could be beneficial.

"I put all my recipes on the computer when Diana was a baby. Every time she took a nap, I typed at least one into the file. It's taken me four years, but it's very convenient to print out a clean copy every time I cook or bake."

"That's something I have to do," Hannah told her. "I have some on my computer, but there are a lot more to type up."

"You said you wanted to wait and see if your daughter's marriage works," Andrea said, getting them back on subject. "Are you worried about the man your daughter is marrying?"

"Not at all," Judy said, sounding very definite. "I met him last weekend and he's just wonderful. He's generous, and kind, and . . . just the nicest person. I . . ." she stopped and took another swallow of her coffee. "It's my daughter I'm worried about. She's just not cut out for marriage."

"Oh?" Hannah questioned. She gave Andrea a look that warned her to be silent, and then they both waited for Judy to explain what she'd meant by *not cut out for marriage.*

Hannah counted the seconds as they ticked by. The hardest thing in the world was to wait for someone to speak. But it was imperative that Judy trust them enough to tell them something, anything, that they could use to stop the marriage between Doctor Bev and Norman. The silence stretched on as the second hand on Judy's kitchen clock made another full round, and then she sighed loudly.

"This is a hard thing for a mother to say," Judy began, but then she was silent again. After a moment or two, she took a deep breath and confessed, "I don't think she loves this man at all. I think she's only marrying him for financial reasons. Of course she doesn't tell *me* that. She says she wants Diana to have a normal family life with a mother and a father."

"But you don't believe her?" Andrea asked.

"No. She'd like me to think that she's turned over a new leaf and she really cares about Diana now. But if she really *did* care about Diana, she'd spend more time with her and less time with her own friends."

It was a harsh assessment, and Hannah could tell that it hurt Judy to say so. Part of her wanted to say something to make Judy feel better, but the other part of her wanted to hear even more negative things about Doctor Bev.

"To tell the truth, I don't think my daughter even *likes* Diana. She was always more interested in going out and having fun than she was in being a good mother to her. It's clear that Diana is a burden to her. And she wants to pass that burden on to me and her new husband."

"And you don't think this man would be a good father to Diana?" Hannah asked. And then she held her breath waiting for the answer.

"Oh, he'd be a wonderful father! I just don't think it's fair, that's all. It's clear to me he doesn't love my daughter, and it's also clear she doesn't love him. Getting married for the sake of a child never works."

"Even if this man is Diana's biological father?"

"That could be different. Then he might feel a certain responsibility, and he'd put up with my daughter for Diana's sake. But he's not."

"He's not Diana's biological father?" Hannah asked.

Judy sighed deeply. "I shouldn't say that. I don't really know if he is or he isn't, but he just doesn't fit the other things she's said about the man who fathered her baby. When she came back home pregnant, all she'd say was that she'd made a bad mistake, Diana's father had refused to marry her, and it was too late to do anything about it. That certainly doesn't sound like *this* man. He's just too . . . honorable. If he was Diana's father and Bev asked him to marry her, he would have married her immediately."

*You're right,* Hannah thought. Norman

would have married her. But Doctor Bev didn't ask him, not then. The way Hannah saw it, there were three possibilities. The first was that Doctor Bev had asked Diana's father to marry her, but that man she'd asked wasn't Norman. The second possibility was that Doctor Bev had lied to her mother about asking Diana's father to marry her. And the third possibility was that Doctor Bev had asked Norman to marry her and Norman was lying about being asked. Hannah rejected the third possibility immediately. Norman didn't lie.

"This whole thing must be terribly upsetting for you," Andrea said sympathetically.

"It is." Judy turned to Hannah. "So you'd rather have a smaller house?"

"That's right," Hannah said quickly. It was clear that Judy wanted to change the subject and Hannah was fine with that. They'd gotten much more information from her than they'd expected. It was interesting that Doctor Bev's own mother didn't think that Norman was Diana's father, but that didn't prove anything. The only way to prove it was by DNA testing, and Andrea still hadn't gotten a sample. Somehow they had to get Judy to show them through her house so that . . . but there was a great opportunity just staring her right in the face!

"I'd much rather live in a house like yours," Hannah said, smiling at Judy. "It's so cozy and comfortable. And since I'm a stay-at-home mom, I could keep it up all by myself without hiring a stranger to come in and clean. A house like yours would be perfect for us." Hannah stopped and looked thoughtful. "And you think you might be selling your house in a few months?"

Judy sighed deeply. "I think I'll *have* to sell my house if this marriage actually happens. My daughter plans to keep working, and I don't want a stranger taking care of Diana. In a way, I'm the only mother she's ever known. I've taken care of her from the very beginning, and my daughter doesn't spend that much time here. Take tonight for instance. She's driving here after work to go to a friend's birthday party, but she won't have time to stop by. She said the party is going to run late because they're going out to a club. She said she didn't want to wake us up by coming home that late, so she'll just spend the night with her friend and drive back on Sunday."

Andrea began to frown. "So she'll be in town, but she won't see you or her daughter at all?"

"That's right. She says she'll see us next week, but it'll have to be a rush trip because she's so busy planning the wedding."

Hannah felt like scowling, but somehow she managed to keep a neutral expression on her face. Doctor Bev didn't sound like a good mother at all! It was time to change the subject before she said something she shouldn't. "If you think your house may be up for sale in the next six months or so, I'd love to take a look at it. I really don't think our family will be happy in the house next door."

"How about taking a look right now?" Judy drained her coffee cup and stood up. "I'll show both of you through the house. If you're interested you can leave a number and I'll contact you when I'm ready to sell."

Judy led the way up the front staircase. Hannah made a move to follow, but Andrea pulled her back.

"Good work!" Andrea said softly, very close to Hannah's ear.

"Thanks."

Judy's house was larger than Hannah had thought. There were four bedrooms upstairs, certainly enough for her mythical family. "If the girls double up, I can even have room for an office," she said.

"There's a perfect office space downstairs," Judy told her. "It's the piano room."

"Piano room?" Andrea sounded interested.

"That's what they called it when my husband and I bought this house. It's just off the living room, and it has French doors that can be closed when your child is practicing, or during a piano lesson. And you can open them when your little protégé is playing a recital for your guests. We use it as a playroom for Diana right now, but I'd planned to rent a piano when she turned six. My daughter once said that Diana's father was very musical."

"Really!" Hannah exchanged glances with Andrea. Norman was a lot like her. He couldn't carry a tune in a suitcase, and he'd never mentioned playing any type of musical instrument. Their suspicions were already aroused concerning Norman's role in Diana's paternity. This new piece of information from Judy served to make them even more suspicious.

The master bedroom certainly wasn't as large as the master suite next door. There was no wine cooler, or built-in refrigerator, but there was a dressing room and an attached private bathroom.

"I'm not using these rooms now that my daughter moved away," Judy said, opening the door to a fairly large bedroom with flowered wallpaper and ruffled curtains at the windows. "This was her room as a child, and she used it again when she came back home to live with us."

"It's a nice room," Hannah said, following Judy to another bedroom down the hall. She noticed that Andrea was lagging behind and she wasn't sure why, but she wasn't about to mention it to Judy.

"This is the guest room," Judy said, opening the door so that Hannah could see inside. "There's a connecting bathroom between the two bedrooms."

"That's convenient," Andrea said, joining them so quickly Hannah doubted that Judy had noticed her absence. "Where's your granddaughter's room?"

"Right here, next to my bedroom. It was originally the nursery and there's a connecting door between her bedroom and mine."

"That must have come in very handy when she was a baby," Andrea commented.

"Oh, it did. I left it open for the first few years so that I could hear her if she woke up during the night. Now that she's a big girl, we close it . . . unless there's a storm, of course. Then we leave it open."

"I can tell you're a wonderful grand-mother," Hannah said.

"I hope so. Diana is my life. She's a sweet

girl and I love her so much. You should have seen me the first day I took her to Ready-Set-Learn and left her there. I came home and cried."

"I did the same thing when my daughter went to preschool," Andrea admitted. "You want them to grow up with every advantage, but part of you wants to keep them as babies."

"Exactly!"

Hannah watched as Judy and Andrea shared a smile. She was a bit uncomfortable pretending to feel the same way when a similar occasion hadn't actually happened to her, so she walked over to look at the vertical blinds in Diana's room. "Oh, wow!" she exclaimed, pulling them closed to reveal a large picture of Cinderella getting into the pumpkin coach in the lovely dress she would wear to the ball at the palace. "Where did you get these wonderful blinds?"

"There's a home decorating store at the mall that sells them. Cinderella's on this window, and the Little Mermaid's on the other. They're Diana's favorite Disney characters, and they were her birthday present when she turned three."

Hannah looked around at the rest of the room. The wallpaper was printed with colorful hot air balloons in every shape and size imaginable, floating in a cerulean blue sky dotted with puffy white clouds. The bed was child-size and had a fluffy pink comforter with a white ruffle around the edges. There were two white bookshelves filled with children's books, and one Hannah remembered from her own childhood, *Charlie And The Chocolate Factory,* sat on a bed table next to an adult-size rocking chair.

"Are you reading that for a bedtime story?" she asked Judy.

"Yes, for the third time. Diana just loves it. Next week we're starting the Harry Potter series. It may be a little old for her, but we'll see. If it is, we'll save it for later." Judy motioned to Hannah. "Come downstairs and I'll show you the piano room. It's quite large and it would be perfect for an office."

"I'll join you in just a second," Andrea said, following them into the hallway. "If you don't mind, I'd like to use the bathroom."

"Certainly." Judy pointed to the bathroom at the end of the hall. "Do you want us to wait for you?"

Andrea shook her head. "Go on ahead. I'll find my way, don't worry."

When Judy opened the French doors to the piano room, Hannah was immediately impressed. The room was long and narrow, exactly as Judy had described, but it was also filled with light coming in through the double-paned windows that ran the length of the outside wall. There were blinds you could pull to keep out the hot summer sun, but on a winter day like today, the sun felt good as it fell in patterns on the wooden floor.

"You're right. It's perfect for an office," Hannah told her. "But it's perfect for a playroom, too."

"Diana loves it. She has Saturday play dates with another girl from preschool. One week they're here and the next week they're at her mother's house. I think both of them would rather be here. There's more room for them to play, and we always bake cookies in the afternoons." Judy looked sad for a moment. "That's one of the reasons I really hate to move. This is the only home that Diana has ever known. It's not going to be easy for her to adjust to a new house, a new school, and new friends, not to mention a mother that comes home every night, and a new father who suddenly appears in her life."

"So, did you get it?" Hannah asked the moment Andrea pulled away from the curb.

"Of course I did. I got everything I needed and a lot more besides."

"A lot more?"

"Yes." Andrea took the on-ramp and merged onto the highway. "We stayed a lot longer than I thought we would. It's almost time to go over to Club Nineteen."

"Okay, but what did you mean when you said you got a lot more than just a DNA sample."

"There was a comb on the dressing table in the room Doctor Bev used. I bagged it and put it in my purse."

"Why?"

"It had a couple of hairs in it, and I thought we might need it for her DNA. It can't hurt . . . right?"

"Right. I'm not sure if we need it either, but we might. And you got something to use for Diana's DNA sample?"

"Somethings."

Hannah frowned slightly. "What?"

"Somethings. Plural. I got a sample of Diana's hair from her hairbrush, and a spoon that was next to a bottle of children's cough syrup. I figured that should do it, but then I spotted a band-aid with blood on it in her wastebasket so I took that, too."

"So you got hair, saliva, and blood."

"Yes, and Bill's detective book said that

all three could be used to get samples of DNA. We'll let Doc Knight choose whichever he wants. Did you get anything?"

"Yes."

"What?"

"A guilty conscience. I really liked Judy and I feel terribly guilty about deceiving her."

"Well, don't. We're the best chance she has to be happy again."

Hannah looked at her sister in bewilderment. "What do you mean?"

"I mean Judy doesn't really want to move. She loves that house. When she showed it to us, she was really proud of everything she'd done to it, especially the playroom for Diana and how she'd decorated Diana's bedroom. She's a good mother to Diana, a lot better than Doctor Bev is. Remember when she said that Doctor Bev was more interested in socializing with her friends than she was in spending time with her daughter?"

"I remember."

"I came back in time to hear what she said about reading to Diana every night. That's what parents do. She's taken over as Diana's mother because Doctor Bev doesn't want to be bothered."

It was a harsh assessment, but Hannah

couldn't help but agree. "You're probably right," she said. "While you were upstairs, Judy told me that she baked cookies with Diana and her friends, and how worried she was about the move and whether Diana could adjust to a new home, a new pre-school, making new friends, a mother who came home every night, and a new father."

"I knew I was right!" Andrea signaled and pulled off the freeway. "Judy doesn't want to give up her house and move. She wants to stay right where she is and be Diana's mother. That's why I said that we were her best chance at happiness. If we succeed in breaking up Doctor Bev and Norman, Judy's life with Diana will stay exactly the way she wants it."

# RASPBERRY DROP SANDWICH COOKIES
Preheat oven to 375 degrees F.,
rack in the middle position.

1 and 1/2 cups white *(granulated)* sugar

1 cup *(2 sticks, 8 ounces, 1/2 pound)* salted butter, softened

3 large eggs

1/2 teaspoon salt

1 teaspoon baking soda

1 and 1/2 cups raspberry pie filling *(I used Comstock)*

3 cups all-purpose flour (pack it down in the cup when you measure it)

3/4 cup raspberry cream frosting *(frosting recipe follows the cookie recipe)*

**Hannah's 1st Note: Make the frosting first.**

**Hannah's 2nd Note: Unless you have a very strong stirring arm, use an electric mixer to make this cookie dough.**

Place the sugar in the bowl of an electric mixer.

Place the butter, which must be softened to room temperature, on top of the sugar. *(We're not talking about room temperature in a farm kitchen during a snowstorm — the butter must be easily spreadable.)*

Turn the mixer to LOW and mix for one minute. Gradually increase the speed of the mixer, scraping down the sides of the bowl frequently and beating for one minute at each level, until you arrive at the highest speed.

Beat at the highest speed for at least 2 minutes or until the resulting mixture is very light and fluffy.

Turn the mixer down to LOW and add the eggs, one at time, mixing after each addition. Then add the salt. When that's mixed in, add the baking soda and mix until it's incorporated.

Measure out a cup and a half of raspberry pie filling. Turn the mixer on LOW speed and add the pie filling to your bowl. Shut off the mixer and scrape down the sides of the bowl.

With the mixer running on LOW, add the flour in one-cup increments, mixing after each addition. Shut off the mixer and scrape down the sides of the bowl. Give the mixture a final stir by hand. *(The resulting cookie dough should be fluffy, but not at all stiff like sugar cookie or chocolate chip cookie dough.)*

Line your cookie sheets with parchment paper. It's the easiest way to bake these cookies. If you don't have parchment paper and you really don't want to go out to get any, grease your cookie sheets heavily, or spray them thoroughly with Pam or another nonstick cooking spray.

Using a teaspoon *(not the measuring kind, but one from your silverware drawer)*, drop rounded teaspoons of cookie dough on your baking sheet, 12 to a standard-size sheet.

Bake your Raspberry Drop Cookies at 375 degrees F. for 12 minutes. Take the cookies out of the oven and slide the cookie-laden parchment paper onto a wire rack to cool. *(If you used greased cookie sheets, you're going to have to let the cookies sit on the cookie sheets for 2 minutes and then remove them to a wire rack with a metal spatula.)*

Cool the cookies thoroughly. Frost the bottom of one cookie with Raspberry Cream Frosting and then sandwich the bottom of another cookie on top of it. This will make a little cookie sandwich that is rounded on both the top and the bottom.

Yield: approximately 2 to 2 and 1/2 dozen delicious cookie sandwiches, depending on cookie size.

## Raspberry Cream Frosting:

3 cups powdered *(confectioner's)* sugar
1/4 cup heavy *(whipping)* cream
3 Tablespoons seedless raspberry jam
An additional cup of powdered sugar, if
  needed.

Measure 3 cups powdered sugar and place them in a small bowl. Do not pack the sugar down in the cup when you measure it, but do level the top off with a table knife.

Whisk the heavy cream into the powdered sugar.

Heat the 3 Tablespoons of seedless raspberry jam in a small microwave-safe bowl for 15 to 20 seconds or until it melts a bit. Mix the warm raspberry jam into the cream and powdered sugar mixture.

If the frosting is too thick, add a little more cream. If the frosting is too thin, add a little more powdered sugar.

Cover the bowl with plastic wrap and set it aside to wait for the cookies to be baked.

**Hannah's 3rd Note: If there's any frosting left over, frost some graham crackers as a special treat for the kids when they come home from school. You can also frost soda crackers, salt side down, or gingersnaps.**

Yield: Approximately 3 cups of frosting.

# CHAPTER NINETEEN

The interior of Club Nineteen reminded Hannah of the Eden Lake Pavilion except that it was three times larger. The outside was stucco, nondescript grey stucco, but the interior was wood. There was a wooden floor that had been polished to a full gleam, and wooden walls that were hung with framed posters and signed pictures of every jazz group and luminary that had performed there. The tables were small and square, seating four people, but Hannah noticed that they had four hinged and rounded leaves. Once the catches on two opposite leaves were released, the table could be made into an oval that would seat six people. If all four leaves were released, the resulting round table could seat eight people. It was a clever design and Hannah wondered why more restaurants didn't use it.

"Hi, I'm Shelby," their waitress said,

bustling up to their table. "Can I get you a drink?"

*I imagine you* **can** *or you wouldn't be working here,* Hannah's pedantic mind said, and Hannah did her best to tune it out. Of course the grammatically correct question should have been, **May** *I get you a drink?* but it wouldn't be wise to correct their waitress and alienate her right off the bat.

"Iced tea for me," Andrea said. "I'm driving."

Hannah was about to ask for the same when she reconsidered. It was a cold day and she wanted something warm. "Do you have any nonalcoholic coffee drinks?" she asked.

"Yes, we do. We have a raspberry latte, a caramel latte, and a chocolate apricot latte. They're all made with flavored syrups and milk that's been frothed in our espresso machine."

"Could I change my order to a raspberry latte?" Andrea asked, giving Shelby an apologetic smile.

"Sure, Honey. No problem. And you, ma'am?"

Hannah wondered just when she'd graduated from honey to ma'am. Or was it an elevation in status? It could be a demotion because she looked older than Andrea, more matron than miss. Perhaps she should have worn the wig inside, and put on makeup, and . . .

"Ma'am?"

"Oh! Sorry. I'd like to have a chocolate apricot latte. And . . . when we called in for reservations, we were told the owner might be here and that perhaps we might be able to speak to him. It's about Cinnamon Roll Six."

"Just my favorite group in the whole world!" Shelby exclaimed. And then she looked slightly embarrassed. "They're *so* good. When they were here, everybody loved them. Where are they playing now?"

"The Lake Eden Inn," Andrea answered. "The owners hired them to headline their weekend jazz festival."

"They deserve it!" Shelby smiled. "We're going to be asking them to come back next month. They were huge hits and everybody loved . . . what's wrong?"

She'd obviously gotten a cue from Andrea's distressed expression, and Hannah reached out to pull out a chair. "Sit," she said, brooking no nonsense. "You obviously haven't heard, and I'm afraid we've got some bad news for you."

"About Cinnamon Roll Six?" Shelby asked, sinking down in the chair that Hannah had pulled out for her.

"That's right. There was a bad accident on the highway, a multi-car pileup. The band bus was in that accident."

Shelby's face went so pale, her bright red lipstick stood out like a beacon. "Buddy?" she asked, clasping her hands together.

Hannah shot Andrea a glance that said, *Let me handle this,* and then she turned her attention to Shelby. "Buddy is dead," she said.

"Oh, no!" Shelby gasped, slumping in her chair. "Buddy just *can't* be dead! I saw him last week. He came in to hear a new jazz group." Shelby gave her a pleading glance. "Are you sure?"

"I'm sorry, Shelby, but yes, I'm sure. Buddy's dead. He died the night of the accident at Lake Eden Memorial Hospital."

Although Hannah hadn't thought it possible, Shelby's face turned even paler. Her skin was now the color of the freshly fallen snow outside, and Hannah wondered if they'd have to pick her up off the floor.

"Buddy died in the accident?" Shelby asked in a voice that shook with emotion.

"No. Buddy died later, at Lake Eden Memorial Hospital."

"But . . . what happened to him? I need to *know!*"

Hannah gave a slight nod to Andrea. It was her turn to take over when affairs of the heart came into play. And Shelby obviously had more than a *I'm-a-fan-of-your-music* relationship with Buddy.

"You loved him." Andrea reached out to put her hand over Shelby's. "I'm so sorry we had to be the ones to tell you about his death."

"Thanks, but . . . how? How did he die? Was he hurt that bad in the accident?"

Andrea nodded to Hannah, and Hannah took the lead again. "No. All he had was a sprained wrist. But while he was in a treatment room waiting for someone to come and put a splint on it, he was . . . murdered."

"Who would murder Buddy?" Shelby cried, staring at them in shock. "Buddy was wonderful! Buddy was sweet! Buddy was . . . who would do something awful like . . ."

Both sisters stopped as Shelby's eyes narrowed and her expression turned from grieving to hard and cynical. "*She* did it!" Shelby said.

"Who?" Hannah asked, holding her breath. This could be the best clue they'd gotten so far.

"That woman, the one who came here around Valentine's Day. She killed Buddy. I know she did. He told her he didn't want anything to do with her, and . . . and she *murdered* him!"

"You saw this woman?" Hannah asked her.

"I saw her. She was one of those women who like to pick up the musicians. You know the type. Dressed all sexy in a tight sweater and a skirt that barely covered . . . well, you know. She couldn't take her eyes off Buddy. I noticed because . . . well . . . I had a thing going with Buddy at the time. After the show I saw her go backstage. I wanted to go back there to see what was going on, but I was clearing tables and I couldn't find anybody to fill in for me. But later, when I took a smoke break, I saw them in the parking lot. She was hanging onto his arm and Buddy was trying to shake her off. She said, *I'd know you anywhere,* whatever that meant."

Hannah and Andrea exchanged glances. Was it possible this woman had known Buddy's real identity?

"What did Buddy say?" Hannah asked.

"He said, *You got the wrong guy, lady. Leave me alone!* And then she said something, and Buddy tried to shake her hand off his arm, but she wouldn't let go of him. He finally hollered at her to let go, and she did. And then he shouted, *I'm not the guy you think I am!* And she shouted right back and this time I heard her. She said, *Yes you are! I know you are!* really loud. And then she slapped him and walked away."

"Did you see where she went?"

"I think she went to a car. There's no exit to the parking lot in the direction she was walking. But I didn't stick around to find out which car or anything like that. I saw that Buddy was heading my way, so I ducked back inside the club. I didn't want him to know I'd been listening to them fighting."

"Did he mention anything about it to you?" Hannah asked, hoping that Buddy had let something slip about the woman Shelby had seen.

"He didn't bring it up when he came in, but I did," Shelby admitted. "His cheek was red from where she slapped it, and I asked him what happened."

"What did he say?" Andrea asked, leaning forward expectantly.

"He said there was a crazy lady who came backstage and harassed him. He went out to the parking lot to get away from her, but she followed him and slapped him. I asked him why some lady would harass him, and he said that she seemed to think he was someone from her past. *It's just plain weird,* Buddy said. *Especially since I'm sure I've never seen her before in my life.*"

"Can you describe the woman you saw in the parking lot in a little more detail?" Hannah asked her.

"Not really. I already told you what she was wearing. She wasn't a real looker, just kind of average, but she had on a ton of makeup. And dark hair. She had dark hair. I took her picture with my cell phone when she was hanging onto Buddy in the parking lot, but it didn't turn out very good. Hold on a second and I'll find it for you."

Hannah held her breath as Shelby clicked through the photos on her phone. This could be a real breakthrough! When Shelby found the one she was looking for, she gave a satisfied sigh. "Here it is," she said. "There were over a hundred pictures on there, but I found it. The light was kind of bad in the parking lot and I was a ways away, but you can sort of see what she looks like. I was afraid to get any closer because I thought they might spot me, and I didn't dare use the flash. If Buddy had seen me taking their picture, he would have thought it was a jealousy thing, you know?"

*And Buddy would have been right,* Hannah thought, but she didn't say it. Instead she said, "I understand," and took the phone from Shelby.

"Let me see, too." Andrea moved her chair close to Hannah's so that she could take a look. "It's great that you took a picture, Shelby. And I think you're right. This woman could have something to do with Buddy's murder."

Hannah felt like groaning as she stared at the small screen on Shelby's phone. She could see two figures standing near a row of cars in the background, but neither one was close enough to be recognizable. "Is there any way to enlarge this?" she asked.

Shelby shrugged her shoulders. "I don't know. Maybe. The guy at the phone store told me this phone had a pretty good camera."

"Can you e-mail this photo to me?" Andrea asked.

"I think so, but I'm not sure how to do it. The phone store guy said I could send people photos right from my phone."

"Do you mind if I try?" Andrea asked.

"Knock yourself out!" Shelby gave a little laugh. "I'll go get your drinks while you try. If my phone rings, just don't answer it. They'll leave a message and I'll get it on my break."

Hannah watched as Andrea did things she didn't understand to Shelby's phone. It was a much fancier model than the one she owned, but she wasn't a bit envious. All she really wanted to do was make calls and answer calls. Any other tricky features would just get in the way.

"Got it!" Andrea said, looking up with a grin. "I sent it to my e-mail at home, and then I sent it to my phone. Do you want me to send it to your phone?"

"You can't."

"Sure I can."

"No, you can't. My phone's just a phone. It doesn't do anything else."

Andrea rolled her eyes. "You're in the Stone Age, Hannah. You really should replace it with a newer model."

"Why? It works just fine the way it is as long as I remember to charge it."

"But really, Hannah. There are newer models that do so much more."

"I'm sure there are, but I finally figured out this phone and I don't want to switch."

"All right. Fine. Stay behind the times. I bet you still have a typewriter somewhere in your closet."

Hannah had a clear mental picture of the portable Olivetti she'd used to type her college term papers. It was perfectly good, and she kept it in a cabinet in her laundry room.

"Well? *Do* you still have a typewriter in your closet?"

"No," Hannah said quite truthfully. "I don't."

"Well, I'm glad to hear that! Maybe there's hope for you yet." Andrea glanced down at Shelby's phone again. "Do you want to know what date Shelby saw this unrecognizable woman with Buddy?"

"Yes. That's very important. We'll ask her when she comes back."

"We don't need to ask her. I know."

"You're psychic?"

"No, I'm smart. And I'm in step with the new technology. The photos are grouped in her phone by date. All I had to do was access the date menu to find out it was taken on the second Saturday in February."

"Sally and Dick were here!"

"What?"

"I asked Sally when she hired Cinnamon Roll Six to headline her jazz festival and she said it was right after the show on the second Saturday in February."

Andrea tapped the screen of Shelby's phone. "So Sally or Dick might have seen this woman?"

"It's possible. We can go out to the Inn and ask."

"There's something else we can do first. We can ask Norman if he can enlarge this photo, or sharpen it, or do something so that we can recognize the woman."

"I'm not sure that Norman can do that."

"Why not? He's always helped you with photographs before."

"I know, but . . . I'm not sure Doctor Bev will let him help us."

"You're not sure, so you're not going to *ask?*" Andrea looked incredulous. "What happened to the woman who was going to fight for Norman? Did she turn back into a doormat when I wasn't looking?"

Hannah sighed deeply. "No, she didn't. *I* didn't. I'll call him myself and tell him we need his help."

Shelby came up to their table carrying a tray with two tall glass cups. "One raspberry latte, and one chocolate and apricot latte," she announced placing them on the table. Then she turned to Andrea. "Did you manage to send that picture?"

"Yes. Don't erase it though, just in case. Okay?"

"Okay. I wouldn't erase it anyway. It's the last picture of Buddy I've got." Shelby's lip quivered and she blinked several times. Then she took a deep breath and set two small plates in front of them. "We started serving the appetizers, so I brought you some. This is Nancy's Piggy Chicken. Nancy's the owner's wife and it's made from her recipe."

"Piggy Chicken?" Hannah looked down at her plate. The aroma wafting up to her was heavenly. "It looks like rouladen."

"What's that?" Shelby looked puzzled.

"It's meat that's been pounded thin and rolled up with some kind of filling inside. Then it's baked, or fried."

"That sounds a lot like this."

"Is the *piggy* part of Piggy Chicken the bacon that's wrapped around the outside?" Andrea asked her.

"That's right. And the *chicken* part is chicken tenders pounded flat in the kitchen. I watched the cook make them once. The stuff inside is cream cheese and chives. He spreads the cream cheese on the chicken, and snips the chives off with scissors over the top. Then he rolls them up with a strip of bacon, sticks in a toothpick, and bakes them in the oven. I think Tom, he's the owner, is going to ask the cook if he can make them bigger so we can serve them for dinner."

Hannah just couldn't take it anymore. She cut off a piece and put it in her mouth. The Piggy Chicken had been baked to perfection. The bacon was crispy, the chicken was tender and the cream cheese and chive filling just melted in her mouth. "These are really great!" she said, already planning out how to make them at home.

"There's another one they make sometimes called Piggy Moo."

"Beef instead of chicken?" Hannah guessed.

"That's right. And we've got another appetizer coming up soon," Shelby said, obviously pleased that Hannah liked their first one. "I'll bring it as soon as they plate it. It's Janet's Texas Jalapeno Pimento Cheese. She's Tom's daughter, and she lives in Dallas. It comes with crackers and a little knife, and everybody loves it."

"I'll bet they do," Hannah said. "I can hardly wait to taste it. Is it fiery hot?"

"It's not that hot. They're pickled jalapenos and that takes away some of the heat. The cheese part helps, too. We do sell a lot of drinks after people eat it, though."

Hannah grinned, but she didn't say anything. She knew a bit about restaurant sales, and she'd been told that there was more profit to be made on the drinks than there was on the food. It seemed that Tom, the owner of Club Nineteen, was a good businessman.

"I'll be back," Shelby said, picking up her tray and preparing to leave.

"Just a second," Hannah stopped her.

"Please don't tell the owner, or anyone else for that matter, that Buddy's dead. My sister and I would like to tell him ourselves."

"Sure thing," Shelby said. "I don't want to talk about it anyway. Maybe we never would have gotten together the way I wanted us to, but just thinking about Buddy being gone makes me too sad for words."

# PIGGY CHICKEN
Preheat oven to 375 degrees F.,
rack in the middle position.

**Hannah's 1st Note: This recipe is from
my friend, Nancy Sapir. Nancy's family
just loves Piggy Chicken. Nancy wrote
"Sooo good!" on the bottom of her
recipe. This recipe may sound complicated, but it's not. Once you do it you'll
laugh at how delicious and easy it is.
(And it looks gorgeous and very difficult, as if you spent all day working in
the kitchen — don't tell ANYONE you
didn't! It's Nancy's secret . . . right?)**

1 to 1 and 1/2 pounds boneless, skinless
   chicken tenders
8 ounces cream cheese *(NOT whipped, NOT
   low fat — use the brick type of cream
   cheese, not the plastic tub) (I used an
   8-ounce box of Philadelphia Cream
   Cheese.)*
1/8 cup *(2 Tablespoons)* dried chopped
   chives
1/3 cup dried minced onions (optional)
salt
freshly ground pepper
1 pound regular-sliced bacon *(Don't use
   microwave bacon or thick-sliced bacon.*

*The thick-sliced bacon may not get crisp, and the microwave bacon may get too crisp since it's been precooked.)*

**Hannah's 2nd Note: I added the minced dried onions to Nancy's recipe because the whole Swensen clan likes onions. Since I was the one who added it, I made it optional.**

Lay each skinless, boneless chicken tender between two sheets of plastic wrap and place them on a cutting board or a bread board on the counter. Use a meat hammer to pound them as flat as you can get them without creating holes. If you pound on the undersides, instead of on the tops, they're less apt to fall apart.

**Hannah's 3rd Note: If you don't have a meat hammer, you can smack the chicken tenders flat with a rolling pin. (I saw that on the Food Channel.) You can also use a thin board on top of the plastic wrap covered chicken tender and hit the board all over with a hammer. You can even do what I did and hit the plastic wrapped chicken tender with a rubber mallet. And here's some marriage-saving advice: If you choose this last option, don't tell your husband that you used his rubber mallet!**

Once you've pounded the chicken tenders thin and stacked them *(still inside the plastic wrap)* on the counter, it's time to prepare your baking pan.

Eyeball the pile of pounded chicken tenders. Once you've assessed how much space they'll take, find a shallow pan *(or two)* that will hold them all with **at least one inch between them on all sides.** *(Nancy says the space between them is very important so that the bacon can get crispy.)* Spray this pan *(or both pans)* with Pam or another nonstick cooking spray.

Move one flattened chicken tender to the cutting board or bread board. Take off the top sheet of plastic wrap.

If your cream cheese isn't softened, put it in a microwave-safe bowl and heat it on HIGH for 25 seconds. If you can't stir it smooth at the end of that time, microwave it on HIGH at 20-second intervals until you can stir it smooth.

Add the chives plus the dried onions if you used them. Mix them into the cream cheese thoroughly.

Use a rubber spatula or a frosting knife to spread approximately 2 teaspoons of softened cream cheese on the flattened chicken tender.

**Hannah's 4th Note: Don't worry about**

contaminating your cream cheese with raw chicken juice. If there's any cream cheese left over, you're going to throw it away rather than risk whatever dire disease you might get from raw chicken. You're also going to wash the cutting board, the rubber spatula or frosting knife, and the bowl holding the cream cheese very thoroughly. (Washing them in the dishwasher is best.)

Sprinkle the dried chopped chives with minced dried onions *(if you decided to use them)*.

Sprinkle the cream cheese mixture with salt and freshly ground pepper.

Roll up the loaded-with-goodness chicken tender like a jelly roll. Pick it up and move it to the bottom of the cutting board.

Bring one piece of bacon on the cutting board. Pick up the piece of bacon and wrap it around the chicken roll, trying to angle it so that you cover as much of the chicken tender roll as possible.

When you're finished rolling the bacon around the chicken roll, place it in the pan you've prepared with at least one end of the bacon under the chicken tender roll. *(If you can get both ends under, that's great. If you can't, don't worry about it.)*

Repeat this process until all of the flattened chicken tenders have been rolled and covered with bacon.

Slip the pan *(or pans)* into a 375 degree F. preheated oven for 25 minutes. Then turn the oven up to 425 degrees F. for 5 additional minutes, or until the bacon is crisp.

Serve just the way they are, or with Champagne Mushroom Sauce to pour on top.

## Champagne Mushroom Sauce:

1/2 cup salted butter *(1 stick, 4 ounces, 1/4 pound)*

1 eight-ounce container sliced fresh button mushrooms *(you can also use well-drained canned mushrooms)*

1/2 cup domestic champagne *(or white wine)*

1 packet *(.88-ounce net weight)* of brown gravy mix *(I used Lawry's)*

Melt the butter in a saucepan on the stove over MEDIUM heat.

Add the mushrooms and sauté lightly.

Add the champagne *(or white wine)* and stir well.

Sprinkle in the gravy mix. Stir the mixture until it bubbles.

Cook this mixture, stirring constantly, for one minute.

Pour the Champagne Mushroom Sauce

into a gravy boat, and serve it when you serve the Piggy Chicken.

**Hannah's Note: If you don't want to use anything alcoholic, you can use 1/2 cup of chicken stock as an alternative.**

**Jo Fluke's Note: If I'm serving this for company, I spoon on the mushroom sauce and then sprinkle on chopped parsley.**

# JANET'S TEXAS JALAPENO PIMENTO CHEESE

No need to preheat your oven. This recipe requires chilling, not baking.

**Hannah's 1st Note: This recipe is from Janet McLeod.**

8 ounces *(that's a half pound)* mild cheddar cheese, shredded

16 ounces *(that's a whole pound)* sharp cheddar cheese, shredded

8-ounce package softened cream cheese *(the brick kind, not the whipped kind)(I used Philadelphia Cream Cheese in the rectangular silver package.)*

two 7-ounce jars of diced pimiento, drained

12-ounce jar roasted red bell peppers, drained

1/4 cup *(4 Tablespoons)* mayonnaise *(I used Hellman's)*

2 Tablespoons *(1/8 cup)* Worcestershire sauce *(I used Lea & Perrins)*

1/2 cup pickled jalapeno pepper slices

basket of assorted crackers, your choice

**Hannah's 2nd Note: Janet says that a home-size food processor won't hold all the cheeses at once, so you'll have to**

**process them in 3 batches.**

Place one-third of the shredded mild cheddar cheese, one-third of the shredded sharp cheddar cheese, and one-third of the softened cream cheese in the bowl of a food processor equipped with the steel blade. Process the cheeses for approximately 45 seconds, or until they are the same color and consistency.

Use a rubber spatula to remove the cheese from the bowl of the food processor and store it in a bowl on the counter. The bowl you choose should have a cover and hold about 5 cups.

Process the second batch of cheeses. When you're finished, use the rubber spatula to add it to the first batch you processed.

Process the third batch of cheese, and add it to the bowl on the counter.

**Hannah's 3rd Note: Don't worry about washing out the food processor bowl. You're going to process the rest of the ingredients, but it's just fine if there's a little cheese in the bowl.**

Drain the pimentos and place them in the bowl of the food processor.

Drain the roasted red peppers and place them in the bowl of the food processor.

Add the mayonnaise and the Worcestershire sauce.

Drain the pickled jalapeno pepper slices and place them in the bowl of the food processor.

With the steel blade in place, process the ingredients with an on-and-off motion 6 to 8 times, or until everything has been chopped into small pieces.

Use the rubber spatula to scrape the final ingredients from the bowl of the food processor. Stir them into the bowl with the cheeses, and mix until they're evenly distributed.

Cover the bowl and place it in the refrigerator for at least 3 hours. This will keep in the refrigerator for up to 24 hours, but no longer.

Serve in a pretty bowl with knives for each person to use for spreading it on crackers.

Yield: This recipe will serve at least 6 people as an appetizer, but only if Mike Kingston's not invited. If he is, you'd better make double!

**Hannah's 4th Note: This is Mike's favorite snack. I made it for him to take to a Winnetka County Sheriff's Detectives meeting, and everyone raved about it.**

# Chapter Twenty

"So what now?" Andrea asked as they drove away from Club Nineteen. "We didn't get anything important from the owner or his assistant."

"I know. All we got was a repeat that Buddy was talented on keyboards, and a real ladies' man."

"So? What do we do next?"

"I guess we go back home," Hannah said, holding her head in her hands. She felt adrift in a choppy sea without a lifeboat or any other means of support. "But first could we stop off for chocolate?"

"I thought you'd never ask," Andrea said, taking a sharp left off the highway and heading for the nearest ice cream place. "Let's get a gigantic mud slide. My mouth's still on fire from the Texas Jalapeno Pimento Cheese."

"What's a mud slide?"

"It's a hot fudge sundae with caramel

sauce and chopped pecans over mounds of coffee ice cream."

"Sounds good to me," Hannah said, unbuckling her seatbelt as they pulled into a parking spot in front of Dreamery Creamery, a chain of ice cream parlors that dotted the highway.

"Hi," a cheery voice greeted them as they pushed open the door, and Hannah turned to see a pretty girl in a pink and white apron behind the cash register. "Would you like something to go, or would you like to be seated?"

"We'd like to be seated," Andrea said.

"Where *is* everybody?" Hannah asked, as the girl led them to a pink vinyl-covered booth. "Every time I've been in one of your shops, it's been packed with customers."

"It's the weather. People think it's still too cold to go out for ice cream. Just as soon as the weather warms up a little, they'll be back. Right now our business is mostly for hot chocolate and coffee to go."

"But you still make mud slides, don't you?" Andrea asked.

"Yes. Is that what you two want? A mud slide with two spoons?"

"She'll have a mud slide with coffee ice cream and one spoon," Hannah said, pointing to Andrea. "And I'll have a mud slide with chocolate ice cream and one spoon. We've had a rough day. We need lots of chocolate."

"How about drinks? Coffee?" she turned to Andrea.

"Yes, please."

"And you?" She turned to Hannah.

"Hot chocolate. And make it a double with whipped cream and shaved chocolate on top. And when we're ready to leave?"

"Yes?" The girl waited, pencil poised.

"I'll have a double hot chocolate to go. And one for her, too." Hannah pointed to Andrea. "That way we won't have to stop again to get chocolate."

"Wow!" The girl looked very sympathetic. "I'll give you some chocolate cookie wafers, too. You must have had a *really* rough day!"

"We're here," Andrea said, quite unnecessarily, as they pulled into a parking spot in back of The Cookie Jar. She drained the last little bit of hot chocolate in the bottom of her to-go cup, and smiled. "The chocolate held out."

"And it's a really good thing," Hannah said, releasing her seatbelt and opening the car door. "Coming in?"

"You bet. I want to make sure you call Norman and get him to come down here.

We need him to look at that photo and see if he can do anything with it."

Hannah glanced at her watch. "It's four o'clock. He's probably got patients."

"Then he can give them to *her*. This is more important than his dental practice. What we're doing for him could affect the rest of his life!"

"You're not going to tell him you got the DNA samples, are you?" Hannah turned to her sister in shock.

"Of course not. Come on, Hannah. Let's go in. I need a fresh cup of coffee."

When they entered the kitchen, The Cookie Jar smelled the way it always did. There was only one word to describe it, and that word was *mouthwatering*.

"Cinnamon," Andrea breathed.

"And apple," Hannah added. "Lisa or Marge must have made your Apple Cinnamon Whippersnappers."

Andrea looked pleased. "I still can't believe you're using *my* cookie recipe."

"Why wouldn't we use it? It's a great recipe. And it's something we can bake really fast if we're running low on cookies. All we have to do is make sure we keep some spice cake mix on hand." Hannah gave Andrea a little push toward the swinging door that separated the coffee shop from the kitchen. "Let's go say hello to Lisa and everybody and get that fresh coffee. All that chocolate made me think that everything is going to turn out just fine, and I need some caffeine to jolt me back to reality."

"Hannah!" Lisa greeted her with a big smile as they came into the coffee shop. "I didn't think you'd be back before we left."

"Quick trip," Hannah said.

"Mission accomplished," Andrea added.

And then the sole occupants of the coffee shop, Delores, Carrie, Earl, and even Lisa broke into applause.

"Good heavens!" Andrea said, preening a little at the unexpected tribute. "Thank you." And then she turned to Hannah. "You'd better go make that call before Norman goes somewhere with Doctor Bev, or *she* won't let him out of her sight."

It took a moment for Andrea to react. Then Hannah watched her sister's face turn red. Andrea hadn't really registered the fact that Norman's mother was sitting next to Delores, and Carrie might not appreciate the tone Andrea had used when she'd practically spit out the word *she*.

"I'm sorry, Carrie," Andrea said. "I didn't really mean to . . ." and then she stopped, and Hannah knew that her sister couldn't think of any way to smooth the feathers she might have ruffled.

That was when Carrie laughed, surprising everyone except Delores and Earl, who were also smiling. "It's all right, Andrea," Carrie told her. "We're all on the same page. Earl and I think Norman is making a big mistake, and both of us will be very grateful if you girls can do something to break them up before the wedding."

"Did you get the DNA samples?" Delores asked.

"Mother! Maybe now isn't the time to . . ."

"You can talk in front of Carrie and Earl," Delores interrupted her. "They know exactly what we're doing. And they're going to help by getting Norman's DNA sample tonight."

"How?" Hannah asked, turning to Carrie.

"Earl and I are taking Norman out to dinner since he's going to be all alone. *She's* going to be gone most of the weekend visiting her mother and her daughter."

"I see," Hannah said, shooting Andrea a warning look. They knew that Doctor Bev was going to a party and wouldn't be seeing her mother and daughter at all. It might have been gratifying to share this information, but this wasn't the time to tell Carrie and Earl that their future daughter-in-law was a liar.

"Doc and I are going out to the Inn, too," Delores informed them. "And we're going to join Carrie, Earl, and Norman for dessert. That way Doc will have Norman's sample and he can take everything to his friend at the lab tomorrow."

"How long will it take to get an answer?" Lisa asked the question they all wanted to know.

"Doc's not sure. It all depends on how busy they are, but his friend knows how important this is and he's promised to speed things up any way he can."

"That's good!" Andrea looked relieved. "I just hope we can get an answer before the wedding."

"So do I!" Carrie said. "And thank you so much for what you did today. Delores told me all about it."

"Why don't you girls join us for dinner tonight?" Delores suggested. "It'll be my treat. And then *all* of us can join Carrie and Earl's table for dessert."

"Wonderful!" Carrie turned to Hannah. "Andrea said that you needed to talk to Norman anyway."

"That's right. It's about the murder. One of the waitresses at Club Nineteen took a photo of Buddy and a woman arguing in the parking lot the night before Buddy told the band's manager that he wanted to leave Cinnamon Roll Six."

"And you think this woman might have something to do with his murder?"

"It's possible. We're just following every lead we can get. The photo's really dark and it's taken from a distance. We know how good Norman is with photography, and we thought maybe he could do something to the photo to make her more recognizable."

Carrie nodded. "If anyone can, Norman can. He's switched over to digital and he's getting really good at it. It's a pity *she* doesn't appreciate his talents."

"Carrie." Earl reached out and put his hand on her shoulder.

"You're right, dear," Carrie said, sighing deeply. "That's their business and I shouldn't be talking about it."

There was an uncomfortable silence for a moment and then Delores stepped in. "Girls? Are you joining us for dinner at the Inn?"

"Thanks, Mother. I will," Hannah said quickly. "You'll come with me, won't you, Michelle?"

"Sure. Thanks for asking us, Mother."

"Andrea?" Delores turned to her.

"I'll be happy to come. Bill won't be home until late anyway. Thank you for inviting me, Mother."

Delores turned to Lisa. "How about you, Lisa? You're part of the family, too. Will you join us?"

"I can't, but thanks for asking. Herb gets off work early tonight, and he's bringing home a pizza. We're going to cuddle up with Dillon and Sammy and watch a movie."

Hannah felt a stab of envy over Lisa's plan for the evening. She wished she could go back in time to only a few months ago when she'd cuddled up on the couch with Norman, Moishe and Cuddles to watch a movie. But that was impossible now. Norman was embroiled in a lose-lose relationship with Doctor Bev, and she wouldn't let him come over to watch a movie with Hannah. Cuddles and Moishe would cuddle up on the couch with her, but then Cuddles would entice Moishe into a game of chase all over the condo, and Hannah would miss the end of the movie because she'd have to clean up whatever they spilled or broke.

"Oh, by the way, Hannah," Lisa said. "I found your coat."

"You . . . did?" Hannah felt as if reality was slipping away from her. She'd gone through every inch of The Cookie Jar looking for her parka yesterday, and she was ninety-nine point nine percent positive it hadn't been anywhere in the building. "Where did you find it?"

"In the shower, hanging on a hanger. I was going to rinse out some towels and I figured the shower was the quickest way to do it. And there it was, as big as you please."

Hannah covered her eyes with her hands. It was a pose of abject embarrassment, and it was precisely how she was feeling. She hadn't thought of it at the time, but now she remembered hanging it there herself after someone had come in the back door and tossed a very wet, snow-covered parka over hers on the rack.

"I did that," she admitted. "And then I forgot all about it." She turned to Delores. "I apologize, Mother. I thought maybe you . . . but I was wrong."

"You thought I stole your parka so that I could buy you one that I liked better?" Delores asked, but she looked much more amused than angry.

"Well . . . yes. That's what I thought. But it was just a *fleeting* thought. Really it was."

"I know how much you love your old parka," Delores said. "Do you want me to try to return the new one?"

"No! Don't do that!" Hannah stopped and gave a sheepish grin. "I love my new parka. It's perfect for me. It makes me feel special, and loved, and . . . I've never had a parka that made me feel that way before."

"That's wonderful, dear." Delores gave a little smile. "Now the only question is, what are you going to do with your old parka?"

"I'm going to ask you to take it back to Helping Hands, Mother. It's not in any worse shape than it was when I bought it. Maybe someone else can use it."

"Nice idea," Delores said, giving her daughter an approving nod. "And don't forget to take the charity write-off when Stan does your income tax. I'm sure Helping Hands will value it at least a nickel, maybe even as much as a dime."

# APPLE CINNAMON WHIPPERSNAPPERS

Preheat oven to 350 degrees F.,
rack in the middle position.

## For the Cookies:

1 large egg

2 cups Cool Whip **(measure this — Andrea said her tub of Cool Whip contained a little over 3 cups.)**

1/3 cup apple pie filling **(Andrea uses Comstock)**

1 package (approximately 18 ounces) spice cake mix **(Andrea used Betty Crocker)**

## For Rolling Cookie Balls:

1/2 cup powdered **(confectioners)** sugar

1/2 teaspoon ground cinnamon

Prepare your cookie sheets by spraying them with Pam or another nonstick cooking spray, or lining them with parchment paper, which you then spray with Pam or another nonstick cooking spray.

First of all, chill 2 teaspoons from your silverware drawer by sticking them in the freezer. You want them really icy cold. This will make it lot easier to form the cookies after the dough is mixed.

Whisk the egg in a large mixing bowl.

Measure out 2 cups of Cool Whip and stir

them into the egg.

Place the 1/3 cup of apple pie filling in a small bowl. Cut the apples with a sharp knife until they're in quarter-inch pieces. *(The object here is to make small enough pieces so that you'll get some apple in every cookie.)*

Add the apples to the mixing bowl and stir them in by hand. Mix very gently and don't over-stir. You don't want to stir all the air out of the Cool Whip.

Sprinkle the cake mix over the top of your mixing bowl. Fold it in very gently, mixing only until everything is combined. The object here is to keep as much air in the cookie batter as possible.

Place the 1/2 cup of powdered sugar in a separate small bowl *(you don't have to sift it unless it's got big lumps).*

Add the cinnamon to the bowl and stir it all up with a fork. Mix until the cinnamon is thoroughly combined with the sugar.

Drop the cookie dough by chilled and rounded teaspoonfuls into the bowl of powdered sugar and cinnamon. Roll the cookie dough ball around in the bowl with your fingers to coat it on all sides.

**Hannah's 1st Note: Roll only one cookie dough ball at a time. If you roll too many, they'll stick together and**

you'll have a real mess. This dough is very sticky, so you must keep your fingers coated with the sugar-cinnamon mixture.

**Hannah's 2nd Note: If you're really having trouble with the sticky dough, refrigerate your mixing bowl and dough for one hour. Then take it out and try it again. If you do this, don't forget to turn off your oven. You can preheat it again a few minutes before you take the cookie dough out of the refrigerator.**

Place each coated cookie dough ball on the cookie sheets you've prepared, 12 cookies to each standard-size sheet.

Bake the cookies at 350 degrees F. for 12 to 15 minutes, or until they are firm to the touch when tapped very lightly on the top with a fingertip.

When the cookies have baked, take them out of the oven and let them cool on the cookie sheets for 2 minutes. Then move them to a wire rack to cool completely.

**Hannah's 3rd Note: If you used parchment paper, all you have to do is wait 2 minutes and then pull the whole sheet onto a wire cooling rack. Just leave the Apple Cinnamon Whippersnappers on the parchment paper until they're cool, and then simply peel them off.**

Yield: 3 to 4 dozen delicious cookies, depending on cookie size.

**Hannah's 4th Note: Andrea says these are Bill's favorite cookies. He likes to have two with a cup of hot chocolate when he's watching the Vikings play.**

# CHAPTER TWENTY-ONE

They'd almost finished their entrees when Andrea turned to Doc. "The samples I got are in my car."

"Samples?" Doc gave her a questioning look.

"I wasn't sure exactly what to get, so I collected Diana's hair, saliva, and blood. And I got some of Doctor Bev's hair. Is that all right?"

"That's fine, Andrea. Better too much than too little." Doc turned to Delores. "Right, Lori?"

That was when something happened that shocked all three Swensen sisters. Their mother giggled. Hannah stared at Delores as if she'd suddenly grown wings and a tail, and she knew that Michelle and Andrea were staring at Delores in the very same way. No one had ever made their mother giggle like a schoolgirl before!

"I was, of course, referring to this incredible salmon," Doc explained, popping the last bite in his mouth.

"I knew that," Delores said. And then, to Michelle's, Andrea's, and Hannah's surprise, she giggled again.

All this was a bit much for Hannah. She didn't really mind that Delores and Doc had shared a private joke, but it was a little embarrassing to see her mother so giddy, especially since they hadn't had anything except bottled water to drink. "Are you going to submit the sample you took from Buddy. . . ." She stopped, rephrasing what she'd said in her mind. "Are you going to submit the sample that you took from the man we thought was Buddy to the lab at the same time?"

"Yes." Doc was suddenly all business. "Unless he was in the military in the last couple of years, his DNA won't be on file. But I think it's worth a try. Some of our government agencies are building up DNA banks, and perhaps he was involved with one of them. I've got to tell you, I'm curious. I want to know why he was using a fake name and what he was doing here in Minnesota. But it's not just a matter of simple curiosity. He may have family looking for him, or someone else who'd like to know what became of him."

"What did his driver's license say?" Michelle asked.

"It was a Minnesota license issued to Bernard Alan Neiman. It was Buddy's picture and the physical description matched the man we thought was Buddy Neiman."

"But not his blood type," Hannah pointed out.

"That's true. We got that from a Red Cross blood donor card. The name on the card was Bernard Alan Neiman, and it was stamped on the back with the name of a Seattle, Washington blood bank."

*Seattle again!* Hannah filed the information away for future reference. Cammy had said Buddy mentioned some trouble in Seattle at one of the breakfasts they'd shared. She had to remember to ask Norman if he'd ever come into contact with Buddy Neiman, since Norman had lived in Seattle when he'd gone to dental school.

"I have a question for you, Hannah," Doc said, leaning forward to garner her attention. "Is there any way to make a good bran cookie?"

It was so far removed from their discussion about the murder that Hannah was startled. "Do you mean a bran cookie that tastes good?"

"That's exactly what I mean. I have quite

a few patients who need to have more whole grain in their diets. I asked my hospital cooks to make bran cookies, but the ones they made were so awful, nobody would eat them."

"I told Doc that if anybody could make a bran cookie taste good, you could," Delores told her.

"I can try. What ingredients do I have to use?"

"Bran, oatmeal, and that's it. You can put in anything else you want."

"How about eggs?"

"Eggs are fine."

"Butter?"

"Certainly. Just don't use margarine."

"Can they have some raisins?" Michelle asked.

"Raisins." Doc looked thoughtful. "Yes. Raisins would be good. And you can put in any spices you like. Those are fine."

"I think we can do it," Michelle said, smiling at Hannah. "What do you think?"

"I agree. I think we can do it if we can have a couple of days to experiment."

"Great!" Doc turned to Delores. "I wonder if those awful bran cookies are one of the reasons Ben is leaving."

"I doubt that."

"Did you ever taste one of those bran

cookies?" Doc asked her.

"No."

"Then you don't know how bad they were."

"Are you talking about Ben Matson?" Hannah asked, very surprised when Delores and Doc nodded. The last time she'd seen Ben, only two nights ago at the hospital, he'd seemed content with his job.

"Ben landed a much better internship," Doc explained. "He wants to make plastic surgery his specialty, and something opened up at one of the most prestigious hospitals in Los Angeles. I can understand why he felt he had to jump at the chance."

Hannah knew when it was time to keep silent, and when it was time to speak up This was one of those times to speak up. "What hospital is he going to?" she asked.

"Rolling Hills Vista Clinic. They're leaders in the field of facial reconstruction. You've heard about the remarkable new face transplants, haven't you?"

Hannah had. She was certainly in favor of transplants in general. She even had a donor card. But she wasn't sure exactly how she felt about face transplants. It seemed almost like stealing a dead person's identity, and she balked at the idea of someone else walking around wearing her face. On the other hand, if her face were destroyed through some horrible circumstance, she wouldn't be eager to spend the rest of her life locked indoors where no one could see her, or hidden behind a dark veil. Then she might embrace the idea of wearing a donor's face, but it still gave her shivers just thinking about it.

"Doc explained it to me on the drive out here," Delores told them. "This isn't a clinic that does ordinary facelifts, or nose jobs, or anything like that. They work with the most serious cases, and their goal is to give their patients a better life."

"It'll be a great opportunity for Ben," Doc said. "I'm just glad Marlene is staying. She's a real help to me. But enough about my interns. Who's going to get the DNA sample from Norman?"

"Carrie volunteered to do it after we join their table for dessert," Delores told him. "When Norman finishes his, she's going to snitch his dessert fork and slip it to me under the table. I'm going to bag it and put it in my purse. I'll give it to you when we get to the car."

"Thank you, Natasha," Doc said, winking at Delores.

"You're welcome, Boris," Delores said, winking right back.

Then both of them laughed, and Hannah laughed, too. Delores seemed happy and carefree tonight, even after a long day of work. Spending time with Doc Knight was obviously good for her.

Hannah watched as several of Sally's busboys took extra chairs to Carrie and Earl's table. Once everything was arranged, Carrie motioned to Delores's party and they all got up and crossed the dining room.

Andrea took the chair next to Delores, while Michelle took the one next to Doc. There was only one chair left, the one between Carrie and Norman. Hannah walked over to it, wondering if the placement had been arranged in advance.

She felt a lump in her throat as big as a baked potato with a slew of toppings when she sat down next to Norman. It was difficult to speak around the potato-sized lump, but she managed to croak out a *hello* and a *how are you?*

"I'm fine," Norman replied, but Hannah didn't think he looked fine. He had dark circles under his eyes, and he reminded her of a man facing a hanging jury. Of course that could have been her imagination, but she was convinced that he wasn't *fine.* "Mother said you needed my help?"

It was clearly a question and Hannah nodded. "That's right. Andrea has a digital photo of a woman talking to the man we thought was Buddy Neiman. It was taken the night before he told his band manager that he had to get out of the Minneapolis area."

"Whoa!" Norman stopped her by putting his hand over hers. "Buddy Neiman wasn't really Buddy Neiman?"

"No. Doc discovered that his blood type didn't match his donor card. We don't know who he actually was."

"Have you looked into Buddy Neiman's background? The real Buddy Neiman, I mean?"

"There hasn't been time. All I know about the real Buddy Neiman is his blood type and the fact that he gave blood at a blood bank in Seattle. You didn't run into him while you were there, did you?"

"I don't think so. I saw him with you that night at the hospital, but he didn't look familiar. And I don't recognize the name at all."

"That may not be the name he used in Seattle. All we know is that he used that name when he joined Cinnamon Roll Six. He had a Minnesota driver's license so he must have had his fake identification in place when he applied for that."

"That makes sense, but wouldn't he have used his own blood type on that blood donor card he carried?"

Hannah gave a little shrug. "Maybe, if he knew it. A lot of people don't know their own blood type."

"You're probably right. Do you want me to do a little research on the real Buddy Neiman if there is one?"

"That would be wonderful! But . . . do you have time?"

"I have plenty of time. Bev's spending most of the weekend in the Cities. She wants to see her mother and her daughter, and discuss their move up here."

Hannah had all she could do not to frown. Doctor Bev was already lying to Norman about where she was going and why. But there was no way Hannah was going to tell Norman that now. She'd wait until she had the complete picture before she hit him with the truth.

"What's the matter? Is something wrong?" Norman asked.

"No. I was just thinking, that's all. So . . . you're free tonight?"

"As free as a bird."

*You mean, As free as a jailbird!* Hannah's mind corrected him, but she didn't repeat it out loud. She was too busy glorying in the fact that Norman wasn't tied up with Doctor Bev for the weekend.

"Bev's not coming back until three on Sunday afternoon. That's when Claire asked her to come down to the dress shop to try on the dress she's wearing to the wedding."

"Oh," Hannah said, wondering why he was telling her all this.

"That means I'm free until then. I can help you with the investigation if you want me."

"Oh, yes!" Hannah said smiling at him. "You *bet* I want you!"

Her words fell into a vat of silence. That was when Hannah realized that everyone else at the table was looking at them with expressions of undisguised interest.

It was not a comfortable thing to know that you were blushing. Hannah attempted to stop the heat of extreme embarrassment from reddening her cheeks, but of course that didn't work. She could tell that she was as red as her hair and that couldn't have been an attractive sight.

"Norman just offered to help me with the investigation into Buddy's murder," Hannah explained to everyone else, hoping against hope that her cheeks were returning to a color approaching normal. "And I just told him that I want his help."

"Hello, everyone!" Dot Truman Larson, Sally's head waitress, arrived at their table in her usual breezy and friendly way. "How are you all tonight?"

"We're fine," Hannah said, so grateful for the interruption that she could have given Dot a giant bear hug and might have even offered to babysit her toddler for a period of no less than a solid month.

"Sally's got something special planned for you," Dot told them. "She made her Mom's Apple Pie just for you."

"I love apple pie," Doc said.

"Me, too," Norman added, and there were nods all the way around the table. It seemed that apple pie was everyone's favorite.

"Great. We've got it warm with vanilla ice cream, cinnamon ice cream, sweetened whipped cream, and crème fraiche. We've also got sharp cheddar cheese for those who want it. Coffee?"

"Coffee all around," Earl said, speaking for all of them.

Carrie waited until Dot had left and then she gave a contented smile. "This is just like old times. It feels so good to be with all of you again."

Norman didn't say anything. He just

smiled, reached out, and squeezed Hannah's hand.

# Mom's Apple Pie
Preheat oven to 350 degrees F.,
rack in the middle position.

2 frozen deep dish piecrusts **(or make your own)**

3/4 cup white sugar

1/4 cup flour

1/4 teaspoon ground nutmeg **(freshly ground is best, of course)**

1/2 teaspoon cinnamon **(if it's been sitting in your cupboard for years, buy fresh!)**

1/4 teaspoon cardamom

1/4 teaspoon salt

6 cups sliced, peeled apples **(I use 3 Granny Smith and 3 Fuji or Gala)**

1 teaspoon lemon juice

1/2 stick cold salted butter **(1/4 cup, 2 ounces, 1/8 pound)**

Prepare your crusts:

If you use homemade piecrust, roll out two rounds. Line a 9-inch pie pan with one round, and reserve the other for the top crust.

If you use frozen piecrust, buy the 8-inch deep dish kind. Leave one right in its pan and let it thaw on the counter. Loosen the second one from the pan while it's still frozen, flip over the pan, and tip the piecrust out on a floured board. When it thaws and flattens, it'll become your top crust.

Mix the sugar, flour, spices, and salt together in a small bowl.

Prepare the apples by coring them, peeling them, and slicing them into a large bowl. When they're all done, toss them with the teaspoon of lemon juice. *(Just dump on the lemon juice and use your impeccably clean fingers to toss the apple slices — it's easier.)*

Dump the small bowl with the dry ingredients on top of the apples and toss them to coat the slices. *(Again, use your fingers.)*

Put the coated apple slices in the pan with the piecrust. You can arrange them symmetrically if you like, or just dump them in as best you can. There will probably be some leftover dry ingredients at the bottom of the bowl. Just sprinkle those on top of the apple slices in the pie pan.

Cut the cold butter into 4 pieces and then cut those pieces in half. Place the pieces on top of the apples just as if you were dotting the apples with butter.

Fold your top crust in half. Move it over to the apple laden pie pan and plunk it on top. Unfold it and spread it out on top of the pie. Squeeze the edges from the top crust and the edges from the bottom crust together. *(Use a little water for "glue" if the crust just won't cooperate.)*

With a sharp knife, cut 4 slits in the top crust about 3 inches long, starting near the top and extending down the sides. *(This is a very important step. Not only does it let out the steam when the pie bakes, releasing a delicious aroma that'll have the neighbors knocking at your door, it also provides a way to sneak in those pieces of butter you cut if you forgot to put them on the apples before you covered your pie with the top crust. Don't laugh. I've done it.)*

Put your pie on a baking sheet with sides that will catch any drips. Bake it at 350 degrees F. for approximately one hour, or until the top crust is a nice golden brown and the apples are tender when you pierce them with the tip of a sharp knife.

Alternatively, you can leave off the top crust and top your apple pie with French Crumble.

**French Crumble:**
1 cup all-purpose flour
1/2 cup cold butter
1/2 cup brown sugar

Put the flour into the bowl of a food

processor with the steel blade attached. Cut the stick of butter *(1/2 cup, 4 ounces, 1/4 pound)* into 8 pieces and add them to the bowl. Cover with the 1/2 cup of firmly-packed brown sugar.

Process with the steel blade in an on and off motion until the resulting mixture is in uniform small pieces.

Remove the mixture from the food processor and place it in a bowl.

Pat handfuls of the French Crumble in a mound over your pie. With a sharp knife, poke several slits near the top to let out the steam.

Place your pie on a baking sheet with sides that will catch any drips. Bake it at 350 degrees F. for 50 to 60 minutes or until the apples are tender when pierced with the tip of a sharp knife and the French Crumble is golden brown.

**Hannah's Note: Sally always serves this pie with all the sides people could possibly want. She has vanilla ice cream, cinnamon ice cream, sweetened whipped cream, crème fraiche, and sharp cheddar cheese. She also offers plenty of strong coffee, or her Special Cinnamon Coffee.**

# CHAPTER TWENTY-TWO

Hannah could barely believe the change she saw in Devin Murphy. Only two nights ago, when Devin had first met the keyboard player from Cinnamon Roll Six, he'd been as awestruck and as eager as a puppy wanting to please. Tonight, as he took his place with the rest of the band, he seemed completely self-assured. "I think Devin just grew up," Hannah whispered to Michelle.

"I know," Michelle whispered back. "Lonnie says the only time he's ever really confident is when he's playing his music."

The program started with several classic jazz numbers, and Hannah watched Devin with interest. He was good, very good, and she was proud that Kirby Welles at the Jordan High music department had helped to produce such a talented performer.

Hannah watched with interest as Sally got up from her front row seat and walked to the microphone. But instead of saying a few words about their featured band as everyone expected, she just smiled at her husband and said, "Most of you don't know this, but I used to sing at a club in Minneapolis. I was singing *Something Cool* by Billy Barnes when Dick walked in one night, and ever since then, it's been our song."

That was the Cinnamon Roll Six's cue to start playing, and Hannah was amazed as Sally began to sing the song that June Christy had made famous. She'd never guessed that Sally could sing so well. The whole audience was silent, mesmerized by the song and Sally's melodic voice.

"That was terrific!" Michelle exclaimed when the last note had faded away.

"Yes, it was," Hannah responded, wondering why Sally had given up what must have been a promising signing career to become a chef. They were friends, and it was something Hannah would ask when the time was right.

Once the applause had dwindled and Sally had taken her seat next to Dick again, the band began another number.

*"Take Five,"* Michelle whispered, and Hannah knew that her youngest sister wasn't suggesting a five-minute break. It was the jazz piece that Paul Desmond had written and the Dave Brubeck Quartet had made

famous in the sixties. It showcased the alto sax and keyboard players, and Hannah crossed her fingers for luck. This was Devin's chance to show how talented he really was.

Hannah found that she was holding her breath as Devin picked up the unusual time signature and superimposed contrasting rhythms and meters. Instead of simply duplicating what Brubeck had done, which would be no easy task in itself, Devin put his own twist on it.

She gave a little smile as Tommy Asch joined in on the alto sax, playing the Paul Desmond part. He was excellent, but Devin was the real star of the piece.

And then she was lost in the music, the rhythms, the complicated and intricate interplay of the instruments. It was a world of bright shining notes sequencing as trippingly as glissandos, intricate and unexpected harmonies, and pure melodic pleasure. And then the final note sounded, tugging her back to reality as applause filled the room.

"Wow!" she mouthed, turning to Norman.

"Wow is right!" he said, close to her ear. "I had no idea Devin was *that* good!"

"Neither did I. And to think all he needed was a chance to . . ." Hannah stopped speaking, suddenly realizing that she hadn't checked to see if Devin had an alibi for the time of Buddy's murder.

"You're not thinking what I think you're thinking, are you?" Norman asked.

"I probably am. Of course I don't believe it for a second, but I have to check it out."

"It's okay," Michelle said, leaning close to Hannah. "Lonnie already checked it out."

"He investigated his own cousin?"

"Yes. Devin asked him to check out his alibi. He knew what it would look like since he was hanging around with Buddy in the hospital and then he got Buddy's job when he was killed."

"Where was Devin when Buddy was murdered?" Norman asked as they followed the crowd out of the room.

"With Felicia Berger. She's a nurse's aide this year at the hospital, and she came in to tell Buddy that a doctor would come in to splint his hand in a few minutes. Felicia knew Devin from high school, and she asked him if he'd help her fold up some of the chairs they didn't need in triage any longer and take them to storage."

"And he left Buddy there in the room alone?" Hannah asked.

"That's right. Buddy told him to go ahead, that he'd be leaving for the Inn as

soon as he got the splint on his wrist anyway."

"How long was Devin with Felicia?"

"They were still together loading folding
chairs on the racks when they heard that
Buddy was dead. Devin's in the clear, Hannah. You can cross him off your suspect list."

"With pleasure."

"Are you sure you don't mind if we bake
at your house?" Michelle asked Norman as
they entered the lobby.

"I don't mind at all. Nobody's baked in
that great double oven since the last
time . . ." Norman stopped and cleared his
throat, ". . . since the last time Hannah
came over."

"Doctor Bev doesn't bake?" Michelle
asked, and Hannah felt like handing her the
Academy Award for looking so surprised
even though Hannah had told her that Doctor Bev didn't bake.

"No. She doesn't really cook either. We go
out a lot."

"That must get boring."

"Sometimes it does."

Hannah suspected that Michelle was
really asking questions to make Norman realize how empty his life would be when Bev
lived in his house. She applauded the effort,
but she couldn't help feeling sorry for

Norman. He looked uncomfortable as he answered Michelle's questions, but she wasn't about to interfere with whatever Michelle had in mind.

As she watched, Michelle reached out and patted Norman on the shoulder. "Well, we're going to bake you some cookies tonight."

"I thought you had to bake bran cookies for Doc Knight."

"We do, but we'll bake something for you, too. What's your favorite fruit?"

Norman thought about that for a moment while they walked through the lobby toward the front door. "Peaches," he said, stopping at the coat rack to pick up his coat. "I haven't had anything with peaches for a long time."

"Then we'll bake you some peach cookies. How about that?"

"Sounds good."

Norman's response came fast, and Hannah knew he was looking forward to the night ahead. But she still wasn't sure exactly what Michelle was trying to accomplish.

Once they'd put on their coats and pulled on their boots, they stepped out into the crisp night air and began the short walk to the parking lot. In colder weather and snowy conditions, Dick hired someone to ferry customers back and forth to the parking lot, but it was well above forty degrees tonight, and Norman shook his head when the college kid offered to take them to their cars. "We'll walk," he said, and then he turned to Michelle and Hannah. "Is that okay with you?"

"Fine with me," Hannah said quickly.

"Me, too," Michelle responded, falling into step with Norman as they began to walk down the lighted path to the parking lot.

Michelle and Norman made polite conversation as they walked, but Hannah didn't say a word. She was much more interested in seeing what Michelle would do and say next. But nothing of import happened until they entered the parking lot.

"How about taking Hannah home with you?" Michelle said as they reached Hannah's cookie truck. "That way I can run out for baking supplies and we won't waste any time. You can get started on that photo Andrea's going to send you," she said to Norman. "And Hannah can start pulling out all the utensils and small appliances we need in the kitchen."

"Good idea!" Norman said, taking Hannah's arm.

"Do you want me to get the supplies first

and then stop off at the condo to get the cats?" Michelle asked him. "I bet they'd like to visit while we bake."

"You can't," Hannah said quickly. "Doctor Bev's allergic."

"But she's in the Cities," Michelle pointed out. "What do you say, Norman?"

Norman thought about it for all of a second or two, and then he said, "I say yes. I haven't seen Cuddles and Moishe in way too long."

"But . . . what about her allergy?" Hannah asked him.

"Let's see if it really *is* an allergy. If Bev comes over on Sunday night and she doesn't have any reaction, I'll know it's not an allergy."

*When the cat's away, the mice will play,* Hannah thought, hiding a grin. Or in this case, *When the fiancée's away, our cats will play!* She was proud of Norman for showing some backbone instead of just believing everything Doctor Bev told him. "Can you handle the cats alone?" she asked Michelle.

"Of course. I'll use the carrier for Cuddles, and I'll put Moishe on his harness and leash. When I get back to Norman's house, I'll beep the horn, and you can come out and help me get them into the house."

"We'll both help," Norman offered

quickly. "Come on, Hannah. Let's go. I want to get all the cat toys out of the garage and put out the scratching post again." Then he turned to Michelle. "Thanks for thinking of it, Michelle. It's the best idea I've heard in a very long time."

"So! We're all ready," Norman said, positioning the scratching post by the window in the den. "Do you think they'd like a fire in the fireplace?"

"I don't know about them, but I would," Hannah said, laughing a little. She was very encouraged by the fact that Norman had kept all of the cat toys. She just hoped it meant that he was having second thoughts about giving up the cat he loved so much.

"This has got to be moved," Norman said, picking up a glass-topped end table and putting it in a closet. "It's Bev's. She moved it over here last week. If Cuddles starts playing chase with Moishe, they could break it and hurt themselves."

Hannah smiled. She noticed that Norman had said, *They could break it and hurt themselves,* not *They could break Bev's table.* At least for now, he had his priorities straight.

"Do you need me to find anything else for you in the kitchen?" Norman asked.

"I don't think so. We've got the mixer,

344

food processor, mixing bowls, measuring cups, and measuring spoons. And all your spoons, spatulas, and whisks are in the drawer in the kitchen. Your cookie sheets are still in that flat drawer under the ovens, aren't they?"

"Nothing's changed, at least not yet. And actually . . . I don't think it will change. Since Bev's not going to be cooking in the kitchen anyway, I'm not going to let her remodel it. It seems like a waste, doesn't it?"

"It does to me."

"Then we're agreed. I'll start in on that background check for Buddy Neiman if you don't need me for anything else."

"That's fine. The first name on his driver's license was Bernard so you might try that, too. It's Bernard Alan Neiman."

"Okay. I'll be in my office."

"I'll bring you a fresh cup of coffee when it's ready." Hannah walked over to the espresso machine on the counter, poured in some bottled water, and flicked it on.

"That would be great! And . . ." Norman paused to listen. "Was that a car horn I heard?"

"I think it was. And that means Michelle must be here. Let's go help her bring in the cats!"

Hannah eyed the huge box of ingredients that Michelle carried into Norman's kitchen. "Where did you get all that?"

"At the Red Owl."

"They were open past eight at night?"

"I drove past on the off-chance Florence might be there, and she was in the back, unpacking some boxes. When I told her I needed lots of stuff, she was happy to let me shop."

"Just look at all this!" Hannah started to pull ingredients from the box. "Cream cheese, peach jam, peach pie filling, white sugar, flour, baking soda, two pounds of salted butter, ground cinnamon, whole nutmeg, and a nutmeg grater?"

"That's only the first layer. I've also got pecans, eggs, and sliced canned peaches. And in that second box over there," Michelle pointed to another box, "I've got bran flakes, oatmeal, raisins, brown sugar, and vanilla. I figured Norman must have salt so I didn't buy that."

"This must have cost you a fortune!"

"Oh, it did. But that's okay. I can afford it."

"How? You don't earn much working part-time at the college."

Michelle laughed. "I can afford it because I charged it to Mother."

"But . . . but . . ."

"You sound like a motorboat," Michelle interrupted with the tease they'd used as children. "It's okay, Hannah. Mother told me to charge all expenses to her. She wants us to break up Norman and Doctor Bev, and she also wants us to solve Buddy's murder. She said it's her assignment to us and she's happy to pay for it."

Hannah felt a little like a kid stealing money from her mother's purse, something she'd never dreamed of doing when she was growing up. It made her very uncomfortable. "Maybe I should pay Mother back."

"Absolutely not. It would only make her mad. Mother gave me her credit card and told me to use it. Besides, Mother can afford it. I can't, and you can't."

"You've got a point." Hannah gave a little shrug. "Okay. I'll buy that. What kind of cookie are we going to make for Norman?"

"We're making Peaches And Cream Cookies. I thought it all out when I was shopping in the store. They're going to be soft, creamy, delicious cookies. Just wait and see."

"You're the boss on this one. I don't think I've ever made peach cookies in my life."

"There's always a first time," Michelle said, tossing Hannah a can of sliced peaches. "Open these and drain them, will you? I'm going to start softening the salted butter and the cream cheese."

Thirty minutes later, Norman looked happier than Hannah had seen him look in several months. He was sitting at the kitchen table watching them mix up cookie dough, and Cuddles was in his lap. Hannah could hear her purring even over the whine of Norman's stand mixer, and Moishe was purring too. Perhaps she was anthropomorphizing, but Hannah was convinced that her own cat was purring because he was happy to see his friend, Cuddles, so happy.

As Hannah watched, Cuddles jumped down from Norman's lap and walked over to rub noses with Moishe. Then she turned, swished her tail, and wiggled her rear as she walked away.

"She wants Moishe to follow her," Norman explained his cat's actions. And to Hannah amazement, Moishe jumped up and padded after her.

"Where are they going?" Michelle asked.

"They're going to check out the house to see if anything's changed. And now that I put that silly table in the closet, they're going to find out everything's exactly the same. Cuddles is leading the way because she still considers it to be *her* house."

*From your lips to God's ears,* Hannah thought, remembering the phrase her neighbor used to use when she wanted things to be as she said they were.

There was a loud thump from the den and then a startled meow. A scant second later, there was the sound of running footfalls on the stairway Norman had built for Moishe before he'd adopted Cuddles.

"The chase is on," Norman said. There was another loud thump and then the sound of footfalls running down the circular staircase.

"And the chase has picked up speed," Hannah commented. "Any second now they'll probably . . . feet up everybody! Here they come!"

Hannah and Michelle hopped up to sit on the kitchen counter. Norman lifted his feet to the seat of a neighboring chair. They were just in time as the two cats rounded the corner into the kitchen and skidded across the tiles.

"Careful, guys!" Norman warned, but of course they didn't listen. Norman didn't speak cat and the cats didn't speak caution. They slid past the refrigerator, rounded the center island on three paws, and ran smack dab into the cupboard under the sink.

"Rrrrow!" Moishe yowled, sounding dazed.

"Merrrowww," Cuddles moaned, adding her voice to the complaint.

"Are they hurt?" Michelle asked, preparing to jump down from the counter.

"I really don't think so," Norman said with a chuckle, as the two cats shook their heads, regained their feet, and started to chase each other all over again. "Do they do this at your house?" he asked Hannah.

"Oh, yes. Every night."

"But your place is so much smaller! How do they manage it?"

"They fly," Hannah said, and left it at that.

# PEACHES AND CREAM COOKIES
Preheat oven to 375 degrees F.,
rack in the middle position.

15 canned peach slices to garnish your cookies

1 and 1/4 cups white *(granulated)* sugar

1/2 cup *(1 stick, 4 ounces, 1/4 pound)* salted butter, softened

4 ounces cream cheese, softened *(the brick kind, not the whipped kind — I used Philadelphia Cream Cheese in the silver box)*

3 large eggs

1/2 teaspoon salt

1 teaspoon cinnamon

1/2 teaspoon nutmeg *(freshly grated is best, of course)*

1 teaspoon baking soda

1 and 1/2 cups peach pie filling *(I used Comstock — my can was 15.5 ounces net weight, and it was exactly 1 and 1/2 cups)*

2 Tablespoons *(that's 1/8 cup)* peach jam

3 and 1/2 cups all-purpose flour *(pack it down in the cup when you measure it)*

1 cup finely chopped pecans

Drain the can of peach slices in a strainer over the sink, or over a bowl. You do not need to reserve the juice. Let the peaches drain while you mix up your cookie dough.

**Hannah's 1st Note: Unless you have a very strong stirring arm, use an electric mixer to make this cookie dough.**

Place the sugar in the bowl of an electric mixer.

Place the butter and the cream cheese, which must be softened to room temperature, on top of the sugar.

Turn the mixer to LOW and mix for one minute. Gradually increase the speed of the mixer, scraping down the sides of the bowl frequently and beating for one minute at each level, until you arrive at the highest speed.

Beat at the highest speed for at least 2 minutes or until the resulting mixture is very light and fluffy.

Turn the mixer down to LOW, and add the eggs, one at a time, beating after each addition.

Continue to mix on LOW speed while you add the salt, cinnamon, nutmeg, and baking soda. Mix until they are thoroughly incorporated.

Measure out a cup and a half of peach pie filling. If there are any large pieces of peach, chop them up with a knife into small pieces about the size of mini chocolate chips. The goal is to get some into each cookie.

With the mixer on LOW speed, add the peach pie filling to your bowl and mix it in.

Measure out the peach jam. If there are any large pieces of peach, chop them up with a knife just like you did with the peaches in the pie filling.

With the mixer on LOW speed, add the peach jam to your bowl and mix it in thoroughly.

Mix in the flour, one cup at a time, mixing on LOW after each addition. (**You don't have to be exact — just add the flour in 4 increments**)

Shut off the mixer and scrape down the sides of the bowl. Then give the mixture a final stir by hand. The resulting cookie dough should be fluffy, but not at all stiff like sugar cookie or chocolate chip cookie dough. Let the bowl sit on the counter while you . . .

Line your cookie sheets with parchment paper. It's the easiest way to bake these cookies. If you don't have parchment paper and you really don't want to go out to get any, grease your cookie sheets heavily, or spray them thoroughly with Pam or another nonstick cooking spray.

If you haven't already done so, put the pecans in the bowl of a food processor with the steel blade in place, and process them with an on-and-off motion into fine pieces.

When the pecans are ready, place them in a shallow bowl. This is what you'll use to coat the outside of your Peaches And Cream Cookies.

Using a teaspoon *(not the measuring kind, but one from your silverware drawer),* drop a rounded teaspoon of cookie dough into the bowl of finely chopped pecans. Use your fingers and a light touch to form the cookie dough into a ball. Lift the ball gently and place it on your baking sheet. Continue to form dough balls covered with finely chopped pecans, 12 to a standard-size cookie sheet.

Lay your peach slices out on layers of paper towels on the counter. Pat them dry and then cut each one into two pieces, making thinner slices.

Top each Peaches And Cream cookie dough ball with a thin peach slice, cut side up. Press it down gently.

Bake your Peaches And Cream Cookies at 375 degrees F. for 12 minutes. Take them out of the oven and slide the cookie-laden parchment paper onto a wire rack to cool. If you used greased cookie sheets, you're going to have to let the cookies sit on the cookie sheets for 2 minutes and then remove them to a wire rack with a metal spatula.

Let the cookies cool completely before you attempt to remove them from the wire rack.

Yield: Approximately 4 to 5 dozen soft and moist cookies, depending on cookie size.

# CHAPTER TWENTY-THREE

"One thing's for sure," Norman said grinning at Hannah. "These are the best peach cookies I ever ate."

"These are the *only* peach cookies I ever ate. But I agree that they're wonderful. Michelle is really talented at making up recipes. These are so good, I think I might have to serve them at The Cookie Jar."

"Not these!" Norman jerked the plate away from her. "These are *my* cookies. You'll have to get the recipe from Michelle and bake your *own* cookies."

A message flashed on Norman's computer monitor and he gave a little sigh. They were in his home office, a large room with a sofa, chairs, a spectacular view of the woods, a fireplace, and two walls of floor to ceiling bookcases. "I'm sorry, Hannah. None of the hits I got on Bernard Alan Neiman panned out."

"That's okay. It just goes a little further

toward proving my fake name theory."

"But we may never know who Buddy actually was."

"I know that, but Doc and Mike are working on identifying him too, and they may have gotten some leads we don't know about. Mike's running his fingerprints and he's got deputies checking for anyone who fits Buddy's description in the missing person's records."

"That's a big job."

"Yes it is, but Andrea says Bill's all for it. He even called in some retired deputies to work on it."

"Is Doc helping the deputies?"

"No, he's got his own plan. He told Mother that he was going to post Buddy's picture in something called *Hospital News*. It's a magazine like those airline magazines you read when you're on a plane. Hospitals subscribe to *Hospital News* and put it in their waiting rooms. Lots of people see it, and one of them might recognize Buddy and know who he really is."

"Doc really wants to know, doesn't he?"

"Yes. He says that since Buddy died in his hospital, he feels a certain responsibility. And that responsibility is doubled because Mother was the one who discovered Buddy's body. Both of them think that

Buddy may have family or someone who needs to know what happened to him."

"They're probably right. Human beings don't live in a vacuum."

Norman's computer gave a little ding, and Hannah turned to look at the screen. "What does that ding mean?"

"It means I have an e-mail message. It's probably Andrea with the photo. Time to get busy, Hannah. I'll download the photo and we'll see if we can find out more about the woman in Shelby's photograph."

Hannah watched with envy as Norman called up his e-mail program and signed in. She really ought to learn to do some of these things. He'd offered to teach her on several occasions, and she simply hadn't gotten around to taking him up on his offer. Now it was too late if his marriage to Doctor Bev went off as planned. *If,* she reminded herself. Those two little letters contained a world of possibilities, and she intended to take full advantage of them.

"Here we go, Hannah." Norman said, gesturing toward his large computer screen. "See that little circle with all the little lines radiating out from it in the center of the screen?"

"I see it."

"That means the JPEG Andrea sent me is

downloading."

"Oh," Hannah said, trying to sound as if she knew exactly what *JPEG* and *downloading* meant.

It wasn't the same magic as watching a print come up in the developer, but Hannah decided that it was magic nonetheless as the image on the screen became detailed before her very eyes. She could see a woman and a man standing in the parking lot of Club Nineteen, in the same row that Andrea had parked her Volvo less than twelve hours ago. Was the man Buddy Neiman? She'd be hard-pressed to give a definitive answer. The best she could do was say that it *could* be Buddy Neiman.

"Let me see if I can make the woman any clearer," Norman said, pulling down a menu from the top of the screen and clicking on several selections.

As Hannah watched, the dark background lightened slightly and she was now able to see the evergreen shrubs lining the parking lot and the arc light glinting off the hoods and fenders of the cars. She still could not have positively identified Buddy from the photo, but luckily that wasn't necessary. Shelby had identified Buddy for them, and she had been an eyewitness. Not only that, she'd heard part of their conversation, which Hannah had written down.

"Are they arguing?" Norman asked, as he worked on the contrast of the photograph.

"Yes. Hold on and I'll tell you what the waitress overheard them say."

Out came the murder book, and Hannah flipped to the correct page. "She said, *I'd know you anywhere,* and Buddy said, *You got the wrong guy, lady. Leave me alone!* Then she said something that Shelby couldn't hear. Buddy hollered at her to let go, she did, and then he shouted, *I'm not the guy you think I am!* And she shouted, *Yes you are! I know you are!* Then she slapped him and walked away. Shelby thinks she went to a parked car, but she didn't see which one."

"Interesting."

"The argument?"

"No, look at this." Norman used the mouse to point to a section of the photograph on the screen. "See these three spots of light here?"

"On the woman's wrist?"

"Yes."

"I see them. They're a reflection of some type, aren't they?"

"Exactly right. They must have caught the light from the arc light in the parking lot behind them. The reflection is clearer than the rest of the photo."

Hannah's mind was going so fast, she felt dizzy. This very same thing had happened with the photo of Boyd Watson's killer. In that case, it had been one spot of light from the moon, and it had reflected off a cufflink that had led them to the killer. Could they be lucky enough to identify the woman who'd argued with Buddy by a reflection?

"This should work," Norman said. "I'll select the area of her wrist and start by enlarging two hundred percent."

Hannah watched as the section of the photo Norman had selected filled more of the screen. "Could it be her watch? Or maybe a bracelet?"

"It could be, but it looks to me like something on the watch or bracelet is catching the light."

"Can you enlarge it even more?"

"I think so. Those spots are bright."

"And they're in sharper focus than the rest of the photo?" Hannah asked.

"That's right! How did you know that?"

"You told me when we were working on the photo Lucy took of the killer. You said that since the cufflink emitted reflective light of its own, it was sharper than the rest of the photo."

Norman began to smile. "Do you remember everything I say?"

"Not everything. Sometimes I forget on purpose."

"Give me an example of what you forget on purpose."

*The fact that you're getting married and I'm losing you forever,* Hannah thought, but of course she didn't say that. "I'm forgetting the fact you said I should have my teeth checked."

Norman laughed. "Okay. That's fair. But you probably should have . . ."

"I know. I know. One of these days when I have more time . . . okay?"

While they were talking, Norman had changed the percentage of enlargement until it now stood at four hundred percent.

"They look like little starbursts," Hannah said, but they're getting a little . . . what do you call that?"

"Grainy, if you're doing print photography. Since this is digital photography, I think we could say that we've enlarged so much, the image is breaking up into pixels."

"Would that be like Pointillism? It looks a little like George Seurat's painting of boats on the Seine, except that the dots are like stars and all three of them are pinkish-orange."

"That's it exactly. The color is from the arc light. And you're right when you say they look like starbursts. They're snowflake ornaments on a silver bracelet."

Hannah turned to stare at him in shock. "How do you know that?"

"I know because Bev has a bracelet just like it. My mother gave it to her for Christmas."

Hannah was so shocked, she wasn't sure what to say. "Do you . . . do you think the woman in the photo is *Bev?!*"

"No," Norman gave a little laugh. "You said this was taken at a jazz club, didn't you?"

"Yes. Club Nineteen."

"Well, Bev doesn't really like jazz and I can't imagine her going to a place like that. If you'd said it was taken outside Orchestra Hall, I would have believed it, but definitely not a jazz club."

*Don't push it,* Hannah's better sense put the warning in her mind. *The seed of doubt has been planted. Now let it grow. You already know she's a liar, but he doesn't know that yet.*

"I wonder where your mother got that bracelet," Hannah said, pushing back the suspicious thoughts that were filling her mind.

"I'm not sure. I know she picked it up at the last minute. It's only nine and I'm sure they're still up. Why don't we call and ask her?"

"The snowflake bracelet?" Carrie repeated when Hannah had posed the question to her. "Of course I remember. Is Norman still on, dear?"

"No. Would you like to . . ."

"No! I just don't want him to know how much I paid for it. You see, I always pick up a few extra Christmas presents every year. People visit over the holidays and if they bring gifts, I like to give them something in return. I call them *Annies,* just like my mother used to. That's for *Annie*-body. Isn't that cute?"

"Yes, it is," Hannah said quite honestly. She also bought some generic gifts for Christmas drop-ins, and so did Delores.

"Well, that bracelet was an *Annie.* I had no idea Norman was going to drop by with her. And since she brought me flowers, I gave her one of my *Annies.*"

"Do you remember where you got it?"

"Oh, yes. It was on-sale at CostMart for twenty-five dollars. I bought three, but that's the only one I used this year."

"Do you know if they were a popular

item?" Hannah asked, hoping that Carrie might have asked at the jewelry counter about them.

"Oh, yes! They were *very* popular. The lady in line ahead of me was buying four, and the lady behind me had two in her cart. I heard the clerk tell the lady in front that they'd gotten in a shipment that morning and they were already almost sold out. They were online, too. Earl checked for me. I don't know where CostMart got them, but they were just darling, the design was gorgeous, and they were a great value for the price."

"Stop, Carrie!"

"What?"

"You're making me want to go to Cost-Mart and see what they've got. And I *hate* to shop."

"Well, just call me any time you want to go and I'll go with you. I've got my Cost-Mart Constant Customer Card, and I get an automatic fifteen percent off."

Hannah gave a little groan, and Norman looked worried. "What is it?" he asked.

"Your mother's convincing me I should go to CostMart with her. She's very convincing."

Carrie laughed on the other end of the line. Of course she'd heard their conversation. "I told you. Anytime you want to go, just call me. Oops! I've got to go. Earl's calling me, and that means his favorite program is on. Talk to you later, Angel."

"What's the matter?" Norman asked, noticing the puzzled expression on Hannah's face as she hung up the phone.

"Nothing really, but . . . your mother just called me *Angel*. She's never called me *Angel* before."

"Are you sure?"

"Yes, I'm sure. She said, *Talk to you later, Angel.* And then she hung up. What does that mean?"

"It means she really likes you."

"I know she likes me."

"You don't understand. It means she *really* likes you. The only people she calls *Angel* are Earl and me. And now you."

"She's *that* pleased that I might want to go to CostMart with her?"

"No, I think it's more than that," Norman said. And then he reached out to give her a hug.

It was precisely nine-thirty when the phone rang. They were in the kitchen, watching Michelle bake Doc's Bran-Oatmeal-Raisin Cookies and Norman reached out to answer it. "Hello. It's Norman," he said. He listened for a minute and then he said, "Hold on for a second, okay? I'll be right back with you."

Hannah knew who it was the moment that Norman got up from the kitchen table and went off into the den with the remote phone. Doctor Bev was checking in on her intended. *Bev,* she mouthed to Michelle, and Michelle nodded. And they were perfectly silent until Norman had closed the door to the den behind him.

"Tight rein," Michelle commented.

"And how! I'm surprised she doesn't have spies out to make sure he's not visiting Cuddles, and . . . uh-oh! There goes my cell phone. I wonder who it is."

"Answer it and you'll know," Michelle suggested, simply stating the obvious.

"Good idea." Hannah pulled her cell phone out of her purse and flipped it open. "Hello?"

"Hannah! Where are you?" *Mike,* Hannah mouthed the word to Michelle. "I'm at Norman's with Michelle. Where are *you?*"

"Between a rock and a hard place."

"No. I mean *where* are you?"

"Oh. I'm about forty-five minutes away. I'm with Lonnie, and he wanted to stop by to see Michelle. Can we come out to Norman's house?"

"Of course," Hannah said, not even thinking twice. "Come on out and we'll see if we can rustle you up something to eat. You're hungry, right?"

"A working detective is always hungry. Wha'cha got?"

"I don't know. I'll have to touch base with Michelle on that."

"Fine. With both of you cooking, it's bound to be good, whatever it is. Thanks, Hannah. Oh . . . is Norman there? I mean *right* there?"

"No, he's on the phone with Bev in the den."

"Good. I just wanted to find out if you got that DNA sample. And before you ask me how I know, let me just remind you that I'm a detective and I can see right through the excuses that Andrea gives Bill. You went to see Bev's mother, didn't you?"

"Of course we did. Does Bill know?"

"If he does, he's never going to admit it. Think about it, Hannah. Bill's the Winnetka County Sheriff. He can't admit he knows his wife entered into a conspiracy with his sister-in-law to do something like that. So did you get it?"

"Just let me repeat Andrea's words when we walked into The Cookie Jar this afternoon. She said, *Mission accomplished.*"

"Good work. Look, Hannah. I can do

368

something to rush this through our DNA lab. And I can pick up the sample tonight."

"Thanks Mike, but we've got it covered. Doc Knight has a friend at a DNA lab, and he's driving the samples there tomorrow. His friend is going to expedite the whole thing."

"That's a relief! I was going to offer to run it through the police DNA lab, but I'd be risking my job on a civilian matter like that."

"But you still would have done it?"

"Sure I would have done it. Norman's my friend and there are some things more important than jobs."

"You're a good guy, Mike."

Mike chuckled. "Only some of the time. And when I'm bad, I'm *really* bad. But that's part of my appeal . . . right, Hannah?"

"Maybe." Hannah began to smile. Mike was attractive when he was being slightly wicked, and he was slightly wicked a lot of the time. She was just getting ready to say goodbye and take a look in Norman's freezer and refrigerator to figure out what they could serve to two very hungry detectives when Norman walked back into the room.

"Hi, Norman," she said, holding out her cell phone. "Mike's on my cell phone. He wants to know if he can come over with Lonnie."

Norman grabbed the cell phone and greeted Mike. "What's your ETA?" he asked. He listened for a moment or two, and then he laughed. "That's fine. I'll start thawing the steaks and see what the girls can put together. See you in about forty-five then."

# CHAPTER TWENTY-FOUR

Precisely forty minutes later, Hannah took a pan of Cheese and Green Chilies Biscuits out of the oven.

"Those smell great!" Norman said, coming up behind her and wrapping his arms around her waist. "I just want to lean over you and sniff."

"I'm leaving now. I'm too young to hear things like this," Michelle said with a perfectly deadpan expression.

Both Hannah and Norman started to laugh. They laughed so hard, Michelle just had to join in. When they'd calmed down a bit, Michelle said, "They *do* smell good, Hannah. And this is an experiment?"

"Yes. Shall we cut one in thirds and try it before Lonnie and Mike get here?"

"Best idea I've heard all night," Norman said, watching as Hannah cut a biscuit in three pieces and buttered them.

Michelle was the first to taste hers.

"Mmmm," she said. "I think I just burned my lip, but it was worth it."

"Excellent!" Norman pronounced, wolfing down another bite.

"Oh, boy!" Hannah said, knowing that it might be impolite to praise her own baking, but unable to keep her enjoyment nonverbal. The richness of the cheese and the mild heat of the green chilies were perfect with the flaky biscuits.

"What did you do for a salad, Michelle?" Norman asked her. "I know I didn't have any lettuce."

"You didn't have any cabbage either, so I made Carrot Slaw."

"Carrot Slaw?" Hannah stared at her sister, intrigued. "What's in it?"

Michelle gave a little shrug. "Anything I could find in Norman's refrigerator and freezer that I thought would go with carrots."

"Can we taste it?" Hannah asked.

"Sure. I want to taste it, too. I have absolutely no idea how it turned out."

Hannah and Norman watched while Michelle put servings of her Carrot Slaw in small bowls. "Here you go," she said, passing the bowls around. "Tell me what you think."

Hannah smiled as she tasted a bite. Michelle had a natural sense of food combinations and the salad was wonderful. "Crunchy, salty, sweet . . . it's great, Michelle. I've never had anything like it before."

"I thought it should work, but I wasn't completely sure."

"Well, I'm sure it worked," Norman gave his approval. "There's a pad of paper in the drawer next to the sink. Write down what's in it before you forget. You don't want to lose this recipe."

Michelle had just finished jotting down the ingredients and the dressing when the doorbell rang. "That must be Lonnie and Mike," she said. "I'll go let them in."

"And I'll put on the steaks," Norman said, getting up to don a chef's apron.

Hannah felt a warm glow when she saw the apron. It said FOOD BY NORMAN on the front in block letters, and it was the one she'd given him the first time he'd barbecued at the Fourth of July celebration at Eden Lake. "You still have the apron," she said.

"Of course I do. You gave it to me. I'll never give it up."

Their eyes locked and a wealth of emotions welled up in Norman. Hannah could tell that because the same emotions were welling up in her. He knew it shouldn't end like this. She knew it shouldn't end like this. There was too much history, too much laughter, too much love to separate them forever.

"Hey, you two!" Mike burst into the kitchen. "What's cooking? I'm hungry as a bear."

"You'd better be," Hannah warned him. "I just made eleven huge Cheese and Green Chiles Biscuits."

"And I just made a big bowl of Carrot Slaw," Michelle added, smiling at Lonnie.

"I love your Carrot Slaw," Lonnie said, smiling back.

Michelle burst into peals of laughter and Lonnie looked puzzled. "Did I say something funny?"

"Yes. You said you loved my Carrot Slaw, and tonight is the first time I've ever made it."

"Oh. Well . . . how about this? I love *anything* you make, Michelle." That said, Lonnie walked over to her and gave her a kiss.

Hannah felt good, watching her sister and Lonnie interact. They appeared to have a clear understanding between them, and they were definitely a couple.

"Okay, guys. Five minutes to dinner."

Norman flipped the steaks on the grills. "I just want you to know that we expect you to do justice to this meal."

"Oh, we will," Mike promised, reaching out to snag a biscuit.

"You'll spoil your dinner!" Hannah warned, but it wasn't until the words left her mouth that she realized she sounded exactly like Delores when she'd caught them snacking on cookies an hour before dinner. "Forget I said that. If you want a biscuit now, eat a biscuit. There's softened butter on the counter."

The kitchen was filled with the mouth-watering smells of prime-cut steak cooking on a grill. Hannah's stomach growled even though she'd eaten Sally's excellent dinner less than three hours ago and sampled the Peaches and Cream Cookies even more recently than that. She certainly wasn't hungry, but she knew that this was going to be a wonderful meal.

Since both Lonnie and Mike liked their steaks rare, it didn't take long before they were cutting off chunks of rare beef and washing them down with fresh, hot coffee. There wasn't much time for conversation between bites of steak, biscuit, and slaw, but Mike finally stopped eating long enough to say, "There was a partial print on the murder weapon, but it belonged to the nurse who brought supplies to the treatment room."

"How about defensive wounds?" Hannah asked, even though she'd read the autopsy report and knew there hadn't been any.

"No. That's probably because the victim was tranquilized. Doc's theory is that he didn't even see it coming."

"Do you think that the killer had some kind of medical training so that he knew exactly where to stab Buddy?" Hannah asked.

"Maybe. It was a hospital, after all. There are a lot of people with medical training at a hospital. Either that, or the killer simply got lucky. We won't know until we catch him."

"Or her," Hannah added.

"Or her." Mike gave a little nod. "It could have been a woman. It didn't take that much strength. The scissors were very sharp." Mike looked down and grinned. "Hi, Moishe. Hi, Cuddles. Are you two sniffing around my steak?"

"Rowwww!" Moishe said, rubbing up against Mike's ankle.

"Sorry, Big Guy. I'm not going to give you anything quite yet. Go over and see if Lonnie's a softer touch."

Michelle laughed. "Lonnie's a softer touch," she said. "He's been feeding them both little pieces of meat for a couple of minutes now."

"That's it, though," Lonnie said, pushing back his plate. "My steak is history."

"I still have some left, but you two aren't getting any," Mike said, "not until the last bite. Then I might reconsider if you stop bugging me now."

Hannah watched the two cats in amazement as they backed off, turned tail, and walked out of the kitchen.

"How did you *do* that?" she asked Mike.

"It was cop to cat. They understood that they couldn't sway me, so they gave up. It's my commanding manner."

"Right," Hannah said, almost believing it, but not quite.

"Did you have any luck finding out who Buddy really was?" Michelle asked Lonnie.

"Not yet, but we're working on it."

Hannah was silent. It was Doc's place to tell Mike he was posting Buddy's photo in the *Hospital News,* not hers.

"How about you, Hannah?" Mike asked her. "Any luck?"

"I don't know who he really was, either. Norman tried to find out online tonight."

Mike turned to Norman. "What did you find?"

"Basically . . . nothing. When I go back to the office, I'm going to go at it another way."

"What way is that?"

"I'm going to approach it from the jazz keyboard player angle. There's got to be some kind of organization Buddy might have joined. Or maybe there's a list of jazz keyboard players posted online somewhere."

"You'll let me know if you find anything?"

"Absolutely."

Hannah heard the sound before anyone else did. It was the scratching, scrabbling noise two cats make when they run at top speed across wall-to-wall carpeting. The sound was coming closer and she shouted out a warning. "Feet up, everybody. Quick!"

"Is it chase?" Mike asked, and Hannah knew he remembered the chase game he'd seen Cuddles and Moishe play at her condo.

"Yes."

"Put your legs up Lonnie," Mike ordered. "The cats are coming through, and they'll total out on your feet."

Lonnie didn't wait for a second invitation. He tucked his feet up on the rungs of his stool while Hannah and Michelle made a beeline for the counter and hopped up.

They hadn't been in position for more

than a second before the feline racing team of Swensen and Rhodes roared around the corner and careened into the kitchen.

"Whoa!" Lonnie exclaimed, rocking a bit on his stool as Moishe crashed into the table leg, skidded on three legs, recovered his balance, and raced off after the blur that was Cuddles.

"How fast do you think they were going?" Norman asked Mike.

"I don't know. Too bad I didn't bring the radar gun. Where are they now?"

"Anywhere they want to be," Hannah said with a laugh. "I think it's the den, but . . . feet up! Here they come again."

The two cats dashed into the kitchen for the second time, and there was a flying hurdle, a near-miss collision, several yowls, and then both cats rammed into the table leg closest to Mike. The table shook with the force of the blow and teetered on its legs. Mike reached out to grab his plate, but it was too late.

"No!" Mike yelped as his plate hit the floor and the steak slid off. And then, before any of the four of them could grasp what was happening, Moishe grabbed the steak in his mouth and tore off after Cuddles who was speeding toward the doorway.

There was a long moment of silence as

the scrabbling sound of cat claws digging into expensive carpeting faded into the distance. The cats were gone, and so was the remainder of Mike's steak.

They simply stared at each other for a moment, and then Norman broke the silence. "Do you think . . . ?" and his voice trailed off.

"Oh, yes," Hannah replied to his half-formed question. "I'm almost sure of it."

Lonnie nodded, looking a bit dazed. "They planned it, didn't they?"

"I believe they did," Michelle said with a grin. "When it didn't work the first time, they went back to regroup, and then they tried it again."

"Well, I'll be!" Mike said, just shaking his head. "Do you think I should go and try to get it back from them? I mean, I don't want it, but it's the principle of the thing."

"Cats don't understand principles," Hannah told him.

"Don't bother unless you've got some kitty handcuffs in your pocket," Norman advised.

"But where did they go?" Lonnie asked. "I don't hear a thing now."

"They're somewhere safe," Hannah answered him.

"Like under my bed, gnawing on that

steak bone," Norman added. "They won't come out until they're good and ready."

"But what should we do about it?" Mike asked.

"We should have dessert," Hannah answered him. "I'll put on a fresh pot of coffee, and Michelle can get out some of Norman's cookies. There's plenty since she made a double batch."

Mike looked upset. "So we're just going to let them get away with it?"

"Of course not," Hannah said, biting back a grin. "When they finish the steak and come out from under the bed, you can have a cop-to-cat talk with them."

# CHEESE AND GREEN CHILES BISCUITS
Preheat oven to 425 degrees F.,
rack in the middle position.

3 and 1/2 cups all purpose flour *(pack it down in the cup when you measure it)*

1 teaspoon salt

2 teaspoons cream of tartar *(this is important)*

1 teaspoon baking powder

1 teaspoon baking soda

1/2 cup salted softened butter *(1 stick, 4 ounces, 1/4 pound)*

1 cup shredded sharp cheddar cheese

1 can *(4 ounces)* diced green chiles, drained and patted dry with a paper towel *(I used Ortega Diced Green Chiles)*

2 large eggs, beaten *(just whip them up in a glass with a fork)*

1 cup sour cream *(8 ounces)*

1/2 cup whole milk

1/2 cup shredded cheddar cheese

FIRST STEP

Use a medium-size mixing bowl to combine the flour, salt, cream of tartar, baking powder, and baking soda. Stir them all up together. Cut in the salted butter just as you would for piecrust dough.

**Hannah's 1st Note: If you have a food**

processor, you can use it for the first step. Cut 1/2 cup COLD salted butter into 8 chunks. Layer them with the dry ingredients in the bowl of the food processor. Process with the steel blade until the mixture has the texture of cornmeal. Transfer the mixture to a medium-sized mixing bowl and proceed to the second step.

SECOND STEP
Stir in the shredded cheddar cheese and the drained, chopped green chiles. Mix everything up thoroughly.

Add the beaten eggs and the sour cream, in that order. Mix everything all up together.

Add the milk and stir until everything is thoroughly combined.

THIRD STEP
Drop the biscuits by Tablespoonfuls onto ungreased baking sheets, 12 biscuits to a sheet.

**Hannah's 2nd Note: I use an air-bake cookie sheet lined with parchment paper when I bake these. I measured the cookie sheet and it's 14 inches by 15 and 1/2 inches. It works perfectly for 12 large biscuits. If you want smaller biscuits, use 2 cookie sheets and make**

your biscuits smaller. If you have only one oven, bake one sheet on the upper rack and the other sheet on the lower rack, switching places halfway through the baking time.

Once the biscuits are on the baking sheet *(or sheets if you decided to use two)* you can wet your fingers with a little water and shape them if you like. *(I leave mine slightly irregular so everyone knows they're homemade.)*

Sprinkle the tops of the biscuits with shredded cheese.

Bake the biscuits at 425 degrees F. for 12 to14 minutes, or until they're golden brown on top. For 2 sheets of smaller biscuits, reduce the baking time to 10 to 12 minutes. They're done when they're golden brown on top.

Cool the biscuits for at least five minutes on the cookie sheet, and then remove them to a wire rack. Let them cool for at least another 2 minutes before you serve them. **(I place mine in a towel-lined basket so they stay warm.)**

Yield: Makes 12 large Cheese and Green Chiles Biscuits, or 18 to 24 smaller biscuits that are equally delicious.

**Hannah's 3rd Note: When I make these for Mike, he really likes them with**

diced Jalapenos instead of green chiles. He takes the leftovers home and eats them for breakfast. He says eating something spicy for breakfast really perks him up. He's the only man I know who carries around a bottle of "Slap Ya Mama" Cajun pepper sauce in his Winnetka County cruiser to sprinkle on his scrambled eggs when he goes out for breakfast.

Hannah's 4th Note: If there are any leftovers that Mike doesn't get, they're wonderful to use for sandwiches. Just split them in half lengthwise, slather them with mayonnaise, and put some sliced lunchmeat in the center. Cheese and Green Chiles Biscuits will make an ordinary sandwich into a special treat.

# CARROT SLAW

Preheat the oven to 325 degrees F.,
rack in the middle position.

**The Carrot Slaw Topping:**
1/2 cup chopped pecans
1 egg white
1/4 cup white *(granulated)* sugar
1/4 cup melted butter *(1/2 stick, 2 ounces, 1/8 pound)*

**Hannah's 1st Note: You'll start the Carrot Slaw topping first. It takes the most time, from 30 to 35 minutes, but 25 minutes of that is baking time. Once your pecan pieces are in the oven, you can start in on the slaw. *However,* if you know you'll be pressed for time, you can always buy candied pecans and chop them up to use for the topping.**

Spray a pie tin or an 8-inch square pan with Pam or another nonstick cooking spray. Sprinkle in the chopped pecans. Toast them at 325 degrees F. for 5 minutes.

While the pecans are toasting, beat the egg white with a whisk or a hand mixer until it's stiff but not dry. Fold in the sugar and then fold in the toasted pecan pieces when they come out of the oven.

Pour the melted butter in the bottom of your pan. Fold the pecan mixture into the melted butter with a wooden spoon or spatula.

Bake at 325 degrees F., uncovered, for 10 minutes. Stir.

Bake another 10 minutes. Stir.

Bake an additional 10 minutes. Stir.

Remove the pan from the oven and spread the contents out on wax paper.

**Hannah's 2nd Note: Careful! This is very hot!**

Let the pecan pieces cool for at least two minutes, and then separate them into small chunks with a wooden spoon or a wooden spatula. Leave them on the counter to cool completely. Your yummy topping is finished.

**The Slaw:**

2 cups frozen petite peas *(I used Green Giant Baby Sweet Peas)*

3 cups peeled and shredded carrots

1/4 cup finely chopped green onion *(You can use up to 2 inches of the stem)*

1/8 cup fresh parsley, finely chopped *(optional)*

1/8 teaspoon nutmeg *(freshly grated is best, of course)*

1/2 teaspoon salt

1/2 teaspoon ground black pepper *(Of*

*course freshly ground is best)*

**Hannah's 3rd Note: If you want to save time, buy the baby carrots that are already peeled and shred them in your food processor with the shredding blade. It's faster than doing it all by hand.**

Cook the frozen peas according to the package directions, BUT give them a minute or two less than it suggests on the package. Overcooked peas are not good in this slaw. Once the peas have been cooked, drain them quickly and place them in ice water to cool down.

Measure out 3 cups of shredded carrots, and place them in a large mixing bowl.

Sprinkle in the finely chopped green onions and the finely chopped parsley **(if you decided to use it).**

Add the nutmeg, salt and the pepper and mix it all up.

**Hannah's 4th Note: No, we didn't forget the peas that are chilling out in that bowl of ice water. We're just not quite ready for them yet.**

**The Dressing:**
1/4 cup white *(granulated)* sugar
1/2 cup mayonnaise *(I use Hellmann's —*

*it's called Best Foods west of the Rock-*
*ies — you can use any brand you like,*
*but don't use salad dressing!)*

1 Tablespoon cider vinegar *(I used cham-*
*pagne vinegar once, and it was great!*
*Just plain vinegar will also work.)*

Take out a smaller bowl or a quart measuring cup to hold your Carrot Slaw dressing.

Combine the sugar, mayonnaise, and
vinegar. Mix it with a rubber spatula or
whisk it until it's smooth.

**Hannah's 5th Note: That's it! You just
made the dressing. How simple is that?**

Pour the dressing you just made over the
salad in the large bowl. Toss it with your
fingers, or stir it with a spoon or spatula
until it's coated with the dressing.

At last! The peas! Drain the peas in a
strainer or colander and gently pat them
dry with paper towels.

Add the peas to the top of your bowl.
DON'T mix them in yet. Since the peas are
the most fragile ingredient, you won't mix
them in until you're ready to serve the Carrot Slaw.

Cover the bowl with plastic wrap and
refrigerate it until it's time to serve your
salad.

**Hannah's 6th Note: It's just fine to make this in the morning and leave it in the refrigerator all day until dinnertime. You may have to use a slotted spoon to remove it to the salad bowl so that it isn't too wet, but that's simple to do.**

When you're ready to serve, give the Carrot Slaw a final toss to mix in those fragile peas. *(They're a little extra work, but they make the salad juicy and give a little burst of flavor when you bite them.)*

Transfer the Carrot Slaw to a pretty salad bowl, and sprinkle the candied pecan pieces over the top.

**Hannah's 7th Note: If your family and guests like the candied pecan pieces on top, you may want to make double the amount next time you make them and keep half in a freezer bag so they're all ready to go.**

Yield: This salad will serve at least 4 people as a side dish unless Lonnie's included in your dinner party. He just loves Michelle's Carrot Slaw and I don't think he's just saying that because he loves Michelle.

# Chapter Twenty-Five

The church was crowded with men in suits, ladies dressed in their very best, and children who had been warned not to wiggle, chew gum, or otherwise call attention to themselves. The scent of the perfumes that the ladies were wearing had merged into one cloud of sweetness that made her want to sneeze.

But she couldn't sneeze. No one could know she was here in the choir loft, watching the spectacle that enfolded before her. No one could know that she just had to see him one last time before he was transformed into a married man with a family. Most of all, no one could know how desperately she wanted something to happen to stop the ceremony before he committed himself forever by saying *I do.*

There he was at the front of the church, looking unbelievably handsome in his groom's tuxedo. And his best friend, the cop, was standing next to him, acting as his best man. The organ music swelled and then broke into the triumphant strains of Mendelssohn's *Wedding March*. The bride was entering the church, and soon she'd be walking down the white-covered aisle to meet him. She was carrying a huge bouquet of lilacs. She could smell their scent all the way up here in the choir loft. They were *her* favorite flower, and that was just plain wrong. The dark-haired woman she saw below her couldn't be the bride. She was wearing a low-cut red sweater, a short black skirt, and boots with stiletto heels. This was wrong. *She* was the bride, not the woman who was walking up the aisle toward Norman. She had to do something to stop the wedding!

She screamed several times to get Norman's attention, but he didn't seem to hear her. In desperation, she began pounding her fists against the stained glass window that had suddenly appeared to separate the choir loft from the body of the church.

Row by row, the congregation turned to see her spread-eagled and pounding on the stained glass window. They looked horrified, but she couldn't help that. She had to stop the wedding. The false bride was going to take him away from her.

And then the cop was running up the stairs to tackle her and snap on cuffs. And now he was leading her away, pulling her forward. But she held back to look down at the false bride and listen as she opened her mouth to speak the words that would seal his fate forever.

"Noooooo!" she shouted again. "Nooooo!"

"Hannah? Wake up, Hannah! You must be dreaming. Are you all right?"

It was Michelle, and Hannah sat bolt upright in bed. "Dreaming," she repeated.

"Yes. I heard you thrashing around in here. And then you started moaning and crying. When I got to the doorway, you shouted, *Noooo!* like you were in terrible pain. That must have been a really awful nightmare!"

"Oh, it was," Hannah said, remembering Norman's wedding to Doctor Bev in full color, sound, and even smell.

Michelle walked over to sit on the side of the bed. "If you tell me about it, you probably won't dream it again when you go back to sleep. How about it?"

Hannah didn't say anything. She just shook her head. Perhaps Michelle was right, but she'd just have to take her chances. There was no way she was going to tell her

393

baby sister that she'd been dreaming the final scene of *The Graduate,* and she'd botched the ending by going off to jail instead of running away with the man she loved and jumping on a bus in her bridal dress.

It was difficult to get out of bed the next morning and that wasn't entirely the fault of the two cats who were sleeping on her chest. Hannah shooed them away, sat up in bed, and punched the alarm clock to shut it off. It was eight-thirty in the morning, but it was Sunday and she didn't have to go to work.

It was odd to see lights on in the house when she emerged from her bedroom. It was also nice to see lights on in the house when she emerged from her bedroom. Michelle was up and Hannah could smell the welcome scent of Swedish Plasma in the air. There was another scent too, and it smelled like cinnamon and sugar.

"Coffee?" she asked, hoping it was ready as she shuffled through the kitchen doorway.

"Coming right up. Sit down and I'll pour some for you."

Hannah sat. Gratefully. And then she glanced over at Michelle. Her youngest sister's cheeks were pink, her eyes were sparkling, and her hair was curling gently around her pretty face. Oh, to be young again! But Hannah knew she'd never looked as beautiful as Michelle did, even when she was young.

"You're scowling." Michelle set a mug of coffee directly in front of Hannah. "What's the matter?"

"I was trying to figure out how you can look so good in the morning when I feel so dragged out."

"Clean living. If you'd lay off the booze and drugs for a while, you'd probably start to look better." Michelle burst into peals of laughter. "You should see your face. You look absolutely dumbfounded. I'm kidding, okay? It's just a joke, Hannah."

"Don't joke with your elder in the morning or she may turn on you like a ravening beast."

"Nicely put," Michelle sat down and took a sip of her coffee, "but what's a ravening beast anyway?"

"It's too early for me to define a word. You'll have to wait until I can remember my name."

"Okay. Drink coffee. Get those brain cells dancing. I really want to know what it is."

Hannah took a big swallow of coffee. It was hot, and it was good. There was nothing like coffee on a cold spring morning that still felt like winter.

"More," Michelle said.

Hannah took another swallow. And then another. Caffeine was starting to work its magic on her tired brain.

"Name?" Michelle prodded her.

"Hannah."

"Middle name?"

"Louise."

"Last name?"

"Swensen."

"Occupation?"

"Cookies."

"Age?"

"I don't want to think about that."

"Weight?"

"Michelle! Cut that out!"

"Okay. Your brain seems to be working again now. What's a ravening beast?"

"Ravening comes from the Middle French word *raviner,* which means to rush or take by force. It was first used in the sixteenth century. Ravening means to possess the ability to devour greedily, or to prowl for prey. In other words, I'll crush you like a bug if you mess with me first thing in the morning."

"Forewarned is forearmed. What are you doing today? Or is it too early to ask?"

"I'm finishing my coffee so that I can stay awake and not drown in the shower. And then I'm going to get dressed and see if I can find something for breakfast."

"I've got that covered. I'll make another pot of coffee while you shower. And then we can taste the bran cookies I baked this morning."

"You baked this morning?" Hannah asked, and then she remembered smelling the sweet scent of cinnamon and sugar when she came into the kitchen.

"I was up early thinking about the cookies we promised to bake for Doc. And I had a brainstorm, so I got up and tried out a recipe."

"What kind of a brainstorm?"

"I'll tell you after you taste them. Now hurry up and take your shower."

Less than ten minutes later Hannah came back into the kitchen. She was dressed in clean jeans and a long-sleeved sweater. She was wearing her moccasin boots, the ones with the fringe on the sides, and Moishe and Cuddles were on her heels, one on the left and the other on the right, trying to capture the fringe as she walked.

"How about one of those cookies?" she asked, refilling her coffee mug and then sitting down at the kitchen table.

"Do you like bran?"

"Not particularly. I don't hate it, but I wouldn't choose it."

"Good."

"Why good?"

"Because if you really loved bran you might love the cookies even though they weren't that tasty. Let's see if you like these." Michelle walked over with a napkin containing two cookies.

Hannah took a bite and chewed. "Nice aftertaste," she said. "These are really good cookies, and I love the cinnamon and the raisins. They remind me of something, but I don't know what."

"Think back to your childhood," Michelle advised, "and try another bite."

"With pleasure." Hannah took another bite. Then she took another, bigger bite and the cookie was gone.

"Did you remember?"

"No." Hannah picked up a second cookie. "These are definitely winners, Michelle. I like these as much as I used to love . . ." She stopped and looked up at her sister in shock as the light dawned. "Grandma Ingrid's bran muffins?"

"That's right. I just made a couple of changes and baked her bran muffins as bran cookies."

"That's brilliant," Hannah said, and then she looked puzzled. "Where did you get her recipe?"

"It was in one of those shoe boxes on your bookshelf."

"Really? I didn't even know I had it!"

"It was in the third box I tried."

"Well, good for you! These are definitely great cookies, and Doc's going to absolutely love them!"

"Shall I pack them up so we can take them out to the hospital today?"

"Sure. We should do a little more snooping around out there anyway. If we talk to the right person, maybe we can learn something new."

The phone rang, and Hannah reached up, grabbed the wall phone over her head, and answered, "Hello?"

"Hello, dear," her mother's cheerful voice greeted her. "I'm here at the hospital and we wanted to know if you and Michelle would like to join us for Sunday brunch at the Inn."

Hannah thought about it for a nanosecond. Two bran cookies, no matter how tasty, did not a breakfast make. "We'd love to. Thanks for asking, Mother. But who's *we*?"

"Doc, Marlene, Vonnie, and me. I'm going to call Andrea, too. She said that Bill's going out to the station today, and she loves Sally's brunch."

"We *all* love Sally's brunch," Hannah said, and as she did so, visions of popovers swimming in butter and freshly made preserves danced through Hannah's head. They were followed by crisp strips of bacon that twirled like prima ballerinas, succulent sausages strutting their stuff, pancakes as light as a feather wheeling up like doves toward the sky, and homemade crullers rolling like wheels on a path to her plate.

"Bring your murder book," Delores reminded her. "Vonnie checked Buddy in, and she remembers something that might help you. And Marlene was with him part of the time in the hospital. She could have new information for us."

"There's Doc, too. He may know something new."

"He doesn't," Delores said.

Her mother answered so fast, Hannah frowned. "How do you know that?"

"If Doc knew something new, he would have told me. He doesn't have any secrets from me."

"Really?"

"No. Well . . . not unless it involves a patient. Then it's confidential. Meet us at ten-thirty in the lobby, dear. And do dress up a little. It *is* Sunday, you know."

# DOC'S BRAN-OATMEAL-RAISIN COOKIES

Preheat oven to 350 degrees F.,
rack in the middle position.

3/4 cup raisins *(either regular or golden, your choice)*

3/4 cup boiling water

1 cup white *(granulated)* sugar

1/2 cup brown sugar *(pack it down when you measure it)*

3/4 cup *(1 and 1/2 sticks, 6 ounces)* salted butter, softened to room temperature

2 large eggs

1/2 teaspoon salt

1 teaspoon baking soda

1 teaspoon ground cinnamon

1/4 teaspoon grated nutmeg *(freshly grated is best)*

1 teaspoon vanilla extract

2 cups all-purpose flour *(pack it down in the cup when you measure it)*

1 and 1/2 cups dry quick oatmeal *(I used Quaker Quick 1-Minute)*

2 cups bran flake cereal

Place 3/4 cup of raisins in a 2-cup Pyrex measuring cup or a small bowl that can tolerate boiling water without cracking.

Pour the 3/4 cup boiling water over the

raisins in the cup. Stir a bit with a fork so they don't stick together, and then leave them, uncovered, on the counter to plump up.

Prepare your cookie sheets by spraying them with Pam or another nonstick cooking spray, or lining them with parchment paper that you also spray with Pam or another nonstick cooking spray.

**Hannah's 1st Note: This cookie dough is a lot easier to make if you use an electric mixer.**

Place the cup of white sugar in the bottom of a mixing bowl. Add the half-cup of brown sugar. Mix them together until they're a uniform color.

Place the softened butter in the mixer bowl and beat it together with the sugars until the mixture is nice and fluffy.

Mix in the eggs, one at a time, beating after each addition.

Add the salt, baking soda, cinnamon, nutmeg and vanilla extract. Beat until the mixture is smooth and well incorporated.

On LOW speed, add the flour, one-half cup at a time, beating after each addition. Continue to beat until everything is well blended.

Drain the raisins by dumping them in a strainer. Throw away any liquid that remains, then gently pat the raisins dry with a paper towel.

With the mixer running on LOW speed, add the raisins to the cookie dough.

With the mixer remaining on LOW speed, add the dry oatmeal in half-cup increments, mixing after each increment.

Turn the mixer OFF, and let the dough rest while you prepare the bran flakes.

Measure 2 cups of bran flake cereal and place them in a 1-quart freezer bag. Roll the bag up from the bottom, getting out as much air as possible, and then seal it with the bran flakes inside.

Squeeze the bran flakes with your fingers, crushing them inside the bag. Place the bag on the counter and squash the bran flakes with your hands. Once they're in fairly small pieces, take the bag over to the mixer.

Turn the mixer on LOW speed. Open the bag and add the crushed bran flakes to your cookie dough, mixing until they're well incorporated.

Turn off the mixer, scrape down the sides of the bowl with a rubber spatula, and give the bowl a final stir by hand.

Drop the dough by rounded Tablespoonfuls *(use a Tablespoon from your silverware drawer, not one you'd use for measuring ingredients)* onto your prepared cookie sheet. There should be 12 cookie dough mounds on every standard-size cookie sheet.

**Hannah's 2nd Note: Lisa and I use a level 2-Tablespoon scooper to form these cookies down at The Cookie Jar.**

Bake Doc's Bran-Oatmeal-Raisin Cookies at 350 degrees F. for 13 to 15 minutes, or until golden brown on top.

Remove the cookies from the oven, and let them cool on the cookie sheets for 2 minutes. Then remove them to a wire rack to cool completely.

Yield: 2 to 3 dozen delicious cookies, depending on cookie size.

**Hannah's 3rd Note: Doc had to warn the Lake Eden Memorial Hospital cooks not to let the patients have more than two cookies. Since they contain bran and bran is an aid to the digestive system, patients who eat a lot of these cookies could be spending a lot of time in the little room with the porcelain fixtures.**

# CHAPTER TWENTY-SIX

"I hate pantyhose!"

Michelle looked over at Hannah and laughed. "They're a necessary evil. And they *do* keep your legs warm in the winter."

"So do long woolen socks," Hannah grumbled, but she was smiling as she got out of her cookie truck in the parking lot of the Lake Eden Inn. They were being treated to Sally's brunch and that, by itself, was a reason to embrace the whole dress-up-and-wear-pantyhose thing.

"How about a ride, ladies?" Sally's husband, Dick, asked them as he pulled up behind Hannah's cookie truck.

"Thanks, Dick. We'll take it," Hannah said, glancing down at Michelle's dress flats. "I forgot to drop her off at the door and she'll never make it up the hill in those."

"But you'd make it up the hill," Michelle said, eyeing Hannah's moose-hide boots. "We should drop by the mall this afternoon and get you a pair of dress shoes."

"No way! I never wear anything I can't run in. And I can't run in dress shoes. Unless I'm locked in my condo, it's boots, tennis shoes, and moccasins for me."

Dick laughed. "Knowing you, you'd probably wear boots or tennis shoes to your own wedding."

Hannah had an uncomfortable feeling as she got into his tram. The dream she'd had early this morning was still with her, but she knew she had to make light of it in front of Dick. He was a kind man and he'd never knowingly hurt her feelings. "Boots to my own wedding? Really Dick! I'd never do that!"

"Well, that's a surprise." Dick looked down at her scuffed, secondhand moosehide boots and smiled as he climbed into the driver's seat.

"But tennis shoes to my own wedding? I might do that. They'd be a lot more comfortable than satin shoes. And most wedding gowns are so long, nobody can see the bride's feet anyway."

Luckily, Sally was mixing up a pitcher of mimosas at the bar. "Would you like a mimosa?" she asked.

"No thanks. I'm drinking plain orange

juice today. Do you have a minute, Sally?"

"Sure." Sally motioned for one of the waitresses to pick up the pitcher, and then she came out from behind the bar to slide onto the stool next to Hannah's. "What gives?"

"I've got another mystery on my hands. The night you and Dick booked Cinnamon Roll Six at Club Nineteen, Buddy Neiman was seen arguing with a dark-haired woman."

"And she figures into his murder somehow?"

"I don't know. She *could* figure in, and that means I have to find out who she was. Did you or Dick happen to see a dark-haired woman with Buddy that night?"

Sally shut her eyes for a moment, and then she shook her head. "Not that I recall. Can you describe her?"

"Red sweater, black skirt, high-heeled boots, and a lot of makeup. She was sitting near the stage. I have a picture, but it's not very good."

"That's the understatement of the year!" Sally said as she glanced down at the photo Hannah placed on the bar. "Her own mother couldn't recognize her. But I did see the woman you described. She was sitting near the stage watching the show. I thought she was . . . never mind." Sally looked down at the picture again. "What is this glitter on her wrist?"

"It's a bracelet with silver snowflakes. It was sold at . . ."

"*That's* where I saw her before!" Sally interrupted. "When Norman brought her out here to dinner the first time, I knew I'd seen her somewhere. But she was dressed so differently then, and I didn't realize it was her until now." Sally tapped the photo with her finger. "That's Doctor Bev!"

There it was! The confirmation of all her suspicions! Hannah drew a deep breath and asked, "Are you sure?"

"Yes, I'm sure. I know because I recognized her bracelet. She wore it out here the first time they came to dinner with Carrie and Earl."

"Doctor Bev was the woman you saw at Club Nineteen?" Hannah asked again, just to be sure.

"Yes, she was. Of course she looked a lot different then, and that's probably why I didn't put it all together until you showed me that photo. It's like Doctor Jekyll and Mr. Hyde. Here in Lake Eden she's Miss Goody Two Shoes. But that night at Club Nineteen, she was the Woman in Red."

"Is it possible that you could be mistaken?"

Sally thought about it for a moment and then she shook her head. "No. It was Doctor Bev. I'm ninety-nine point nine percent positive of that!"

Michelle was eating an omelet from the special order breakfast bar when Hannah got back to their table. To Hannah's way of thinking, ordering an omelet at one of Sally's breakfast buffets was a waste. Not that they weren't good. They were. It was just that anybody could make an omelet for breakfast, but it was unlikely that you'd make Swedish pancakes, blintzes, maple sugar glazed ham, and crullers with three different glazes for your own breakfast at home.

Hannah was having a little of all of the above except the omelet. The old adage, *Her eyes were bigger than her stomach* always came into play when she attended a buffet. She wanted to taste everything, and her plate became loaded with so many different types of food, that it ended up being a crowded palette of foods that failed to retain their individual identity.

"Vonnie?" Delores spoke to Doc Knight's secretary. "Tell Hannah what you told me about the night of the accident."

"It's probably nothing, but I thought it was a little unusual," Vonnie began, putting down her fork. "When Buddy Neiman came up with his paperwork, I checked through it to make sure that nothing was missing. He'd filled out everything, but I noticed that he had the zip code for Minneapolis wrong. I asked him about it and he looked a little embarrassed. He said he should have written five-five-four-oh-three, but he kept forgetting the zip code. I crossed it out when he gave me the correct one."

Hannah nodded. So far there wasn't anything interesting in what Vonnie had told her.

"Well, I got to thinking about his admission form, so I pulled it today to take another look at it. The incorrect zip code Buddy put on his form wasn't anywhere near Minneapolis. I looked it up and it was a zip code from Seattle."

Seattle again. Hannah gave a little shake of her head. Seattle just kept cropping up in her investigation.

"That's not really that unusual," Doc said, before Hannah could respond. "He was probably in shock due to his injury and the trauma of the accident, and an old zip code popped into his head."

Delores gave a little laugh. "I did something similar to that once. I was filling out the insurance forms after your dad died, and I put the phone number I had when I was in high school."

"Lori." Doc reached out to cover her hand with his. "That was shock, too. You'd just lost your husband, and you wanted to go back to happier times."

Delores gave him a poignant smile. "You're right. You always understand."

"I'm just trying to get onto your good side. I hate to travel alone and I want you to ride down to the lab with me when I take in those DNA samples."

Delores laughed and the poignant moment dissipated. "Why didn't you just come out and ask me? I'd love to go with you."

"I'm going to get another potato pancake," Vonnie announced, standing up.

"I'll go with you," Andrea said, pushing back her chair. "I want more eggs Benedict. That's something I never get unless I'm out somewhere for breakfast."

They ate in silence for another couple of minutes, and then Hannah pushed back her chair. She'd tasted everything on her plate, and now it was time for dessert. "I'm going to get one of Sally's fresh crullers."

"Wait up, Hannah." Marlene stood up.

"I'll go with you. I want to get another waffle."

Hannah glanced over at Marlene's plate. There was a half-finished waffle on it, but she didn't point that out. Perhaps Marlene wanted to tell her something in private that she didn't want the rest of the group to hear.

There was a line at the buffet table. The people ahead of them were deep in their own conversation and there was no one behind them. Hannah turned to Marlene. "What is it?" she asked.

"What is what?"

"You still had half a waffle on your plate. I figured you just wanted the chance to talk to me alone."

"That must be why you're such a good detective," Marlene said, smiling at Hannah. "I don't know if this is important, but something's bothering me about Ben."

"What's that?"

"I know he got that plum internship in Los Angeles and everything, and I can't fault him for leaving. Facial reconstruction is his specialty, you know. But before you got here, Doc said he was glad that Ben would be able to spend some time with his family. And Ben told me he didn't *have* any family. We stopped for a pizza after work one night, and we got a pitcher of beer to go with our pizza. I don't like beer very much, so Ben drank most of it. And that was when he told me that his parents died a couple of years ago, and now that his older brother was dead, he didn't have any family."

"But Doc said Ben told him he'd get a chance to see his family while he was in California?"

"I know. Maybe Ben was talking about an uncle, or cousins, or something like that. Or maybe he felt he had to give Doc an excuse for leaving so suddenly. There's also the possibility that Doc got it wrong. It might have been Ben's friends he was talking about, not his family. It just struck me as inconsistent, that's all. And things that are inconsistent bother me."

"Did you mention this to Ben?"

"No, and I won't. He probably doesn't even remember he told me that he didn't have any family. He was pretty buzzed that night. And maybe he just fed me a line to get my sympathy and make me feel closer to him. If that was his intention, it worked."

"Oh," Hannah said, catching the implication and settling for a comment that was perfectly noncommittal.

"It was just one of those things that seemed right at the time. And then later, I found myself wishing it had never happened. Do you know what I mean?"

"Yes, I do."

"I don't know why I felt I should tell you all this. It probably doesn't mean anything at all. But your mother said we should tell you anything out of the ordinary that we noticed at the hospital, and this seemed to fit into that category."

"What's next?" Michelle asked, as they got out of the tram next to Hannah's cookie truck and Andrea's Volvo.

"Doctor Bev," Hannah said, taking her keys out of her saddlebag purse.

Andrea and Michelle turned to look at Hannah in shock. "Did you just say what I thought you said?" Andrea asked.

"Yes. I have to question Doctor Bev and I know she'll be at Claire's dress shop at three o'clock. Norman said she was driving back from the Cities for a wedding dress fitting."

Andrea put her hands over her eyes and gave a little moan. "So you're going to question Doctor Bev in her wedding dress?"

"Yes, as long as Claire agrees." Hannah opened the door to her cookie truck and climbed up into the driver's seat. "You're going with me, aren't you, Michelle?"

"I think I'd better be there. Claire might

need help to break up the fight."

"What fight?"

"The fight you're bound to have if you see Doctor Bev in her wedding dress."

"There won't be any fight. We're just going to have a nice, civilized question and answer session," Hannah gave a little smile that belied her words. "Or perhaps I should say I'm planning to grill her within an inch of her life! Would you like to come along, Andrea?"

"No way!" Andrea said emphatically. And then she gave a little sigh. "I'm going to make a quick stop at the mall, and then I'm going home to wait for you to call me. I'll be a wreck for the rest of the day if I'm not the first to know what happened!"

# CHAPTER TWENTY-SEVEN

"So what are we going to do?" Michelle asked as they parked in the back of The Cookie Jar.

"I'm not sure, but we've got . . ." Hannah glanced at her watch. ". . . eight minutes to figure it out. The first thing we have to do is tell Claire what's happening."

"You're right. And after we do that, I think you should take three or four outfits into a dressing room and try them on."

"But I don't *need* a new outfit."

"I know that, but if you were Doctor Bev and you saw Hannah Swensen and her sister Michelle waiting for you in Claire's dress shop, would you go in?"

"Probably not. I'd wait until they left."

"Exactly! So the two of us will be in a dressing room when Doctor Bev walks in."

"And she won't know we're there," Hannah picked up the idea and ran with it. "We'll wait until she tries on her dress and then I'll come out."

"Not me?"

"No, you stay in the dressing room and take notes for me. I'll give you my murder book. We need a record of exactly what she says."

"I can do that. Anything else?"

"Yes. I'm going to ask Claire to keep her with her back to our dressing room. That way you can peek out and let me know when she's dressed. Then I'll step out and confront her."

*"Confront?"*

"Sorry. I meant *greet.* I'll step out and greet her. And then I'll start questioning her about Seattle and Buddy Neiman. I might even show her the copy of the photo Norman printed for me. Sally's positive it's her."

"Do you think she'll admit that she was there at Club Nineteen that night?"

"Probably not. She'll try to tell me it's not her, and she's never been to Club Nineteen in her life. I'm looking forward to that part of it." Hannah gave another hard-edged smile. "She's going to get really nervous before I'm through with her."

"All you have to do is smile at her like that and she's going to get nervous. *I'm* getting nervous and I haven't even done anything wrong!"

"It's called intimidation. Mike taught me that smile."

"Well it's a good one. Let's go, Hannah." Michelle got out of the cookie truck. "We've only got a couple of minutes to talk to Claire and tell her what we're doing. Let's get in there in case Doctor Bev is early."

Of course Doctor Bev wasn't early. She was five minutes late. And that gave Michelle and Hannah plenty of time to explain to Claire exactly what they were doing.

"Here," Claire said, thrusting four outfits into Hannah's arms. "Keep the door to the dressing room closed. It'll be easier if I cue you. Get into one of these now and stay put until I ask you how you like the selections I've made for you. And then come out."

Hannah sat down on the bench in the dressing room while Michelle took up a cross-legged position on the floor. "You'd better get one of those outfits on," Michelle said.

"I guess," Hannah said, hanging her parka on a hook, divesting herself of the clothes she'd worn to the brunch, and slipping one of the outfits Claire had chosen for her over her head.

"Nice color," Michelle commented, eyeing the rich turquoise. "I like the fact it's a pantsuit and you can wear it with dress flats."

"I don't have any dress flats."

"We'll get some." Michelle got up to zip the tunic top of Hannah's outfit. "It looks good on you, Hannah.

"Of course it does. Claire chose it for me. If I ever get rich, I'm going to hire Claire to be my personal fashion consultant."

"I wonder if Doc will like the cookies I made," Michelle said. "I wanted to give him samples right away, but it seemed wrong to take them in to brunch."

"We'll take some out to the hospital in the morning. Mother said they'd be there early, and they can have a couple for breakfast."

"Just like we did this morning, before we found out we were going to brunch."

"Right."

Claire gave a little knock on the dressing room door. "Here she comes. She's just getting out of her car. I can hardly wait to see her face when she realizes that you're here. This is going to be fun!"

"Do you get the feeling that Claire doesn't like her either?" Michelle asked when Claire had left.

"I know for a fact that Claire doesn't like her. She told me that she thought Doctor

Bev was a phony from the word go. She said it was probably uncharitable, and unchristian, and all the other bad un-things, but she never liked Doctor Bev and she never would. And then she said she had half a notion to put a stop to the wedding."

"How?"

"She said that when Reverend Bob gets to the part, *If any person can show just cause why they may not be joined together, let them speak now or forever hold their peace,* she wants to stand up and tell Norman he shouldn't marry Doctor Bev."

"Claire wouldn't actually do that, would she?"

"I don't know. Probably not, but it's good to know that she feels the same way we do."

The two sisters fell silent as they heard voices. Claire was greeting Doctor Bev, and Doctor Bev was being her sweet, nice, fake self. At least that's the way Hannah thought of her now. *Sweet by day, strumpet by night,* Hannah thought, *and unless I'm completely mistaken, Norman isn't even the strumpee!* She could hardly wait to see what Doctor Bev had to say for herself.

"Are you excited about the wedding?" Claire asked, and Hannah tried not to grit her teeth.

"Oh, yes! It'll be wonderful to have all our

friends there. I do hope my mother can make it, but Diana's been down with the flu. It's the reason I drove to Minneapolis for the weekend. The poor baby was still running a fever when I left this morning."

*And just how would you know that since you didn't even bother to see her?* Hannah thought exchanging glances with Michelle. Doctor Bev was an accomplished liar. Perhaps it was because she got so much practice lying to everyone in Lake Eden.

"I'm sorry your daughter's sick," Claire said, and Hannah heard a garment bag unzip. "Just let me put this dress over your head and we'll check to make sure the alterations are done correctly."

"Oh, I'm sure they are if *you* did them, Claire," Doctor Bev said sweetly. "I just hope Norman likes this dress. I know it's bad luck for the groom to see the bridal dress before the wedding, but I'd feel more confident if he had come here with me when I chose it."

"It's a beautiful color," Claire said. "Ice blue looks lovely on you."

"Thank you. Blue is my favorite color."

*Wrong,* Hannah thought frowning deeply. *Beige is your favorite color. That's what you wrote on the Rhodes Dental Clinic website. If you're going to lie about everything, you'd bet-*

*ter keep your lies straight!*

There was the sound of another zipper. Claire must be zipping up the back of Doctor Bev's dress. Hannah stood up, raring to go. The liar was in the box, and it was time for the turquoise-clad detective to interrogate her.

"Just step out and we'll take a peek in the mirror," Claire said, and Hannah knew she was about to position Doctor Bev in front of the three-way mirror in the back of the *Beau Monde* Dress Shop.

"Showtime!" Hannah mouthed.

"Almost," Michelle mouthed back as she flipped to a blank page in Hannah's steno pad and picked up the pen.

"Are you ready in there, dear?" Claire called out. "I hope you like the selections I made for you."

"They're great," Hannah said, marching out the door and straight for the ice blue vision in the mirror. "Well hello, Doctor Bev. Fancy meeting you here."

If ever a woman looked as if she'd just swallowed a cow, it was Doctor Bev. She gaped at Hannah as if she couldn't believe her own eyes. "What are *you* doing here?" she asked in a tone that was decidedly unsweet.

"Why I'm looking for an outfit to wear to

your wedding. That is, if your wedding is still on."

"Of course it's on! What do you mean?"

*Once you get them rattled, you've got to keep them rattled,* Hannah's mind repeated the advice Mike had once given her about conducting interrogations. "I thought you might be too busy to get married, since your daughter's so sick. Or perhaps she's not sick at all. Perhaps you're too busy because you're spending time at Club Nineteen."

"*What* are you talking about? You're crazy, Hannah. I don't know any place called Club Nineteen. I've never heard of it."

"Just like you've never heard of the tight red sweater and high-heeled boots you wore when you went there on the second Saturday in February?" Hannah whipped the photo out of her folder and handed it to Doctor Bev. "There you are with Buddy Neiman, but that's not his real name. Of course you knew that, didn't you? And you knew he was from Seattle because both of you were there at the same time!"

Doctor Bev glanced down at the photo and her face turned a bit paler. She swallowed hard, and then she raised her eyes to Hannah again. "This isn't me. This isn't anybody I know. And it's ridiculous to think I knew Buddy Neiman or whatever his

424

name was."

"Is it? When I passed by with Buddy at the hospital, you were pretty quick to step behind Norman so that Buddy didn't see you."

"You're imagining things."

"I thought I was for a while. But now I know there's a connection. Can you look me straight in the eye and swear you didn't know Buddy in Seattle?"

"Certainly!" Doctor Bev faced Hannah squarely. "I didn't know Buddy in Seattle. I might have passed him on the street, but even that's doubtful. There are over six hundred thousand people in Seattle. Any *intelligent* person should realize that I couldn't possibly have known *all* of them."

"But I'm not concerned with all of them. I'm only concerned with one of them. What was his name back then? You knew it."

"This conversation is absurd. I'm leaving!"

"Not in that dress, you're not!" Hannah warned her. Then she turned to Claire. "Has she paid for it?"

"Not yet."

Doctor Bev shot Hannah a scathing look, and then she turned back to Claire. "Just put it on my bill, please."

Hannah noticed that Doctor Bev's hands

were shaking slightly. This was the time to really put her on the defensive. *Once a subject begins to crack, all you have to do is widen the crack,* Mike's words echoed in her mind. "Just tell me Buddy's real name and you can go."

"How should *I* know?"

"You know because you said you did," Hannah stated, "on the second Saturday in February when you argued with him in the parking lot at Club Nineteen. You said, *I'd know you anywhere.*"

"How do you know *that?*"

"Someone overheard you. And after you said, *I'd know you anywhere,* Buddy said, *You got the wrong guy, lady. Leave me alone! I'm not the guy you think I am!* And you shouted, *Yes you are! I know you are!* And then you slapped him and walked away."

"That's . . . that's . . . ridiculous! You made that whole thing up because you're jealous that I'm marrying Norman!"

"No, I didn't make it up. I got it from a waitress at Club Nineteen who just happened to be out in the parking lot taking a break when you were there arguing with Buddy."

"I told you before. I don't like jazz, I've never been to Club Nineteen, and I don't own a red sweater, a black leather skirt, or a pair of high-heeled boots. And I've *never* slapped anyone in my life!"

"A black leather skirt? It's interesting you should mention that. I didn't say anything about a black leather skirt. Since you knew without me telling you, I'd say that proves you were there."

Doctor Bev grabbed her purse, pulled out a credit card, and tossed it on a chair. "There! Now I've paid for the dress and I'm out of here!"

Michelle emerged from the dressing room just as the front door slammed behind Doctor Bev. "Uh-oh," she said glancing at the coat rack by the front door. "Doctor Bev stormed out of here in such a hurry, she forgot her coat."

"That's okay," Hannah told her. "She's hot enough under the collar without it."

"Well, I'll be!" Claire walked over to pick up the credit card. "You nailed her, Hannah. And you did it in front of me. Thank you!"

"Why are you thanking me?"

"Because this has got to be the most fun I've ever had collecting a bill."

# CHAPTER TWENTY-EIGHT

Hannah's eyes burned from lack of sleep when her alarm went off the next morning. It was five o'clock, and she'd tossed and turned most of the night, thinking about Buddy Neiman's murder case. At one in the morning, she'd been sure that there was something she was missing, so she'd padded out to the living room, retrieved her steno pad, and gone over every note she'd taken. There was a Seattle connection. She was sure of that now, despite Doctor Bev's initial attempt to convince her that she'd never encountered Buddy in Seattle, a city of six hundred thousand.

At two in the morning, Hannah had gone back to bed, but her mind wouldn't sleep. She kept going over the clues, one at a time, trying to decide if Doctor Bev could be the killer. She'd slapped Buddy at Club Nineteen, and Shelby, the waitress, had told them that Buddy still had a red mark on his face when she saw him at least fifteen minutes later. Slapping was an act of physical aggression. It was clear that Doctor Bev wasn't shy about confronting Buddy and using force when she didn't get whatever it was she wanted. The red mark on Buddy's face proved that she'd delivered a forceful slap. But what if just slapping Buddy hadn't been enough for her. What if Doctor Bev had initiated an even more violent encounter, an encounter that ended with surgical scissors thrust into Buddy's chest?

Perhaps she'd slept for a while. Hannah had no way of knowing. But she did know that she was wide awake at four in the morning, wondering where Doctor Bev had gone when she'd fled Claire's dress shop in her bridal finery. She wasn't at her own apartment and she wasn't at Norman's house. Hannah knew that for a fact because when she'd called Andrea to tell her about the confrontation, Andrea had driven around town looking for Doctor Bev's car. It had vanished. She was no longer in Lake Eden and that, to Hannah's way of thinking, was also suspicious.

And now it was five minutes past five. She could smell the coffee, and even though it was on an automatic timer, she suspected that Michelle was already up.

It was a struggle to get out of bed, but Hannah made it. It was also a struggle to put the correct arm in the correct sleeve of her robe. After three attempts, she triumphed.

One glance into the guest room as she passed by told her she was right. The bed was neatly made. Unless Michelle had fallen asleep on the living room couch last night, she was up and dressed, ready to go to the hospital with Hannah.

"Here," Michelle said, taking Hannah's arm as she entered the kitchen and guiding her into a chair. "Drink your coffee. I heard you get up and I poured you a mug. It's not too hot. I put a coffee ice cube in it."

"Thanks." Hannah gulped down the coffee with a speed born of desperation. If there was any coffee left this morning, she'd make more coffee ice cubes. Leftover coffee went into an old-fashioned ice cube tray in her freezer. One coffee ice cube would cool down a large mug of coffee in a hurry without diluting it.

"Now shower and get dressed," Michelle ordered, but she smiled as she gave her command. "We're meeting Mike for breakfast at The Corner Tavern in thirty minutes."

"Mike called here?"

"No, I called Mike. Somebody's got to

tell Norman that Doctor Bev lied about knowing Buddy Neiman, and it would be awkward if you had to do it. As a cop and as Norman's best friend, Mike's the logical choice. And since Doctor Bev wasn't at Norman's last night, and she wasn't at her apartment either, she must have used the excuse that Diana was sick and driven back to the Cities. I think Norman ought to know that Diana's just fine and it's just another one of Bev's lies."

Hannah nodded. Her brain was beginning to work, and what Michelle said made sense. "Okay. You're absolutely right. Mike has to be in the loop at this point." She pushed back her chair. "Will you pour me another mug of coffee, please? I'm going to shower and dress, and I'll be back here to gulp it down in less than ten minutes."

The Corner Tavern was crowded when they walked in, but Mike had already snagged a table in the back room. Hannah sat across from him, directly in front of a planter on top of the room divider that was filled with bright green plastic ivy. She seemed to remember reading somewhere that placing something red next to something green made the red less intense. With the green ivy directly in back of her head, perhaps

Mike wouldn't notice her red, scratchy, didn't-sleep-a-wink eyes.

"Nice job, Hannah," Mike said, handing the steno book back to her. "Of course you shouldn't have handled it yourself. You know that, don't you?"

"I know." Hannah did her best to look contrite. This was difficult because she felt like smiling at Mike's praise.

"You don't contact her again. Okay?"

"Okay," Hannah agreed quickly. "Are *you* going to contact her and follow up?"

"You bet I am! It's pretty clear she knows Buddy Neiman's real name, and I need to have it."

"But will she tell you?" Michelle asked. "She wasn't exactly what I'd call forthcoming. Hannah had to trick her to get her to admit she was at Club Nineteen that night."

"She'll tell me."

There was a hard glint in Mike's eyes that told Hannah he'd get the information he wanted from Doctor Bev. "Do you think she killed Buddy? It's pretty clear she had some kind of previous relationship with him."

"I agree. She's my number one suspect right now, and I'm going to haul her in for questioning."

"But what if she's left town?" Michelle

asked. "She was so upset after Hannah questioned her, she left Claire's dress shop without her coat."

Hannah was impressed with how innocent Michelle looked, considering the fact that Andrea had driven around looking for Doctor Bev's car and reported back to them.

"Don't worry. I'll find her. And after I do, I'll have a talk with Norman. She's probably fed him a pack of lies, and I need to straighten him out about that and everything else. Norman's a reasonable guy. He'll listen to me."

"Thanks, Mike," Hannah said. She'd expected no less. Although Mike had dated Doctor Bev before her recent engagement to Norman, he was a cop. There was no way any tender feelings he might still harbor for her would affect his ability to put Bev through the wringer.

"These are wonderful, Michelle!" Delores beamed at her youngest daughter. They were sitting in Doc Knight's office, and Michelle had just given her mother a box of the bran cookies she'd made.

"Do you think Doc will like them?"

"I know he will. He likes bran a lot better than I do. He eats a big bowl of bran flakes every morning for breakfast. Are you sure these have bran in them?"

"I *know* they do. I measured out the bran flakes myself."

"Well, all I can say is they're *very* good. And I haven't liked bran since Grandma Ingrid made those wonderful . . ." Delores stopped speaking, and Hannah watched the light dawn on her face. "They're Grandma Ingrid's Bran Muffins!"

"You got it!" Hannah said, giving her the high sign. "I had the recipe and I didn't even know it. Michelle found it and baked it in cookie form."

"I'll give one to Doc the moment he gets back here," Delores said, putting the cover on the cookie tin. "It'll cheer him up."

"What's wrong with Doc?" Hannah asked.

"It's just this whole intern thing. He's going to have to interview candidates again, and that takes time. He'd much rather spend that time with his patients. And then he'll have to train the new intern he chooses. Of course Marlene will help. Thank goodness she's staying. It's just that it's all so sudden. When the clinic called Ben, they told him they needed him to start next week. It's just a pity that they gave him such short notice, and he had to turn around and give Doc such short notice."

*Short notice.* The words repeated themselves several times in Hannah's mind. Short notice was what Lee complained about when Buddy gave notice right after his argument with the dark-haired woman they now knew was Doctor Bev. If Buddy had trusted his instincts and left right away instead of giving Lee the time to find his replacement, he'd probably be alive today. But that wasn't the situation with Ben. He had to leave Lake Eden right away because he took another job.

"What's the matter, dear?" Delores asked.

"I don't know. Something just struck me. You said something about Ben's new internship, that the clinic had given him such short notice and that's why he had to give Doc such short notice. Did Doc talk to the clinic to see why there was such a rush?"

"No, dear. Ben talked to them. They called him directly."

"Did they know he was working here?"

"Of course. Ben told Doc they asked for a recommendation, and Doc wrote one and gave it to him. Ben faxed it to the clinic."

"So Doc has never spoken to the doctors at the clinic. Is that right?"

"That's right." Delores began to frown. "I see where you're going with this. It *is* a little odd that the doctors at the clinic didn't speak to Doc directly. It would have been the courteous thing to do. I think we should call the clinic."

"Do you want to do it, or shall I?" Hannah asked.

"I will. I'll say I'm Doc's secretary. What was the name of that clinic again?"

"Rolling Hills Vista Clinic," Michelle said promptly. "I remembered it because I thought it sounded fake."

Five minutes later, they had their answers. Hannah's head was reeling and she knew that Michelle and their mother felt the same way. There was a Rolling Hills Vista Clinic and it was a leader in the field of facial reconstruction. They did have several interns at the clinic, but none of them had left recently. There were no vacancies for interns, and they'd never heard of Doctor Ben Matson.

"So what does this mean?" Delores asked, "other than the fact Ben lied to us."

"It means he wants to get out of Dodge for some reason," Hannah speculated.

Michelle looked puzzled. "Get out of *Dodge?*"

"Dodge City, Kansas. That phrase comes from the Old West. Dodge City became a law-abiding town when Marshall Dillon took over, and all the criminals had to get out of Dodge."

"How do you know that?"

"Lisa told me. Herb loves to watch re-runs of *Gunsmoke* while she's fixing supper. That's where she heard it. Dillon loves *Gunsmoke,* too. He gives a little woof every time he hears his name."

"That's cute," Delores said. "Doc and I watch *M\*A\*S\*H.* He says it relaxes him. But let's get back to business. Why would Ben want to get away from Lake Eden?"

Hannah shrugged. "I don't know, but I think we'd better find out. Maybe there's a clue somewhere in his background. Can you get his personnel file?"

"That's easy." Delores swiveled in her chair and switched on the computer. "All the employee records are accessible from Doc's computer. I'll pull it up."

Hannah and Michelle waited as Delores located and pulled up the file. "That's interesting," she said.

"What's interesting?" Hannah asked her.

"Ben's from Seattle."

"Seattle *again?!*" Hannah was dumbstruck. There were just too many people from Seattle. It was like a Washington State invasion in their own little town! "That settles it!" she said.

"Settles what?" Michelle asked.

Hannah was at a loss to explain. Her mind

was churning too fast. It was all about opportunity, and coincidence that might not be coincidence, and things they had yet to discover. The key to Buddy Neiman's murder was missing, but there might be a place they could find it.

"Settles what, dear?" Delores asked, repeating Michelle's question.

"It settles what we're going to do next. Ben's working all day today, right?"

"I believe so. At least that's the way the schedule stood yesterday. Let me check to see if there are any changes."

Hannah waited impatiently as her mother pulled up another file. It seemed to take forever, but at last Delores nodded.

"Ben's scheduled for a twelve-hour shift from eight this morning until eight tonight. Then Marlene comes on. She works until eight tomorrow morning."

"Great. Do you know where Ben lives?"

Delores looked puzzled. "Of course I do. Ben lives here in the intern quarters. There are two one-bedroom apartments built at the end of the middle corridor. Ben lives in the one to the right, facing the lake. Marlene lives in the one on the left, facing the pine grove. They're lovely little apartments. Marlene showed me hers."

"Okay. We're all set." Hannah got up from

her chair. "Let's go, Michelle."

"Sit!" Delores said, motioning her back down in her chair. "You're not going anywhere until you tell me *where* you're going!"

Hannah sat back down. She knew adamant when she heard it. "We're going to break into Ben's apartment. And then we're going to toss it for clues."

"Why?"

"Because I can't think of anything else to do. And I'm hoping we'll find something that'll help us put the pieces together."

Delores reached into Doc's center desk drawer and pulled out a key. "You don't have to break in. I'm coming with you, and I've got the master key."

# CHAPTER TWENTY-NINE

The first thing they saw when they entered Ben's apartment was a huge pile of cardboard boxes in the center of the room, waiting to be assembled. A roll of packing tape sat on top of the boxes, and a black felt-tipped marker was next to it. One box was already closed and labeled. It had the word *Mementos* written on all four sides, and Hannah made a mental note not to leave Ben's apartment without opening it and taking a look.

"This is your show, Hannah," Delores said. "What do you want us to do?"

"You take the kitchen," Hannah said to Michelle. "Call me if you find anything that has to do with Seattle, jazz clubs, Buddy Neiman, or Doctor Bev."

"Or anything else that piques her curiosity?" Delores asked.

"Exactly right. You get the bedroom, Mother. Just call out if you need us for

440

anything. I'll take the bathroom and the living room, in that order. When we're through, we'll all meet in the hallway by the back entrance."

"Got it," Michelle said, heading off to the kitchen.

"Seattle, jazz clubs, Buddy, or Doctor Bev," Delores repeated, walking toward the bedroom.

Hannah didn't really expect to find anything in the bathroom, and she wasn't wrong. The only item of interest was an expensive-looking silver watch that was nestled around the bottom of a replica of the Seattle Space Needle. Hannah picked it up and saw that it was engraved with a name, Dr. Gene Burroughs, on the back.

The living room was next, and it was devoid of personal items. If there had been any, they were probably already sequestered in the box marked *Mementos*. The bookshelves contained nothing but books, the coffee table had a plant that looked in dire need of water, and since there was a half-empty bottle of water nearby, Hannah watered it. The entertainment center housed nothing but DVDs, the wicker chest by the window was empty, and the closet by the front door accommodated only a coat, a windbreaker, and a parka.

"Hannah!" Delores rushed in with a large binder in her hands. "It's a scrapbook. Is this the sort of thing you want to see?"

"It's perfect," Hannah said, reaching out to give her mother a little hug. "This could be important, Mother."

Michelle came in just then. "Nothing in the kitchen. There aren't even any frying pans. I think it's safe to say that Ben didn't cook." She noticed the scrapbook in Hannah's hands and hurried over. "What's that?"

"A scrapbook."

"There are photos, clippings, and some other things," Delores reported. "I just flipped through it, and then I brought it right out here to Hannah."

"Let's take a look," Hannah said, taking a seat on the couch and waiting until her mother and sister had taken places on either side of her. She flipped the book open to the first page, and they saw a photo of two boys, one a toddler and the other about ten years older."

"Ben and Gene," Delores read the caption. "They were cute kids. Gene must be his brother."

"I think Gene was his stepbrother," Hannah told her. "At least they had different last names. I found a silver watch in the bathroom, and it was engraved, *Dr. Gene Burroughs.*"

"I wonder if he's a medical doctor," Delores said. "It could explain why Ben went into medicine. They might be planning to open a practice together. Sometimes families do things like that."

Hannah shook her head. "Not this time," she said. "I'm pretty sure Dr. Gene Burroughs is dead. Marlene said Ben told her his brother was dead."

"Oh, that's sad," Michelle said.

Hannah flipped through the pages. There were family photos, school portraits, snapshots of Christmas and other holidays. They were followed by graduation pictures and announcements. There was Dr. Gene Burroughs standing with a class of graduates, and an announcement of his graduation from medical school. Then there was the same type of photo of Ben, and the announcement of his medical school graduation.

"Here's the last page," Hannah said, flipping it over and staring at a clipping from the *Seattle Times.* The headline read, *Local Doctor Murdered In Alley Behind Jazz Club,* and there was a picture of Dr. Gene Burroughs.

"What is it?" Delores asked as Hannah gasped.

"It's an article about Ben's brother Gene. He's dead. He was stabbed in the chest with a broken beer bottle in the alley behind a Seattle jazz club called *Jazzmen*."

"Did they catch the killer?" Michelle asked.

"I don't know. It doesn't say. And there's nothing else here except . . ." Hannah stopped speaking and unfolded a piece of paper that was stuck to the back cover of the album.

"What is it?" Michelle asked when Hannah was silent.

"It's a photo of the band that was playing the night that Ben's brother was stabbed. They're called *Ticket To Tulsa*."

Michelle leaned closer to look at the photo. "That's Buddy!" she said, and her voice was shaking. "His hair's blond in the photo, but it's him."

"You're right," Hannah said. "It's definitely Buddy. I wonder if Ben recognized him."

"It's Ben's photo," Delores pointed out. "I'm sure he must have noticed the resemblance. Even *I* noticed it and I only saw Buddy after he was . . ." Delores stopped speaking and gave a little gulp. "Girls!"

"What is it, Mother?" Hannah asked.

"Ben must have known Buddy in Seattle. That much is clear. You don't think that Ben . . . that *Ben* killed Buddy, do you?"

Hannah was speechless for a moment and then she reached a conclusion. "I don't know," she said, "but we'd better show this photo album to Mike."

"And we'd better get out of here," Michelle added, grabbing the book from Hannah's hands. "Let's go, Mother."

"Come on, Hannah." Delores motioned to her. "Hurry! It's too dangerous to stay here. Ben could be the killer!"

Hannah shook her head. "You two go and find Mike. Give him that scrapbook and tell him everything you know. I'll be along in a minute. I just want to go through that box marked *Mementos.* There could be something important in there."

"I think you should come with us now," Delores argued.

"It's okay, Mother. Ben's working until eight tonight, and it's only eleven in the morning. You know his schedule. You looked it up yourself. Just go on ahead with Michelle and I'll meet you later."

The first thing Hannah did after her mother and Michelle left was to get the silver watch and slip it into her purse. If Ben had killed Buddy, it could be important to the murder investigation. Then she went into Ben's living room and dragged the heavy box to the couch. She had no intention of leaving Ben's apartment. She was going to stay right here, gathering possible evidence, until her sister and her mother got back with Mike.

A little tingle of apprehension gave Hannah pause. She would have felt more secure if Ben's apartment had been several miles from his workplace, but she convinced herself that she was perfectly safe. Ben was busy seeing patients and he had no idea that she was searching his apartment.

Hannah used the scissors on the coffee table to slit the tape on the box. So far everything they'd found was circumstantial. She didn't expect to find a handwritten confession in the box, or the pair of gloves that Ben had worn when he stabbed Buddy Neiman in the treatment room, but a box labeled *Mementos* might contain something from Ben's life in Seattle that would be useful.

Once she'd opened the box, Hannah removed the items one by one. She found photos of Ben's parents, smiling at the camera, and one of the family dog romping with Gene. There was another of Ben and

Gene in a rowboat on a lake. They were smiling and holding up fish on a stringer.

A stuffed toy cat was near the bottom of the box. One ear was shorter than the other. It had been mended with black thread, and Hannah decided that it had probably been a childhood toy. And then, very near the bottom, she pulled out a framed photo of Gene standing on stage with the man Hannah had known as Buddy Neiman. The photo was inscribed near the bottom right corner in silver ink. It read *For my good friend, Gene.* And it was signed *Chaz Peyton.*

That was when she heard it, a key in the lock. It wasn't Mike. Even if they'd found him right away, he couldn't have gotten here that fast. And it couldn't be Michelle or Delores. There was no reason for them to come back. And if it wasn't any of them, it had to be . . .

Ben! No time to put things back in the box and tape it up. She had to get out. Now! He'd spot her if she tried to go out the back way. Ben had what was called a shotgun apartment. If you opened the front door and opened the back door, anyone standing on the steps outside could fire a shotgun straight through the apartment without hitting anything. No time to get out. And that meant she had to hide.

*Quick as a bunny,* the phrase flew through Hannah's mind. But didn't a very frightened bunny freeze? Her feet felt frozen to the floor, but she forced them to move to a spot just to the left of the front door. When Ben opened it, she'd be hidden. He'd spot the open box, walk over to it, and she'd slip out the door while his back was turned, and make a run for it.

The door opened. Hannah caught the knob so that it wouldn't bounce back and close. Then she counted to five, just time enough for Ben to spot the box and walk over to it.

Cautiously, she peeked out. Yes! Just as she'd expected, he'd walked across the floor to the box. He was standing there staring at the contents, his back to her. It was time to get out. Now!

Hannah stepped out, her heart pounding so hard she was afraid he'd hear it, and slipped out the open doorway. And then she broke into a run for her very life.

# CHAPTER THIRTY

He'd seen her. She knew that from the pounding footfalls she heard behind her. Hannah ran down the hallway as fast as she could. She opened the door to the hospital corridor, dashed through, and made a sharp turn to the left, thanking her lucky stars that she was wearing her tennis shoes.

She'd never been down this corridor before. Lake Eden Memorial Hospital was expanding and this section was still under construction. Her hope was that Ben would expect her to flee in a straight line and not to veer off into a construction zone.

The lighting was dim in this section. The overhead fluorescents had yet to be installed, and only the occasional bare incandescent bulb hung from the open ceiling. This was uncharted territory for her, and her hope was that it would be uncharted territory for Ben as well.

Hannah rounded a corner and saw a door.

It was painted bright yellow, and that was a good sign, wasn't it? She paused, wondering if she should take a chance and go in.

The running footfalls she heard behind her were the deciding factor. Hannah yanked the door open and ran into another corridor. This one seemed to be leading downward and it was tiled. The walls were painted institutional green, and she passed another door with a stenciled sign on it that read *Engine Room,* and she knew where she was.

She was in the basement of the hospital. She remembered taking a tour when it was first built and the tour had included the basement. It ran under the entire hospital and it housed the power plant, the backup generators, the furnace, and the air conditioners. If she remembered correctly, there were also several storerooms for things like medical and janitorial supplies. There had once been a cafeteria in the corner of the basement, but it had closed several years ago and a new cafeteria for visitors and hospital workers was under construction on the ground floor as part of the expansion project.

Ben was gaining on her and Hannah didn't know what to do. It had been over ten years since she'd taken the tour of the hospital basement and she couldn't remember how to get up to the ground floor. Even if she did manage to locate a stairway, he'd catch her going up the stairs. It would be smarter to hide down here and use her cell phone to let Mike know where she was.

As she rounded the next corner, she saw a another door. She skidded to a stop, tugged it open, and ran into a large room. Then she stood leaning against the closed door, catching her breath, and hoping he hadn't spotted her. She couldn't keep running like this forever. There was a limit to her endurance.

Someone ran past the door. It had to be Ben. She heard his footfalls fade into the distance, and gave a sigh of relief. She was safe, at least for a while. But she didn't know where she was.

It was quite dark in the cavernous room, and it took a few moments for her eyes to adjust to the dim light. Low wattage bulbs were glowing in some ceiling fixtures, and Hannah could make out massive brushed steel cabinets with pull out drawers against the back wall. Perhaps this was a supply room?

A steel shelving unit sat against the wall, just to her left. It contained pairs of folded scrubs and plastic aprons. There were masks on the top shelf, along with booties, the type that operating room doctors wore, and there was a large sink on the opposite wall, the kind you'd find just outside an operating room.

A steel operating table was positioned in the center of the room. Next to it was a rolling cart that held a scale. A second steel cart was filled with various basins, beakers, and glass containers.

The tiled floor sloped down to a line of drains, the type you'd see in showers or locker rooms. It was clear that this room had been designed for easy cleaning. All you'd really have to do was hose it down. Any debris on the floor would wash down the drains.

Hannah spotted a microphone hanging from the ceiling over the operating table. There was also something that looked like a video recorder. What type of patient would give his doctor permission to record his surgery? And what type of operating room would be equipped this way?

She walked over to take a look as the two questions circled in her mind. She was stymied for a brief moment. and then she had the answer. A dead patient wouldn't object if the doctor recorded his operation, and the pull-out drawers were built to contain dead bodies waiting for autopsies. She'd never seen this room before because it hadn't been included in the tour she'd taken. She was hiding in the Lake Eden Hospital morgue!

# CHAPTER THIRTY-ONE

Hannah whirled as the door crashed open and the bright overhead lights flashed on, nearly blinding her. She blinked, and then, when she saw who was standing there, she gasped in fear. He'd found her! Ben had found her!

"Did you really think you could hide from me?" he asked.

"I . . . yes! Yes, I did!" There was a button on the side of the autopsy table and Hannah surreptitiously reached out to press it. She hoped that it was the right button to turn on the microphone and the video camera. If Ben killed her, Mike would know who did it.

"I saw you duck in here. I would have come in right away, but I wanted to get a little something for you." Ben held up his hand so she could see the syringe he carried. "I need to leave Lake Eden right now. And you're trying to stop me."

"No! No, I'm not. Go ahead. Leave!"

Ben laughed, but there was no humor in it. "I've got a little unfinished business first, and my unfinished business is you. I know you saw that photo, and I know you figured it out. Doc told me you were a good detective."

"Figured *what* out" Hannah asked, stalling for time even though she hadn't had the chance to call Mike to tell him where she was.

"That I killed Chaz. You put it all together when you saw that picture of Gene and Chaz, didn't you?" Ben took a step closer, and Hannah backed up. "Come on now. I've got a nice injection for you. It won't hurt a bit, I promise."

"No!" Hannah shouted as loud as she could.

"Screaming won't do you any good. Freddy's already been down here to get supplies, and we don't have any autopsies scheduled for today."

*Keep him talking,* Hannah's mind advised. So she asked, "Are you sure Buddy killed your stepbrother?"

"I'm sure. I was there at Jazzmen that night and they were arguing when I walked in."

"What about?"

"They didn't say anything in front of me, but I think it was about the dentist."

"What dentist?"

"A dentist they both knew. Gene met her at the free clinic. He volunteered there one afternoon a week, and so did she. She told him she liked jazz, and he took her to Jazzmen. Ticket To Tulsa was playing, and Gene introduced her to Chaz. And a couple of weeks later, she dumped Gene and started going out with Chaz."

A terrible suspicion crossed Hannah's mind. "What was her name?" she asked.

"I don't know. They never talked about her in front of me, and I never met her."

"Then you didn't hang out with Gene at Jazzmen?"

Ben shook his head. "I was in med school, and I didn't have much free time. And I've never been a big jazz fan like Gene was. I just dropped in that night to have a quick drink with him, and then I left because I had to study for a chem test. Now I wish I'd stayed. Then everybody would still be alive."

Hannah was silent, and so was Ben. They both stood there like statues, unmoving and barely breathing. Hannah was afraid to ask any more questions. She didn't want to break the spell. And then Ben spoke again.

"I wish I hadn't killed him. I wasn't going to, you know. I just wanted him to tell me what happened. But then he said something about Gene that made me see red. And the next thing I knew, he was dead."

"You snapped. That's temporary insanity, and it's your defense. Put the syringe down and let me call the best lawyer in town for you."

"I can't go to jail. It'll kill me. I couldn't stand to be locked up! My way's better. I'll get out of here and no one will ever find me."

"Listen to me," Hannah said, but she could tell it wouldn't work. Ben's eyes had turned hard and cold again, and he took another step closer.

"Noooo!" Hannah shouted. She tried to back up, but there was nowhere to go. She was up against the stationery autopsy table. Ben had her cornered. "Somebody! Help me!"

"What are you doing, Doctor Ben?"

Both Hannah and Ben turned toward the door. Freddy Sawyer was there, and he was pushing a gurney into the room.

"Get out of here, Freddy!" Ben ordered.

"No, Freddy. Don't go!" Hannah contradicted him. "Doctor Ben is trying to hurt me."

457

Freddy looked at Ben with a puzzled expression. "You can't hurt people, Doctor Ben. Doctors are supposed to help people."

"I *am* helping her, Freddy. She's sick and I'm going to give her some medicine."

"I'm not sick," Hannah insisted.

"Isn't that silly, Freddy? Hannah's afraid to get an injection. I'm a doctor. All I want to do is help her."

"He's lying to you, Freddy. He's going to hurt me. Doctor Ben is just like your cousin Jed."

"Jed?!" Freddy began to frown. "I remember Jed. He was bad!"

"Get out of here, Freddy! I'm a doctor. You have to obey the doctor's orders. Now leave or I'll make sure Doc fires you!"

"I won't leave. Not if you're going to hurt Hannah. She said you're like Jed. And Hannah doesn't lie."

Ben took another step toward Hannah, and that was when Freddy went into action. He shoved the gurney forward with such force, it knocked Ben right off his feet, and he landed hard on the tile floor. At the same time, the syringe went flying, Hannah ducked, and it landed next to Ben's unconscious body.

For a moment, Hannah was too shocked to react, but she quickly recovered. "Help me get him on the gurney, Freddy. We have to strap him down before he wakes up."

"I can do it," Freddy said, picking Ben up like a sack of potatoes and dumping him on the gurney. "Doctor Marlene taught me how. She said I was the best gurney strapper she'd ever seen."

Hannah watched, fascinated, as Freddy secured a maze of straps around Ben's arms and legs. "You have to do this so they won't hurt themselves," he explained.

"Exactly right," Hannah told him, and then she gave him a little hug. "And now Doctor Ben can't hurt me either. Marlene is right. You're the best gurney strapper I've ever seen."

# Chapter Thirty-Two

It was Friday morning and it seemed that spring was finally here. It was a balmy forty-nine degrees outside, and Hannah felt like opening the back door to let in the air, but she had six pans of Angel Kisses cooling on the baker's rack, and it was important to keep meringue cookies out of drafts until they were completely cool.

A lot had happened since her chase down the hospital corridors. Ben Matson was in jail awaiting trial, but his defense lawyer was hopeful. Just as Hannah had thought, his lawyer would claim temporary insanity. The police lab had tested the syringe he'd attempted to use on Hannah, and they'd discovered that it contained a powerful sedative, enough to knock her out for three or four hours, but not enough to kill her. All Ben had intended to do was to give himself time to get away.

The button Hannah had pressed on the

side of the autopsy table had indeed activated the microphone and the video camera.
Ben's confession that he'd killed the man
they now knew was Chaz Peyton had recorded in sound and full color. The only
unanswered question was whether the
dentist that Gene and Chaz had both dated
was Doctor Bev Thorndike.

"Your mother and Doc are coming over,"
Lisa said, coming through the swinging
door into the kitchen. "They got the DNA
test results."

"So soon?"

"Your mother said Doc's friend at the lab
walked it through personally. She also said
that paternity tests don't take as long as
some other DNA tests."

"Okay."

"You'll tell me, won't you?"

Lisa sounded a bit worried, so Hannah
smiled to reassure her. "Of course I will!"

"Good. I really hope Norman's in the
clear."

*So do I,* Hannah thought, but she didn't
say it. Lisa already knew how she felt.

Hannah had just poured coffee and set
out a plate of her newest creation, Chocolate
Caramel Pecan Bars, when there was a
knock on the back door. Delores and Doc
had arrived.

"Coffee?" Hannah asked, ushering them in.

"Always," Delores responded, smiling at Hannah.

Doc nodded. "Thanks, Hannah. I could use a cup."

"Good, because I already poured it." Hannah gestured toward the coffee mugs and cookies on the stainless steel work island. "Pull up a stool. And please . . . give me some *good* news."

"Relax, dear," Delores told her, but there was no way Hannah could relax until they told her everything.

"It's a little complicated," Doc told her, "but Rye expained it to me."

"Rye is your friend at the lab?"

"Yes. Tom Ryan. He was my roommate in med school."

"Then he's a doctor?"

"Yes, but he doesn't have a practice. He discovered he really didn't like dealing with patients that much, so he went into research. Rye had his technicians run a basic paternity test with the samples we provided. There are more complicated tests, but I told him we needed a quick answer."

"Doc told him it was a matter of *wife* and death," Delores said, smiling at Doc.

"I *did* say that. Rye always liked a good joke."

"That's clever," Hannah said, even though she wished that Doc would get to the point.

"When we took in the samples, Rye was very pleased. He said he had plenty to work with."

"Andrea gets the credit for that," Hannah said, remembering all the samples that they'd turned over to Doc.

"Well, she did a good job. They used the mother's sample, the child's sample, and the potential father's sample."

Delores nodded. "Rye said that when they do paternity tests, they divide the potential fathers' samples into two categories, *inclusions* and *exclusions*."

"That's right," Doc took over. "The first test they ran doesn't legally prove that a candidate is the father. But it can prove that a candidate is *not* the father."

Hannah crossed the fingers on both hands for luck. "How did Norman's sample turn out?"

"Norman couldn't possibly be the father."

"Norman's an *exclusion?*" Hannah asked. She needed to make dead certain she'd understood.

"That's right," Doc confirmed it. "Norman is not Diana's father."

463

A giant weight slipped off Hannah's shoulders and fluttered away on a breeze of relief. Doctor Bev had been lying about everything, including the identity of Diana's father!

"Tell her about the mistake," Delores said, nudging Doc.

"Remember that DNA sample I took from the man we thought was Buddy Neiman?" Doc waited until Hannah had nodded, and then he continued. "The lab tech thought he was supposed to run the first paternity test on Buddy's sample, too. So he did, and it turned out that Buddy was an *inclusion*."

"Let me tell her!" Delores said, practically jumping up and down on her stool.

"Go ahead, Lori," Doc said indulgently.

"Oh, Hannah! It's just like Doc said! The lab tech ran the second paternity test on Buddy's sample. And it's ninety-nine point nine percent positive that *he* was Diana's father!"

Hannah paced the floor of the kitchen. She started at the back door, made a path from the industrial oven to the crate where Sammy lay on his velvet dog bed. He was chewing on the ear of a teddy bear squeaky toy and Hannah paused to squeak it for him. Then she executed a smart, military-style turn on her heel, and made the return trip to the back door again. She was sure she'd logged at least a mile since she'd called Norman and asked him if he'd please meet her in the kitchen at The Cookie Jar.

As she turned and headed toward Sammy's crate again, she glanced at the clock. Fifteen minutes had passed, and Norman should be there any second. She wished she knew exactly what to say to him, but she didn't. And time was running out.

They'd left it all up to her. Carrie, Earl, Andrea, Michelle, Delores, Doc, Lisa, Herb, and even Mike had decided not to say a word about the DNA samples they'd collected for the tests the lab had run. They'd all agreed that Hannah should be the one to tell Norman whatever she wanted him to know. The ball was in her court, the bow was drawn back with the arrow in place, and the die was cast. Everything was up to Hannah, and she still wasn't sure how much or how little she should tell Norman.

Sammy gave a little woof and Hannah reached down to pet him. The door to the crate was open, but he seemed perfectly content to stay inside. Perhaps he thought that she might trip over him in her pacing.

There was a knock on the back door, and Hannah rushed to open it. Norman was standing there and he looked very serious.

"Come on in, Norman," Hannah said. "I've got fresh coffee."

"Great." Norman hung his jacket on the hooks by the back door and took a stool at the stainless steel work island. "I'm glad you called me, Hannah. I was just about to pick up the phone and call you."

"Oh?" Hannah delivered his coffee, and then she sat down on the stool across from Norman. He looked so serious, she felt a little weak in the knees.

"This is serious, Hannah," he said.

*I can see that,* her mind said, but her mouth was so dry that all she could do was nod.

"I'm not Diana's father."

*Uh-oh!* her mind flashed a warning. Had Norman found out about the paternity tests they'd run? Was he about to tell her he'd never forgive her for interfering in his life?

"Did you hear me, Hannah?"

"Oh, yes," Hannah said in a voice that trembled slightly. "How did you find out?"

"I had the lab run a paternity test, and I got the results in the mail yesterday. With my DNA, I couldn't possibly be Diana's father."

"You . . ." Hannah stopped and swallowed hard. She took a deep breath and started again. "You sent in a sample and they ran a paternity test?"

"Of course I did. You didn't think I'd simply accept Bev's word for it, did you?"

"I . . . I didn't know."

"Well, you should have known. Give me a little credit, Hannah. I wasn't born yesterday. I thought it was odd that she waited that long to tell me about Diana, and I decided I'd rather be safe than sorry. As it turned out, I would have been sorry. *Very* sorry." Norman stopped and reached out for Hannah's hand. "Are you okay?"

"Yes. Yes, I'm okay." Hannah took another deep breath. "Did you tell *her* yet?"

"I drove to Minneapolis and told her last night. Of course I had to find her first. She wasn't at her mother's house, and Diana wasn't sick. She lied to me about that, too."

"Did she tell you who Diana's father really was?"

"No, and I didn't ask. That doesn't really matter."

Hannah made a snap decision. There was no reason to give Norman the name of Diana's father. "It doesn't matter to you?"

"No. What matters is that Bev lied to me, and she tried to trick me into marrying her."

"Then . . . you're *not* getting married

467

tomorrow?" Hannah asked, just to make sure.

"That's right. I'm not getting married tomorrow. I haven't told anyone else, Hannah. I wanted to tell you first." Norman reached out and captured her other hand. "I love you, Hannah. I always will. We were so good together before all this happened. Do you think that with a little time . . . we can get back to being *us* again?"

Hannah wasn't sure she could speak past the lump in her throat, but she knew she had to try. "We never stopped being *us*," she told him. "Even when you were with her, I never stopped believing in *us*."

They sat there, hands clasped, for a long moment, just breathing the same air and being together. And then Norman gave a deep sigh.

"I'd better get over to Granny's Attic," he said. "I have to ask Mother and Delores to activate the gossip hotline."

"Why?"

"I want them to tell everyone in town that the wedding's canceled. I don't have the list of addresses Bev used when she sent out the invitations, and I know it's impossible to contact everyone. So I'm going to go down to the community center tomorrow to tell anybody who shows up that there won't be a wedding."

"But can't you just put a notice on the door?"

"No. I have to be there. It's the right thing to do, Hannah. If people show up, they're going to want to know what happened."

"And you're going to tell them?"

"Not all of it. They don't need to know the details. I'll just say that we decided to call off the wedding, and that Bev left Lake Eden and she won't be back."

Hannah wasn't sure what to say. As far as she was concerned, Norman was the bravest man she knew. Most people who found themselves in a similar situation would put a sign on the door, and hide at home with the curtains drawn. "You're not going down there alone, are you?" she asked.

"Yes. I cancelled the wedding, and it's my responsibility."

Hannah thought about that for a moment. Norman had a point, but greeting people at your own canceled wedding would be the height of humiliation. "You're not going to go down there alone," she said, making another snap decision. "I'm going with you."

"But you don't have to. Really, Hannah. I'd love it if you came with me, but I can handle it alone."

"No, you can't."

"Why not?"

Hannah gave him a little smile. Things were getting back to normal again. "You don't know your way around the community center kitchen. And *somebody's* got to put on the coffee."

# CHOCOLATE CARAMEL PECAN BARS
Preheat oven to 350 degrees F.,
rack in the middle position.

4 one-ounce squares semi-sweet baking chocolate *(or the equivalent — 3/4 cup regular chocolate chips will do fine)*

3/4 cup butter *(1 and 1/2 sticks, 6 ounces)*

1 and 1/2 cups white *(granulated)* sugar

1/8 cup *(2 Tablespoons)* caramel ice cream topping

3 beaten eggs *(just whip them up in a glass with a fork)*

1/4 teaspoon salt

1 teaspoon vanilla extract

1 and 1/2 cups flour *(pack it down in the cup when you measure it)*

1 and 1/2 cups chocolate chips *(that's 3/4 of a 12-ounce package — I used Ghirardelli)*

1 and 1/2 cups pecans

Prepare a 9-inch by 13-inch cake pan by lining it with a piece of heavy-duty foil large enough to flap over the sides. Spray the foil-lined pan with Pam or another nonstick cooking spray.

Microwave the chocolate squares and butter in a microwave-safe mixing bowl for one minute. Stir. *(Since chocolate frequently maintains its shape even when melted, you have to stir to make sure.)* If it's not melted, microwave for an additional 20 seconds and stir again. Repeat if necessary.

Place the sugar in a mixing bowl. Stir in the chocolate and butter mixture, and continue stirring until it's well combined.

**Hannah's 1st Note: The caramel ice cream topping comes next. It will stick to your measuring cup unless you first spray the inside of the cup with Pam or another nonstick cooking spray.**

Add the caramel ice cream topping to your bowl and mix it in thoroughly.

Feel the bowl. If it's not so hot it'll cook the eggs, add them now, stirring thoroughly.

Mix in the salt and the vanilla extract.

Mix in the flour, 1/2 cup at a time, stirring just until it's moistened.

**Hannah's 2nd Note: These are a form of brownies, and you don't want to stir the batter any more than necessary.**

Put the chocolate chips and the pecans in the bowl of a food processor. Using an on and off motion, chop them together with the steel blade. *(If you don't have a food processor, you don't have to buy one just for this recipe — simply chop everything up as well as you can with a sharp knife.)*

Mix in the ingredients you just chopped,

give one final stir, and spread the batter out in the pan you prepared earlier.

Bake the Chocolate Caramel Pecan Bars at 350 degrees F. for 30 minutes.

Cool your yummy creation in the pan on a metal rack. When the bar cookies are cool, slip them into the refrigerator at least an hour for ease in cutting.

When you're ready to serve them, lift the chilled cookie bars out of the pan, using the "ears" of foil you left at the sides. Place them face-down on a cutting board, peel the foil off the back, and cut them into brownie-sized pieces.

Place the squares on a plate and dust them lightly with powdered sugar. Everyone will think you're a genius when they taste them.

# CINNAMON ROLL MURDER
# RECIPE INDEX

# BAKING CONVERSION CHART

These conversions are approximate, but they'll work just fine for Hannah Swensen's recipes.

## VOLUME:

| U.S. | Metric |
|------|--------|
| 1/2 teaspoon | 2 milliliters |
| 1 teaspoon | 5 milliliters |
| 1 tablespoon | 15 milliliters |
| 1/4 cup | 50 milliliters |
| 1/3 cup | 75 milliliters |
| 1/2 cup | 125 milliliters |
| 3/4 cup | 175 milliliters |
| 1 cup | 1/4 liter |

## WEIGHT:

| U.S. | Metric |
|------|--------|
| 1 ounce | 28 grams |
| 1 pound | 454 grams |

## OVEN TEMPERATURE:

*Degrees Fahrenheit*   325 degrees F.
*Degrees Centigrade*   165 degrees C.
*British (Regulo)*       3
  *Gas Mark*

*Degrees Fahrenheit*   350 degrees F.
*Degrees Centigrade*   175 degrees C.
*British (Regulo)*       4
  *Gas Mark*

*Degrees Fahrenheit*   375 degrees F.
*Degrees Centigrade*   190 degrees C.
*British (Regulo)*       5
  *Gas Mark*

Note: Hannah's rectangular sheet cake pan, 9 inches by 13 inches, is approximately 23 centimeters by 32.5 centimeters.

# ABOUT THE AUTHOR

Like Hannah Swensen, **Joanne Fluke** was born and raised in a small town in rural Minnesota, but now lives in sunny Southern California. She is currently working on her next Hannah Swensen mystery and readers are welcome to contact her at Gr8Clues@aol.com, or by visiting her website, murdershebaked.com.

The employees of Thorndike Press hope you have enjoyed this Large Print book. All our Thorndike, Wheeler, and Kennebec Large Print titles are designed for easy reading, and all our books are made to last. Other Thorndike Press Large Print books are available at your library, through selected bookstores, or directly from us.

For information about titles, please call:
(800) 223-1244

or visit our Web site at:
http://gale.cengage.com/thorndike

To share your comments, please write:
Publisher
Thorndike Press
10 Water St., Suite 310
Waterville, ME 04901